LIVING IN THE RAW WIND

A JOSEPH F. DELGADO OMNIBUS

Joseph F. Delgado

Living in the

Raw Wind

A Joseph F. Delgado Omnibus

Edited by Javier Toro-Boland

El Bohío Press

El Bohío Press

P. O. Box 592
Hudson, NH 03051

filmproject@sc.rr.com

Cover Photograph: Adele Romens
Cover Design: Mark Proudfoot
Interior Design: Susan Elfstrom

Printed in the United States of America

CONTENTS

Joseph Figueroa Delgado
(Humacao, Puerto Rico, 1950)

"Don't be afraid; people are so afraid; don't be afraid to live in the raw wind, naked, alone…"

Tony Kushner,
Angels in America, Part One: Millennium Approaches

FOREWORD

The task of organizing the contents of an anthology is generally a difficult one. Should the sequence be presented in chronological order to provide a glimpse at the author's evolution? Could stories be clustered topically? The difficulty is not simplified when the general theme is consistent throughout a volume. In the case of Joseph F. Delgado's work, the short stories are not gay-*themed*: they are about the LGBTQ experience. Although some of the stories are set in American environments, Delgado bestows upon each story an undeniable touch of the queer Latino perspective. He seems to know first-hand what it is like to be forced into a life of inauhtenticity lest an individual suffer the scorn and mockery of those who object to an existence separate from the one demanded by the unyielding heterosexual norm. Perhaps more than anyone else who has not had to endure a machocentric tyranny, Delgado is familiar with social contexts in which queer people are shoved into a lie in the darkness of their closets by those who often use the fag in secret for their sexual satisfaction, but date and marry the girl next door while deriding and humiiating their same-sex partner in public.

The organization of the book is therefore a matter of categorizing specific facets of our experience as human beings who defy heteronormative expectations. Within the broad thematic framework the stories span the human life cycle from childhood to death. Sometimes the stories convey a message of hope and optimism even under inhumane circumstances; in others the author portrays unsavory situations and characters who act on the basis of despair and thoughtless reactions against the powers that asphyxiate and crush them mercilessly.

I was left with the feeling that most of these stories are intimately autobiographical. The author has not dispeled my impression. Reading his *Coming of Queer Age in Puerto Rico* certainly confirmed my suspicions. It's a cliché in the world of literary creation that we should write about what we know. To a great extent Delgado elaborates a fictional world out of the joyless, sometimes hopeful, world he inhabited as a child and as a young man, all the way into maturity.

Specific foci of interest guide the stories' plots: surviving violence and prejudice, the effects on self and others of moral duplicity and hypocrisy, the consequences of isolation and physical or mental abuse, the psychology of self-loathing, and loving self-sacrifice that triumphs over intolerance and ignorance. Joseph Delgado treats those topics as they manifest themselves in diverse geographical locations and life stages.

The short stories have appeared before in the author's collections and in national LGBTQ-oriented magazines such as *The Lower Stumpf Lake Review* (1972),

The James White Review (1991) and *Raspa* (2018); a poetic excerpt in one of the stories appeared in *A&U* magazine (2018). Several of them have been published only in Spanish-language collections and are included here in their English version for the first time.

Although it might seem inappropriate for an editor to express his or her preferences regarding a text, I will do so presently: stating my preferences cannot be construed in any way as a slight against the rest of the stories, of course. The sustained fantasy plot of "Man of His Dreams" (perhaps an example of magical realism with a queer bend, some would say) captivated my attention due to its original storyline and subtle message in a sort of queer *Twilight Zone* episode. "Toyland" struck a chord of painful personal experience with which many queer men can identify, particularly those who, like me, were raised in homophobic fundamentalist family settings: the final realization of what is happening came as a surprise that both startled and saddened me, but which rang true. "Heartbreak at Plaza Las Americas" is a first-person stream of consciousness account of a cat-and-mouse cruising game reminiscent of Delgado's novella *The Silence Barrier*. "Self-Stolen Identity" conjures images of ambivalence and the fluidity of human sexuality in a narrative instance of reverse category crisis, a lapse in gay identity, a subject seldom addressed in LGBTQ literature. Two stories address the impact of AIDS on the lives of gay men: "Survived by Those Who Loved Him" does so obliquely, narrated by a presumably straight man in love with the main male character, and "And Now, What?" in which a long-term survivor of HIV looks back at his life and wonders about his future while living a life of uncertainty and sexual frustration. Delgado himself made an independent film of "Survived by Those Who Loved Him" in 2012, titled *Mr. Doppler's Effect*.

The stories were written over a period of 47 years and are thus, as a collection, a historical survey of where we have been and where we are, collectively and individually. I hope every reader experiences the literary epiphany I have at reading each of the stories in this collection.

Javier Toro-Boland
Rice Lake, Wisconsin
February, 2019

TOYLAND

Shortly after he turned twelve Jason Prince told his mother, Paula.

"Are you sure you know what you're saying?" his mom asked him. She had stopped mashing potatoes to sit down by him at the kitchen table.

"I'm pretty sure," Jason said.

"Now, Jason," his mom said, looking directly at his eyes, "what makes you say that? How do you know?"

Jason paused for a while, looked up at the ceiling, then out the window, where the oak tree shaded the kitchen side of the house.

"Other kids in school talk about girls. They brag about the girls that let them do things to them. You know. Make out, touch them there and stuff," Jason explained.

"And you're not curious about that?" Mrs. Prince asked.

"I don't care what they do," Jason said. "I'm not interested. I don't think about girls. You know what I think about?"

Mrs. Prince remained silent, waiting for the answer.

"Alan. Alan Beamon. I think about him all the time. Since third grade. I think of Alan, what he's doing, what he thinks about, what he likes to do. That's what I think about," Jason said. Mrs. Prince detected the same enthusiasm Jason displayed for Little League baseball. "When he's at bat I feel so proud of him. I wish I were as good as he is, mom."

"You're pretty good yourself, Jason," Mrs. Prince said.

"Yeah, but he's better. I don't want to compete against him. He's fourth at bat. I'm happy to be sixth. I don't want him to be mad at me. He's the reason I try so hard, because if he's on base and I don't run him in he'll be mad at me."

"What does that have to do with what you just told me?" Mrs. Prince asked.

"Everything, Mom, everything! When he runs from third to home plate, I want to go hug him. I want to tell him how proud he makes me," Jason explained. "And I want to kiss him right on the lips."

"I see. You've never told him how you feel, have you?"

"Of course I have, Mom, duh?" Jason said, rolling his eyes.

"And what did he say?" Mrs. Prince asked, full of anxiety. This could not be good, she feared.

"I told him behind the bleachers after practice a couple of weeks ago. We kissed. He told me he loved me too, and that we better keep it to ourselves."

Mrs. Prince was at a loss. It was not something she had expected from Jason. He had never expressed any interest in the things she had always thought gay boys liked: dolls, girls' dresses, Britney Spears. He had never worn her clothes or her makeup. She remembered her uncle Luke Kendrick. He was married to June Dillon; they had five children together. She always thought he held his cigarette funny, just like her own mother. When he sat down and crossed his legs, he always swung the top leg back and forth, just like the other women in the room. He'd talk with his hands and threw his head back while gossiping about the neighbors.

"He's like a woman," Paula told her mother one day after he and his family left.

"That's unkind," Paula's mother said. A few years later she remembered overhearing a conversation her mother and her aunt were having about Uncle Luke and the trouble he was in. None of it was clear to her until some years later when her brother Roger told her: Uncle Luke had been arrested in a rest area off I-95. He had solicited sex from an undercover cop in Virginia. When he got caught he was wearing women's stockings and panties. The arrest made it to the local news in Virginia, but no one in Whitsett heard about it. Paula's dad bailed him out, forced him to declare himself guilty and then paid his fine so it wouldn't go to trial.

For years after that it was what Mrs. Prince thought men who had sex with other men did, dressed up in ladies' garments and hung out in bathrooms trying to seduce men. Her husband, of all people, was the one who told her that was all a story people told to scare and disgust others. Mr. Prince had a gay cousin who had played college football and was even more masculine than he. His cousin had also lived with the same companion in Kentucky for at least twelve years.

"Well, Jason, you told me for a reason, didn't you," Mrs. Prince asked. Jason nodded. "What would that be?"

"I want to be honest with you. You know, in case you try to set me up with girls," Jason said. He felt encouraged when Mrs. Prince smacked her tongue and shook her head. "And because people will start to talk like they talk about Wendell Clapp."

"I know. People fear what they don't understand. And what the Bible tells them to hate," Mrs. Prince said.

"Those are the people who are missing pages from their Bible. Sometimes they rip out all four gospels."

Jason smiled. "Thank you, Mom. I didn't know what you'd say. I'm glad I told you."

"You know you can always tell me anything. No matter how bad you think it is, I'll be here for you. And I will always love you," Mrs. Prince said. She stood up and held his head in her hands, then bent down to kiss Jason on his head. "Now go wash up for dinner. Your brothers and your dad will be here any minute."

Besides the mashed potatoes, broiled fish and vegetables that night they also had Jason's favorite dessert: a slice of warm apple pie with a scoop of vanilla ice cream melting on top.

"I have an announcement to make," Mrs. Prince said at the table. "But maybe I should let Jason give it." She looked at Jason while his dad and two brothers waited for him to speak.

"Are you sure, Mom?" Jason asked. He blushed.

"Yes, I am. Go ahead."

"Okay, I guess you all need to know. I'm gay," Jason said. He surveyed the faces at the table.

"Wow," said Gene, his older brother. "I never suspected."

"Me neither," said Tim, Jason's younger brother. "That's cool."

Dad had laid his fork down. He swallowed the morsel of apple pie and looked at Jason. "I don't think it's anything to celebrate, just like it's nothing worthy of praise that your brothers are straight." Mr. Prince then looked at both of his other sons. "Are you?"

Tim and Gene nodded.

"You are what you are. We can't change nature. You are certain of this?" Mr. Prince asked.

"Yes, I am," Jason affirmed.

"Well, son, thanks for the trust you've had in us to share this. You are going to need a lot of strength to deal with the opinions of others and the prejudices of ignorant people," Mr. Prince said. "I can't control that, but I can promise you that we will stand by you and support you." Mr. Prince stretched out his hand and patted Jason in the back. Tim and Luke stood up and hugged him at the same time.

His dad had been right. He thought everyone else would be as accepting as his immediate family and thus felt comfortable sharing the information with others in school. No one wasted time to call him names. No one would sit by him at the lunch table. Alan Beamon—and this was the most hurtful of all the rejection—stopped talking to him. "The Bible says that is wrong" was all Alan said before walking away looking around him to make sure no one saw him speaking to Jason. Jason thought Alan would react differently in baseball practice, however. But Alan sat at the other end of the bench. When Jason couldn't see clear enough to focus his attention on the direction of the baseball at the next game against Newberry's Bulldogs he batted directly into the glove of the short stop, who quickly threw the ball to the catcher: Alan tried to slide home, but the catcher tagged him. He was out.

"You faggot!" Alan yelled at Jason. The rest of the team echoed the word.

"Okay, cut it out," the coach said after a round of name-calling that lasted for an infinity.

Mr. Prince walked up to the coach. "Are you going to let those kids yell and bully Jason? What are you here for?"

"I'm here to coach. You better get out of my face," the coach said.

"You don't know in your face! I demand you reprimand those kids. What kind of message is this about sportsmanship and respect for others?" Mr. Prince asked.

"Your kid is funny. You don't really expect boys that are normal to tolerate him, do you?"

Mr. Prince decided it was not worth it, this attempt to bring the troglodyte into the 21st century. Jason quit Little League.

"There are other sports, champ," Mr. Prince said, and put his arm around Jason's shoulders on the way to the car.

School was different, though. Jason's teachers unanimously supported him. Any attempt at name-calling was immediately squashed. Jason didn't have to complain: his teachers were always on the lookout for anyone who tried to belittle him. Jason felt secure. His grades, already outstanding, became even better. When he tried out for junior varsity basketball, the coach praised his natural ability to play the game. When some of his teammates gave any indication that Jason was less than normal, the rest of the players stood by Jason and put an end to it.

His basketball achievements earned him even more acceptance among the students. He was, after all, the stop scorer, the leader in rebounds and turnovers. For the first time in five seasons the Laurel Junior High School Huskies were in the finals. For the first time ever they won the regional championship and went on to the state competition. They came in second in that one, but it did not diminish Jason's approval by everyone in school, from the principal to the maintenance staff.

"I was unfair with you," Alan Beamon told him one day when he caught up with Jason on their way home. "I'm sorry. I hope you can forgive me."

"Of course, Alan. Don't even think about it! I'm so happy you are speaking to me!" Jason said.

"I'm glad also," said Alan. "Do you mind?"

"What?"

"A peck in the cheek. You know, to make up," Alan said.

"Out here?" Jason asked.

"Behind that tree," Jason said.

They walked behind the tree. Jason placed his cheek where Alan could kiss it, but Alan put his lips on Jason's. It was a soft kiss that made Jason quiver inside. He had closed his eyes, but he opened them to catch a glimpse of Alan's countenance, so beautiful and tender, and—

"Hey, Jason Prince," called the woman after unlocking the door. "Dr. Pence is waiting for you."

Jason turned on his side. It was that woman in the pilgrim's collar dress to her shins. She looked as unhappy as always. He propped himself up on his elbow, dropped his legs to the floor and got into his slippers. He felt he had lost weight. His shirt felt larger; his pants could not stay on him even with a belt on the last notch.

"You know what room we're going to," the woman said as Jason walked to her right. He knew: of course he knew. The room with the machine and those wires on the gurney, that chamber that smelled of burnt cloth and stagnant water. Jason had been there two days before. After the first time he tried to refuse to return, but Dr. Pence sent for two men dressed in white to force him out of his room and tie him to the gurney.

"This is for your own good," Dr. Pence said. "Your parents know this is best for you. By the time you leave here you will be cured of those bad habits."

Now he didn't feel like fighting them. It wasn't that he had learned to like it, but rather that he knew how useless it was to fight it. He had not learned how to lie, either. When Dr. Pence called him to his office to ask him if he wanted to date a girl, Jason still answered, "No. I would date a boy, though." The answer exasperated Dr. Pence.

"Then tomorrow we will fry you again, you little faggot. You'll get over that abomination if it kills you."

When Dr. Pence and the nurse secured him to the gurney and gave him the shot—a muscle relaxant, they told him it was—he started dreaming again that same dream, interrupted by the convulsion. He had to complete it in his room later, because while they prepared him and stuck that rubber stick in his mouth before sending the current through his body he only got to the part where his mom said. "I'll be here for you. And I will always love you."

It's Much Better Now

"Shake it!"

"Swisher, Leandra!

"Swing that ass!

"Thow thweet, Leandra!"

"Look here, faggot, look at what I got here for you, just what you like. It's nice and thick. It'll stretch that ass of yours just right!"

"That hole has seen a lot of action!"

"Leandra, you filthy queer, come suck it!"

That's what he heard behind him when he walked across the city park or when he went by the street corners where the bums and the idle of the town gathered. He asked himself what would happen if he picked up stones and started pitching them at the bastards' heads. What would they say then? Of course, he knew what would happen. The guy who owned the Red Mill Lounge would call the police when he'd crack his glass window. He'd only look ridiculous and end up in jail, if not kicked and punched and left near dead for daring to challenge the machos poisoned by their own insecurity and hypocrisy.

Leandrito did nothing. He sped up or turned a corner he hadn't planned to turn, just to stop listening to them, but he went on hearing their mocking and cackles, an echo no one else could hear, the way only dogs can hear certain pitches.

He was named Leandro Armando Vega Cruz: Leandro after his paternal grandfather and Armando because it sounded to his mother like a Mexican matinee idol's name. The elder Leandro Vega had married three times. One of his brides was his mistress during his second marriage. Grandpa Leandro had nine children, two of them illegitimate who had to use their mother's maiden name until she married their father. They were in their 20s when that happened. The old man's name was a synonym for horny in their town.

"And this, what do you want it for?" grandpa Leandro would ask little Leandrito when the boy was still in Kindergarten, grabbing him by his genitals without squeezing. "This is for sticking it into little girls' pussies, you hear?"

Leandrito would then look at him when he laughed with that "hee-hee-hee" and gave Leandrito a glimpse of the spot where he was missing a canine and the neighboring incisor.

Leandrito, however, grew up without any interest in his grandfather's lesson.

His family lived on the Corchado Street hill when the neighbor's son gave him a taste of what had fed his curiosity. At ten he understood it as the appropriate way to show Amaury that he was in love with him. Amaury came home from high school and Leandrito rushed to his house while Amaury's parents were working. Leandrito teased him. He waited for Amaury to sit in the sofa to pretend he would stumble and fall on Amaury's lap. Amaury did nothing to stop him or push him away. Leandrito did not want to make his intention obvious for fear Amaury might reject him, but neither did he want Amaury to ignore him. His was a premature feel for subtlety, but his immaturity was insufficient for its execution. Leandrito became aware that his pee-pee was minute, compared to Amaury's, big, fat and after a while, hard, when Amaury pulled it out of his underwear after removing his grey school-uniform pants.

Leandrito did everything Amaury asked of him. He wasn't sure whether this was one of those bad things he was not supposed to do, but somehow he understood that this was not something he could tell anyone about. He felt accepted by his boyfriend Amaury and felt this was how love was expressed. Nonetheless, he knew he had to hide to do it. If someone else found out he would be ashamed. Mommy would give him a belting like the ones she gave him when he threw a tantrum or failed to clean his room, with one of Daddy's leather belts. And Daddy—he didn't want to think about what Daddy would do to him. His love for Amaury had to be kept a secret and shown only in the isolation of the house next door.

"Is it true that Amaury has been checking your oil?" Carlitos Ruibal asked him one Saturday afternoon when they were sitting around a street lamppost with Amaury himself. With them was Con, the son of a man who cleaned septic tanks for a living and lived in the slum two streets away from theirs. The Varona twins were also sitting there. They all laughed. Leandrito's face turned red and hot. He had walked up to the group because he used to follow them during their innocent adventures through neighborhood backyards and when they'd walk down to the river to climb boulders where the water flow turned into rapids.

Denying it was useless. It would be his word against Amaury's. Amaury was the oldest of all and the group's admired leader. Leandrito returned home. Behind him he heard the mortifying chorus.

"Hey, don't go! I got something here for you."

"Oh, so it's okay to do it with Amaury, but not with me, is that it?"

"Darling, come back here!"

"Come suck this I got for you here!"

His chest filled up with the terror that a neighbor could hear. He wanted to run away far, where no one would be able to tell it was he the boys were addressing. He locked himself in his bedroom to cry. What hurt most was knowing that Amaury had betrayed him. In the future he would not allow Amaury to touch him, even if he called from the porch, as he always did.

In that dusty four-street town that fancied itself a miniature Paris after a local poet had dubbed it such in a poem that was nothing but pretentious doggerel verses, it wasn't long before he started hearing the same taunts.

"Girlie boy! Sissy!"

"Come on, fag, come here and blow my dick!"

"You little queer!"

No one yelled at him when he was with Mommy. Just as old Leandro had the reputation of a stud on two legs, hers was of a humorless, aggressive woman. She kept strict discipline in the elementary school where she was principal with a hardened countenance and rigid judgments.

"I don't care if they don't love me, but they will respect me!" was her dictum when someone called her attention to the stern manner in which she looked at students and even some of the teachers. Leandrito noticed at an early age that she was neither loved nor respected: she was feared with the same intensity of the love she demonstrated toward her only son. Offending her son, who was a pupil in her school, casting doubts on his early heterosexuality, would have resulted in a merciless barrage of punches and slaps to the face of the offender.

Leandrito lived near the town's movie theater. Already when he was in fifth grade sometimes in the afternoon he would go see the second-run movies the theater showed on a double bill. There he had to switch seats several times, because he was followed by teenagers and grown men who would sit by him to try to grab his hand

26

and place it on their erections. They were the same ones who called him names on the street, the ones who didn't want to have anything to do with him in public for being queer, and at least two who would not let their children be his friends in school because of his bad habits. Freckles, one of Daddy's employees, attempted to get Leandrito to keep a hand on his erect penis, surprising Leandrito that his pee-pee was almost the same size as his. If he stood behind the partition that separated the gallery from the seating area, he'd feel César Torres brushing and rubbing against his back. Monchito Correa, Papo Ruiz, Goyito García, Toñito Flores—the son of the owner of the grocery store where his parents shopped—, anonymous men of all ages he would recognize because of the reiteration of their attempts: they all sought the same thing.

Leandrito wanted to do it. What stopped him and drove him to feign repugnance was thinking more voices would be added to the tormenting chorus, detailing what he had done with them, always alleging he had initiated whatever they had done.

Leandrito stopped going to the movies. He couldn't remember the plot of any of them: he either left early or could not concentrate on the movie while changing seats to avoid his pursuers. He buried himself in books; he turned into a prisoner of his own house. If his parents took him to visit relatives in another town he anguished at the thought that he had an invisible mark on his body that identified him and screamed his abnormality. He would stay in the car reading, the windows rolled up, he on the verge of suffocation.

"Boy, don't be so bashful," was what his dad's uncle Fefé always came to tell him at the car. He would rap on the window. Leandrito shook his head and pressed the safety lock on the door.

When he reached sixth grade he had taken up magic as a pastime. With the allowance his dad gave him every week Leandrito would send for mail-order tricks from a supplier in Aibonito, up in the mountains past the city of Cayey. He practiced an act that included *abracadabra* and *shazam!* as he performed the tricks to make coins disappear from his hands and produce smoke by tapping one finger against another. Most of all he liked the cup trick, which involved the disappearance of a globe when he removed the lid. The secret was that what seemed to be a white sphere on the red plastic cup was actually a hemisphere whose edge he would hold when he lifted the lid again, the hemisphere hidden inside the equally-shaped lid, thus leaving an empty bowl. He also liked, although not as much as the cup trick, a trick with four metal rings, bigger around than his hands, that seemed solid, joined one inside another, but that the magician would pull apart and join again by crossing the hidden cut in each ring.

He made a rubber chicken disappear and reappear form a deep top hat. He would stir his magic wand inside the hat and turn it upside down, "Nothing here, nothing there," shake it and then with a strike on the hat with the magic wand he would pull out the rubber chicken, stretched out like the ones that hung, feathers plucked and the neck twisted, on the butcher shop window.

His sixth-grade teacher learned of his magic skills and invited him to perform his act for his classmates. Leandrito was filled with terror: he would have to stand in front of the class, among whom were some of the ones who yelled the nasty words on the street and whispered among themselves in the schoolyard during recess, pointing at him and laughing, their arms raised with wrists as limp as if they had no tendons in them.

He refused. The teacher, however, continued to insist.

"Don't be so antisocial, Leandrito," she said. "Your classmates will be very impressed with your ability. Maybe they will even lay off."

In the end he yielded. He set up his equipment on a table covered with a red cloth that Rosa Dávila, a neighbor, had cut for him from remnants of a gown she had sewn for a client at her workshop. He wore a short black cape, part of a costume he had never worn after refusing to go to the school's Halloween party.

He opened his performance with a card trick. When he tried to separate them to show the same card he had shown before, his shaking hand dropped the pack of cards that scattered all over the floor. Amidst guffaws and mocking noises he crouched to pick them up in silence. Then, facing his classmates, he spread his arms open with his hands raised, as if to say "Wait! The best is coming!"

He pulled out the handkerchief trick. He showed each individually. After squeezing them into his hand and a shake of the magic wand they would come out like a seven-piece garland. When he stretched out the handkerchiefs, only two were tied together; the rest floated away until they reached the ground. Again he picked up the pieces in silence, accompanied by a dissonance of snorts and cackles. Fatso Mora was the loudest. He was one of those who pilloried him in front of others and later, in the boys' bathroom demanded that Leandrito prove to him that Leandrito was that which he accused him of in public without knowing whether it was true or false.

Leandrito repeated the previous gesture to ask for patience. He went back to the table and lifted the rings. When he tried to separate them the rings remained imprisoned within each other. He didn't want to look at anyone. The heat on his face was the same as if he had his head in a broiler. Fatso Mora's laughter was seconded by Elizabeth Pagán's, a cutup who used to look for Leandrito's score in tests to compare and confirm that she was the most intelligent of her classmates. She was always disappointed, and that was when she would turn around so quickly that her skirt went in the opposite direction. At her retreat she would make a limp wrist and murmured "Thilly boy."

The last illusion was yet to come: it was the hat and chicken trick. He had set it up before his performance began. Now that several were yawning or talking among themselves he would have to take advantage of the moment to vindicate himself and dispel any notion of failure.

He followed the same procedure he had when he practiced the trick by himself or for family guests in the living room at home. He made the "Nothing here, nothing there" motions. He took the hat by the brim with one hand and shook the magic wand with the other. He stuck his hand in the hat's false bottom. Nothing. Nothing was in there. He looked inside, confused.

"Are you looking for this?" Fatso Mora asked, holding the rubber chicken high by its neck.

The resonance of the laughter paralyzed him. He took his hands to his face and started sobbing. It was then that he heard the chorus that Fatso Mora led. Soon everyone was yelling, their voices blending.

"Queer, queer, queer..."

"Girlie boy!"

"Cry-baby!"

"*Maricón, maricón!*" yelled with her hands in a megaphone the daughter of the Spanish doctor in town.

"*Pájaro, pájaro, pájaro!*" screamed the son of a Cuban merchant who owned a five and dime shop on Main Street, *La Nueva Habana*.

And the son of a New York based singer who had moved back to the island a couple months ago could be heard in the middle of the front row, where the teacher sat him because he was as tall as a second grader:

"Fag, fag, fag! He would alternate with the equivalent in the island, "*Pato, pato, pato!* in a Brooklyn accent.

Leandrito ran out. He left his equipment behind. Before he reached the building's first floor he had torn off the cape and pitched it on the steps. He didn't stop running until he got home.

The next six years were not that different, except for the polishing and refinement of his faux dark arts. He set up demonstrations in the backyard for neighborhood children, mostly girls younger than he. Every once in a while someone's mother would ask him to perform for guests at a birthday party where everyone applauded him and his illusions always came out right. Sometimes moms would try to pay him, but The Great Leander would refuse it in his professional magician's cape and white gloves, a red bow tie under the collar of his long-sleeve white shirt.

Serving as an artist of innocent deceit, fascinating children for an hour during which they believed him to hold the secrets he claimed to be so exotic and arcane that they were impossible to explain: that made him feel fulfilled. It convinced him he was in charge and control of something in his life, that not everything was living in the shame of public derision.

Nothing changed on the town's streets, which he traveled in an old Volkswagen van his dad had bought him. On the contrary: his reputation had extended to the generation before his and stretched toward the next one. He hated stopping to wait for a traffic light to change or to check for oncoming vehicles when he drove home. On the corner there was a bar so long and narrow that clients had to stand on the sidewalk to drink from the Corona cans and Michelob bottles. Some were classmates of his in high school. As was common throughout Puerto Rico, laws forbidding the sale of liquor to minors were only stated on statutes, seldom enforced. In reality, if the client was tall enough to place the money on the counter, he was old enough to be served. The same applied to cigarettes.

Sometimes his friend Ivonne, from the neighborhood, rode with him. They had become close friends since seventh grade, and she often served as his magician's assistant. When he came to a stop in front of the bar, he could hear the same epithets as always. From the corner of his eye he would look to see who was among the tormentors. Like a breathing fixture he could see Fatso Mora, his belly like a sack of potatoes over his belt, and Ramón Caloca, the one with bad breath. Occasionally he would see among the mob one or two of the ones who tried to persuade him to do privately what they condemned him for in public, He wished his magic were strong enough to turn Ivonne deaf.

"Don't pay attention to them, Leandro. They're just envious. They wish they were as smart and talented as you," Ivonne would say. He wouldn't reply. He just sighed deeply and tried to speed off as soon as possible.

For the hat illusion he now used a white turtledove he cared for like a pet. Dad looked at him suspiciously: for sure this one was not going to work with him at the bank, regardless of how he had reserved a position for him already. Mom didn't mind the magic foolishness as long as he graduated high school and pursued a career in law or diplomacy.

The second semester of twelfth grade he himself suggested to the principal, Mrs. Toyéns, that he set up his show some afternoon. So far his life had been ruled by insecurity and torment. He needed to convince himself that he could change the opinion of those who saw him as something less than human, unworthy of being among them. With his art and the refinement of his illusions he could turn his classmates' contempt into admiration. They would spread the word through town and soon everyone would be proud that someone as talented as he lived in their midst, someone who would go far with his mastery of the white occult.

"I don't know, Vega," Mrs. Toyéns said. "These kids go wild and there's no controlling them. And if you fail at anything, who knows."

"No, ma'am. I am in complete command of what I do. Let me show you I can do it. School is almost out and there's not much else to do. It's free entertainment."

"What would you need?" asked Mrs. Toyéns. "I ask you, because we don't have a red cent to pay for anything."

Leandro explained that he needed nothing. He would bring all of his equipment and even a folding table on which to put it. All he needed were a location and time enough to set up.

Mrs. Toyéns' resistance began to falter. Perhaps it wasn't a bad idea after all. Or maybe not: it sounded like an absurd idea that would be good only for exposing him to the same harassment. Then again, it could be a heavenly sign to make him give up the nonsense for good.

"Well, okay, but... Huh... I'm not so sure. You know what you're doing."

They agreed on a date. The performance would be the following Monday, the last week that students would come to school, because once the final exams were done with three weeks before the official close of the school year, who would show up? Teachers spent their time on attendance and grade reports and taking inventory of books after the students turned in their textbooks. When they were done they'd sit in empty classrooms playing cards or, like Mr. Martínez, would pull out a bottle of cheap Llave rum from the drawer where they kept it in a desk drawer, to pass the time anesthetized. Some others, Mr. Echandi in particular, tried to brush against as many female teachers allowed him to, now that students could not wag their tongues to talk about it.

Leandro suggested opening the folding blackboard walls that divided classrooms and using the stage on the last classroom for his performance. Mrs. Toyéns rejected the idea. Teachers had already collected supplies and whatever they wanted to take home for the summer. They would not want that mess to impede their efforts. It would have to be at the basketball court, outdoors.

The sun was going to scorch them, Leandro thought, but he agreed to it. Everything was set.

After lunch the following Monday afternoon The Great Leander went home and drove his Volkswagen back to school. The show was scheduled for two o'clock.

Before donning his attire, which by then included a tuxedo over which he threw the red-lined back cape, The Great Leander carried by himself what he needed to a spot under a basket. Students would sit in the bleachers on opposite sides of the court. He grabbed four stones from the ground to weigh down the tablecloth and prevent the wind from flying it away. At the foot of the table he placed a sign: "Presenting... The Great Leander!"

He didn't unload everything from the van at once. In between the six illusions he would take out what he needed and bring back what the following tricks required. He had a method.

Close to the starting time for the performance he felt upset. A threat of doubt about the wisdom of that experiment began digging into his certainty. His mind shook as much as his knees. He refused to let it intimidate him.

No, it wouldn't. This was his great opportunity, and he was not about to waste it with mental nonsense and spinelessness.

The bleachers started filling up, boys in their blue short-sleeved shirts and drill gray pants like the ones Amaury used to wear. The girls were in their brown pleated skirts and white blouses that had been the high school uniform when the school was still in town and had a different name. Several among them called him the usual names while others cheered them on, but The Great Leander also heard others ask them to hush. He felt more secure.

Everything went just as he had dreamed in his most optimistic moments. He performed his tricks with self-trust and a certain degree of ostentation he recognized as insincere and hammy, but still made him feel magnificent, spectacular. His audience was mesmerized; they applauded, listened to his prologue and the fantasies he weaved to enliven the tricks. He no longer heard anyone yelling sissy or fag or queer or Leandra.

Still to come was the impressive illusion with which to close his act. What he had used he carried back to the Volkswagen, parked right behind him. From the rear of the van he started preparing what followed, the illusion with the turtledove, which he would pull out from the hat after a member of the audience came to check it. He had abandoned long before the tastelessness of the rubber chicken. The turtledove, which he pulled from the false bottom with his hand, granted the trick a touch of life, of truly magic authenticity. Where did that dove come from? How does he do it? The lack of answers to those questions conferred upon him an aura of mystic mystery.

He pulled out the hat from a large box and from a plastic box he took the second of three magic wands he used in his shows. He lifted the secret compartment where he'd hide the dove. From the box with the holes carved on the sides and the lid he meant to pull the turtledove when he discovered that the poor bird had fallen prey to the suffocating heat in the Volkswagen and lay on its back, legs sticking up, flaccid and still.

Boundless sadness overwhelmed The Great Leander, dejected over the loss of his pet, confused and trembling. He realized there would be no closing act. He looked at the cement bleachers, where all faces were turned toward him, waiting for what was to come.

Dismay took hold of the last bastion of control he still had. He took the turtledove in both hands above his head, carried it to the spot under the basket and started weeping while his entire body convulsed.

"It has died on me," he tried to say, but only produced choked syllables.

Some remained silent, perhaps saddened and relating to Leandrito's pain. Soon someone somewhere in the bleachers started clapping and yelling.

"Sissy! Faggot, faggot, faggot... Girlie cry-baby, Leandra!"

The Great Leander recognized the voice. It was Fatso Mora, with his nasal shrill just like a child whose testicles have not yet descended. Anger was The Great Leander's first reaction: how dare that moron behave with such blasphemy, that callousness in the presence of his pet's cadaver? He stopped crying. It wasn't long before he realized his anger was useless. Others joined Fatso Mora's taunts. Among them sat teachers: none stood up or did anything to stop the mob. Fatso Mora's was an aria initiated by the opera's villain, but it was not a solo. Soon it rose in crescendo from a, off-pitch chorus to support him by repeating the damned refrain. Several teachers joined them.

The rabble did not stop at the epithets: The Great Leander saw them rising and walking in his direction. He took some backwards steps. They noticed it. They were going to catch up with him who knew with what intention.

He turned around and ran to the Volkswagen without letting go the dead turtledove. He searched in his pocket for the key he quickly stuck in the ignition. The crowd banged on the windows; some tried to get into the sliding door The Great Leander had left open when he discovered, devastated, the dove's death. He feared running over them. He dropped the dove's cadaver on the passenger's seat.

"Faggot, faggot, faggot, faggot, faggot!

Hearing the name so close to him filled him with dread. Someone was trying to open his door. He held on to it and was able to shut it back in the three attempts the person on the other side of the door made to open it.

He slammed on the brakes as far down as he could. The ones who had tried to get in the sliding door on the side, still hanging on to it, got hit with the door frame. When he accelerated the intruders fell off the van. Someone stood in front of him to keep him from leaving while another boy was trying to rip out the windshield wiper on the passenger's side.

He thought no more. He shot the accelerator and gave the fool standing ahead just enough time to get out of the way. He looked on the rearview mirror and saw the brown and gray mass raising fists in the air and yelling threats and tormenting names.

That evening Mrs. Toyéns came to his house with the folding table and the folded tablecloth. She said nothing about the incident. She didn't apologize. She didn't berate him for hurting several students. She just dropped the table and the folded tablecloth on the porch.

"You left this behind," she said. She ignored his dad, who was in a rocking chair on the opposite side of the porch. "I didn't want someone to steal it."

Then she turned around and left.

He studied neither finance nor accounting, as his dad had foreseen; he studied nothing that prepared him to argue cases in any court. He majored in humanities, which, mom and dad agreed, was a waste of time and the waiting room in unemployment hell.

He graduated college and put his diploma in his mom's hand. With money Ivonne lent him he left for Las Vegas. Ten years later The Great Leander's name was on the marquee of one of the better hotels, where he appeared in one of the nightclubs. Five years later he was appearing in television variety shows. He appeared on Broadway three years after his debut on *The Tonight Show* with Jay Leno. He was considered one of the best illusionists in the world, at the same level, if not higher, as David Copperfield and David Blaine. He was a technical advisor on the set of *The Illusionist*, where he trained Edward Norton. At the Olympia in Paris he did sold-out shows for two weeks. The same happened when he appeared on stage at the Theatre Des Westens in Berlin. Milan recognized him by granting him the privilege of performing at Il Teatro alla Scala. Even Queen Elizabeth II was a guest in a commend performance at the Royal Albert Hall in London.

The Great Leander no longer performed hat tricks with birds or rabbits and much less with rubber chickens. He was an artiste of international fame, wealthy and set up in New York City's Upper East Side, where he never met with people from his hometown. They would find out his address through his mother, then showed up the way they did on the island, unannounced and uninvited.

"When you see people at the door who show up without previous notice, send them off," he told Henry, his business manager and companion, after Henry made the mistake of thinking that, if they knew the artist's name and claimed to know him from back home, it was alright to let them in. "Don't even bother to let me know. If I'm not expecting them, they're trespassers, a nuisance. Don't let them in the door."

They would appear every so often as if conjured by black magic. He asked them once how they made it past the doorman and found out they dropped the magician's mother's name and assured him they had known him since childhood. Then he gave the doorman the same instructions he had given Henry.

"Ask them whether I am expecting them. If they say yes, call up. Chances are they are lying."

Those people were the sewer flies in the ointment of his happiness.

After his third show at Madrid's Zarzuela Theatre he decided to return to Puerto Rico, where he performed at the Luis A. Ferré Fine Arts Center in San Juan for a single night. More than an interest in his illusions, the audience wanted to see this Puerto Rican who had conquered the world, this queer Rita Moreno who had to leave his land of origin to rise above its pettiness.

At the end of his performance, before granting press interviews and receiving local dignitaries he retired briefly to his dressing room. He wanted to relax a bit and drink a glass of water.

Someone walked in while he urinated. Whoever it was did not hesitate. The Great Leander shook his penis, zipped up and walked out of the bathroom, intent on admonishing the intruder, whose back was toward him, crouching, a small broom in one hand and a long-handled dust pan in the other, sweeping out a corner of the room. The intruder's belly almost touched the floor in front of him.

"How dare you come in without knocking or permission?" asked The Great Leander. "Are you used to this lack of discretion?"

"Hey, you'll have to excuse me, but this is my job," the man said without looking back or stopping the sweeping by the large garbage can on wheels. "If I don't do it, I get fired."

Many years had slipped by, but this voice that now sounded somewhat harsher was familiar.

The man stood up, still with his back to The Great Leander. The artist noticed with some repugnance the man's arm covered in crude tattoos in green ink of a crucifix and stars out of proportion. With that same arm he hung the dust pan on a hook on the side of the trash can he started pushing out. He wore a soiled yellow cap from whose edges stuck out curly strands of greasy hair, a cap that wasn't deep enough to cover the other tattoo on his neck, under the left ear. It was another sketch in green ink of something resembling a lizard.

The man turned sideways to walk out. The Great Leander was able to confirm that the man was, no doubt about it, Fatso Mora.

It Happened This Way

*"He wears a mask and his
face grows to fit it."*

George Orwell

Back in the neighborhood on B Street in the subdivision known as the hangout of the rich and influential everyone knew or thought they knew who the Piñeros were. The wife, Mariíta, had been a social worker in the local elementary school. Among the comments she included when she evaluated school children were "He comes from the slum and he shows it. He will grow up to be a thief or something worse. He will end up in juvenile detention before he turns eleven."

The visionary's husband, Don Daniel Piñero— Danny, to Mariíta—was known as forward and something of a dirty old man. Neighborhood husbands feared him and women avoided him. He bragged about his likeness to a Mexican actor by the name of Arturo de Córdova and, as a matter of fact, there was a resemblance, mostly in the phony bedroom eyes he had for women after whom he lusted and the graying thin moustache. He mostly wore jeans or khaki work slacks, plaid shirts, a high-brimmed straw hat and work boots. That is what he wore to work at the family dairy farm, where he made sure not to become involved in tasks that would ruin his manicure.

Danny and Mariíta had two children, Junior, around eleven, and María Julia, five years younger than her brother. Neighborhood children's parents frowned upon a friendship with the Piñero children. Rumor was, justifiably, that the father would ask his daughter to call other girls to come play with her when her mother was not home. In the midst of games and merrymaking the father could not restrain himself from placing his hands where he shouldn't on his daughter's playmates.

From the Piñeros' rooftop, a flat cement surface lower than the exterior walls that formed a low fence around it, baseball games at the city park were visible. Minor-league games were played there Sundays during baseball season. Sometimes Junior and Robertito, who was more or less Junior's age, would go up a wooden ladder behind the house to climb to the roof and watch the game. The last time Robertito joined Junior up there Don Danny, in pajamas and a bathrobe when it was already mid-afternoon, climbed up behind the two boys to watch the game with them.

"I have to take a piss," Don Danny said at the top of the second inning. He squatted low enough that neighbors would not have seen him, pulled up his robe to his chest, pulled down his pajama bottoms. He gave the boys a clear view of his genitals and the urine stream while staring them in the face. At first Junior feigned indifference, but when Don Danny was done peeing and remained in the same spot, fondling his penis, Junior smacked his lips.

"I gotta go," the son said. He climbed over the rooftop edge to get on the ladder. "You can stay if you want, Robertito."

Robertito followed Junior down the ladder. Don Danny did not descend behind them.

Robertito thought about telling his parents. Instead he chose not to climb on the rooftop again for any reason.

Weeks later Mariíta had to attend an evening meeting of the Parents and Teachers' Association. Junior asked several boys in the neighborhood to join him to play in the carport. Robertito thought about it. As long as he was not alone with Junior and his dad, the old man would not have a chance to give him anatomy lessons, he figured.

"Come over to the porch," Don Danny ordered when a group of six or seven children had gathered in the carport. "You're going to scratch my Jeep."

A little later Don Danny whispered loudly enough for the children to perceive the urgency without the neighbors hearing anything Don Danny said:

"Children, get in the house! I hear noises in the backyard. It could be some thief, a marauder of some kind. Get in, get in right away!"

Persuaded by the seriousness of the matter the children rushed into the house, Robertito among them.

"Junior, go see what's back there," Don Danny told his son at the same time he placed a flashlight in the boy's hand.

"Why should I?" Junior asked.

"Because I have to look after your little friends and no one else can go," Don Danny replied.

Protesting under his breath Junior went off to inspect the backyard.

"Don't make any noise! Shh!" Don Danny ordered the children." Let's go to the last room in the back to look out the window and see what Junior finds.

Sheep under the spell of the shepherd, the children followed Don Danny to the back of the house. They gathered against the window slats to get a clear view of whatever Junior found with his flashlight.

"Shine to the left," Junior's father ordered in a tone that would have alerted any intruders. "Now toward the back fence."

Meanwhile Don Danny had shifted to stand right behind Robertito. He had contorted himself to press his crotch against the boy's buttocks. Robertito stiffened, not knowing what to do. The rest of the boys were in front of him searching out the window for the elusive intruder, nervous over the possibility that, if someone was on the prowl back there, he could hurt Junior while Don Danny remained inside the house.

"You haven't shone yet to the right, Junior," Don Danny ordered his son while he rubbed in gyrations against Robertito and held him by his shoulders, the other boys still in front and glued to the window. Robertito tried to let loose and Don Danny held him back. He held Robertito's right arm with one hand and held the boy by the chest with the other.

"I don't see anything," Junior said. "There's no one here. I'm going back inside."

Robertito went home feeling confused. No one had done that to him before. His classmates talked about things. They shared among themselves what they learned from older brothers, things he had not tried out or had any interest in. They all seemed as exotic as Kipling's tales and the short stories of Jorge Luis Borges, which he read without understanding completely from a book his teacher had lent him.

He would never go back to play with Junior Piñero or step into that house even if mother went with him.

The following afternoon, close to dinner time, Robertito was returning home from a Boy Scouts meeting in the local Catholic parish. He wore his uniform and the badge sash he was so proud of. He walked down the Piñeros' sidewalk, on the same side of the street as his house. He heard Doña Mariíta call him. He turned toward her. She asked him to come into the house. As long as she was there, he thought, he'd be safe from Don Danny. He walked up. When he followed her into the dining room he removed his cap.

"My husband told me what you did to him last night," Doña Mariíta said in a tone Robertito identified as the same one his mother used when he did something of which she disapproved. Doña Mariíta was on her feet close to him, her right fist on her hip. She shook her left finger at his face.

"What was that, ma'am?" asked Robertito. If he had stood in front of a camp bonfire his face would not have burned as much.

"Touching him down there." She frowned, pursed her lips and looked at Robertito's groin.

Robertito remained silent for a moment, wondering when his face would melt.

"I did not touch him, ma'am," he said staring her in the face. "It was he who...

"You disrespectful brat! I thought you had been raised better than this. Now you're going to deny it and blame him? I should tell your mom and dad and make sure they fix you up," she said, her mouth stretched out from side to side as if she needed to make room for everything she needed to say. He continued to stare at her. "That is a nasty habit. I'm not going to tell them. I don't want to embarrass them when they learn they have a son who goes around doing filthy things."

Doña Mariíta was right: his parents would believe her and belt him in between slaps to the face and sermons. They had both done it for minor infractions against house rules. This could cost him his life. His fear soared.

From the corner of his eye where they stood in the dining room he noticed something moving in the living room. Don Danny was reading the newspaper in silence, as if none of that had anything to do with him. His wife could have just as easily been pressing burning coals against his cheeks for all that man seemed to care. Robertito did not know whether to cry or drop dead from shame, It wasn't so much because of the imputations the unwary wife was making as for his lack of understanding of what that rubbing against someone else's butt was all about or why anyone would want to do it. He was disgusted when Don Danny held him back after he refused Don Danny's contact against him.

"I don't want to see you again in this house. I don't want you playing with my children, you hear?" Doña Mariíta finally said. She shook her finger even closer to Robertito's face.

The boy walked out of the house invaded by an overwhelming confusion that he would not be able to disentangle fully until several years later. He asked himself whether Doña Mariíta inhabited an isolation chamber with lead walls that kept her from becoming aware that not everyone could have been guilty of getting fresh with her husband.

As an adult Robertito, a physician married to another physician, Federico, came from Virginia for a short visit to the old neighborhood. He walked past the Piñeros' house. Doña Mariíta sat in a rocking chair in her porch. She was in conversation with another María, Doña María Ramos, whom Robertito remembered as the neighborhood gossip monger everyone feared. Doña Mariíta recognized Robertito and jumped from her rocking chair to run out to the sidewalk and kissed him on the cheek. Robertito was speechless. Maybe the woman thought he was rehabilitated from his antisocial habits, all of it a phase he had overcome. He regretted that Federico had been too busy to join him on his visit: Robertito would have had the immense pleasure of introducing him as his husband to Doña Mariíta.

"Now, this one I did touch. I'm still touching it," he would have said to her face.

As he walked away he waited for a discreet moment to rub with the palm of his hand the spot where she had kissed him. He needed to obliterate the invisible imprint she had left on him.

Don Danny had died. She lived alone. Junior was an engineer and had moved to Texas; María Julia was a psychologist in Arizona. The day her father was buried she was scheduled to take a final exam for one of her college classes and decided that the test was more important than burying him. Neither of them returned to the town after graduating college until Doña Mariíta died. She had lost her mind and was practically blind. She would cause a commotion when she'd run out of the nursing home screaming "All I need is a good fuck!"

Neither Junior nor María Julia claimed their inheritance. María Julia said she did not even want to ever hear again her parents' names. The house remained vacant, fully furnished and abandoned. It became a shelter for homeless people first, then a shooting gallery for heroin addicts and a crack house in the midst of the neighborhood's opulence. Sometimes crackheads under the influence would come out of the house naked to perform dance routines and often ended up performing sex acts that scandalized some neighbors while others watched from behind their windows. Eventually someone would call the police, who did nothing.

The city seized the property and had the house razed. All that remains of it is a miniature jungle full of weeds and vines.

Bodies That Should Not Return with Dawn

The sky has shores where to avoid life
And there are bodies that should not return with
dawn.

El cielo tiene playas donde evitar la vida
y hay cuerpos que no deben repetirse en la aurora.

Federico García Lorca,
"Oda a Walt Whitman"

José Francisco was the first.

Not the first with whom I did it, but certainly the first one with whom I wanted to do it with the hormonal despair that only a twelve-year old boy can experience. He was my obsession, the boy I would glance at furtively during recess and when he walked past my house. He was a grade ahead of me in school, fit, popular with girls, admired by boys, an athlete, a leader. His eyes were almost black, of the type they call wild, sheltered under long eyelashes and set against caramel-colored skin that I longed to touch. I wanted him to notice me, but not from so close or with such intimacy forced upon him that he would react by punching me in the face.

He lived next door. Every night I searched from our bathroom's window for the light of José Francisco's bedroom. From there I could see the inside of his room across the alley. Behind a locked door, in the darkness I waited until José Francisco undressed, visible through windows free from the obstruction of curtains, and wrapped a white towel around his waist to go shower. I would wait as long as I had to, my heart drumming a rumba, against the Persian-slatted window, until José Francisco returned from his bath, dried off with the towel and offered me, without knowing it I thought, the fleeting vision of his genitals, hardly discernible against a dense, black pubic mat.

My father had finally yielded to my unrelenting request for a pair of binoculars. They were inexpensive ones he had found in a store close to his factories on Padial Street, in Caguas. The binoculars had turned out to be of little help. José Francisco would not stand still while putting on his clothes. He paced around the room and too soon after removing the towel it seemed to me he had pulled up his white shorts.

I had put a great deal of effort in adopting a masculine tone of voice and gestures, perhaps too much. I feared that someone would see through my performance as a transvestite in reverse. I would ask José Francisco to wrestle in the front yard. I strove to ignore the sharp stones that often broke my skin. I pretended to remove his body from mine when he held me in a chokehold, then later yelled "Surrender! Surrender!" when he pinned me down under his body.

One summer my father bought me a BB gun. I showed it to José Francisco, who offered to give me shooting lessons in a wooded area not too far from our neighborhood, on the other side of the Brook of the Dead. The first lesson consisted of pointing the gun at a rusty can on a wooden picket, part of a barbed-wire fence that separated city land from the Méndez farm. The second lesson, two days later, required José Francisco to support my hand with his to stabilize my wrist while he stood behind me rubbing against my butt. At first it would have been difficult to determine whether he did it on purpose or because it was a cosequential aspect of the learning experience. After some time the student felt the instructor's hardened underbelly pressuring against his buttocks. It was so obvious that I asked him not to do it, betraying my desire and with my every instinct contorted under the petition. José Francisco withdrew. He said nothing. His silence evinced his awareness of what he was doing. We crossed the miniature jungle and walked back home in silence.

One night when my drool moistened the window screen I noticed under José Francisco's towel the undeniable profile of an erection. A choked sigh escaped my mouth. I saw José Francisco look toward my window. I pulled away into the deeper darkness of the bathroom. I feared, with the contradictory hope that he had, that José Francisco heard me. Perhaps he had always known that there was someone with his face stuck against the window screen and that was why he had left his windows open and the light on.

Instead of pulling up his underwear, he put on a pair of jeans and a T-shirt. He walked out of his bedroom.

It was a Tuesday. Neighbors knew that my parents went to a special church service Tuesday night. José Francisco also knew I was home alone.

The doorbell rang. On the other side of the door stood José Francisco. Through the peep hole José Francisco looked upset, threatening.

"Yes?" I asked, my voice uncertain, as if I had no idea who it might be. He turned the doorknob, pushed the door open and walked in.

"Do you still have the *Superman* comic books?" he asked.

"Yes, sure. They are in my bedroom. I'll go get them," I replied, trying to keep the lid on my fear braided in desire, not knowing which would prevail if I let myself go.

José Francisco followed me to my bedroom. We had to walk no more than thirty feet, for me six inches alternating with seven miles, in any case fueled by a tempting and ambivalent dread that overwhelmed me with the suspicion that this was all a ruse. José Francisco knew where the pile of comic books was: he had seen it during other visits to my house without paying any attention to it. I was anguished by the troubling thought that José Francisco could tell anyone else what my jumble of feelings both feared and craved, the same confusion that had led me to reject the overture during the shooting lesson.

While I was excited by the idea that José Francisco had found me worthy of this kind of attention, instead of seeing me as just the neighbor, now the dream and its possible fulfillment were crossing from one dimension to another, but crushed under the weight of a duality imposed by the need to balance instinct and my secret's potential publication.

I bent over in a corner to pick up the comic books. Before I could straighten up again José Francisco had closed in to rub his crotch against my buttocks. He took me by my waist and started to sway his hips with obvious excitement. I was completely aware that I could no longer pretend that I did not know what this was about. I had to stop him at that precise moment, turn around and push him back to make it clear I was not one of *those* people.

Or I could let José Francisco continue to loosen my belt, unbutton my pants until they dropped at my feet. That is what I did. He had not done the same with his clothes: he went on pressing against my back, his hands on my waist, rubbing vertically, softly caressing my skin. He said nothing. I could feel his warm breath on my nape; I could hear his panting murmur.

He finally unbuttoned his pants and approached me without the interference of fabric. My blood abandoned the rest of my body and gathered in throbs in my temples.

José Francisco walked toward the opposite wall, where he flipped the ceiling light off. The only light in the room was a blade of cerulean moonlight, sliced by the slats of the windows. In the semidarkness José Francisco took me by my shoulders. Saying nothing, he led me to the edge of my bed. Filled with terror I felt José Francisco pressing his naked glans against my clenched teeth. As grandma Lola used to say, one thing is to call for the devil, a much different one to see him approaching. I felt like the bullfighter who enters the ring barely hiding his hesitation, motivated by a fondness for a fear bordering on the erotic, to provoke the bull with the sharp horns, without knowing what the goring feels like.

"No, no," I tried to say with a tightened jaw while José Francisco grabbed me by my head to prevent my rejection. He must have been sure I was not going to bite him. I shook my head, but did not defend myself with my hands. I was sitting on them. This was a new experience for me. As an elementary-school child I had explored alternative forms of penetration with my cousins Edwin and Manolín, with Danilo Román and Rafita Ochoa, experiments mostly failed and painful due to a lack of physical maturity and the ignorance of sexual mechanics.

José Francisco broke the silence. As if to make sure that no one else could hear him in a house that only he and I occupied at the moment, he said, "Don't pretend. I knew you were peeping at me through the window. Wasn't this what you were looking for? If you already have it against your lips, what does it matter if you have it in your mouth?"

My emotional conflict was thus resolved. Aristotle could not have appealed to sounder logic. I yielded, but faking objections to the surrender with light moaning and attempts to put as little effort into it as possible. It was a drama only I had believed, credible in my histrionic deceit. My audience of one had seen right through it.

While I tried lip and tongue movements, I was not sure of mastering for José Francisco's benefit, I felt my own excitement. I raised a thigh to loosen my hand. I grabbed myself, but José Francisco slapped my hand and pushed away my arm to make me let go. I thought it was part of the journey on which I had just sailed to deny the subjugated the recognition of his own masculine sexuality. Perhaps it was necessary to preserve the illusion that it was not another man who was manipulating his sexual organs, but rather a facsimile of a woman.

"You can't touch yourself there. I don't have sex with males, get it?" he said without pulling away from my mouth, which emitted a vague affirmation without interrupting the rhythm of the operation.

At his climax I did not know what I was supposed to do with something that tasted like salty castor oil.

"Swallow," he said when he pulled away, flaccid, and held my head with one hand while covering my mouth with the other.

He pulled up his jeans. Still in a state of partial tumescence, I did not dare stand up. I slowly spread my legs until I felt it slide between my thighs, becoming invisible between my sparse pubes. I pulled my legs together again and formed a sort of crackless vagina. I waited for José Francisco to leave before slipping into my underwear. I did not know what protocol I was supposed to follow. I wanted to satisfy my own need, but felt shame at the thought I would be betraying José Francisco.

That night I dreamt in reverse: I lived again the scene with him in my unconsciousness. The emission awoke me, a thick moisture in my crotch that wet my pajama bottoms. Several days went by before I was able to materialize my urgency for self-satisfaction, at the end of which I felt the remorse that overwhelms when the conscience cries out in a voice stronger than that of the flesh, with a draped scream.

With a few exceptions, that was Tuesday night for me until I turned fourteen. Later, when I had gone to boarding school and only came home for a few weeks in the summer, José Francisco tried to restart those encounters that eventually turned monotonous for the lack of affective and sensual variety and that never lasted more than three or four minutes.

I no longer peeped from the window. The concretion of the longing for an object of desire unbound by reciprocal tenderness tends to placate curiosity to engender in its stead the substitute of indifference. Besides, in boarding school, where we all undressed, walked around naked with impudence and bathed in open showers, I had lost interest in José Francisco's possible uniqueness, which then became much less impressive. I had reoriented my appetite, sublimated as friendship with classmates incapable of suspecting my repressed hunger. Crushing the core of my being without mercy allowed me to broaden my feelings beyond the possibility of zipper teeth scratching my lips.

By then José Francisco had a formal girlfriend, Nilda. She had been a grade behind me in school. She was one of those who yelled "Faggot, queer!" at other boys as synonyms of jerk, asshole, stupid or son of a bitch or, in some cases, as an accusation of something that could or not be true.

I felt the unjustified sting of betrayal. I did not want to repeat an instance of José Francisco, eyes shut, lying on his back in my bed on a Tuesday night, the physical fulfillment of his fantasies, what he would not be able to do with virginal Nilda.

A decade later I was living far from the town, on Pez Street in the gay district of Chueca, Madrid. On the few times that sleeplessness assailed me since my marriage to Manolo, I looked into my spouse's countenance, sleeping in his innocence by my side, with a light snore, to me a lovely, rhythmic tune. He would not wake up when I ran my fingers gingerly down his arms to convince myself that my happiness was not fiction. Javier was the second man I had kissed. The first one had been a Jesuit priest during a spiritual retreat at San Ildefonso's Seminary in Aibonito, in Puerto Rico.

By then I had understood that denying another man a tender kiss or caress is not what makes a man straight after subduing and using another man's affection to deposit in him fluids during a convulsive and passing

reflex. That only was irrefutable evidence of the inhumane hollowness that inhabits the space where others
have their heart.

A Yearning Draped in Silence

The boy is about to have his first cocktail. Two months ago he turned thirteen. It's going to be a *Cuba libre* in a disposable waxed-cardboard Solo cup. That's what he asks Lope for, a rum and Coke with a small wedge of lime and a wooden swizzle stick, the way his dad has them.

"Your dad lets you drink?" Lope asks. The boy nods. His hands are shaking; his legs too. Anyone would think it's because he's so excited about having his first drink. It's a rite of passage in Puerto Rico. You're not a man until you've had your first taste of rum. No, beer will not do: it must be rum, preferably Don Q, the good stuff. The next evolutionary task, deflowering a girl, is proof irrefutable you're a man; if a hymen is not available, then it must be a visit to one of Tony Tursi's establishments of ill repute, escorted by an older brother or cousin—sometimes your own dad. The boy needs to take this step. He doubts he will want to walk through the next gate.

However, he trembles at being before Lope. It's his first taste of alcohol and the first time he has been this close to Lope, although they are separated by the makeshift bar his dad set up in the garage. Lope had been to their house many times to sit in the terrace and drink with the boy's dad. The boy would peek out the window to look at Lope, but had never dared sit in the terrace and listen to their conversations. His mom wouldn't let him, for one. "Your dad's family blood is 80° proof. You don't need to fulfill that prophecy." For another, the boy would not dare look at Lope. That would have encouraged Lope to start up a conversation with him. His tongue would have dried up and twisted. He wouldn't have been able to say anything and come across as mentally defective. He had to be happy watching Lope without being seen. Even the cigarette glued to Lope's lip gave the boy an image to sleep to at night.

Lope has his own drink to the side of the bar. It looks like gin and something else. A clear drink with a twist of lemon rind at the bottom and a wooden swizzle stick.

"Now, take it easy, okay? Don't drink fast and let it last," Lope says. The boy nods and smiles. He cannot look at Lope in the face. With his eyes he follows Lope's hands mixing the drink and imagines those hands are caressing him, that Lope's arms are around his shoulders holding him tight to his side as they take a stroll around *La Selvita*, the Little Jungle, on the other side of the mountain behind their subdivision. No one will see them walking back there. The boy has not yet dared imagine his lips against Lope's. He only sees himself staring into Lope's face as the older man speaks to him of love and its inexplicable hold on humans, the things we do in its name and the uselessness of questioning why. Lying unseen in the thicket the boy looks to the sky and then turns his head toward Lope again, mistrusting his own eyes. How can it be that Lope is here with him? He must be dreaming.

"I was your age when dad sent me off to Colegio San José," Lope says. "That's a boys' school in Río Piedras, you know. You must have seen it from the freeway, close to where it turns into 65ᵗʰ Infantry Avenue?" Of course the boy has. He did not know Lope had been there. Hence whenever he sees the school building from the road he'll think that Lope once walked its halls and slept in one of its beds. "That's where I learned to drink. So if you go to that boarding school your dad told me about, don't start drinking. Once you have a taste, hell, you can't give it up." Lope handed the boy the *Cuba libre*. Their hands brush and the boy feels a quiver rise from his fingers to his heart. Lope lowers his voice so the boy can still hear him above the Christmas carols, the *aguinaldos* on the record player and speaks in his ear. "It's like sex, you know." He laughs. The boy blushes and laughs a little, but won't dare look at Lope in the face. Then he looks anyway. For the first time he notices Lope's perfect teeth behind the lips somewhat covered by a thick graying moustache. How old can he be? Not that old. His mother says he was in her first-grade class when she started teaching. That was in 1946. Lope can't be more than 28, but his hair is almost all completely gray. So is Lope's father's. It must be a genetic thing.

The boy comes back for a refill. His legs are a little wobbly, perhaps because he has been dancing the mashed potato with Angie Cruz. The dance floor is the carport's, connected to the garage by a cement slab. Back in the garage is where Lope is still bartending. He hadn't done that before at his parents' annual Christmas party. All the neighbors were invited. His dad had a pig roasted and hired cooks to take care of the rest. He also got someone who worked a club in town to do the bartending. Lope and his wife had always been guests. The boy doesn't know why he is doing that job tonight. Maybe the bartender didn't show up. Maybe he wants to: then he can be closer to the liquor. His wife Manuela is chatting with *señora* Monina and *doña* Leonor in the porch. The boy dances facing the garage. While Angie tries her best to keep her rhythm to Dee Dee Sharp's singing the boy is following Lope's every move in the garage. Lope takes a break from his duties, lifts a leg and props his foot against the edge of a small barrel on the floor, his right elbow resting on the bar and his left hand holding a drink and a cigarette. He looks in the boy's direction, so the boy looks elsewhere. Sometimes one of the guests walks up for a drink and strikes up a conversation. It's then that the boy can look at Lope knowing the man's talking with someone and will not notice the boy's pining eyes fixed on him. If Lope did, what would the boy do? How frightening the thought.

The boy does not ask for another drink. Maybe Lope will tell him he's had enough. Or the boy will get so drunk he will tell Lope how he feels. Then God only knows what will happen. Lope will scold him and reject him and never again even look in his direction and tell his father what the boy said and the news will spread around town when Lope tells the story in some bar or at a Rotary Club gathering.

Every weekday afternoon the boy sits in the front porch to do his homework. He checks his Mickey Mouse watch every so often. Close to 5:30 he stops working math problems to focus on the sidewalk across the street. Soon he sees Lope approaching. He's coming from work and headed home, four houses down from the boy's on the other side of the street. He's a supervisor in a hairpin factory in town where his brother-in-law is manager. The boy can't see him on his way to work in the morning: by the time he leaves his house the boy is on the school bus. On Catholic holy days when school does not meet the boy sits early in the morning in the dining room facing the street, waiting for Lope to walk up to work. The boy likes days off in honor of some Catholic saint, but not because school is out.

Lope looks not where the boy sits. He looks straight ahead and smokes his cigarette. While still in Lope's field of vision the boy lowers his head as if reading some word problem and forces his eyes to the upper corner to follow Lope. The boy looks across the porch and sees Aida García and her friend from secretarial school Olga Escobar next door. He can hear them clearing their throats, trying to get him to look at the porch where they are sitting. They, too, follow Lope as he walks down toward his house. When he has gone past them Aida looks at Olga and curls up her tongue against her upper lip. The boy only looks at Lope from behind until the man reaches his front fence and walks in. He's afraid Lope would catch him looking and greet or wave at him, and he would not know what to do, probably freeze, and next time Lope walks by he won't bother with the greeting.

"Where did these cigarette butts come from?" the boy's mother asks him one afternoon after storming into his bedroom. "Have you been smoking, boy?"

In her hand his mother has his wallet. She has been going through it. His mother's tone, he knows, is meant to keep him from asking her what she's been doing going through his things. He sees through the intimidation tactic and decides to challenge it anyway.

"Why are you going through my wallet?" the boy asks.

"Doing what a concerned mother does," she shouts. "And it seems I need to do it! Answer me now!"

"Those are Dad's," the boy says.

"Dad's? Why the hell would you be keeping your dad's cigarette butts in your wallet?" As she asks it he realizes how borderline creepy that sounds.

"They are Dad's. I just picked them up and put them there, that's all," the boy says. He tries to sound reasonable. It's lucky for him that Lope and his dad both smoke Winston.

His mother turns around to face the hall, where his dad is standing.

"He says these cigarette butts are yours. Why would he keep them if not to smoke what's left? Or maybe he's smoked them himself and can't think what to do with them," his mother says.

"Oh, leave him alone. The boy's growing up. That's what boys do," his father says.

"Not this boy! He better not start smoking," his mother says. "If I ever catch you smoking you're going to get what's coming to you." She then takes the three cigarette butts and throws the empty wallet at him. He watches her retreat with the cigarette butts in her hand, and his heart goes with them.

The boy is relieved that his father somehow put an end to the interrogation. Getting a belting for smoking would be preferable to what would happen if he tells the truth. Three times when Lope has gone by on his way home the boy has noticed that Lope throws his cigarette on the ground and keeps on walking. The boy has waited until he is out of Lope's sight. He has walked across the street and looked for the discarded butt. He has picked it up and walked home with it. If the cigarette butt still has enough tobacco in it he takes a drag from it. In any case, he presses the cigarette filter against his mouth, knowing that Lope's lips have been on it.

Now his mother has taken away the mementos of his fanciful lovemaking. He will not pick up any more. Regardless of where he hides them, his mother's harassment would exceed the value of the fantasy.

The boy is now fifteen. One Sunday morning, while the boy and his mother are having a late breakfast and his father is still in bed they hear a knock at the door. It's

Manuela, Lope's wife, looking as if God has told her she will be struck dead in three minutes.

"Is your husband home?" Manuela asks his mother.

"Yes, he's still in bed," his mother replies. "Do you need to talk to him?"

"I'd like to, but if he's asleep, then don't bother him," Manuela says. She's smoking and the boy knows it's not a cigarette butt he wants to put away in his wallet. "Actually, I just wanted to know whether he knows where Lope might be."

"Come in," his mother says. She shuts the door. The boy returns to the dining room. He has lost his appetite. He suspects something terrible has happened to Lope. His soul tarnishes with the pain of the mere thought that Lope could be injured in any way, worse if the thought he refuses to allow into his mind were the case. "Where did he say he was going?"

"He said he was going out for cigarettes. That was last night. The place where he usually buys them hasn't opened yet. I was there already," Lope's wife says, "I haven't slept all night." She puts out her cigarette in an ashtray and pulls out another one from her dress pocket. She strikes a match and lights it before continuing. "I guess he went somewhere else from there, probably a bar, but they are all closed, and no one is going to give me any information." The boy notices her hands were shaking. His are doing likewise.

"Don't worry, Manuela," the boy's mother says. "He probably fell asleep somewhere. Just wait.

Something will come up. Everyone knows his family in this town." She's right. Lope's dad owned the land where their house's development is. He had also owned a rum distillery and much real estate. None of the old man's three children had amounted to much when judged as academic or labor achievements. One of his daughters had married a Peruvian mechanic who then took advantage of his father-in-law's money to improve his social and financial status. The other daughter married a clerk in a paint shop; they got a large lot and a big house to go with it as a wedding present. When the old man died they all inherited his properties. But while the daughters kept a low profile and associated only with members of their own social class, Lope had taken to heavy drinking in sleazy dives. Lope's job was a favor from his Peruvian brother-in-law: he really didn't do anything at the factory except pace and stand at the main gate smoking. Sometimes when walking downtown the boy would detour from the shortest route to go past the factory in the hope of catching a glimpse of Lope. He had married Manuela, the daughter of another Asturian entrepreneur who, like Lope's own father, had traveled from the Bay of Biscay to Puerto Rico in steerage and wearing *alpargatas*, Asturian slippers, then married into creole wealth. Lope's drinking buddies includes people his siblings would have never allowed past the front gate.

In chats with other neighbors Manuela often says casually that when he gets home in the afternoon Lope showers, then goes to their air-conditioned bedroom and asks her to come play Battleship with him, but she's busy cooking and he starts whining that he wants her to come play Battleship while he drinks his whiskey on the rocks. After dinner he wants to play Battleship again and it's surprising they managed to have two children. If it weren't for her nagging him in the morning, he'd miss work. It's easier to prepare their twins for school than getting him out of bed, she says.

"If you hear anything, please, call me," Lope's wife tells the boy's mother. "I'm going insane! He's done some crazy stuff before, but never like this!"

"When my husband gets up I'll ask him. Don't worry. He'll show up," the boy's mother says.

The boy does his best to conceal his despair.

"Where could he be?" the boy asks his mother with feigned lack of concern.

"Who knows. He's nothing but a drunk. Probably passed out and locked up in some bar where the bartender couldn't get him to wake up," the boy's mother says.

The boy's father walks up to the dining room looking hung over. He asks for a cup of coffee and lights a cigarette. The boy tells him what Manuela just came over for.

"We were at Monche's last night," the boy's father says. "I don't know what happened to him. I got in my car and drove home. I left him there."

"Why didn't you leave your car parked somewhere and walk home?" the boy's mother asks.

"And risk getting mugged? Monche's is down there in that slum. Hell no. I drove home," the boy's father says.

"If it's so unsafe, why do you two go drinking down there?" the boy's mother asks. He drinks his coffee and provides no answer.

"Do you think they locked him up in there?" the boy asks. He chuckles as if he finds it funny.

"How the hell would I know? He's a big boy," his father says.

"But what if someone mugged him or stabbed him?" the boy asks.

"As I said, he's a big boy," the boy's father says. "And what do you care?"

"I don't give a damn one way or another," the boy lies. "Just curious."

"Learn a lesson from that," his mother says, her coffee cup to her mouth. "It's what happens to deadbeats and drunks. And it doesn't matter how much money they came from."

The boy walks out of the house and goes to the workshop next to the garage to look for a hammer. He's been trying to fix the bottom of a drawer in his desk. He walks back toward the house past his father's car and notices something unusual in the back seat. He approaches the car. There in a twisted bundle that hardly fits in the seat: it is Lope, sleeping. The boy is about to run back in the house to tell his parents, but decides not to do it right away. Lope's face looks peaceful, undisturbed by his wife's panic, of which Lope knows nothing. He notices the windows are rolled down as his father usually leaves them, inimical as he has always been to air conditioning. The boy sets the hammer on the ground and opens the passenger side door making only the most necessary and unavoidable noise. He pulls the passenger seat's back forward. His hand reaches for Lope's face and touches it lightly. Lope does not seem to notice anything. The boy runs his finger across Lope's lips. Lope does not notice anything. The boy places the palm of his hand against Lope's jaw and caresses it. His stubble feels like silk to the boy. Lope does not notice anything. The boy pushes through to the back seat. There's hardly any room for him to lean over, but he carefully manages to bring his face closer to Lope's. He waits for a sign that Lope is waking up. Lope notices nothing. The boy closes in on Lope's lips with his own and places a soft kiss on them. A tremor overtakes his entire body; he feels the impulse to give him another, but fear fetters his desire. He just pulls back. Lope does not notice anything. The boy straightens up and steps backward to reach the carport floor. He brings the passenger side door toward the frame, but does not shut it. He takes a last look at the back seat, where the fallen angel has been his alone for an instant. He picks up the hammer, walks back into the house and tells his parents of his discovery.

The boy goes back to prep school. His longing for Lope is tempered by incipient maturity. He remembers picking up the cigarette butts and the intensity of his attraction, but when he comes home on vacation he's content just to see Lope sitting in his porch down the street. The boy can almost see the cocktail glass in Lope's hand. He's drinking something, whatever it is. He pitches his cigarette butt to the street and lights another one. Manuela is often sitting in a rocker across the porch from him.

The boy returns after finishing college in Vermont, but he does not come back to the same town. He settles in Guaynabo, a city close to the capital. He visits his parents a couple of times a month. Lope's wife has become close friends with his mother. She visits often. The boy is surprised at her sense of humor. Funny things happen to her, she says. The boy realizes she really is a ditz, but a funny one. When she leaves after a visit the boy always tells her to say hello to Lope and the children. One day Lope sends his wife over to ask the boy to join him for a drink. The boy is flustered.

"Are you sure he wants me over?" he asks Manuela. If he wants to see the boy, why doesn't he come himself and sit in his parents' porch?

"Yes, yes, he was asking about you, and I told him you were here for a visit. He wants to see you," Lope's wife replies.

Awkwardness overwhelms the boy, but he walks down the street and sits down in a rocker across the porch from Lope. The boy strains to find anything they can talk about. Lope asks the boy about his days in Vermont; the boy exaggerates his tone, pretending he is excited about those days, as if he had to keep Lope entertained. Lope sits there nodding and looking at him. Manuela fills the void with anecdotes she finds funnier than either of the two men listening to them. Lope is curious about the boy's occupation now. The boy fills him in. Lope sips from his cocktail glass and keeps looking directly at the boy, sometimes above the rim of his cocktail glass. Every once in a while he nods again and makes a gravel-like sound at what the boy describes.

"I remember the morning you found me in your dad's car," Lope says.

"Oh, I had forgotten about that," the boy lies. The image of Lope sleeping so angelically in that back seat has haunted him for the past ten years. It had been his first kiss, even if he is still ashamed at the other person's lack of awareness. It had been almost like kissing a breathing corpse, but a breathtakingly beautiful one with ruddy cherubic cheeks.

"Who can forget, oh, my God!" Manuela says, her voice dampened by the smoke she puffs out. "I was a wreck! Thank God he was there," adds Manuela, referring to Lope as if he weren't present.

"I can't remember too well how I got there," Lope says. He takes a swig of his whiskey and looks at the boy. "I must have been with your dad and slipped into the back seat before he noticed and took off."

"Oh, how worried I was! You know," his wife says, "that bar where they were is in a pretty nasty neighborhood."

"I remember waking up and remaining quiet in the car with my eyes shut," Lope says. He stares into the boy's eyes. The boy blushes so fiercely he feels his cheeks afire. Lope takes the last drag from his cigarette and tosses it to the sidewalk; the boy follows its trajectory and sees exactly where it falls, still smoldering. Lope drinks from his glass. "I thought it was a dream, but it wasn't."

"And thank God that you found him and let me know right away," Lope's wife says, addressing the boy. "I was going crazy. You were so helpful! I've never forgotten how kind you were."

"It never happened again," Lope says. He is still staring at the boy, who is now petrified. "I wish it had."

"What are you talking about, Lope?" his wife says and puts out her cigarette in a small porcelain ashtray on a wrought iron table next to her. "What do you mean?"

"It was nice. I was too old for that, though. It was too late for me," Lope says. He drinks again. His eyes are fixed on the boy's smile.

"Nice? Are you nuts, Lope? I swear, sometimes you say such things," his wife says. "You've had enough to drink, honey."

"I could offer little in return," Lope says, then looks at his wife. "It was nice. It was sweet. Impossible to forget."

Fireworks have gone off in the boy's chest.

Lope's wife's jaw drops. "I swear, honey, you are going senile." She takes a drag from her cigarette and shakes her head.

The boy's eyes brighten. He cocks his head almost imperceptibly and keeps on smiling. Lope's faint smile is redolent of grateful nostalgia.

FOOLS GOLD

"Fools rush in, so here I am,
awfully glad to be unhappy…
Unrequited love's a bore,
but for someone you adore
it's a pleasure to be sad."

Rodgers and Heart

He asked for it, he decided in the end. He didn't
know any better, and that's what happens when immaturity blends with desire, when love is confused with manipulation. It's possible Job Carretero reached old age
and never fully understood that. Some people mistakenly
follow what they think is a solid road that turns out to be
a shallow path of deceitful affection and stray in their
search of an elusive romantic chimera.

The only ugly thing about Filiberto Montalvo was
his first name. His nickname, Goyo, was even uglier. Job
was fourteen and a sophomore when he started sighing
secretly for Filiberto. The object of his respiratory distress was a year ahead of him in boarding school. Job
could not stand the thought of summer vacation at the
end of tenth grade. He had to wait until Labor Day to see
Filiberto again: They lived three hours away from each

other; Job could not travel to the other end of the island to visit. They were not close friends, but they teased each other playfully. Filiberto eventually became a sort of older brother who looked after him during football practice, providing tips and making suggestions. That filial link was not deep, nonetheless. Job observed from a prudent distance when Filiberto shared free time with his classmates, sometimes also with younger students who were from the same city as Filiberto.

"You're always chasing after Goyo," Felipe García told him one day in the refectory. Job blushed. Felipe was in ninth grade when Job was a junior. He was a neighbor of Filiberto's back home. Job felt Felipe was often staring at him with his acne-scarred face that did not spell friend.

"Why is that any fucking business of yours?" Job asked.

"It looks strange," Felipe replied.

"To you, maybe, because you're a zit-ridden creep," Job said.

Job was a defensive linebacker, Filiberto an offensive tackle. They seldom met on the football field. After practice they showered with the rest of the players. Off season Job tried to figure out when Filiberto showered if they weren't playing intramural sports. He managed to arrange it so that they would coincide alone in the shower. Job looked at Filiberto from the corner of his eye. When Filiberto turned his back to the wall and rinsed shampoo off his head, his eyes closed, Job stared unencumbered by any need to cloak his interest. To Job Filiberto looked like one of those Greek statues he had seen in museums in Spain. His olive skin was partially hidden by a coat of dark hair that made Job wonder how it would feel against his own skin. Job was almost indifferent to Filiberto's penis. After two years seeing genitals of every size in the open showers, it would have been a novelty when seen for the first time, perhaps, but his curiosity had been more than sated over the years. His only interest in Filiberto's genitals and butt had to do with the fact that they were Filiberto's, and some day Job had hoped to have them against him—but not just them: Filiberto's entire body while they were lost in a passionate kiss.

The second-floor slat windows overlooking the tennis courts and the football field in the distance from the locker room occupied about one-fourth of the wall. Looking out from them required stretching up while standing on one of the locker room benches. One afternoon Job left the shower room earlier than Filiberto and went upstairs to the locker room. He stood naked on the bench pretending to be looking out the window. He knew Filiberto had come up. He pretended he couldn't tell Filiberto was climbing the bench and pressing his naked body against Job's back.

"Oh, stop that, you pervert!" Job shouted. "I don't like it."

Filiberto smiled and chuckled. "You didn't mind it that much. I stood there long enough to see your ears redden before you moved away."

"What the hell are you talking about?" Job said as he pulled up his shorts. "You're sick, you know that?"

Filiberto then grabbed Job's mouth and squeezed his lips. "One of these days I'm going to suck the life out of those luscious lips!" Filiberto said in a tone meant to strip the threat of any serious intent. "Uh? Whatcha say? Yeah, you'd like that!" Filiberto said and started laughing as Job pulled his head away from Filiberto's hand.

Job said nothing. He simply imagined what it would be like if Filiberto did deliver on the promise. He would let him try, then pull away full of dread that his mouth could also expose Filiberto to contagion.

Once in a while and in public, perhaps meant to deflect the notion that he meant anything by it, Filiberto would squeeze his lips and repeat the promise. Some laughed, Job included; others turned their heads away in disgust. When Felipe García was nearby he would just stare stone-faced at Job.

During evening study hall juniors and seniors could go to the library to study instead of staying at their carrels. The library was air-conditioned, unlike the study hall, where the fluorescent lighting attracted flying bugs. Job would wait for Filiberto to come in to sit in one of the individual tables along the longer side walls. Job would sit behind him and run a pencil's eraser lightly from one side of Filiberto's nape to the other. He could actually see the goosebumps on Filiberto's hairline. Filiberto would grunt quietly. Job could see him closing and opening his legs repeatedly. One night Filiberto turned around, pointed to his crotch and said, "Look what you've done." His erection was evident. He kept closing and opening his legs nervously. Job's face reddened. He stopped brushing the eraser on Filiberto's nape.

Job knew he could arouse Filiberto, but he would not follow through. It anguished him. His motivation was not hesitancy or shyness. It surely was not lack of desire. Two years before going to prep school he had been performing oral sex on a neighbor, José Francisco, a year older than he, just like Filiberto. He started noticing a severe itch and reddening of his glans under the prepuce. It would come and go, never lasting more than a week. He cleaned himself off meticulously, but the irritation and the itch persisted. Years later he would find out what was causing it, a fungal infection that would have been cured with a prescription ointment when symptoms appeared. Already in his late 20s he was circumcised. The infection never returned.

Yet back then, at thirteen, he was convinced he had a venereal disease. He had no idea how performing oral sex caused lesions and pruritus on his penis. He only knew he had only had sex with José Francisco and José Francisco had given him something. It surprised him that even when José Francisco must have given him the venereal disease he kept coming back for oral sex and never seemed to have any problems. His own uncircumcised penis never showed signs of anything out of the ordinary.

Job was convinced that he would give someone else the same disease if he had sex. He read up on syphilis and gonorrhea in the *World Book Encyclopedia*. None of

the articles explained how oral sex could cause an inflammation so severe where he had it without any direct
contact with anyone, much less the itch. He would not
tell his parents: if he told them, they would take him to a
physician, and they would find out the horrible truth
about his sexually-transmitted disease.

"Why are you always scratching down there?" his
classmate Rafael Dávila asked him one day. "Do you
have crabs or something?"

"No, no crabs, jackass. It just itches."

"You should try being a little more hygienic. It's
disgusting," Rafael said.

But that was not the problem: he knew that. When
he had the inflammation his glans would become painful,
but still he wiped it clean. What if he tried pouring rubbing alcohol on it? He tried that. It burned, but nothing
improved.

His conviction that he could pass on what José Francisco had given him made him realize he could never go
beyond flirting and teasing. He became accustomed to
being satisfied with exciting Filiberto, but could never
cross the line into actual physical intimacy.

Sometimes Job would tickle Filiberto from behind.
Filiberto would turn around, grab him by his shirt and
say, "One of these days you're going to do something
other than tickling." Then Job would laugh and walk
away. He really wanted Filiberto to tell him what he
wanted, what was that something else. He deemed it

safer to withdraw instead of hearing what he knew was coming.

One evening in the library in late April Job went by Filiberto's table and read a name on the back cover of his English book. The spine was blue, the back cover yellow, and in a bright red crooked lettering typical of Filiberto's handwriting Job read, "I love Phyllis Berkowitz." The name was surrounded by drawings of small hearts.

"Who's Phyllis?" Job asked Filiberto. He was blushing, not because he had no right to be reading Filiberto's book cover, but because his heart was now full of lead, falling to the pit of his stomach. He asked the way a cheated lover inquires after finding a love letter addressed to a partner.

"Why do you need to know?" Filiberto asked.

"No reason," Job lied. "I had not seen that before, that's all."

"I'll leave it to your imagination," Filiberto said. It sounded to Job as if Filiberto were embarrassed to tell him who that was. Somehow Job had the feeling Filiberto too was aware that Phyllis Berkowitz's presence in his life represented a betrayal. If that were the case, it softened the blow to Job's ego, because then Filiberto knew that there was more than friendship between them.

That night Job picked up his books and resettled at a table on the opposite side of the library. He lost his concentration. He fought tears and won. When the wake-up bell rang at 6:30 the following morning Job was still waiting for his eyelids to drop over his eyes.

Filiberto's graduation day was on Sunday, May 28th. Students had to wait around until graduation ceremonies were over before getting their final report cards and a copy of the yearbook. Job saw Filiberto gather his books and clothes in preparation for leaving school for good. It was then that Job became fully aware that the man he loved would go off to school elsewhere. The following year Job would be a senior, Filiberto would be a freshman in college. The thought blurred his vision with the moisture of tears.

Job walked into the locker room. Filiberto was there. Job turned around and walked out.

"Hey, come here, Job." Filiberto had walked out of the locker room and followed Job down the terracotta tiles on the hall that ended at the threshold of the second-floor dormitory. Job stopped. "Come here," Filiberto said, trying to drag Job toward the dorm. "I want you to give me a blow job."

"What are you talking about, Goyo? Stop this shit!" Job said. He tried to let his arm loose from Filiberto's grip.

"Come on, you know you want to, come on," Filiberto insisted and grabbed Job closer to him by his shoulders.

"No! Stop, Goyo, please, stop!" Job said. He tried to shake himself out of Filiberto's hold without success.

"Please, make it my graduation present, come on. I've been waiting for this all year, come on, come on, you're not going to see me again, come on, just a blow job," Filiberto said.

"No, no! I don't want to do that, Goyo," pleaded Job. They were now close to the main door to the dorm. There was a half bathroom inside the dorm next to the prefect's room. Filiberto was trying to lead Job toward it.

"Damn it, it's my graduation. You haven't given me anything. This is all I want, come on, suck me off!" Filiberto added. Job was afraid someone would come up the steps and catch them. Even the semblance of Filiberto's intention would have been shameful to him.

"Please, Goyo. We've been friends, don't do this. I'm not going to do it. If you even get me in that bathroom and try to force me I'll bite it off," Job threatened.

Filiberto pushed Job against the granite wall. He almost tumbled, but the wall broke his fall, and he felt pain in his left shoulder joint. When he straightened himself up Filiberto approached him and slapped him hard on the right side of his face.

"You fucking cock teaser. Faggot!" Filiberto said. He walked toward the steps and went down to the first floor.

I can't, my love, I can't. You'd never forgive me, Job wanted to say. The pain in his heart was much worse than the ache in his shoulder.

After graduation a mob of students gathered in front of the auditorium to congratulate graduates as they came out in procession from the building. Job stood to the side. He caught a glimpse of Filiberto with his broad smile and glimmering dark eyes, shaking hands. Parents had not left the building yet: they had to wait for the graduates to file out.

Job wanted to shake Filiberto's hand and hug him. Filiberto looked toward him. Then he turned toward a classmate to shake hands and hug. Job saw him walk away to meet his parents. With them was a short blond female who looked nothing like the Montalvos. Filiberto hugged her and kissed her on the lips.

Every night that summer Job listened to *Don't Let the Sun Catch You Crying* and cried with the lyrics. At the end of his vacation days the pain of Filiberto's absence had refused to abate.

From the yearbook production work Job had kept a copy of Filiberto's three by two-inch black and white graduation photo. He was wearing a coat and tie. His eyes looked brighter than in real life, and his smile was disarmingly sexy, exactly as Job always thought of it. Job kept it in a junior-year geometry book where he knew no one at home would find it. He read an ad in a teen magazine for postage-stamp sized gummed photos made of regular-sized photographs. He ordered a sheet of miniature Filibertos. When the order arrived he put them in an envelope and mailed them to Filiberto at the address in the school directory. He never heard anything from Filiberto about receiving them. Job thought perhaps they got lost in the mail.

School started and Job returned. Returning to a place hitherto saturated with Filiberto's presence, now devoid of the joy of his sight, made it worse. The last words he heard from Filiberto's mouth had almost faded from memory: he had a right to be upset; Job had asked for it.

As a senior he got to share a dorm room with fifteen classmates in his 25-member class. Soon after the beginning of the school year he walked into the room and found Felipe García sitting on one of the top bunks, three or four of Job's classmates sitting or standing around. He had missed the beginning of Felipe's speech, but clearly heard him talk about the stamps Job had sent Filiberto.

"That guy's a fag. Why else would he be sending those pictures to Goyo?" Felipe said. "I tell you, I don't care if he's captain of the football team or becomes Mr. Universe. That guy's queer."

Only Bob Dejay and Hans Meijer had seen Job enter the room. They stared at Job as if waiting for his reaction.

"They're just good friends. What difference does it make? Were the stamps kissed with lipstick?" joked George Munera.

"Good friends?" Felipe asked, his back to Job. "Good friends don't send shit like that to each other. That guy had a thing for Filiberto. He told me himself."

Upon hearing that Job sickened. Filiberto had told Felipe about the stamps. He probably had told him also about Job's teases and embellished them to make Job look worse. What else had he told or aggrandized?

"They weren't fucking, were they?" Frank Armada asked. He had turned around and was now facing Job.

"Because Filiberto refused to, I bet," Felipe said. "I'm sure Job wouldn't have rejected him."

Job had heard enough. He turned toward his locker and started turning the combination lock dial. He did not look at Felipe, who happened to be sitting on Job's bed.

"Jealous, Felipe?" Job asked. Everyone started laughing.

"Go fuck yourself. You're a fairy, not me," Felipe said.

Job removed the padlock and opened the squeaky door, his back still to Felipe.

"Sounds like jealousy to me," Job said. He scratched the itch that was driving him to despair.

"Yeah, sounds like that to me, too!" Frank Armada said.

"Huh, yeah, me too," said George Montijo. "You wanted Filiberto all for yourself, I bet."

"You're a bunch of fuckers. I'm telling you," Felipe said, "this guy's queer." He walked out of the room.

No one ever brought up the subject of the postage-stamp photos. None of his classmates ever questioned his heterosexuality. They cheered for him when he held the line at games against the Richland Bombers and the Kennewick Huskies. They applauded him when he lettered and got the medals for math, speech, newspaper and English on Awards Night in the school auditorium.

He stayed away from his classmates and never stayed with any of them by themselves anywhere. Felipe might think he was putting the make on one of them. "See, I told you he's queer," Felipe would have said.

OF HOW A DICTATOR CRUSHED REBELLIOUS LIAISONS

On October 3, 1968 left-leaning army generals in Peru seized power from President Fernando Belaúnde Terry and installed Juan Francisco Velasco Alvarado in the presidential palace. Following the *coup d'etat* the new government became involved in both political and economic activity in the country, including nationalizing foreign enterprises and imposing socialist labor practices on private businesses of every nature.

Four months earlier, on June 8th, 1968 Joaquín Vargas Acosta Figallo arrived at St. John's University in Minnesota on a Greyhound bus from Minneapolis to work during the summer and then enroll at the university as a special student of theater and communication. He brought with him from Lima his recordings of Peruvian waltzes by Los Morochucos, Barbra Streisand and Edith Piaf, but had no record player. Besides the LPs and his clothes he had also brought his copies of Tennessee Williams and Edward Albee plays. He was assigned to a small one-person dorm room on the third floor of St. Benet Hall, a brick building connected to the university's main quadrangle.

Smoke filled Joaquín's room, just like everyone else's on campus that summer for work-study assignments. Third Bennet should have been renamed Marlboro Country. Directly in front of Joaquín's room was William Maldonado's. William would be a freshman in the fall. Joaquín's main reason for arriving before the start of the school year was to polish his English. William soon realized that before any polishing started its object had to be finished. William had attended private English-speaking schools in Puerto Rico. He was at St. John's University on a partial scholarship. Summer work would help him save for tuition, room and board during the school year.

Joaquín attached himself to William for linguistic support. It defeated the purpose of his presence on campus, this speaking Spanish and associating with William and another Puerto Rican by the name of Pablo Gotay, also on a scholarship for a pre-med degree. William and Joaquín spoke the same language in more than one way, William suspected from the start. William, however, never disclosed to Joaquín that he was gay. They decided to room together in the fall and occupied room number 310 in St. Mary's Hall, whose more spacious accommodations were some thirty years newer than St. Benet Hall, built in 1921 and not refurbished since.

Wherever William was Joaquín could not be far behind. They had their meals together: they hitchhiked, did laundry, went to the Saturday night 25-cent movie at the university auditorium and went together to the campus coffee house to listen to amateur folk singers.

"You two are like twins from different mothers," Ray Herdina said one day. Ray was their neighbor across the hall. They found that funny.

Both Joaquín and William took the same English course, but were in different sections. Joaquín thought in Spanish and wrote in English: unless the reader knew both languages it was next to impossible to decipher his compositions, one of which was assigned weekly that semester on topics related to the works of F. Scott Fitzgerald; the following semester the author would be Ernest Hemingway, the second in the rotation of three that closed with Joseph Conrad. Joaquín was also enrolled in theology 111 ("God and the Human Predicament"), theater 210 ("Stagecraft") and a fourth class that William was also taking, Art 225, "Introduction to Cinema." The only classes that interested Joaquín were cinema and theater. The other two were incidental.

"You have to set your mind to English mode," William would tell him when revising Joaquín's papers. "This is gibberish." William would end up rewriting Joaquín's theme while he smoked, read *Cat on a Hot Tin Roof* or *The Glass Menagerie* for the *n*th time and listened to "My Man" on William's portable record player.

William gave no thought to the reason why he had to stay up late studying after Joaquín went to sleep. Joaquín's parents paid for his every expense. William's parents had refused to help him with anything. "If you stay in Puerto Rico you can attend the university in Río

Piedras and we will pay for that. If you go so far away, you're on your own," his mother had warned him. She could not understand or even know that he had looked forward to college just so that he could get as far away as possible from her. That goal would not be met by going to college in Puerto Rico and living at home. He held a part-time job on campus and did typing at 25 cents a page for other students. That went to pay for personal items and cigarettes.

William was enrolled in sixteen credits, including that freshman English class taught by Bro. Louis Blenkner, the department chair, who had a well-deserved reputation as a merciless prick. Bro. Louis had obtained his Ph.D. at the University of North Carolina on the G.I. Bill after serving in the Army as a drill sergeant. He shaved his head, which glistened above his less than underweight frame. In the dead of winter he wore rubber flip-flops on naked feet and never wore pants under his Benedictine habit. His name was never listed on class schedules, because students would never sign up for his classes. "A is for God, B is for me; the rest of you get F, D and C," he'd say the first day. He meant it. Class only met Monday morning from 8:00 to 8:50, when he would assign the reading and theme for the week. The rest of the week students had to schedule an individual meeting in his office, where he would read the theme for the first time and grade it after pointing out all the flaws in the composition. He chain-smoked and blew his smoke on the faces of students as they waited for his verdict on the other side of his desk.

Thursday afternoon at 2:00 was William's torture time. He sat watching the monk read his theme and chuckle where nothing funny had been written in the theme. At the end of his monologue, upon finishing the reading, he would grade it and hand it back. William, who had graduated high school at the top of his class and had been school paper editor, found nothing comforting in getting C and C+ in his themes—once even a D+.

"You must be really good," a classmate told him one day when they were comparing grades. "C+? That's an A from anyone else."

William confirmed it was true. The same themes he was rewriting for Joaquín earned him an A from Fr. Patrick McDarby while William got his mediocre mark from the fat man. The foreign student who could barely understand English was getting grades that *The Great Gatsby* would not have received from Bro. Louis Blenkner.

The thought never crossed William's mind that what he was doing for Joaquín interfered with his own efforts and required more study time than otherwise necessary. He also had to serve as a living dictionary for Joaquín's theology class.

He was in love with Joaquín. They had become truly inseparable: even showers they took at the same time, albeit in separate stalls. Joaquín couldn't be that dense: he had to be well aware of William's feelings; they did not need to be expressed. William assumed Joaquín reciprocated them tacitly. William wondered when Joaquín would initiate the physical consequences of their mutual attraction.

William's eighteenth birthday was coming up in October. Two weeks before the day they discussed traveling to Minneapolis, eighty miles away, to celebrate. They would have to ride a bus and stay overnight at a hotel, probably the Pick Nicolett, which was close to everything downtown, then spend money on a celebratory meal, pay for movie tickets and spend another night in the hotel, because the Greyhound bus schedule would not allow for an earlier return to St. John's. Perhaps part of the celebration once they were away from the school environment would be conducive to physical intimacy, at long last.

"I want my girlfriend to come along," Joaquín said. William turned toward Joaquín from his desk.

"What girlfriend?" he asked, and he knew the shock was clear in his voice.

"My girlfriend, Louise."

"Where did you meet this girlfriend?" William asked, and before Joaquín replied he added "And when do you see her?"

"We're in the same theology class," said Joaquín. He brought *Night of the Iguana* closer to his face and held his cigarette in his hand even closer, as if the book wanted a drag. Suddenly the human predicament was divested of God.

"Why haven't you invited her to join us at the cafeteria?" William asked. This had to be a ruse, something Joaquín had concocted to force the issue of their relationship, real in every sense but the physical aspect.

"I didn't think you'd care to. I ride the shuttle back to the women's college with her when class is over, then come back for lunch here."

William could not see clearly. He turned his back to continue reading, but instead of text he saw blotches of amorphous black spots. He dropped his eyelids on them, but still saw them in lighter tones. He had nothing else to ask. He didn't care who she was or what she looked like. His ideation of his unmentioned love affair with Joaquín had just been canceled, obliterated. Louise. Even the name repulsed him. He realized that if they stayed in a downtown hotel in Minneapolis Louise would most likely stay in the same room with Joaquín while he slept in the room next door. In his anger he felt taken for a fool.

A senior by the name of Bob Airaghi had posted a "For Sale" ad in a bulletin board behind the Great Hall, a reception center that had been the religious community's first church in 1867. It described a '58 Plymouth, three doors, $60. William called him.

"Is it too rusted out?" William asked. Cars in Minnesota were priced according to the level of corrosion to which they had been exposed due to salt poured on roads to melt the snow and ice in winter.

"It's not rusty at all," Bob said. "Well, except for the one door."

William thought he'd rather see the car than get an absentee description. He told Joaquín: $60 was something they could afford, depending on the car's shape, if each paid $30 for it. They went to see the car, parked on a farm within walking distance from the campus. Parking on the private farm was $10 per semester; on campus it would have been $40, which was not too far from the car's price: for the two semesters parking would cost more than the car was worth. Besides, freshmen were not allowed to park on campus.

It was a manual-transmission Plymouth Fury, dark blue with a white trim and white-wall tires, almost exactly what William's father had owned ten years earlier. Bob did his best to talk up the car.

"This is why it's advertised as a three-door car," Bob said. The passenger side rear door had been crushed in during an accident. It wouldn't open, which rendered the car, effectively, a three-door vehicle. William thought it was ingenious of Bob to advertise it truthfully, but casually. Joaquín, used to limousines and German-made cars in his native San Isidro, an upper-class suburb of Lima, was not as impressed. Nonetheless, he went along.

The two-hour trip was scheduled for Saturday, October 27th. They were to share driving: William would drive out and Joaquín would drive back after dinner at La Casa Coronado and *Rachel, Rachel* with Joanne Woodward, Joaquín's choice for a movie.

Joaquín and Louise rode in the back while William drove. In the rearview mirror William could see the frantic making out, he could hear the panting and the rustling of clothes and felt as if the devil himself had possessed every cell of his body. Louise sat between them at the movie; neither she nor Joaquín saw much of the film or could have summarized the plot. They were too busy kissing and touching each other where they should have explored only in private. William thought of moving to a different seat. It would have been rude, perhaps a signal of his jealousy. On the screen Rachel was just finding out she wasn't pregnant after all when William thought maybe Joaquín was trying to make him jealous to accelerate their own involvement: "Look what I'm going to do if you don't give up your hesitation." Or maybe Louise had detected something and was trying to show William what she could do that he was not equipped to provide—or like a she-wolf marking her territory with saliva instead of urine. No, he decided. None of that. They were insensitive swine.

After the movie they went to pick up the car at the Dayton's parking ramp on 7th Street. William tried to hand Joaquín the car keys.

"Oh, I can't drive this car," Joaquín said, refusing the keys with a gesture of his hand. "I can't drive a stick. Didn't I tell you? Besides, I don't have a driver's license here."

William drove back with the same drive-in show running on the rearview mirror. He slapped the mirror and turned it sideways to spare himself the lack of modesty. He feared the two would be having intercourse by the time they reached Robbinsdale, eight miles north of Minneapolis.

It was William's worst birthday celebration, including his fifth, when his mother belted him. He had thought putting his fist through the cake would be funny.

William's feelings bled. When Joaquín handed him his next theme for rewriting William looked at it, but didn't take it. "You know, I'm so busy now with papers for the end of the semester that I think Louise would do a better job than I at fixing it for you." He was embarrassed at being petty—or perhaps he wasn't petty at all. Maybe he was just reclaiming his dignity. He did have work to do: no more than he had had since September, but work nonetheless. He started going to dinner with other classmates on the same dorm floor. Joaquín wouldn't come along. He thought most of the other floor residents were peasants: after all, they came from rural communities in Minnesota, uncouth and crude. Worst of all was Gordon Karls: he kept chickens in his room and his roommate, Blaine Krogh, had caught him voiding in the sink.

In their room Joaquín and William maintained a superficial civility whose foundation had eroded and would never be as solid as before. Louise was not a factor: Joaquín and she had stopped seeing each other a week after the birthday debacle. William concluded she wasn't the issue. If it wasn't her it would be someone else.

Joaquín was 21 going on 22. He could buy the liquor William could not as an eighteen-year old. One afternoon in mid-November Joaquín took the school shuttle to the next town over, where the women's college was, and bought a pint of Wild Turkey bourbon. He unscrewed the cap and poured a few ounces in a tumbler while William read at his desk. Joaquín dropped the *Funny Girl* soundtrack album on the record player and sat in bed sipping his Wild Turkey.

"Remember when we saw her Central Park concert?" Joaquín asked.

"Yes, I remember the concert in Central Park. It was last September. We watched it on TV," William replied without turning around.

"You wept," Joaquín said.

"I did not."

"Yes, you did. When she sang "People" I looked at you and tears were flowing down your face," Joaquín said.

"I don't recall that, and I doubt it. I don't much care for her."

"What? You don't?" asked Joaquín. "I've heard you humming the songs from this recording. Don't deny it!"

"Liking the melody and liking her singing are two different things."

"I don't know why you deny it. You like her just as much as I. You're just irate at me, that's what it is," said Joaquín, his speech somewhat slurred.

"I'm not fucking pissed off at you."

"Don't be vulgar. And yes, you are. You don't think I've noticed how you've changed? I don't know why, but you have," Joaquín said. "You care to tell me what I've done?"

It was true. Hurt had yielded to anger, but not yet to indifference. William tried to conceal it, but it was evident in his inclusion of other classmates in their activities, inviting the freshmen Joaquín disliked the most for their lack of manners to the potato-chip and Coca-Cola parties they would sometimes have Saturday night, inviting Pablo to bull sessions where Pablo's every other word in his broken English was "fuck," going to the experimental 5:00 afternoon Mass on Sunday in the lower chapel of the abbey church instead of joining him for the 10:30 morning Mass in the main nave, refusing to rewrite his homework, going to the library to study instead of staying in their room and then returning only when the library closed at 11:00 at night.

"I don't know what you're talking about," William said, his back to Joaquín.

Joaquín stood up and poured some more Wild Turkey in his tumbler before sitting back in his bed.

"You've changed, William. I don't know why, but you're not the same."

Hearing that upset William even more. It took the sensitivity of an ox not to know why. Had William done the same to him, would he now feel humiliated and rejected? And on his birthday yet.

"Let's leave it where it is, Joaquín," William said. He stood up and turned off his desk lamp. "I'm tired, and I'm going to bed."

He walked to the sink in the corner of the room, washed his face and brushed his teeth. He pulled back the bedspread from his bed and stripped to his underwear before climbing in. Joaquín's lamp was on, but the light did not shine brightly enough to bother William. He turned his back to Joaquín and pretended to sleep. Joaquín's attempt to get him to open up about something that should have been obvious unnerved him. Joaquín had stuck his finger in William's sore heart to start a brand new hemorrhage. William just wanted to forget it: he had realized that the man he had fallen in love with was a jerk who didn't even know whether he liked snails or oysters, as Joaquín had heard Laurence Olivier's character say to Tony Curtis in *Spartacus*—a reference whose meaning was clear to William in a movie the two of them had seen together, seated in the wooden chairs at the auditorium, their arms touching on the armrest and their knees touching as Joaquín slowly and lightly raised and dropped his thigh to brush William's leg. Joaquín did it each time they sat next to each other at a movie. Sometimes he would complain of pain in his knee and rub it, the edge of his hand sliding up and down William's thigh.

Now William would ride the shuttle to the Saturday night movie at the women's college with Ray Herdina and Mark Loosbrock.

His eyes were wide open, fixed on the white blocks of the wall. He heard Joaquín drop his feet to the floor and put the tumbler on his desk. Joaquín was taking off his shirt. The second rustling sounded as if he were also removing his undershirt. The zipper was getting undone. He dropped his pants on the floor and labored to slip them off his feet. William heard the footsteps approaching his bed. He turned around. Joaquín stood next to his bed, naked and hard. That scene came right out of William's dreams during four months prior to that night. He hesitated before saying anything, unsure of which impulse to follow.

"What are you doing?" William asked him. Joaquín raised his index finger to his lips and made a shooing sound. He lifted his knee and was placing it on the edge of the bed.

"Where the hell do you think you're going?" asked William. Three months before he would have moved to the side and happily made room for Joaquín. Not now, not ever.

Again Joaquín made that noise meant to tell William to be silent.

"Don't ask me to keep quiet. If you don't get away from my bed and go back to yours, I'm going to start shouting. You want to see all of those jocks out there at the door wanting to find out what happened?" William said, not in a loud tone, but in a firm voice that would leave no doubt he meant it.

Joaquín retreated. He returned to his bed. He turned off his desk lamp. William turned away and stared at the wall. A faint light slipped under the window curtains above him. He looked at the overhang from the marble slab at the bottom of the windows that faced the St. Mary Hall parking lot. He tried to find something else he could look at to distract his mind. He wondered what would happen if he got out of bed and walked over to Joaquín's, told him what had upset him and got in bed with the man he had loved and now wasn't sure whether he still disdained or was denying to himself that the love was somewhere in there, hiding from his bruised pride.

He stayed where he was.

The following morning when William got up he looked at the pint of bourbon. It was much more than three-quarters full. The cap was still off on the desk, next to the tumbler. He walked to the sink to wash up. Joaquín woke up.

"What time is it?" Joaquín asked. He stretched noisily.

"Seven."

"Oh, God, I can't believe I had all that bourbon last night," Joaquín said.

William took his toothbrush out of his mouth and said, "You didn't have that much."

"Oh, no, I did. I'm not used to drinking so much," Joaquín replied. William rinsed his mouth and wiped it with his towel. "I can't remember anything!"

William walked around Joaquín's bed to pick up the pint of bourbon.

"There's hardly any missing from this bottle," he told Joaquín; he put the bottle down. "I'm going to refresh your memory." He began telling Joaquín what had happened. Joaquín started making noises with his mouth, covered his ears and shook his head. "I don't give a damn how much you refuse to hear; you know exactly what you did. You're not a good actor, you know."

"Don't tell me what happened! I'd rather not know!" Joaquín kept repeating. William reprised his account of events.

"If you ever try that shit again I'm going to beat the crap out of you," William said, knowing that somewhere at the bottom of his words was a truth he would not bring himself to admit any longer.

The roommate relationship remained strained, but both tried to soften the rougher edges and made a semi-successful attempt at peaceful coexistence.

St. John's operated on what was known as the 4-1-4 calendar: a four-month fall semester, a one-month "January term" and a four-month spring term. During the January term students enrolled in non-traditional coursework either in classroom settings or through independent study on campus or elsewhere. No more than two terms could be taken within a student's major field of study. Some students hitchhiked to Mexico, others blindfolded themselves to write a diary on their blindness. Ray Herdina went to Florida to measure rising tides on Miami Beach; Doug Bancks went ice fishing for a month to record the number of times his spear actually went through a fish; Kevin Twomey went to a parish in the Bronx that St. John's administered to help with the Hispanic outreach program and got mugged right on the Grand Concourse in broad daylight. In some cases the projects enhanced the educational experience, in others they allowed for wasting time. William's chosen major was math, which was why he was taking calculus, physics with lab, English and the cinema class. He chose to complete an independent study on Puerto Rican literature, for which he would remain in the island for four weeks. Returning to his parents' house he was quickly reminded of the reason why he had gone away in the first place, to free himself from bad-tempered parents who spent most of their waking time arguing. He moved his return date a week ahead of the original plan. He finished his project and flew back. In Minneapolis he spent a night at the Pick Nicolett Hotel on Hennepin Avenue and the following afternoon took the Greyhound bus back to campus.

When he opened the bedroom door he saw Joaquín sitting in bed. In his desk chair sat a monk, a member of the the abbey that ran the university. He had seen the young monk around. His name was Bro. James Delisle, as Joaquín introduced him. Bro. James looked 23 or 24. He was a short man with a bowl haircut and thick black-rimmed glasses. His voice was an octave higher than it should have been for anyone over twelve. He held a cigarette between the spots closest to the tips of his fingers, his hand extended back, palm up, one of the standard dorm gold-metal ashtrays in the other hand over the habit's lap.

William felt flustered. His immediate reaction was one of resentment over the intrusion. Where had these two met? Why was Joaquín inviting strangers to their bedroom? Perhaps Joaquín was getting back at William for his slights—most likely not, he knew much too well, but he felt betrayed and dismissed. He wished he had not turned Joaquín away the night of the Wild Turkey pint. He regretted not signing up for basket weaving at the women's college instead of taking off to Puerto Rico.

He went about hanging his clothes in the closet. Joaquín was smoking also. The canopy of smoke was so thick that William walked to the window and lifted the lower pane.

"William! It's January! Shut that window, please!" Joaquín said in a reprimanding tone cushioned on politeness.

"As soon as some of that smoke is gone," he replied. James smacked his tongue against his teeth in disapproval. William ignored him. After a minute he shut the window. "Have you had dinner yet?" William asked. The bus schedule was such that by the time it arrived at the college station the cafeteria had closed. He would have to go to the snack bar on the ground floor of the dorm to have a dry, flat hamburger in a stale bun for dinner.

"Yes, we have," Joaquín answered. He continued his conversation with Bro. James, something about a production of a Christopher Marlowe play. William was too hungry to pay any attention to the details. From the sound of it, however, Bro. James Delisle was an English major who had read Marlowe in one of his courses. It seemed Joaquín and Bro. James were both in the same January term class on contemporary theater at the College of St. Benedict, down the road from St. John's. "But if you want to go ahead, we'll join you in a little while and keep you company."

William left for the gut bomb meal. In the hall Pablo asked him where he was going.

"Fuck, wait for me!" Pablo said. "I haven't had any fucking dinner yet. I didn't want to eat that fucking shit on a shingle they were serving in the fucking cafeteria."

They ate their hamburgers, including the wilted iceberg lettuce leaf and the limp tomato slice. They drank a couple of Pepsi Colas. William smoked two cigarettes. For dessert Pablo got a candy bar from a machine.

"Where the fuck are those two?" Pablo asked. William checked his watch. They had been there for an hour and a half.

"Let's go. I don't want to sit here any longer. I'm pooped from those long flights and all the mess, hauling that luggage around," William said. "I think I'm going to turn in early tonight."

"Do you think he's still in there?" Pablo asked as they approached room 310.

"I don't know. Let's find out," William replied. Without explaining to Pablo why he was doing it he asked Pablo to be quiet. He took his key out, got it close to the lock, inserted it and quickly turned the doorknob. There were Bro. James and Joaquín sitting in William's bed, locked in a kiss. William went back into the hall and shut the door without speaking as Joaquín and Bro. James pulled away from each other and tried to make everything he had seen disappear. He went to Pablo's room. Pablo's roommate, Larry DiMarchi, a wrestler missing his two upper front teeth, was working on a project for his watercolor painting class.

"Fuck, Will! I can't fucking believe it!" Pablo said. "He doesn't look like a fag, you know? I wouldn't have fucking guessed in a million years!" Pablo's speech was in a dual language that only a Spanish speaker who also spoke English could understand, just like Joaquín's compositions: Fuck, *Gweel*! *No puedo* fucking *creerlo!* He doesn't look like a fucking *maricón.*

"Speak English, goddamn it! You're in America now!" Larry shouted.

"Take a hint. We don't fucking want you to know what we're talking about," Pablo shouted back. "It's none of your fucking beeswax, you hick."

Larry muttered something neither of them could understand, and they ignored him.

"I wasn't expecting that," William said. It was true. What he had expected to find was both of them naked, one on top of the other. Maybe he wanted to see something that would turn his feelings off completely, even if at the same time it hurt him in his most intimate pride.

William waited until he heard his bedroom door open and close again. He heard the footsteps going farther. In winter floors were usually gritty: both salt and sand were poured on walkways to provide traction for walking. The melted snow's salt stained shoes and the sand stuck to shoe soles, which dragged it into building interiors. The grit's crunch told him that Joaquín and his boyfriend were walking away

William's sleep was uneasy. He was tired and fell asleep quickly, but woke up often during the night and by morning felt as if he had not slept at all. Joaquín wasn't in bed. William thought that perhaps he had gone to sleep with Bro. James, but that was unlikely, that a monk would bring a student into a shared juniorate room for the night—unless there was something other than brother love manifesting itself in the abbey. By the time William finished dressing to go to breakfast Joaquín walked in from a shower. Joaquín's cheeks were already too red from rosacea. They were impossibly redder now. He greeted William. William did not return the morning greeting.

"I want you to leave this room," he said.

"You can't ask me to do that," Joaquín replied.

"I can and I'm not asking you. I am ordering you to get out." William was standing by the door, a hand on the doorknob. He did not want to prolong the conversation beyond what was necessary.

"Where am I going to go?" Joaquín asked. He was holding the edge of his bathrobe's lapel over his chest as if protecting his nipples from indiscreet eyes.

"That's for you to figure out. I don't want to worry about what I'm going to witness when I open the door to my bedroom," William said. He tried to restrain his anger, but making an effort to subdue it just made it worse.

"If I let this go in time he will be coming here to fuck you while I'm in the other bed."

"Don't be crass," Joaquín said. "You make it sound sordid."

"A monk making out with a male student in a dorm? What is it? Benedictine rites of peace?"

"It's a beautiful thing," Joaquín replied. His face was going to turn purple. At hearing it William had a fleeting vision of how much more beautiful it would have been if instead of Bro. James he would have been the one receiving kisses and caresses from Joaquín. That was, he knew and could not lie to himself, the issue.

"Go practice your beauty elsewhere. Go to the dean of students' office before you go to class and ask for re-location. If he asks you why, tell him I'm a pig, unhygienic, rude beyond belief. I don't care. If he doesn't get you elsewhere, I'll go in myself and tell him why you need to go. I don't want you here any longer than I have to tolerate you," William said and walked out.

Another freshman at the end of the hall, a nursing major by the name of Ray Mattock, had just lost his roommate, Dave Waldoch, a custom-van heir and a slob who had decided to drop out and volunteer for the Army. It was Joaquín's luck that the room was open for another occupant. Otherwise he would have had to go to the fourth floor at St. Benet Hall, where freshmen had to share a tall ceiling, seven by fifteen-foot room with a roommate and had to stack the beds in faux bunks, their clothes in metal cabinets meant for office supplies. It was precisely the kind of slum that would have driven aristocrats of the Peruvian oligarchy to insanity, forced to live like their Inca *cholo* servants.

Before the spring term began Bro. James Delisle had already left the religious order on account of his whirlwind romance. He had remained enrolled as a junior at the university. Just as months before with William, wherever anyone saw Joaquín they also saw Jim Delisle, now defrocked and living among students. Ray Mattock said it was perfect: he had the room all to himself most of the time and still paid for it as a double room.

"He's gone to Wisconsin on Easter break to meet Jim's family," Ray Mattock told William. No one had asked him; he volunteered the information one night in John Zeller's room when some of the residents had gathered for popcorn and pop.

"Maybe Joaquín's going to ask Jim's father for his hand in marriage," Pat Flynn said.

"Hey, Ray, are you going to be best man?" Larry DiMarchi asked. They all laughed. "Or do you want to be godfather to their first kid?"

"Gross!" Ray said, making a face of disgust.

The plan for the following fall term was for both of them to move to a small apartment in the next town over. Jim still had one year to go for his bachelor's degree and after that would take a job somewhere, most likely St. Cloud, to support both of them until Joaquín completed his requirements for graduation. Joaquín had been received warmly by Jim's family, to whom Joaquín was introduced as a foreign student from Peru and thus became an exotic being in Janesville, Wisconsin: his visit was even featured in the *Janesville Daily Gazette*. He had bought toys and other presents for all members of the family, and they could tell he came from money. He was very polite and well-mannered. The whole family was sad that Jim had quit the monastic life, but at least he had this good friend. All that Ray Mattock told William over breakfast laced with a good dose of sarcasm, more than William could stand that early in the day—the content and the style, both.

Joaquín was to remain on campus for the summer months working in the carpentry shop: office jobs were reserved for upper classmen. He had no choice. Jim would not be back until mid-August to go apartment-hunting. Joaquín himself told William one day over lunch in the cafeteria—Joaquín invited himself to sit at the same table. William had also remained on campus to work as a clerk in the Monastic Manuscript Microfilm Library as a Spanish to English translator. William listened to the information pretending he was scraping the edges of indifference to whatever happened to Joaquín and his Jim Delisle.

Joaquín was again in a room on third St. Benet Hall. William had secured a single room in St. Francis House, which had previously been a convent for the nuns who did kitchen work before the university contracted with a food-service company. He only ran into Joaquín during meals. For breakfast he would make sure he ate fast, before Joaquín showed up and sat with him; he had tried to hide in the back lunchroom, but Joaquín found him there, too. For lunch he would get there before Joaquín and started sitting with Frank Baron, a technician for Garrison Keillor's show at the public radio station that broadcast from the university campus. Frank had a long, unkempt beard that tended to get into his food; this nauseated Joaquín and was the best deterrent against his company. For dinner William walked in with a Vietnamese student, Vin Dihn Nguyen, a refugee who was also working on campus for the summer, unable to travel to his country; Herman Guerrero, a soft-spoken student from Micronesia; Abel Laguna, another Peruvian, a senior who during the summer worked in the graduate school library, Sylvester Fernandez, a sophomore from India who was sponsored by a Catholic charity in Calcutta; and Victor Omasaja, from Nigeria, a senior French major. They all lived in St. Francis House. All of them Joaquín considered beneath him, particularly Abel, decidedly middle-class on a full scholarship, majoring in physics, quiet and beneath Joaquín's perceived aristocracy. He sat by himself in a corner table. William pretended not to see him.

In the evening William read. On weekends he rode Abel's '57 Dodge with Victor and Vin Dihn to town for a movie or to shop, or walked down to the lake for a swim when it got too hot. The $60 car owed the second-semester $10 parking fee. When winter hit in earnest and the wind blew across the prairie, the one-mile walk to the farm to pick up the car felt more like a day's walk in Siberia, with which Minnesota shared its latitude. During the winter months the car never started. It would have had to be rolled down a steep hill to get the engine to turn after spraying the carburetor with deicing fluid. Neither William nor Joaquín were interested in getting the car going. William's friends who owned cars either lent him theirs or gave him rides to town. William and Joaquín agreed to turn over the title of the car to the farmer in satisfaction of the parking debt. He was going to salvage it for parts—except, he said, for the fourth door.

On June 24, 1969 the leftist military government of Juan Fernando Velasco Alvarado in Peru announced the enactment of a new law of radical agrarian reform. It included the industrial sector, where workers were to share in profits and receive dividends throughout the year. Since April there had been rumblings that this was coming. Entrepreneurs and men of industry suspected the government would seize their companies if they did not comply. Joaquín's father owned a large glass factory in Cercado de Lima, an industrial zone in the outskirts of Lima. The family feared they would lose the factory to new regulations under what they called "Peru's Stalinesque regime." There were rumors of an imminent uprising by the conservative elements in government and the military, but nothing was certain. Joaquín's father asked his son to return to Lima. Relations with the United States were tenuous at best because of the dictatorship's intention to continue to nationalize and divest foreign investors of their property. The family would feel better if Joaquín returned and finished his degree at the Pontifical Catholic University of Lima in the suburb of San Miguel. Joaquín had attended it for two years before migrating to Minnesota.

***

On June 28th Joaquín Vargas Acosta Figallo boarded a flight from Miami to Lima after flying Northwest Orient from Minneapolis; he never returned. Jim Delisle wrote him letters at the address listed in the student directory; Joaquín never replied to them.

On Saturday, September 19, 1975, a month after the leftist government fell, Joaquín Vargas Acosta Figallo married Teresa Lagos Frei Bachelet Alwyn, a Chilean socialite. William received an invitation in Edina, Minnesota, where he was teaching high-school algebra. He neither confirmed attendance nor expressed his regrets. Sending a silver tray would have been a customs nightmare. He did not send a gift.

Variations on a Theme

One Side

"What has happened to you?" Mom screamed, alarmed at seeing her son's face as it had been through a meat grinder.

"Someone hit me," Frank said.

"Who? Who was capable of this!" Mom said, her voice full of anguish. "You need to go to a hospital!"

"I'll be alright. Just get me an ice pack, please."

"Those cuts and bruises need more than an ice pack, Frank!" Mom said, "You need stitching, at least!"

"I'll be alright," Frank replied. He sat down at the dining room table.

"You haven't told me how this happened," Mom said as she headed to the kitchen to fix the ice pack.

"Some guy. I don't know who he is."

"Where, where, Frank! I can't believe this. Did you do something to him?" Mom yelled from the kitchen. She twisted the plastic ice tray to loosen the cubes into a dish towel.

"In a car. His car. No, I didn't do anything to him," Frank said. He took the ice bundle off Mom's hands and pressed it against his left side, the one that looked the worst.

"What were you doing in his car?" Mom asked, sitting back down.

"I was waiting by the side of the road. Hitchhiking, like I do all the time. I stuck my thumb out and this guy in a blue Volkswagen bug stopped ahead to let me in. He was in a cop's uniform. I think I've seen him around." Frank wiped with his hand the blood dripping out of his nose.

"Let me get something for your nose," Mom said. She ran to the bathroom, then came back with a hand towel. Frank held it to his nostrils. "And then what?"

"He started talking, you know, small talk, about the weather, asking me where I was from and asking how old I am. I told him I'm seventeen and that I am the son of the man who owns the clothing factory on the other side of town, and he said, 'I know who you are,' and then he said, 'I know what you are, too,' and I didn't know what he was talking about. Then he turned off the road and I didn't know where he was going, because I thought he was going down the highway. He had told me that's where he was going when I asked him before getting in the car. Then he went on the shoulder of a side road."

Mom sat with her elbow on the table and her hand to her mouth, eyes wide open. "He hit you then for no reason?"

"No, he didn't hit me first. He got out of the car and walked over to my side, then he opened the door and unzipped his pants, he took his penis out and asked me to put my mouth on it."

"What? This was a cop?" Mom asked even more upset than before.

"Yes. He was in his uniform. It's this town's uniform. I told you, I've seen him around before, but I don't know his name," Frank said. He switched the ice pack to the other side of his face, where the largest bruise was on his cheek. "I told him I wasn't going to do that and I'd rather get out and walk back to the main highway, and he held me by my shirt and pulled me until my face was against his crotch, and he said, 'You're going to suck this right now or you'll see what happens!' and I refused. Right there he pulled me out of the car and started beating on me, punching me with both fists. I screamed at him to stop and let me go, but he just kept punching. Then he got back in the car and drove off."

"How did you get back here, Frank?" Mom asked.

"I walked as I could to the main highway. A classmate's dad stopped and picked me up. I was lucky. I was afraid he'd worry about me getting all this blood on his seats, but he was nice. That's who dropped me off in front of the house," Frank said.

"And you're sure this was a cop who did that to you?" Mom asked.

"Yes, I am. I don't want any trouble, Mom. I'll just take care of this."

"The hell you are! I'm going to police headquarters right now!" Mom said. She stood up. She shook a finger at Frank and said, "Don't you dare stop me! No one does this to a child of mine and gets away with it."

"Please, Mom, don't, please, don't, don't! I don't want any trouble, please, don't!" Frank pleaded.

"You wait until the police chief hears of this. He's a friend of your father's. This is going to be ugly," Mom said. She started walking toward the back to get into her shoes and out of her house slippers.

"No, no, Mom, please don't," Frank said, but it was useless. Mom picked up her purse. As she was about to open the front door Dad walked in.

"Look at this, look at what some cop did to our son!" Mom said.

Dad looked at Frank's face. He became pale. He asked what had happened. Mom recapped Frank's story.

"Now he says he doesn't want any trouble. He doesn't want me to go to see the police chief," Mom said.

"You don't have to. I'll take care of that," Dad said. "And before I get back, take some pictures of his face. Then we'll go to the emergency room."

"Dad, please, don't, don't go, please!" Frank said again. He had removed the ice pack from his face to attempt to convince Dad not to go, but that just made Dad more determined when he saw Frank's swollen and bloodied eyes.

"You stay here. I'll be back when I'm done filing the complaint. If Chief Mundy isn't there I'll go to his house."

Dad walked out, got in his car and drove off.

Another Side

"Sit down, George," Chief Mundy told Dad. He had stayed in his office longer than usual to complete a report he had to turn in the following morning, he said.

"I'm not here on a social call," Dad said. He then told Chief Mundy the account Frank had given of the incident.

"Actually, George, I was expecting you. I thought you'd want to come and file the complaint. You see, the police officer already filed the incident report," Chief Mundy said. He pulled several sheets out of an IN tray and handed them to Dad. "Here, you read it yourself."

Dad took the sheets and read. Past the officer's name, date and location of the incident the report stated:

At approximately 1630 hours at the end of my shift I was driving home on Highway 366 in a westerly direction. I noticed a man in his teenage years hitchhiking near mile marker 23. He was wearing a light green pullover, gray dress slacks and black moccasins. I recognized him as the son of a prominent local family and assumed he was safe to provide a ride for. I stopped and asked him where he was heading. He said where he was going, which coincided with my own direction. He climbed in my vehicle and sat in the front passenger seat. He stated that he had been standing there for a long time, that he was happy to see me and was grateful for the ride, because it looked like rain was approaching. He told me whose son he was; I told him I knew who he was.

He complimented me on my uniform and added that he had always been attracted to men in police uniforms. I did not say anything, but when he asked whether my uniform ever came off I told him I was uncomfortable with his comments and would drop him off on the side of the road if he proceeded to make more comments along those lines. At that point he laughed and stated that there was no one else around to know, that it was not necessary to pretend that I did not like it. At that point he proceeded to place his hand on my thigh and slid it into my crotch. At which point I immediately pulled to the side of the road between mile markers 31 and 32, at the turnoff towards county road 14. I asked him to get off my car. He refused to do so and instead continued to rub my genitals, at which point I got out of the car to walk to his side, opened the door and asked him to get out. He still refused to get out. He extended his arm and tried to unzip my pants, at which point I grabbed him by his shirt. Due to his insistence on touching me and his refusal to go away, I felt in the obligation to take defensive physical action to prevent him from further acts of disrespect to me as a man and as a law-enforcement officer.

The man fell to the ground. I walked back to the car and drove off in the original direction at approximately 1710 hours.

Dad handed the report back to Chief Mundy. He felt humiliated and betrayed. He apologized to Chief Mundy, shook his hand and asked him "Would you do me a favor? Please, don't file that report."

"I wasn't planning to, George. I kept it in the event that you might want to find out what happened," Chief Mundy said. "I will keep it under lock and key in my personal files. Experience tells me that sometimes people change their minds and decide to sue or press criminal charges. I'm not going to file it, but I'm not going to destroy it either. And George, I know this officer very well. I've known his family for a long time. I know he's telling the truth."

"I understand," Dad said. "I'm grateful for your discretion." Then he left the chief's office. It was already cool outside for September, but he felt as if it were the hottest day in July.

Yet Another Side

The cop stopped to pick Frank up. Frank was happy to see the driver. He had seen the cop around and wondered about him. That cop looked really hot in his uniform. Frank thought he might look even hotter out of it. What a lucky break!

"Where you going?" the cop asked him.

"Wherever you're going," said Frank.

He got in the car. The cop started to make small talk about the weather, where he was from, how old he was, and Frank told him he was seventeen and whose son he was.

"I know who you are. And what you are," the cop said.

Frank thought that was promising, if the cop meant what he thought the cop meant. When the cop started rubbing his crotch Frank was sure of the meaning.

"Don't be shy," the cop said. "You can touch it."

Frank placed his hand on the cop's crotch. While still driving the cop raised himself against the back of his seat to unzip. He was hard. Frank put his hand around it and fondled it.

"We don't have room here for this," the cop said. He then turned off to a side county road. During the time they were parked there no cars went by: it was the road to the old mill, closed down some ten years prior. The cop walked around to the passenger side and opened the door.

"Get closer, come on. Get your legs out of the car," he said, swinging his penis in the direction of Frank's face. Frank took it in his hand and wrapped his mouth around it. His fantasy had become partially fulfilled: had they been in bed, where they could make love and carry this several steps farther, it would have been heavenly.

The cop didn't take long to climax.

"Clean it off. I don't want any drips on my underwear," the cop ordered Frank. Then he pulled up his pants and the zipper. As soon as he had smoothed out his uniform he asked Frank to sit closer to the outer edge of the seat. He started punching him in the face.

"You fucking faggot, you filthy piece of queer shit!" he said as he punched him so hard Frank fell to the back. The cop pulled him forward and held him by the shirt while punching him with his right fist. Frank's pullover was specked red. He felt blood streaming out of his nostrils. His left eye was shut. The intensity of the pain, the cop thought, should make the faggot struggle against the punches. Frank did nothing more than try to cover his face, but it didn't work: the cop brushed off his arm and slapped Frank hard on his face, his neck, his ears. By the time he cop stopped hitting him the front of his pullover was no longer specked, but stained dark red.

The cop pushed Frank to the side of the road.

"That'll teach you not to try your shit on men. I'm a man, you hear? I'm not a faggot like you, hunk of scum!"

The cop drove off. Although Frank could barely see through one eye, he noticed that the cop turned back where they had come. He was able to stand up, but his head felt light. He waited a few minutes, until he was stable enough to walk to the main highway and cross it. He was lucky that his classmate's dad stopped to pick him up. He worried that he would stain the seats, but his classmate's dad said it was okay. What was important was that he got home as soon as possible, the father of his classmate said. He asked Frank what had happened. "Some guy gave me a ride and when I told him whose son I was he started beating on me. I don't know why."

It was already dark when his classmate's dad dropped Frank off at home. He opened the front door. Mom was coming down the hall.

"What has happened to you?" Mom screamed.

HEARTBREAK AT PLAZA LAS AMÉRICAS

That man going through the round rack on the other side of this section, that man... Is he? Might he be? He looks straight. Appearances deceive, though. Who knows. Oh, Jesus, he's looking at me. I better pretend I'm looking through these slacks. Wait, what is this? I'm in the 44 section. He must have noticed I'm faking it. Where are they? Oh, here, 34 waist, 32 inseam. No, 33 waist. I did lose a little weight. Better look through these, otherwise he'll know I'm not really looking for pants. Pull this pair out. Set it up so I can look at the waist, just above the size and price tag at the same level as that man's face—and yes! He *is* looking at me. Straight, my ass. There's his left hand—oh, sure there's the wedding band. Is his wife anywhere near here? I don't see any females, just two other guys, a teenager and his dad looking through polo shirts over there. Put this pair of pants back on the rack. Slide another one to the side, open a space so I can look at it. No, I wouldn't buy brown pants, ugh. It doesn't make any difference. I'm not really looking at any to buy. Still. Look at another pair. Bring it up. That man is staring at me. He's holding the hanger above his head and inspecting the cuffs at the height of his head so he can look at me without raising suspicion. From whom? Oh, from me, in case I'm straight. Huh. He's walking around the round rack. Now I can see most of him. The front, that is. I better keep sliding hangers from right to left. I'm not looking at any pants. My head is down, but my eyes are fixed on his crotch. Tight pants. Not jeans? No. Oyster-colored dress pants. Deliciously tight, if I can allow myself to say so. Oh, shit, I've caught myself looking over my eyeglasses at him while shuffling pants from right to left. He's searching for pants himself the same way, looking at me with his head down, his right hand sliding hangers, his left hand grabbing his crotch. I clear my throat. Nothing to clear, actually. Let's see, how about this pair? Let me pull it out. Hold it up where I can still see the man with his hand running up and down his crotch where the nice swelling is. My head still down, my eyes rolled up. Jesus, I'm getting a brain freeze from rolling them up so high and keeping my head down. Let me look at this label. Oh, no, JC Penney's own brand. I hate those. Maybe these are Haggar over here. No, some other brand I don't recognize. Victory? Who the hell makes that? Where are the Dockers? Behind me. Let me walk over here. I'll turn my back on that man. If he comes around to the rack in front of me, then it's undeniable: he's cruising me. Well, it's been undeniable already, so it's kind of a moot exercise. If he's not cruising me, he has jock itch. What's that on the corner of my eye? Sure thing. That man. He's coming around. Oh, shit, he's also looking at slacks on this rack! Right in front of me. Who's faking it now? He can't be more than a 36 waist, maybe. He's looking through pants in the 42 section. What should I do now? Oh, he's slowly walking over to my side. I'm not going to look at him now. I'd have to stare at his face up close. He... oh, if I wasn't sure before, I am now. He's brushed hard against my ass, squeezing between me and the rack behind me. Let me see what he's doing now. His back is toward me. He's shuffling pants around behind me. And there he comes again... Damn! He's rubbed his dick against my crack. He almost stood there too long for being in public. No one else is around. Oh, no, another guy is looking through a Plexiglas cube full of dress shirts on the other side. He's got his back to us. Now he's turning around and looking our way. Hot guy, too. Looks straight, though. This guy is now by me. He stretches out his arm and squeezes my ass! I'm flushed now. My knees are shaking. My hands, too. I'll never get used to this. Twice before I've run out. Literally, run out to my car fearful that the other guy is following me and will want to finish off what we started among the round racks at Sears. JC Penney is a new location, uncharted cruising territory. The guy I ran away from at Sears? He's always there. I don't want to tempt fate. That Sears guy looks rough. I feel an attraction to that, but it also scares me. Probably some married guy who's going to beat me up after his orgasm and leave me for dead in some vacant lot. At least this one is well-scrubbed and his clothes are pressed. He's coming closer. He looks around. Then he takes my right hand, the one hanging by my side, the one I left there so if he went by again I could grab his dick. He places it on his crotch. Actually, on the hardness to the side. He lets go my hand. I keep it there for a few more seconds before I remove it and return it to the rack. My face is burning. Let me pick out a couple of pairs of pants, something that looks as if I were going to buy them. Where are the dressing rooms? Ah, on the other side of the section, across from suits. I'm going to look at the guy in the face. That should let him know I want him to follow me in there. I walk away a bit and stand by the rack where he had been standing before to look at him and make sure he's looking back, then go on walking toward the dressing rooms. He's still in the same spot. Well, he'll follow me there. He probably doesn't want to make it too obvious. Here are the dressing rooms. Let me pick one from the three on each side, one at the end. Could be risky. No doors, just a curtain hanging in front of each stall. God, these are ugly curtains, these cheap flower-print cretonne numbers. But the curtains are shirred in the top bar and easily stretch from one side to the other and reach the floor, though, so that shouldn't be a problem. No one will look in. Just in case I'll hold on to both sides of the frame and hold the curtain in place. Let me hang the two hangers from the hook on the stall wall. Got to take off my shoes before taking off my pants. I should look for pins on the carpet. That's the last thing I need, a pin stab and then having to wait until he's done to take care of it. And blood-soaked socks, a mess. No pins, good. I'll set my pants here on the chair in the corner. Leave my briefs on, but pull the top edge down a bit to show some crack. He'll probably come in with pants on a hanger in hand and push the curtain to the side in the stall across the hall from me. Then he'll pull the curtain some to the side to show me what he's got and I'll fall to my knees over here and wait for him to come over. Maybe I'll bend over. That seems to be what he's after, anyway. For that I have to leave the curtain pulled a bit to the side, to give him a peek this way. I'm not going to put on the pants on the hangers. Well, maybe I should. I will. Here. I can always pull them halfway down and then go at it. Footsteps? Yes, footsteps. Not this far down, though. Is he going to stay in one of the stalls to the front? No, that's not him. Someone is talking to someone else. Oh, it's one of the clerks yelling at a co-worker. Two sets of footsteps walk away. There's no one else in here. How long have I been here? At least fifteen minutes. I'll give him five more, then I'm leaving. It's kind of cold in here. Why do they run the air conditioning so low? I hope that guy has some lubricant with him. I came here to pay a bill on the second floor and got distracted wondering what was new in men's clothes. And maybe in men, got to admit. I wasn't planning on this, so I didn't think to buy any lubrication. And I hope he has something that washes away. Not Vaseline. That stuff is so greasy. I'd end up wiping my butt with one of those pants or the curtain. It stains my white undies and I have to throw them out before Mom sees them and figures out what it is or asks me why my underwear is grease-stained. Maybe we can set up a regular meeting. We can meet here or somewhere safe, more private. Not the roadside motels, though. They only allow men and women. Maybe one of those secluded places off the road from Monacillos to Guaynabo. I wouldn't mind sharing the fee for a room at the San Juan airport hotel. I went there once. No luxury, but who cares. It's got a double bed and a bathroom. Yes, I went there with that slob from Ponce, the traveling salesman. Sounds like a joke, doesn't it? We met at the urinals in the rest room by the mall cafeteria. And he followed me to the hotel in that ridiculous white van full of merchandise. Children's apparel of some kind, he said. I didn't pay much attention. Oh, wait, not there! What am I thinking, what? I got crabs there that time. Never saw the guy again. I still don't know whether the bugs were there already or he gave them to me. Ugh. And Mom... She wanted to know what was in my underwear, those tiny pods, and I didn't know. I just knew I had that itch. Then the face Julio made when I went to his office at the Caguas regional hospital and he made that ugly face and fanned me away when he saw what it was. And that bastard, putting one of the dead bugs in the microscope so I could see how ugly those things are. That was damn embarrassing. No, the airport hotel is out. Maybe we can meet off the road in Piñones and stay in one of the cars, his or mine. We could do it in the back of my hatchback. We'd have to coordinate, that's all. Where is this guy? That's it, I'm going out. Pants on. Shoes on. The pants on the hangers can stay here. I'm not going to buy that junk after all. Some lazy clerk can put them back on the rack. I don't see—oh, there he is. Who's that by him next to the round rack? It's that guy, the one who was looking at the dress shirts before! What the hell?

A Room of His Own

György Sándor had thought perhaps he would miss ambient noise, even music or the images on a TV screen. Immediately after coming into the room off to the side in his bedroom, in the shaded side of the house, and shutting the door it was the first thing he noticed: the abundance of silence, as if the world had stopped turning and everything else around him had died. He liked that. No more noise to upset or startle him, no more embarrassing talk, no more shameful words. He was in a sonic vacuum. It was a nice change.

The limited boundaries of the room afforded him time to think. Undisturbed by the presence of others he could lose himself in memories and thoughts. When remembering became tedious he started weaving stories in his head. He wished he could remember them the next day. They sounded interesting to him, but relying on his memory proved futile: by next morning he only had a vague recollection of the plot. He could have written them down, but that required utensils and light, neither of which he wanted in the room. Besides, there was no one else with whom to share his tales.

The isolation and the lack of anything substantial to do focused his attention on his genitals. Four or five times a day he would fondle them until he achieved an erection and went on to climax. And as he had done since he discovered that pleasure at the age of eleven, when he caressed himself it was his friend from elementary, middle and high school that he was thinking about. He wouldn't see him again except on the movie screen of his mind. His friend had married and left town three years earlier. It was his friend who had spread the rumors that shamed him. He never wanted to see him again in real life, but his mind kept his image alive. That was enough for him now. He didn't hate his friend: that would have been impossible. Even what his friend told others who mocked him he forgave. Even what his friend said that left out the part about his friend's participation, that, too, he forgave.

Pleasuring himself required stripping to keep his clothes from showing evidence of his activity. His mother had to pick up his clothes when he pushed them out the dog door, and he didn't want her to know what he was doing. It became so frequent, however, that he chose to keep off his pants permanently. Then he realized there was nobody there to wear clothes for. He told his mother not to bother with them. The room was warm enough. He needed no covers. Clothing was actually a nuisance.

He scratched his face one morning and felt the length of his beard and moustache. The hair above his upper lip was now covering his mouth down to the crest of his chin. The rest of his facial hair had grown down to his lower neck. When he scratched he cut himself on the side of his face. His fingernails were almost a half-inch long. His toenails had begun curling down over the edge of his toes.

He started standing up for longer periods than he spent sitting on his mat. The lower edge of his buttocks had developed small blisters. They eventually turned into sores that slowly dried and left scabs he could feel when he played with his anus.

His eyes had become so accustomed to the darkness, broken only by a sliver of light under the door and the edges of the dog flap that he could notice the near translucence of his skin, deprived of sunlight. He could follow his swollen blood vessels with a fingernail and wondered whether he could slash them with his index fingernail if he ever thought that to be necessary. It was, however, unlikely: he felt completely satisfied with his new state.

His mother started beating on his door, asking him to please leave the room and come back to normal living. He listened to her and said nothing until he finally got tired of her harassment. He pressed his face against the dog door and told her this was normal for him and she needed to leave him alone. Then he stuck the bucket out the hole in the door. She had not picked it up for a day. He had only noticed when he crouched down to defecate and his penis brushed against the accumulated feces. It surprised him that he had not smelled it. It was evident that his nose had fatigued and no longer needed to enable that sense.

His mother brought his dinner tray one day. She lingered on the other side. He asked her what she wanted.

"The neighbors are talking, They're mocking me," she said. "Myrna next door? She asked where you were. I told her. She laughed at me. She told others. They all laugh at me when I walk to the store. 'Who's he kidding?' that Myrna Kravitz said. You need to come out of there, György."

He didn't answer. He heard her smack her lips, then shuffle her slippers away.

Were there other people in the world who also chose to live in a similar room? He suspected there had to be. He could not be unique in this need to hide away from everything that threatened them. His only regret was that no similar arrangements could be made for his soul so he could also isolate himself from it. He had questioned whether it was a mental disease, some form of paranoia, but had dismissed that concern as just the possible imputations of those who did not understand, the ones who chose to live in what he considered nothing more than a larger room where they were all imprisoned without knowing it. They thought themselves to be on their way somewhere without any awareness that there was nowhere to go, that they walked in circles like donkeys turning a millstone, that each step was a beginning and an end in itself and, if not seen that way, they deluded themselves into thinking there was a real destination.

He couldn't understand why, but he started to feel that the room was becoming narrower and shallower. It couldn't be. The walls were solid framed plywood panels painted black. He shook the notion out of his head.

He no longer slept during set times, because he wasn't sure when night had fallen or day shone bright or even what time it was, whether the wind was blowing or rain fell light or in a torrent. His mother brought him meals at what he figured were the usual times, but he could never be sure. Maybe she was trying to fool him. Confuse him, force him out by befuddling him. She was perhaps bringing breakfast at midnight, for all he knew. The fact was that he had lost the notion of time and the structure his life had known around the regularity of physical activity and social convention.

It looked to him one day that the ceiling was lower. It seemed to be just inches above his head. He stretched his arm upwards and confirmed that the ceiling was still where it had been all along, some two feet above his head. He lowered his arm. The ceiling again felt as if it had dropped. Together with the walls closing in, for the first time since his voluntary confinement he felt uncomfortable, constrained.

He dismissed it as his imagination playing tricks on him. His mind probably missed open spaces. It was a matter of conditioning it to realize that less space was much better, more natural than wandering around vast zones.

No toilet tissue, he discovered one evening. He called for his mother to bring him a roll. No one answered. She must have been out. He had to wait. What seemed like hours went by. He had fallen asleep and woke up to feces crusted in his anus. He needed the tissue. He called again, but no one answered.

He stood up from his mat. Again the roof came down to his head, but as he reached for it he still knew it was where it had been, but the walls: the walls were coming at him. No, they were still where they had been. His arms stretched out to confirm that. He would drop his arms and the walls again came at him. They seemed to be sliding in, all four sides, little by little. He extended his arms. The walls were still in the same place. He dropped his arms. The top was brushing his head, but it was in the same place. Even the floor seemed to rise now attempting to meet the ceiling and crush him. But no. The floor had not risen. But it seemed to rise and the bucket full of feces was rising from the corner of the room, he could feel it next to his leg, he reached for the bucket and it was still in the same place, but he felt it close to his knee and straightened himself again to bump his head on the ceiling that had not really dropped. He crouched on the sleeping mat. He wrapped his arms around his knees. He locked his hands on them. He dropped his head above them. The ceiling, the ceiling was so close to his head he couldn't raise it to struggle against the plank crushing it. He wept when the floor started rising again until he was sandwiched between it and the ceiling and the four walls. He was a beast caged in a cube with a bucket full of feces and urine crushing his shins.

His sobbing and weeping turned into a scream. He yelled for his mother, but no one came. He cried for her again, then again and again, but no one came. He managed to rise and reach for the doorknob. He turned it, but instead of engaging the locking mechanism it spun uselessly in his hand. He banged on the door. He slammed the frame. He looked down on the slot, the dog door that was big enough for the bucket, but not for him to crawl out of it. He kicked the door, banged on it and screamed for his mother. No one came. He didn't know how long he stood there weeping and calling without anyone coming to take him out of that cube that threatened to crush him. He pressed his face against the frame's edge that met the door. He yelled into it: perhaps yelling and screaming against the door just muffled his voice and screaming into that recess stopped it from flowing freely. No one replied, no one came. He tried again to turn the doorknob, with the same result. He had installed a flat-faced knob to make sure he would not be tempted to leave his sanctuary. It was serving its purpose. He held on to the facsimile of a doorknob as he started sliding down toward the floor. He yelled again. No one showed up. The dog door only pushed in, not out: it was framed and sprung with edges against the door to prevent him from opening it. That opening, too, had served its purpose effectively.

He dozed off against the door. When he woke up, his hair covering his face, he had no idea whether he had slept for four hours or twenty seconds. It was the first time he missed any familiar sound, even a car horn, but most of all a distant tune to remind him there was something out there. Now he heard nothing but the terror in his head: the walls were closing on him again, he banged on the door and with the loudest possible voice left after he had injured his throat from an earlier screaming bout he let out what was to be his last call. No one was there. His mother had left him in there. Maybe she had tired of calling on him to leave the room and concluded he never would. She hadn't brought him his meals that day. Or had she brought them, now was night and it wasn't time to bring him breakfast? What was the last meal he had eaten? Was it eggs and toast or chicken with pasta? Orange juice or milk? Ginger root tea? He reached for whatever was still on the plate, but the tray was gone. When did she retrieve it? She could come back any minute. But minutes had lost all reality. It could feel like an hour. By then the walls would have compressed him and the bucket spilled on him and on the sleeping mat. He called again, but his voice was gone: only a harsh whisper came out of his mouth, something no one would hear.

He felt a smothering pressure on his chest. His left arm started shrinking toward his side. His left hand curled into a tight ball against his belly. He couldn't breathe. He tried repeatedly to fill his lungs, but each time he only got halfway there. He felt his last gasp, but he didn't hear it. He collapsed against the door. His sphincters loosened, his bowel and bladder emptied and wet the edge of the sleeping mat.

His mother brought him lunch. She had left the house for some ten minutes to rake a small patch of leaves by the steps into the house. She tried to push the tray through the dog door, but it caught on something.

She called out to him, but got no answer. She knocked on the door, then called out to him again. She turned the doorknob and opened the door. The bundle of pale skin and scraggly hair that had been her son was lying in his own waste on the other side. She lay the tray down and shook him, checked his pulse, called his name, then pressed his face against her bosom, moistening his hair with tears, her chest convulsing with sobbing. She rocked him slowly and hummed the lullaby she had sung for him when he was just days old.

"Why, my son?" she said with a broken voice. "Why did you go into that room? We all knew, we all knew, my beautiful child. We didn't care. We just wanted you to be happy, my son. That's all we wanted for you."

A Lonely Hearts Club for One

The queen of hearts is always
your best bet.
　　　　　–Glenn Frey and Don Henley

Don saw Walt in the lobby as they were getting in the elevator of the building on West Tenth Street where they both lived. He knew he had seen Walt before, and he knew exactly where.

"I saw you at the Brass Rail last Saturday night, didn't I?" Don asked.

Walt chuckled and nodded. His face was like a beetroot, it was so red. Don had to admit it was difficult to see Walt's eyes behind the lenses thick as beer-bottle bottoms, but his persistent stare led Don to Walt's blue eyes.

Although Don had first seen him in the darkness of the back bar at the Brass Rail past two guys who were making out by the pool table, most likely wearing contact lenses instead of those magnifying glasses, he still would have recognized the same red and black checkered flannel shirt and the jeans. They must have been what called his attention. Otherwise, he remembered the frame and the bulk, not exactly his facial features.

Don introduced himself before Walt walked out on the third floor. Walt told him his name and apartment number—Walt Anderson, 305.

The next time Don saw him, a Saturday night, Walt was sitting on the same stool at the Brass Rail. Don put his arm over Walt's shoulders and asked him, "Do you pay rent on this stool?"

Walt chuckled. "I bring my own," he said. He chuckled again.

"I'm sorry, I didn't tell you my name before. Donald. Don Prescott."

Walt was a systems developer with Cray Research, a supercomputer company in Mendota Heights, just south of Minneapolis. He held two degrees from Georgia Tech, one in chemical engineering and another in computer science. He only volunteered information when Don asked him for it. Otherwise, he didn't say much. What he did say was articulate and in a slight drawl.

"Where does that come from?" Don asked him.

"From where did what come?" asked Walt back.

"The lazy vowels," Don said.

"From Atlanta," Walt replied.

"Now, this is a much better match!" someone said behind Don. It was Pat O'Neill, Don's bartender friend. He pinched one of Walt's fleshy cheeks and pushed Don's face closer to Walt's. He said to Don, "I knew sooner or later you'd find someone nice."

The following Monday evening Walt asked Don to stop by his apartment. Don rode the elevator down from the 21st floor. Walt came to the door in gym trunks and barefoot. Two black cats sneaked up. Don tried to pet them, but they ran away.

"Those are Beast and Pest. They are not used to company," Walt said. He chuckled.

The apartment was not in complete disarray, but it wasn't clean, either. A smell Don had perceived on Walt when he approached him to kiss him farewell Saturday night permeated the apartment as well. Don couldn't figure out what it was.

"You play the piano?" Don asked. He referred to a blond Wurlitzer spinet against a wall in the living room.

"Occasionally," Walt said. He chuckled.

"Do you mind if I try it?" Don asked. He had been wanting to play a piano whose keys, unlike his console Lindner upstairs, sprung back when played.

"Please," Walt said.

The first couple of chords put Don's teeth on edge.

"Ugh! Goodness, Walt, this piano is in severe need of tuning!"

Walt chuckled. He had moved it over the years from Atlanta to Lynchburg, Virginia, then to Minneapolis and finally to St. Paul. Not once had he bothered to have it tuned.

"Well, if you ever expect me to come back here to visit, you're going to have that piano tuned!" Don joked.

Late in the afternoon of the following day Walt called Don. "I stayed home today and had the tuner come in this afternoon."

Don was surprised on several counts.

"Wow. That was short notice."

"I paid him three times his fee to postpone his other commitments. Now you have no excuse." He chuckled.

During the next few weeks, they ran into each other often in the building lobby and at the Brass Rail. They met for lunch one Saturday at the Parisian Cafe in Town Square, downtown St. Paul. Even without eyeglasses Walt was not a pretty boy, and it seemed to Don he was aware of it. Occasionally he would have outbursts of arrogance, all dealing with accounts of instances that proved how dumb people could be. The subjects he chose for conversation revealed to Don that Walt was an exceptionally brilliant, but impatient man: listening to him Don felt overwhelmed by the realization of how little he knew, despite his previous career in diplomacy and two advanced degrees. Walt spoke with the refinement and topical breadth men of a technical background usually don't have. His observations were laced with an acrid but witty sarcasm, however, that was often too dark and merciless for Don, and, he suspected, for most other people. At the bar men would walk up, pat him in the back and then never stay too long by his side. When he wasn't on the stool he would stand against a wall, a drink always in hand.

One night Don saw him on his way out.

"Hey, Walt, are you leaving now?"

Walt turned around and nodded. "Are you staying till closing?" Walt asked. Don was sitting with a group of friends and his roommate Joshua, who that night had braved the world beyond his closet door and driven with Don to the Brass Rail.

"Heck, no. I've seen how bouncers treat laggers. Like cattle!" Don said and laughed. "We'll be leaving as soon as I'm done with this beer. I'll give you a call tomorrow." Walt nodded, smiled shyly and went on his way.

When Walt left the bar one of the friends closest to Don asked, "Who is that nerd?"

"Careful! My roommate and occasional sex partner and he are like this," Joshua said, crossing his fingers.

"He's an incredible guy, sweet and just brilliant," Don said.

"You mean a nerd," said another friend, the one in the turquoise Polo top.

"An incredible guy," Don repeated. No one made any more comments.

The following morning close to noon Don called Walt. "You left so quickly. I would have liked to introduce you."

"Not my kind of people, but thanks anyway." Walt chuckled.

A few days later Walt asked Don to join him for lunch at La Fonda de Acebo, a Mexican restaurant on Highway 13 in Mendota Heights, close to where Walt worked. Don drove down from St. Paul; knowing what would ensue, he took the afternoon off: he would have too many margaritas, as indeed he did, three or four giant glasses. They were the only alcoholic drinks for which he had no temperance. Outside the restaurant, in the parking lot behind the building, Walt grabbed him from behind, pulled him up to him and kissed him hard on the lips.

Walt had taken Don by such surprise that he could not think of anything to say. Then he blurted the first thing that came to mind.

"Are you collecting for lunch?"

Walt's face melted. A vague semblance of the shadow of a smile remained on his face, and he muted a chuckle.

"I'm only joking, Walt," Don said. "Don't be mad at me. I'm really sorry for hurting you."

"I'm not hurt," Walt answered. He turned around and walked to his car.

Don waited a few days before talking to him. Walt seemed unconcerned with the parking lot matter.

In the evening sometimes Don would come down to watch TV with him. Every so often he would play some pop song on the piano, aware that the instrument had been tuned for him. Don wondered what the pungent smell could be. Ambergris it sure wasn't. It certainly wasn't a deodorizer, but it smelled chemical; it wasn't a clean smell, either. A sour lining made it repugnant. Don subtly tried to track it down. It wasn't the bathroom, although that itself needed a good scrub, especially the sink on which sat a small case with the remains of a dry set of contact lenses. It wasn't the kitchen: it looked as if Walt used it infrequently. The odor seemed to come from the second bedroom. Don could not pretend he was looking for the bathroom to go in there.

A few days later Walt had to travel to Germany. He went there often on business as the star troubleshooter for Cray Research computers' operating system. He most often went to Stuttgart, to the Max Planck Institute. He was in most demand when the company had a new software release. As Walt explained it, new releases were often plagued with more bugs than Don's old apartment on Lincoln Avenue. He came up after calling to make sure Don's roommate wasn't in.

"Would you be able to look after my cats?" Walt asked him. He usually drove them over for his friend Judy Braun to look after, but she would be traveling as well, and if it weren't too much of a bother Don would prevent him from putting them in a kennel. Don would just have to stop by a couple of times a day, maybe even just once.

"Of course, Walt," Don said. "I have no problem taking care of pussy."

Walt chuckled absently and handed him his door key.

That evening Don went down wondering what taking care of cats entailed. Walt had left a note on the kitchen counter telling Don where the cat litter and food were. Don was to take the litter box to the garbage chute in the hall and dump its contents in there, then put fresh litter in it. It troubled Don that the cats were not visible. Don thought they were hiding as they did since the first time he visited the apartment, only to appear later with their intriguingly annoying antics before again running to hide in one of the bedrooms.

The litter box was not where Don could readily find it: Walt had neglected to tell him where it was. He looked in the pantry, the main closet and under Walt's bed, then in the second bedroom, where the smell that had bothered him became stronger. One of the cats—Pest? Beast?—dashed out when Don lifted the edge of the bedspread. The stench threw him back. The litter box had not been changed for a while, and the cats had taken to pottying anywhere they could around it. Don pulled away before his stomach unloaded right there.

Nose clutched he was able to clean out the floor, change the litter, put out dry food and water in the dishes on the floor and speed out after cracking the sliding door that led to the balcony to air the place. The smell, of course, was a mystery no more.

Early the next day, when it was early afternoon in Stuttgart, Walt called. He wanted to remind Don to pick up his mail. He had forgotten to give Don the mailbox key, but he would find it in the top drawer of the dresser in a corner of his bedroom. When Don returned to the apartment that evening the smell had improved, although not much: he figured the walls and furniture upholstery had probably absorbed it, and even two coats of paint would not rid the apartment of the odor. He headed for the dresser, opened the drawer and found many things other than the mailbox key, which he never did find. Instead, in it Walt had stored several reels of eight-millimeter male porn films, over a dozen half-empty bottles of amyl nitrate and a rubber replica of a male organ so enormously disproportionate to the average actual organ, that it must have been labeled, "Sold only as a novelty item." Nonetheless, it showed signs that the item had served ambitious intentions.

Whenever Don's mother asked him to get something from her purse, he would bring the bag to her and let her open it. Privacy had always been an obsession of his: he only found out about what others did or kept when others wanted to let him know. Even when gossip was meant to save him misery from the company of the wrong person he resented the breach of decency implied in someone else's misguided belief that he had the authority and right to divulge what was none of his business.

Although he was not snooping when he discovered the items, he felt like a heel for knowing a part of Walt's life that he had not freely disclosed. But—Mother Jefferson Davis, that dildo! Walt must have been fearless. And then the thought crossed his mind that Walt had instructed him to look for the key precisely because he wanted Don to find everything.

Don didn't feel offended. Instead he felt great sadness at what the props represented. Walt had to replace human contact with those approximations. He also felt ashamed of himself and for others who had only focused on Walt's physical attributes and found them lacking.

In late January Don made up with the partner from whom he had been estranged since Thanksgiving. He told Walt.

The next morning Don walked out to his car, parked on the opposite side of the street from the apartment building. There was an envelope stuck under one of the windshield wipers. It was from Walt.

He was hurt that Don was going back to Randy, a man who did not deserve him, a man who had treated him like a second-rate trick who had stayed around too long, leaving Don behind while he went out with his female beard to parties where he could pass for straight.

In all that Walt was accurate. Don himself had shared it with Walt.

Walt wrote that perhaps Don should look closer to see who was more willing to spend time with him and give him the respect he deserved. He quoted from "Desperado": Why wouldn't Don come to his senses?

Don thought it was sweet of Walt to be so concerned with his emotional well-being.

He called Walt at work; Walt was silent during most of their conversation. Don thanked him for his words; however, Don felt that his partner and he had spent some good times together and Don wanted to know whether they should still give it another try.

"Well, you know what you are doing," Walt said. He chuckled.

The following morning again Don pulled another envelope out from under the wiper. Walt was in pain, he said. He didn't know whether he loved Don, because he had never loved anyone, but if it hurt like that, like a vise that crushes someone's heart and leaves nothing but its shreds behind, he couldn't see why anyone wanted it so bad. He was starting to believe that one could not always choose to avoid it. What was Don going to do? Waste his life with someone like that other guy, or give him a chance to let his feelings grow into something he had not experienced ever before, if Don could benefit from it as well?

Don couldn't think of anything to reply to that. He dropped by Walt's apartment that evening. His face turned from red to purple as Don spoke: he was very thankful, but he saw Walt as a good friend, a soulmate almost—they could have been brothers, he joked: they were born two weeks apart.

Sadness cloaked Walt's eyes. With a voice deeper than it was already he said, "It's not your gratitude I need, but I will settle for your friendship." He did not chuckle.

Soon after Don and Randy had reestablished their relationship Randy demanded that Don move elsewhere. He didn't trust Joshua and, besides, he couldn't stand Joshua. Don was aware that the dislike would deepen and jeopardize the new attempt if Randy discovered that Joshua had replaced him in bed whenever the need arose.

Moving day approached and still Don had not found help with it. Eventually he got Walt to help together with Tom Reynen, Paul Steffenhagen and Carlos Rodríguez, a Colombian drug counselor whose house's aromas helped anyone get high without ever putting a joint on his lips. Carlos had made several attempts at having sex with Don. He had succeeded finally one evening when he invited Don to his house under the pretense of cooking a large meal for several people. The appetizer would be *ajiaco*, a spicy Colombian soup that Don had tasted in Bogota when he was a U.S. liaison with the Department of State. Carlos had heard Don talk about it and declare himself an *ajiaco* expert. When Don arrived for the banquet the soup was on the menu, but he would be the only guest. Carlos asked him to sit at the head of the table, then crawled underneath, unzipped Don and took him in his mouth while his head bobbed up and down under the tablecloth. Don had taken a break from the hot soup; when it was over he finished the soup and left. Carlos had not given up his notion that sooner or later their shared knowledge of Spanish would bind them as the perfect couple. Don didn't have to give up on the idea, because he never entertained it in the first place.

"Your lingual skills are amazing, but linguistics alone is no basis for a relationship," Don told him. More important yet was Don's fear of junkies, particularly of those who counseled others on how to stop using drugs while doing them themselves. Such duplicity spilled over into other areas of life.

When they were done with the move Don treated everyone to deep-dish pizza at the Green Mill on Grand Avenue, just down the road from his new apartment. It was early April and, although it was still cold, they were overheated from the day-long job. Don's muscular system started to unwind from head to toe when he sat down. He didn't know whether he'd be able to get up after dinner.

Tom and Paul sat on the opposite side of the booth. Walt sat to Don's left and Carlos to his right. During dinner Carlos slipped his hand under the table into Don's crotch. Don was too tired to bother to slap it off. He then felt Walt's hand slithering over his thigh on its way to his crotch. At the unexpected manual encounter Carlos and Walt looked at Don's hands, wondering whether it was one of his they had found under the table. Both hands jerked back to their respective owners. Fatigue was perhaps the cause of Don's uncontrollable laughter. Neither of the other two found it as funny; Paul and Tom thought he had gone mad.

Several months later Don went to work for Cray Research as a human resources development specialist. His office was on the second floor, almost directly above Walt's. They saw each other every day when they converged in the cafeteria at lunchtime. Walt usually sat in a corner reading while Don sat with other colleagues playing gin rummy. Sometimes Don consulted Walt on technical matters he felt he needed to master to better understand the dynamics of the jobs the employees in his care performed. Walt, Don discovered, was also a gifted writer capable of turning the most arcane technical lingo into something the dullest mind could understand.

Over time Don noticed that Walt's interest had cooled down. That did not assuage Don's sense of guilt over his inability to accept Walt's affection. To ease his discomfort and bring him back into his life even if under different circumstances Don invited him to dinner. Randy would be present. He wasted no time cuddling up to Don as if he had to protect his turf. Don suggested watching *Raiders of the Lost Ark*; Walt politely excused himself and left.

When Don left work the next day he found another envelope. Walt had written that he could not believe Don's insensitivity and the additional pain he had caused when he was just beginning to heal. Don had taken him for a slab of stone incapable of any sentiment, a lemon squeezed of everything except the skin. Never was Don to ask him to come along on anything that included that miserable bastard, the insufferable oaf who had even made himself scarce with some lame excuse the day Don had to move at his behest. Don still had his respect and affection, but he thought it would be best if Don stayed away from him except for professional reasons.

Don's truth was that he would have given Walt more than a little time and attention. He admired Walt. Randy was not the type of person with whom he could hold a conversation beyond Randy's family and office politics where he worked at the Burlington Northern Railroad. "He's a mope," Pat O'Neill had told Don one night when they had stopped at the Brass Rail. Without any intention to bring it up completely to his consciousness in a way that would drive him to do something about it, Don surmised that the only satisfactory part of their relationship, and the actual reason he had agreed to resume it, was the sex. Had it been possible, Don would have kept Randy in a vault, unlocked him for sex, put him back and then go have intellectual intercourse with people who could actually think. The world, alas, did not function that way. The only opportunities he had for well-informed exchanges outside of work were the times Randy went out with his beard to a work-related function: whereas he had loathed the pretense as dismissive of his dignity in the past, Walt had opened a world he had not experienced for many years, and then when Randy had to go assemble his portable closet Don would make sure he went out with former colleagues and people he had known but had not seen in a while, gay and straight, singles and couples, sometimes groups whose cultural horizon and wit expanded beyond Randy's family lore and office intrigue while downing cans of Special Export and belching.

Those feelings of Walt's that he could not name for lack of habit and an endearing reticence were evident in Don's eyes, in his entire countenance whenever Don was around, even when he just pretended to be reading his book. Don would look in his direction from the opposite side of the cafeteria and catch Walt looking at him above the edge of his pocket book. Even knowing that Walt's physical needs were met through extraordinary facsimiles made Don feel Walt deserved more than his condescension.

That, Don finally understood, had a name. What had been Walt's unrequited love was in fact reciprocated albeit unexpressed and even unacknowledged. Still, Walt scared Don. His uncommon intelligence, his obdurateness, the intense passion he tried so hard to quell and that tortured his soul, all of it made Don fear that he would overwhelm him and crush his low sense of self-worth. In the best of cases he would end up disappointing Walt. His domestic hygiene they could work on; Don's self-esteem was a completely different matter.

Two months after Walt warned Don about his partner's unworthiness Don was again by himself. They ran into each other at work now and then, but nothing was the same between them. Walt had even stopped going to the cafeteria to read his book during his lunch break.

"He's bought himself this humongous house in Highland Park," David Teeter mentioned one day during a gin rummy game. "I think he wants it so his cats will have more room."

'Maybe he has a beau," Jeanne Zanka ventured. "Oh, damn, another one I don't want," she added after picking up a card from the deck on the table.

"He wouldn't," Don said before realizing it should not have been said.

"Why not?" asked David Teeter, picking up a card and checking where he might put it in his hand.

"Well, you're right. Why not?" asked Don.

"Actually, you may be right. Let's face it, the guy's getting long in the tooth and he's no charmer," said David Teeter. "I'm not queer, but I don't think there would be much demand for someone with his looks among his *compadres.*"

"I saw him at Wild Bill Knowlan's shopping for groceries with some guy a couple of weeks ago," Jeanne

Zanka said, shuffling the cards in her hand. "They looked sort of chummy, if you know what I mean. Gin!"

Don excused himself. Gertrude Sunder took his place at the game table. He climbed the four steps from the sunken cafeteria to the first floor and power walked down the hall to Walt's office. He peeked in the vertical glass pane next to the door. There was Walt reading his book. Don knocked on the door; Walt looked up with those eyes that seemed to say, "I don't ever want to see you again, but come hither and let me touch you." Don opened the door and closed it behind him.

"Is it true that you're dating someone?" Don asked Walt didn't answer. He kept on staring at Don with that same expression. "I need to know, Walt, please." Still no answer. "I need to know, because I'm not going to waste my time and embarrass myself if you are." Walt put the book on his thigh, both sides spread out. "Please, Walt. You may think it's none of my business, and you'd be justified, but I need to know. Are you dating someone?" No reply. "Are you trying to humiliate me? I'm not going to leave this office until you tell me. Are you dating someone, Walt?" Don began to cry. "I am so sorry, Walt. I should have told you I'm sorry I hurt you. You were right about Randy." Walt listened, his arms on his chair's rests. "Aren't you going to say anything?" Walt stared. "Okay, Walt, I've made a fool of myself. I'm not going to apologize for that. You once told me you didn't know whether you loved me. I know I love you. Not because Randy is out of my life. I've walked through your life and mine blindfolded. Now I've made an even bigger idiot of myself."

Don wiped his eyes and sniffled. He turned around to leave. Before he reached the doorknob he heard Walt say, "Why would I be dating someone else?"

Without turning around to face Walt, his hand on the doorknob and feeling defeated Don said, "You were seen at the supermarket with someone."

Walt chuckled.

"My younger brother came up from Lexington. He was going to pick up the Arabian horses he bought in Eau Claire. We had to eat, you know."

Don hesitated. He wasn't sure what any of that really meant. He didn't dare turn around. He could see Walt's reflection on the glass pane in front of him.

Neither said anything. Walt had a streak of stubbornness running through him, Don had perceived during their talks, and Don had one of self-doubt that corroded his soul.

He turned around to look at Walt.

"Are you dating someone?"

Walt chuckled. "I asked you how I would be dating someone? You never answered." His face was two shades darker than crimson.

"Because you are such a special person that someone some day will grab you never to let you go, that's how. I'm afraid someone has."

"Someone already did. He just doesn't know it," Walt said.

Don wasn't sure he understood.

"Who?"

Walt paused. "Why did you come here, Don?"

"To find out something."

"Why?"

"I needed to know."

"Now you know."

"I know nothing!"

"You've known. For a long time you've known, I reckon. Now I know also. Do we really need to say anything else?" Walt asked. "We have come to our senses." He chuckled.

NORTH BY SOUTHEAST

When Juan Julián first walked through the house with the realtor and Arturo he was enraptured with all the closet space. It had a large coat closet in the foyer, one almost as big for linen in a hall on the second floor, a regular-sized one in each of three bedrooms and a Bank of America-vault sized one in the master bedroom. Even the main bathroom had a small closet where a person could fit standing up. The headache he had suffered from all morning practically vanished.

"Who said four bedrooms?" Juan Julián asked in a rhetorical spirit. "You could sleep in one of these closets!"

"I prefer to sleep in rooms with windows," Arturo replied.

And as if all that extra space separated by doors from the rest of the living space weren't enough, the basement was divided into several compartments, each with its own door, separate from the boiler and laundry rooms.

As far as Juan Julián went, the search was over. All the hunting had worsened his frequent cluster headaches. Gone were his concerns about the distance—after all, this was Dutchess County, not the Brooklyn he so adored—and the absence of any Whole Foods or Lands' End stores within a short distance. He would buy a riding mower for the half-acre of land and, as an additional bonus, he would keep it in that closet-like enclosure with its own entrance to the detached garage. He shared the thought with Arturo.

"Yes... You'll look like that guy," Arturo said.

"What guy?" Juan Julián asked.

"You know. The guy in the movie," Arturo said and drew a blank stare from Juan Julián. "*The Straight Story*. The guy who rides a lawn mower to go see his brother. You'd have to get the mower on a ship to see yours."

Juan Julián twisted his mouth and looked away. Arturo's negative thoughts would not dampen his enthusiasm.

"All this room!" Juan Julián said when they inspected the basement. It sounded to Arturo like Pizarro's spirit at the first sight of a roomful of Atahualpa's gold.

"And the floor, look at it," said Myrna, the realtor. "It's so clean, this floor. I tell you, you could eat off it."

"I don't eat off floors," Arturo said, less impressed with the amplitude of non-living space and the pulchritude of bare cement.

"If it were up to me, we'd move in tomorrow," Juan Julián said. He avoided looking at Arturo.

On their way back to Brooklyn Heights Juan Julián felt like a man who wants to scream out his joy in church at getting a marriage proposal from his boyfriend, but realizes the priest is reading the gospel. He feared Arturo's many objections. If it were up to Arturo they would just buy a modest brownstone within a subway hop to the theater district. He had not escaped the poverty and isolation of western Colombia to return to the ruralia of Barrytown.

"Barrytown? So close to Poughkeepsie," Arturo said. "It's like Staten Island without beaches. Or the charm."

"You're such a snob," Juan Julián said. "Who'd think?"

Arturo caught the jab right away.

"I am from Chocó, but Chocó is not in me. After 35 years in the big city I feel no need to go back to the civilized jungle as if it were western Colombia with mildly better architecture," Arturo replied. "You're cruel."

Juan Julián removed his right hand from the steering wheel to pat Arturo's thigh. "I didn't mean it."

"Yes, you did," Arturo said. That was his last utterance until Juan Julián unlocked the apartment door.

They had both retired the year before. Arturo had taught in an elementary school since his graduation from City University of New York. Since arriving in the city from Puerto Rico Juan Julián had been a social worker with the New York City Department of Social Services for so long it took him an entire year to vacate his head of so many sob stories, real and concocted by free-loaders. Neither he nor Arturo considered the possibility of returning to their respective places of origin, especially since their lives were no longer a matter of separate strands—more like a permanent braid fastened by the barrette of a marriage license.

Their mutual frugality had allowed them to save enough to splurge on a dwelling of their own. Juan Julián had the additional benefit of a substantial inheritance from his mother, a small-town heiress who owed her financial comfort to her father's tobacco factories.

"I know why you want to move out there," Arturo said.

"I'm tired of the city, that's all," Juan Julián replied, not entirely convincing. "Finally we'll be able to breathe fresh air."

"More like putting distance between you and the people from your hometown in Puerto Rico," Arturo said. "You know, the ones for whom I am a roommate. You're afraid they'll get on Facebook to say they saw you and your friend. Wink wink. Of course, they can't wink on Facebook. They'll just leave it there. Remember Frankie Valli."

"Frankie Valli?"

"Silence is golden," answered Arturo.

"I had no idea you knew the classics," Juan Julián replied.

Arturo looked out the window. Across the air shaft the Argentinian couple was necking in the kitchen, the lit bare bulb hanging just above their heads. That soft-porn scene was about all he would not miss from Brooklyn Heights. It was just his luck that the kitchen was the only room in the house without window shades: "I like light," Juan Julián replied when Arturo suggested they hang blinds.

"Oh, I remember her! She was so gorgeous! I tried to date her once," Arturo overhead Juan Julián say on the phone one night the previous week. He was talking to a man from his hometown who had found him on Facebook. They were reminiscing about the good old days in a town that, according to Juan Julián's accounts, had very little of goodness to it. Arturo sat reading next to him. Juan Julián was leaning against the couch's armrest with his legs thrown over Arturo's lap. "Yes, yes, I remember him! I dated his sister for a while."

"Probably because his brother was not interested," Arturo said under his breath; Juan Julián covered the mouthpiece, swung his legs away and stood up. Arturo so wanted to cough hard. It would be a coughing fit. A loud one, to make sure the man at the end of the line could hear him. That, however, would be rude.

"You're so wrong!" Juan Julián said, his head buried in the refrigerator. "What did you do with last night's baked beans?"

"Freezer," answered Arturo. He dropped the subject of the real reason for the rush to leave Brooklyn. When they married he had hoped Juan Julián would change his tune. He wasn't expecting Juan Julián to take a one-page ad in *El Diario de Nueva York*. He would have been happy not having to pretend they were *Óscar y Félix*. At least now he wasn't asked to go to a movie while Juan Julián entertained homomisiac relations, his niece Gloria and her husband Luis Rafael Sánchez. Now, that hurt, but not as much as coming home when they were still there. Arturo would go to what was supposed to be his bedroom. From there he would hear Gloria and Luis Rafael telling queer jokes. He could also hear Juan Julián's raucous laughter—and him telling his own joke about a faggot. It had seemed to Arturo as an attempt by his niece and her husband to confirm that the uncle was not *that way*: if he were, he wouldn't be telling those jokes, would he? Arturo had succeeded at preserving his respect for Juan Julián while hoping someday Juan Julián would respect himself.

"They'll follow you there, you know," Arturo said.

"You mean to the bathroom?" Juan Julián asked. Arturo looked at him puzzled. "I never get an upset stomach from them, not even gas."

"Such luck," Arturo said. "I'm not talking about your beans."

Juan Julián caught on.

"It will be more difficult for them to drop by whenever they want," Juan Julián said. He had placed a wet paper towel over the beans container before placing it in the oven.

"You should tell them that in this country people call before showing up at your door with a covered dish of Puerto Rican *tembleque*," Arturo said, referring to coconut custard.

"That would not be hospitable. They are family," Juan Julián said. The beans were now defrosting in the microwave oven.

"My sister always asks. It's courtesy. You know, the old *when in Rome?* Your niece has lived here for what, twelve years? She should be used to that," Arturo said. He had uncorked the bottle of red wine and poured himself a glass. "Don't they realize they'd be wasting a trip if you weren't here?"

Juan Julián said nothing. The microwave bell rang. The kitchen smelled of sweetness and pork. The second bagel popped out of the toaster.

"Like that time when they came knocking and we were making love, and you actually wanted to get up and open the door?" Arturo added. Still Juan Julián said nothing. He grabbed the plates and placed the beans next to the buttered bagels.

Arturo caved in. They made an offer on the house. The owners countered. After several rounds of accusations of low-balling and high-balling they stopped playing the balls game and agreed on a price.

They all met for closing at the attorney's office on the last day of September. It was getting cold. They had walked through the house before closing and noticed that the maples and the oaks were already changing colors.

"You wanted to rake leaves?" Arturo asked Juan Julián. "Just asking, because they're all going to be yours."

"You'll help, won't you?" Juan Julián asked.

"I'll rake as many leaves as I have for the past sixteen years in Brooklyn Heights," Arturo said.

"We can leave them on the ground and have them decompose naturally," Juan Julián said.

"Maybe that's how they do it in Puerto Rico. Oh, wait, you don't have maples down there," Arturo observed. "They won't decompose. They'll collect rain water and grow molds. And you, with all those respiratory allergies and your perennial headaches? Not a pretty picture. I see you raking. *Ruck, ruck, ruck*," Arturo said, holding an air rake and imitating the motion.

The moment came to sign the purchase agreement and the rest of the title paperwork.

"I thought your last name was Madrigal," Mr. Napoli, the attorney, Arturo asked.

"That's my family name," Arturo replied. He had noticed a framed Knights of Columbus parchment of some kind hanging from the wall behind Mr. Napoli. Maybe it was an award. The certificate of membership? A letter from the pope?

"Where did the Correa come from?" Mr. Napoli asked. "I thought that was his last name," he added, pointing at Juan Julián.

"It is. I hyphenate mine since we got married," Arturo replied. Juan Julián's cheeks turned the color of maple leaves in mid-October. Mr. Napoli made a gesture that said, *I get it. I thought you were just queer. Now I want you to get out of here as soon as I have your check in hand.* The sellers looked like something by Grant Wood.

Arturo and Juan Julián followed the Mayflower truck to Barrytown. Juan Julián felt right down bucolic. At every bend he expected to see shepherds and nymphs. He realized he had wanted to get out of the city with its thousands of Puerto Rican prying eyes and wagging tongues for a long time and was finally able to do it. Arturo, however, felt like Dante led by Virgil to hell in a four-wheeled motor boat on a dry riverbed.

"Am I going to have a fake bedroom at the new house also?" Arturo asked. He was looking out the window. The changing leaves did look nice. They would look nicer if this were a sightseeing trip at the end of which they'd be going back to the city.

Living in the Raw Wind

"We've had this conversation," Juan Julián said. "Not everyone is open-minded, Arturo."

"Not everyone is stupid, either," Arturo replied. He often felt like telling Juan Julián he would only pay for a fourth of the rent. While no one was around or when they were in the company of their few gay friends, they shared a home. When Juan Julián's domestic terrorists showed up, he was the other old bachelor, the friend who rented. In the end he would feel guilty for being petty. Instead of making claims he had suggested that Juan Julián go lie in an analyst's couch to clear his mind of foreign occupation.

Four days later they were hanging curtains in the living room. The previous owners had left their tulle drapes on the large window. To Juan Julián they might as well have been see-through. The house had a western exposure: when the sun shone in the afternoon it was almost possible to see right in. When night fell and the lamps were on in the living room anyone going by slowly enough could see what the occupants were doing and even what TV show was on: reruns of *Will and Grace* if Arturo had the remote, *Law & Order Criminal Intent* reruns for Juan Julián.

They drove back to the city amidst Arturo's sighs and cardiac flutter at the sight of the Manhattan skyline. Juan Julián had planned to stop at a mall in White Plains, but Arturo put his foot down and demanded that they drive into the city. After all, the selection would be broader than in White Plains. They went shopping for lined dark-green curtains at Bloomingdale's Third Avenue store. The flimsy tulle would hang from a rod behind them and serve as morning drapery.

Juan Julián was standing on the kitchen foot stool when he noticed a moving object out on the road. It was no object: it was a person coming toward their house. He stepped down and peeked through the corner. It was a woman.

"Someone's approaching," Juan Julián told Arturo.

"A moose?" Arturo asked with no interest whatsoever. He was holding the valance rod. "Really, something human?"

"Could you go to the kitchen?" Juan Julián asked.

"To do what, watch a pot?" Arturo asked.

"While I take care of this woman," Juan Julián said.

"Is she your type?" Arturo asked. "Is she carrying a black naugahyde bag? She could be a Jehova's Witness. I could go down on you when you open the door."

"Don't be funny. Please, go. She's almost at the door," Juan Julián whispered in a Shakespearean aside. "Please, go."

"Are you sure about the kitchen? We have so many walk-in closets!" Arturo said. He let the valance rod fall to the floor and walked away.

The doorbell rang. Juan Julián walked to the foyer and opened the door. The woman, in a plaid dress and a powder-blue sweater, was smiling on the other side of the storm door. She was holding a covered pan with both hands.

"Hello, neighbor!" the woman said. Juan Julián greeted her back and opened the storm door. "I'm Mrs. Provinzino, Mrs. Chuck Provinzino? Rita?" she said in high speak, with a rising intonation when she meant to state the fact. From the kitchen Arturo heard her and wished he were at the door to reply, "No, Arturo, but I could be a Rita. That has a nice ring to it, hon!"

"Pleased to meet you, Mrs. Provinzino..." Juan Julián paused. "Rita. I'm Juan Julián Correa. Would you like to come in?"

"Oh, thank you," she said and climbed the two steps in. "Oh, my! What a tasteful decor! It's so cozy and homey! You can tell it's got a woman's touch to it. Is Mrs. Correa home?"

Juan Julián was about to tell Rita Provinzino that there was no Mrs. Correa when he felt a presence behind him.

"Hello! I believe I heard your name is Rita? I'm Arturo Madrigal-Correa," he said and extended his hand for her to shake. Rita held the pan with one hand and shook Arturo's.

"Nice meeting you," said Rita. "Are you brothers, Juan... What was your second name again?"

"It's Julián," Arturo interjected. "Some people call him Johnny, but he doesn't like it. Not since I have known him, and I have known him, oh, goodness, for years. But not since birth, because no, we are not brothers. I'm flattered you'd think so, though. I live here too."

"Oh?" Rita Provinzino said. After a brief pause she added, "Well, I was just being neighborly? I wanted to welcome you to the neighborhood?" she said, her smile now forced and awkward. In her tone Arturo almost heard a hint of regret. "I brought you this apple pie. I make it with our own apples? I hope you like it." She handed it to Juan Julián.

"Thank you so very much," Juan Julián said. "You're very kind."

"How thoughtful of you!" Arturo said. "We'll have to bake you a fruitcake log, why, with Christmas almost around the corner and all."

"Oh, you don't have to, no, it's not necessary?" Rita Provinzino said. She stepped back and turned halfway toward the door.

"I'll bring the pan over later," Juan Julián said.

"Oh, no, no, no, you don't have to!" Rita said, now close enough to the doorknob that she could turn it. "It's just an old tin pan? You can keep it! And enjoy your home!"

She walked out. Juan Julián followed her with his eyes. He could almost swear she was power walking away.

"Why did you do that?" Juan Julián asked.

"Do what?" Arturo asked. He took the pan off Juan Julián's hand and lifted the foil.

"Show up like that," Juan Julián replied.

Arturo had stuck his nose underneath the foil. "Mmm, this smells so nice! And I know it's not poisoned, because she didn't know who the new owners are. I mean, I am one of the owners, am I not?" He replaced the foil over the pan's rim.

"I just wanted to give our neighbors time to assimilate things instead of popping it out on them this way," Juan Julián said.

"Oh, please. I don't think you have thought this through, Juan Julián. Assimilate? Like babies fed soy milk in case they're allergic to cow milk? At some point everyone in this neighborhood of six will have to know, whether you serve it to them from a dropper or in a *paella* pan," Arturo said. "Are you planning to dress me in camouflage, too?"

"It will take them a little time," Juan Julián said.

"No, honey. It will take *you* a long time. Sooner or later it will happen. It didn't bother you in Brooklyn," Arturo said, less interested now in disguising his hurt with sarcasm.

"They're civilized in Brooklyn."

"No, they mind their own business in Brooklyn, and you got used to that. How do you know these people won't mind theirs?" Arturo said.

"You just saw that one," Juan Julián replied.

"You wanted the country? You wanted a house with lots of storage space? Now you have it. I have it too, whether or not I need it. Just remember: I am part of the package. If I can't live in this house and enjoy our investment together, I'm giving you notice."

At the sound of the last statement Juan Julián recoiled. He had fallen in love with Arturo when they were still in their thirties. Arturo had been the second man he had ever kissed. Their minds were as if traced from the same pattern: they agreed on everything, mostly, except in what regarded his fear of pulling the lid off the boiling pot of his hidden life. They enjoyed so many of the same things. They traveled abroad together: they went to Colombia together, but Arturo stayed home when Juan Julián went to Puerto Rico. Arturo fit his heart snuggly. Arturo's love had been patient with his reluctance to live openly for his family to know. He wished he could: he could not bring himself to let things take their course regardless of where they ended up.

Maybe Arturo was right in suggesting a shrink, but he wasn't sure he could talk about it even to a professional. He lived in crippling fear of his family's rejection. Just below the veneer of his conscience he knew his brother and his sister had to at least suspect. However, one thing was knowing and not acknowledging anything, keeping it an unaddressed secret, and another to make it so obvious his siblings, nephews and nieces would turn their backs on him.

It was easy for Arturo. He only had the one sister. He had told her about him; she didn't care. She had never treated him or Juan Julián any different. Juan Julián wasn't so sure his relatives would be that accepting.

"I'm sorry, Arturo. I'm awkward. I'll get over it, you'll see," Juan Julián said.

"I hope so. It's been a long time I've been living like this. I love you, you know that. It's love that keeps me wanting to hold you and spend every minute of my life with you," Arturo said. "I survive on the hope that someday you'll surprise me and let me sit at your table instead of having my dinner in the servants' quarters."

The strain softened with lovemaking that night. Once the lights were turned off Arturo pulled back the curtains: it was a clear night, stars filled the sky and a harvest moon brightened the room. Arturo was thankful that Juan Julián was not suffering from one of his headaches. At first he thought it was just an excuse to keep him at bay, but that idea dissipated when Arturo realized the headaches were there often and during the day when Arturo was not threatening with a sexual assault. In bed Juan Julián's stress unwound with such tenderness that whatever discrepancies they had experienced up to that point were evanescent memories that seemed to involve some other people, not them. Juan Julián offered so much of himself in his passionate embraces. They became two vines finding each other and intertwining inseparably. At the moment when they had to withdraw from each other the feeling of togetherness remained, surviving the physical reality.

Arturo turned toward the end table on his side of the bed, where he kept the small tray with the ear plugs. Juan Julián had relaxed too much too quickly, and his snoring showed it.

October proved to be rainier than it was snowy. By the first week of November the entire lot was blanketed in a quilt of fading wet golds and crispy reds. Raking, whether done by one of them or both, was out of the question. Juan Julián decided the exercise would be good, but when he had contemplated becoming a monk in his late teens he had learned that St. Benedict's *Rule* recommended all things in moderation. He would not hire landscapers: they wanted contracts and then showed up on a schedule instead of when they were needed.

At the Poughkeepsie Lowe's he bought the John Deere riding mower he had envisioned for the room in the garage.

"Isn't it kind of late in the season for mowers?" Arturo asked.

"I have a plan," Juan Julián said.

He would mow the leaves instead of raking them. They would turn into minute pieces that would mulch the soil and stop being unsightly. On the raised northeastern corner of the lot where the mower would not climb Juan Julián applied the rake. He built four mounds of leaves that he then bagged. The leaves defied the rake: they were wet and stuck to the ground. He gathered the recalcitrant ones by hand.

Before he was done he had started coughing. It was a scratchy cough, as if he had dust in his throat. He hadn't had a fit like that one since he used to visit his grandmother in the country as a child. His eyes would redden, and his chest felt constricted. He wasn't sure his eyes were red now, but they were itchy.

He left the bagged leaves on the curb, drove the mower back to the garage and walked into the house. He drank some tap water. Arturo heard him and gave him a cough drop. A few weeks earlier Arturo had asked Juan Julián how he felt about getting a dog: a black Labrador or a Dalmatian to go with the landscape.

"You want me dead?" Juan Julián replied to the suggestion. "I'm so allergic to dog dander my throat would close up and I'd choke."

Arturo remembered a vague reference to that early on in their relationship. It was one allergen in a long list of such. Juan Julián had suffered from recurrent bouts of allergic reactions that most often would cause respiratory infections, especially in the spring. They had often turned into bronchitis, twice to pneumonia. Arturo thought Juan Julián's frequent irritable bowel syndrome problems were also related to food allergies and not to stress, as Juan Julián claimed.

Juan Julián spent a restless night. By early morning he sounded as if oxygen were not reaching his lungs. Arturo thought of calling an ambulance. It would take too long to reach the hamlet. He helped Juan Julián get dressed and drove him to a hospital in Rhinebeck. As soon as they arrived in the emergency room the nursing staff put him on oxygen and did an allergy workout.

Arturo waited by his gurney.

"Who's his next of kin?" asked a woman who rolled a computer on wheels into the examination area.

"I am," Arturo said.

"Are you his brother?" the woman asked.

"No, I'm his husband."

The woman said nothing. Arturo had given her Juan Julián's driver's license and health insurance cards. Shortly after she left the same nurse who had received them walked in.

"Has he been tested for HIV?" the nurse asked.

"Yes. We are both negative," Arturo said. He surmised the question was meant to rule out pneumocystis, an assumption he wasn't sure was warranted or just part of the general ambiance of ignorance.

Juan Julián was admitted. Arturo followed the gurney to his room, a private cubicle almost the size of the master bedroom closet. This one, however, had a window. Morning had broken. A haze enveloped the landscape of barren trees. Frost framed the window.

Whatever they had given him opened up his chest. He was breathing almost normally. A young Dominican doctor named Guarionex Ibáñez walked in to examine the patient. He performed the usual *Take a deep breath* routine

"I hear some wheezing," the doctor said.

"*Y a qué se puede deber?*" asked Arturo to let Dr. Ibáñez know they shared a common language. "What may be causing it?"

"It may be a number of things," replied Ibáñez in the type of English *Saturday Night Live* comedians use to ridicule Spanish speakers. "The blood work came back fine."

The doctor said he was going to send Juan Julián home that morning with an inhaler and an antibiotic, just in case. He never did say what he was treating Juan Julián for.

After Juan Julián ate his breakfast of thick oatmeal, prune juice and coffee thick as spring water an orderly came by to wheel him down to the hospital entrance.

Three days later Juan Julián sounded worse. Arturo noticed the labored breathing and the red eyes.

"We're going to civilization," Arturo said. "You need a real doctor."

Arturo drove him back to Brooklyn, to the emergency room at Mount Sinai.

"Who's the next of kin?" the registration clerk asked.

"I am," Arturo said.

"Partner?" the clerk asked.

"Husband."

"Does he have a living will or power of attorney?" the clerk asked.

"Both," Arturo replied.

Juan Julián went through the same examination as he had at Rhinebeck. The doctor, an intern by the name of Ramírez, ordered x rays.

Minutes later Dr. Ramírez returned. "He has some funky gunk in his lungs," she said. "Has he been exposed to mold?"

"Probably. He's got a lot of respiratory allergies. A few days ago he was raking leaves," Arturo said.

"That's probably the problem," she said. "He may have inhaled some of those mold spores. We're going to admit him and see what we can do to clear this up. And," she added, looking at Juan Julián, "get yourself a lawn service."

Juan Julián had remained silent through most of the hospital visits. He seemed worried to Arturo. It was usually how he reacted when he was uncertain about what could come next.

"You need to call my niece," Juan Julián told Arturo.

"Why? This is just a breathing problem."

"I don't know that. It could be serious. Maybe the doctor is trying to be tactful. I don't know," Juan Julián said.

"You think it's okay to alarm your niece over something that could turn out to be mild?" Arturo asked.

"I don't know, neither do you. I want you to call her. Here," Juan Julián said, handing Arturo his cell phone. "Look her up under contacts. Gloria Sánchez."

"I don't think it's a good idea," Arturo said. "I'm not going to hide if she comes to see you. Are you ready for that?"

"Please call her," Juan Julián said, ignoring the question.

Arturo called her. When Juan Julián was taken up to his room Arturo thought of going home for a while, then returning in the evening to spend the night with Juan Julián. He thought of himself alone in that house that was already too big for just the two of them. Fear overtook him. He thought of the possibility that this could turn out to be a serious problem, something perhaps even fatal. He brushed the thought out of his mind. Without even knowing what this was, possibly some self-limiting problem that would not recur, his own throat started constricting as he involuntarily conjured the image of him without Juan Julián. He had trouble breathing, but talked himself into calmness and recalled his old yoga instructor's words to invoke a relaxation response.

He decided not to go home.

After dinner he sat in bed next to Juan Julián, who had been dozing off for brief periods of time. An oxygen cannula crossed his face. Whatever Dr. Ramírez had ordered for an intravenous therapy had made him drowsy and helped him stabilize his breathing, although it was not yet normal.

Juan Julián opened his eyes. "Why haven't you gone home to rest?" he asked Arturo.

"Because I'm afraid of large spaces," Arturo replied. Juan Julián stared at Arturo with that look of confusion that likened him to a helpless child. "I'm not going somewhere you are not."

"You may have to get used to that," Juan Julián said.

"Please, please, don't start that and don't go there. This is not the time for it. Stop getting ahead of events," Arturo pleaded. He took Juan Julián's hand. "You don't need those negative thoughts. I know I don't. Let's focus on getting medication to work."

"I'm being realistic," Juan Julián said.

"You're being an *istic* alright. Pessim-," replied Arturo. "The drama queen shtick becomes you not," Arturo fake-scolded him.

"We all have to go sometime. After fifty every day is a gift," Juan Julián said. "And I've had sixteen years' worth of daily gifts."

"Let's make a deal. When you feel that the world is closing in on you and all goes dark, then we'll talk about this. Right now you're breathing and connected to an IV," Arturo said. "Now you need to shut up. Give yourself some peace of mind and let me have mine."

Arturo leaned over. Making sure that he did not displace the cannula going up Juan Julián's nostrils Arturo kissed Juan Julián softly on the lips.

"That felt like a motherly kiss to a three year old. Could you kiss me like you mean it?" Juan Julián asked. "We don't know how many of those we have left."

"I'm going to ignore that," Arturo said. "I don't want to choke you." He got closer to Juan Julián's face, looked directly into his husband's eyes and said, "I do love you." He then kissed Juan Julián harder.

The din in the hall became louder than before. Neither of them heard the door open.

"What the hell are you doing to my uncle?" Gloria shouted.

Arturo turned around and rose from the bed. Juan Julián raised his head.

"I'm kissing him," Arturo said.

"While he was unconscious?" Luis Rafael asked, his voice strained with anger.

Juan Julián had dropped his head back on the pillow.

"He's sick, but not unconscious. It was quite consensual," Arturo said without any defensive excitement.

"Are you trying to turn my uncle queer?" Gloria asked in a tone that evinced her realization that she was in a hospital, not on the Grand Concourse. "I knew there was something strange about you. Didn't I tell you, Luis Rafael?" she asked her husband, standing next to her.

"You did. Now I see how it is, this depraved Colombian taking advantage of a sick man," Luis Rafael said, his tone not quite as aware as his wife's that he was in a hospital.

"I don't have to turn your uncle queer. He already is. So am I. We both are," Arturo said, again without demonstrating neither anger nor a great need to defend himself.

"Queer, you *maricón*? My uncle *pato*? He is a full, complete *macho*, just so you know. There's not a drop of fairy in him. There are no *maricones* in my family, you hear!"

"Except for your uncle," Arturo said.

"You are disrespecting my wife, you fag!" Luis Rafael shouted.

Juan Julián followed the dialogue from what he now wished was his deathbed.

"First of all, don't call me fag. We prefer queer. Or gay. Or homosexual, if you want to get clinical. Fag is just not politically correct. Second, lower your voice. Third, I am not disrespecting anyone. If anything, she's doing it to me."

"You don't deserve any respect!" Gloria yelled, abandoning her previous restraint. "You know, back where I'm from, we ran fags like you out of town."

"Then I guess that's how your uncle ended up in New York," Arturo said.

Juan Julián pressed the button on the right of his bed rail to raise his head.

"I see what you're doing here," Luis Rafael said. "You're trying to sneak into his life with your bad habits, that's what. You probably want to rob him of his money if this thing disables him. You're some shady faggot!"

"Yeah," Gloria added. "You think you're going to stay in his house if he dies, don't you? Well, think again, because my dad and my aunt are going to inherit whatever he leaves behind when he dies. Not even a shyster lawyer will get away with stealing from us!"

"You really don't know what the hell you're talking about, you greedy witch," Arturo said. He had not raised his voice. Gloria and Luis Rafael must have noticed the smirk on his face.

"Oh, you think you're so smart, don't you? We're smarter than you. We know our rights. We've done the research, just in case," Gloria said.

Juan Julián's eyes followed the ping-pong ball as it crossed the room back and forth.

"You've done the research, have you?" Arturo asked.

"You bet we have! If he's single when he dies and has no direct heirs, his siblings inherit, not some room-mate. We will have you evicted, you'll see," Luis Rafael clarified.

"Evicted, will I?" said Arturo with more than a little condescension. He felt tempted to explain why their plans were wrong, but he was enjoying the cat and mouse game neither niece nor nephew suspected they were playing. He had waited over twelve years for this.

"You better clear out before we throw you out!" Gloria ordered.

Juan Julián's chest felt less tight. Arturo had been afraid that this scene would agitate him, perhaps worsening his condition. Juan Julián, however, were it not for the breathing difficulty, felt as if he had fallen from space onto firm ground and yet still floated lightly on a field painted with pansies in full bloom. It may have been the medication in the IV bag, but that was not completely it. His chest was constricted on the inside, but on the outside someone had loosened tight straps.

"What are you doing here, anyway?" Luis Rafael asked of Arturo. "Honey," he said, looking at Gloria," go to the nurses' station and tell them we want this creep out of here."

"Call her from Uncle Juan's button," Gloria said. "There, by his side," she added, pointing at the calling control.

Luis Rafael approached Juan Julián's bed and pressed the red button. Juan Julián made no effort to stop him: he moved his hand away from the control. His intuition told him Arturo needed this moment.

"You really have some freaking nerve, you know?" Gloria told Arturo. "I never liked you. There's something about you. I couldn't put my finger on it, but now..."

"Mr. Correa, did you call?" asked Stephanie, the head nurse. "Is your bag empty?" she asked again, looking at the IV pole. "Oh, no, that's okay. What can I do for you?"

Juan Julián said nothing.

"We called you," Luis Rafael said, standing in the middle of the room and pointing at Arturo. "You need to call security to have this man removed.

"Why would I do that?" Stephanie asked.

"We walked in and caught him... I think he was kissing my... our uncle," Luis Rafael explained.

"And?" asked Stephanie.

"I don't know where to begin, but I don't think I need to go into disgusting details," Gloria said. "It should be enough to say that he needs to go right now!" she shouted.

"Don't shout, miss. You're in a hospital, and this is not a street brawl," Stephanie said. "If this gentleman is bothering Mr. Correa, it would be up to the patient to decide who stays and who goes. Right now, you are the ones causing the commotion."

"He's not a relative, he's nothing, just a... a creepy fag!" Luis Rafael shouted.

"That's a nasty word we don't use around here," Stephanie said. "I thought you said Mr. Correa is your uncle."

"He is," Luis Rafael and Gloria said at the same time.

"Then why are you calling him that word?" Stephanie asked.

"We're not talking about him. We're talking about this guy," Luis Rafael said, clicking his head toward Arturo.

"What's the difference?" Stephanie asked.

"You don't understand, do you? Do we have to call security ourselves?" Gloria asked.

"If someone doesn't understand it may be the two of you," Stephanie said. She looked at Juan Julián. "They don't know, do they?"

Juan Julián shook his head.

"May I?" Stephanie asked Juan Julián.

"No, that's okay. I will," Juan Julián said. He stretched out his hand to reach Arturo. Arturo gave him his to hold.

"Call me if you need me. I think you may," Stephanie said, and walked out of the room.

"What the hell does this mean, Uncle Juancito?" Gloria asked.

"What does it look like?" Juan Julián said. He couldn't raise his voice much. "This is not my roommate. This is my husband, Arturo Madrigal-Correa. I am not single. If I die first, our house—*our* house—is registered in common tenancy: our house passes to him, not to you vultures. Neither of us owns anything separately. What we own is ours. There. Do you get it now?"

Arturo looked at Juan Julián. A smile was etched on his face.

"I am gay. *Pato*. A *maricón*, as you said. A *partido*. A queen, a *loca*, whatever you wish. It doesn't change anything. The same blood runs through our veins, but if you don't want exposure to my contagion, I'll live with that," he added.

"Oh, my God, wait till Dad hears about this!" Gloria said.

"He's going to be disgusted and disappointed," Luis Rafael said.

"Frankly? I don't give a shit," Juan Julián said. It surprised Arturo. It was the first time he had heard that word come from Juan Julián's mouth.

"This is against God's will, you know," Gloria said. "You are living in sin!"

"Yes. Just as your parents. You were born a healthy full-term baby six months after their wedding," Juan Julián said. While he talked, he pressed the calling button.

"Well, at least they were a man and a woman, not two fags," Gloria said. Juan Julián did not reply right away.

"Now that you've shown me who you are, I need you to get lost and let me rest," José Julián said, an edge of relief cutting through his voice.

"You called, Mr. Correa?" Stephanie asked from the door. "Your IV bag…"

"No, you need to escort these people out of my room," Juan Julián said.

Stephanie looked at Gloria and Luis Rafael. "You heard the patient. Do I need to call security?"

"My pleasure," Luis Rafael said. "It smells like burning faggot feathers in here."

"You'll regret this," Gloria said. "Oh, yes, you're going to regret this!"

Stephanie held the door open. Gloria and Luis Rafael walked out. Arturo thanked Stephanie.

"No problem. Just call if you need me again," she said.

Arturo turned toward Juan Julián. "Thank you too."

"No, thank you," Juan Julián said, his hand still in Arturo's. "Come sit by me." When Arturo sat by him, he added, "I hope this is nothing. Now I really hope this is nothing. We have a lot of catching up to do. We never sent in our wedding picture to the *Times*. It's overdue."

"Does that catching up include both walking over to Mrs. Provinzino to hand her the fruitcake log?"

"That too," Juan Julián said.

"We were interrupted before."

"Yes, we were. Rudely," Juan Julián said.

"May I kiss you again?" asked Arturo without any concern for who else might hear him.

"Don't ask, don't tell, just pursue."

Unhappy Hour at the Cantina

Now you're going to see. What's wrong with you, turds? How dare you mess with me? Don't you know in this house I am the bossy boss, the big fucker? Learn your lesson and learn it well. Let's see who yells at whom. Who's the boss here, huh? Did you think I was going to go on taking your whining and your pissing and moaning? That I was going to hug you and forget how you fuck? I've had enough! You, living here. ripping me off, here living for free and squeezing my balls? That's over, motherfuckers, you're totally screwed! I'm going to take a few more of these little pills and running off to the club. Now you're going to cut off your balls. I'm going to leave you down here. And whom are you going to complain to? Ha, ha, ha, ha, ha, ho, ho, ho. When I get back you better be where I'm leaving you, bustards, ha, ha, ha, ha, you thought I was going to keep taking this bullshit day after day, night after night? That the music is too loud, that the walls are shaking, buh, buh, buh, enough with the fucking fucks. I'm leaving, but I'll be back. Don't you go hide, ha, ha, ha, ha, ha! because I will find you, hee, hee, hee, hee, sons of bitches, kuh, kuh, kuh, bwahahahaha!

He paced erratically around the bar, other patrons noticed. Drunk? So early? It wasn't even ten yet. The club wouldn't get busy until about eleven on Fridays, not until after *Falcon Crest* was over. They needed time to shower, throw on themselves the latest Perry Ellis and

180

Alexander Julian, spray with Grey Flannel or Vetiver by Guerlain or the harness and the chaps.

This guy crossed over into both sides of the Grand Finale. Fashion didn't seem to matter to him. Or hygiene. He held a glass containing something purplish. With his other hand, when he paused, he held himself against one of the pillars that separated the raised platform from the bar, across the way from the dance floor, an area lit by the disco ball turning its glimmer over the dancers.

Whenever the back door opened the man jumped as if startled and turned as if he were waiting for someone who had parked in the lot behind the building. It was the side that faced city police headquarters. Inadvertently the police had offered security services for the cars. Some were not concerned about the lack of security when they parked on the street. More than vandalism they feared a co-worker, a relative or acquaintance, a son or wife would drive by and find out about their secret life from the car's location: if they had parked there, they could be nowhere else other than at the Grand Finale.

Every so often the man wiped his mouth with his plaid-shirt sleeve, the shirt tails hanging out over his pants. He sipped from the glass. He ran his fingers through his full head of black hair, shiny with natural grease. He turned his head from one side to the other. He wiped his mouth. Sipped. Ran his fingers through his hair. Looked behind him. Sipped. Looked toward the dance floor, where six couples and a partnerless man twirled to *Rock the Kasbah*. That was strange. The DJ played that kind of music near closing time, when the customers' plasma was saturated with booze and had lost their inhibitions. Then they hopped, arms in the air above their heads, the bodies clustered in a sweaty mass. Summer nights the exhibitionists removed their shirts to show off their pecs and biceps while dancing in tandem with a partner whose butt was pressed against the other man's crotch.

The man wiped his whole face with the sleeve. He breathed as if something were making it difficult. He approached the counter. He pushed out someone who stood where he wanted to get, nearer to the counter. The other guy gave him a dirty look. He didn't give a rat's ass.

"Hey!" he yelled at the bartender standing at the other end of the bar. Aren't you tending?"

The bartender got closer.

"Haven't you had enough?" the bartender asked him. The bartender was responsible for verifying, as much as possible, the degree of drunkenness of the clients. If they were visibly intoxicated, he could not serve them any more: he ran the risk of being charged with negligence and sued in civil court.

"Don't give me that shit! I haven't started yet! Get me vodka with cranberry juice, fast!" he yelled in the bartender's face. From his mud-stained jeans' pocket he pulled out a pack of folded dollar bills.

The bartender thought about it.

"This is the last one," he told the man. "And if you don't behave, I'll let the bouncer know." He pointed at a muscle-bound giant standing in a corner from where he observed the patrons.

The man dismissed him with a hand gesture.

"I'm not afraid of any asshole," the man replied, leaning forward against the bar to get closer to the bartender's face. The bartender pulled away to go mix the man's drink.

The man placed the money on the counter. When the bartender came back the man walked away. He stood near the bar. He sipped looking over the rim of the glass still stuck to his lips, in a 120-degree arc. He wiped his face with the sleeve. Sipped. Pulled out the swizzle stick from the glass and threw it to the side after licking it.

Swigged. An ice cube slipped into his mouth. He spat it on the floor.

Since I was a skinny kid, not even this tall, look, then, look how you've fucked me over, bastards, forcing me to work in that warehouse, not even school I attended. Yeah, there in that mud hole of a village full of huts and penniless people. And this bitch, my so-called sister, pretty dresses from the capital city, I, in rags and broke. You, not even money for beans you gave me of the money I turned over to you, drinking coffee from a pot and stuffing your faces with chilaquiles *when I was killing myself carrying flour sacks in the warehouse, and this fucker you call my father, screwing around to drop a dozen bastard kids, sons of the bitches who bore them and you, so pretty, wasn't it? taking his cheating and even handing him the* pesos *I was earning so he could go do whatever the fuck he wanted and feed his little bastards. And I eating basket tacos on my break from the warehouse if I had a couple of* pesos *to pay for them, there in the city park, under an almond tree, not even taking a nap, swallowing like a hungry dog to get back to carry boxes larger than I. And you, shitty mother, pimping, that I had to be nice to Don Inés, that he helped us with what he could, that I shouldn't be disrespectful with the nice boss or think I could rise above my station with that gentleman, so nice, so generous, the fucking degenerate. I'm starting to believe you always knew that old fart was fucking me in the back of the warehouse after he locked up for the day. And I, I didn't dare say anything, motherfuckers, because the son of a bitch would fire me, that hairy ape, he'd fire me if anyone complained and I let him drop my pants even when I just wanted to take a shit and that pig took my breath away, nailing me with that thing, the thing with the hanging skin and he made me take it in my mouth after he stuck it in me to clean it off, he said, so his wife wouldn't smell shit when he went to bed with her. It's all your fault, you were the ones who made me go to work so you would live off me until I said fuck it, this is enough, I wised up and crossed over to the north and here I had to clean toilets and even shitty pigsties and send you dough, bastards, you lived off me and didn't even let me learn to read and I learned from the nuns at the Church of the Guadalupe, here, the ones who taught me to read, yeah, them, not you, fucking freeloaders. Fucking faggots!*

He looked toward the raised platform. He noticed someone who was dressed more or less like them, except the other guy must have had a washing machine. Probably used his bathtub more than he, too. Fuck it. He walked up to him and whispered in the man's ear. The other man pulled away and looked at him confused. He made a face of disgust and shook his head, then walked to the lower level.

The man stayed there for a while. He then went to the other side of the dance floor, the one closest to the front wall of the building. He walked up to another guy, whispered in this guy's ear and this guy cackled heartily. The man remained in the same place. This other guy could tell the man was not joking. This other guy looked in the opposite direction and yelled a clear and loud no. The man walked back to the column. He leaned against it. He wiped off the sweat from his forehead with a shirt sleeve. Sipped. He looked toward the bar. Someone wearing tight black jeans, black boots and a plaid flannel shirt was leaning against the bar. He didn't look like one of those young misses, white and blue-eyed. He didn't seem to gesture with a limp wrist: he seemed to be alone, drinking beer from the bottle, watching the dancers.

The man walked toward the other guy and stood behind him without saying anything. Little by little he got closer until his legs were against the other guy's and he could polish his belt buckle against the other guy's shirt. The other guy turned around.

"I'm sorry," the other guy said in an accent different from the local one. "I didn't mean to."

"But I did," the man said to the other guy, who smiled to acknowledge the joke, but without any intention to encourage the man to try it again. He turned the other way.

The man pressed against the other guy again. He whispered something in the other guy's ear. The other guy turned around with a knitted brow and a face of confusion.

"What did you say?"

"What you heard," the man replied.

"I don't think I heard you right," the other guy said. The man was pretty sure English was not what he spoke as a child. You didn't need to be a stuck-up school teacher to figure that out.

"Where are you from," the man asked.

"From here. I live here."

"I suspected as much," the man said as he brushed the shirt sleeve's cuff against his face to wipe the sweat.

"Are you hot?" the other guy asked. "The air conditioning here is set at a glacial setting."

"I'm like this," the man said. He ran his fingers through his hair. That had not felt the buzz of clippers for a long time. Strands clustered above the top edge of his ears. "Where did you come here from?"

"I grew up in Philadelphia."

The man sipped. He shook his head as if he had spiders in his hair. He wiped his forehead with his shirt sleeve. He inhaled between his teeth, producing a smothered hiss.

"But you are not from Philadelphia," the man replied in Spanish.

"No. I'm from Peñuelas. It's a town in Puerto Rico. Not near San Juan," the other guy said with a hint of surprise at finding someone who spoke his language. The conversation continued in their common language.

"I'm from Michoacán," the man said.

"I've been to Michoacán. Where in Michoacán?"

"Tacámbaro," the man said.

"Ah, there I'm not sure I've been, but it doesn't sound familiar."

"No one goes there. They all come from there," the man said. He shook his head like a dog under the rain. He sucked in again through clenched teeth, and the same muffled hiss.

"Anything wrong?" the guy from Peñuelas asked.

"No... I'm just a little... agitated."

"Oh," the other guy said. He felt he had run out of subjects and wasn't sure whether asking something else could seem an indiscretion to the man.

"Do me a favor," the man said. "This fuckard bartender doesn't want to serve me a drink."

"Maybe you've had enough," the other guy said. He noticed the man's shaking hands when he pulled out the pack of bills.

The man looked at him with eyes wide open. Even in the semidarkness of the bar the other guy could tell his pupils were so dilated they were almost the size of the iris.

"I can take ten more."

The other guy smiled with skepticism.

"Here," the man said. He handed the other guy a $20 bill. "Ask him for a vodka with *arándano* juice and as many beers as you want for yourself."

"*Arándano*? What's that in English? the other guy asked.

"Cranberry. What do you call it back in Philadelphia?"

"*Cramberee*," the other guy said. He followed that with a vague smile.

The man's expression was as blank as the first time the other guy saw his face.

The other guy asked the bartender for the vodka and cranberry juice and a Miller Lite for himself.

"Do you dance?" the other guy asked the man.

"No," the man's reply came out as dry as the Sonora desert he probably crossed to enter the United States.

The bartender approached with the drinks and the change, which the man picked up before the bartender could take out his tip. The other guy thanked them both.

"Cheers," the other guy said, lifting his bottle to the point where the man could reach with his glass. Perhaps the man had not heard the attempt at a toast. Instead of replying he stretched his eyes larger than the other guy could have thought possible for a human being and shook his head at the same time he hissed the same way as before.

Let's see, come over here. Don't get all sad. Come on, come on! Oh, yeah, you can't, ha, ha, ha, ho, ho, hee, hee, ha, ha. Don't' move, then. You moved back then, when I had enough dough to bring you here and this old fart for a change started working in the strawberry fields instead of running around with nothing to do and looking for broads to make more kids with them and here he'd

get more fucked than he would fuck, here he has to sup-
port the bastard or you end up behind bars, and those
niggers in there were going to fuck you the way Don Inés
fucked me and break your hole just like Don Inés broke
mine, he first and then that pervert of his son, that stuck-
up prick who turned out as sick as the motherfucker who
made him. May the whore of death have taken them! You,
you son of a bitch and you, you bitch, you didn't want to
know what had happened to me when I had to see the
doctor to cure what one of those two gave me and me
with that pus and blood coming out of my ass that hurt
me when I took a shit, motherfuckers, because if you
claimed anything you'd have to stop pimping me out and
looking the other way and you'd have to admit you knew
what those two bastards were doing to me, who knows,
you'd probably call me a dirty liar just so you could deny
to yourselves what you had to know, because innocent
little doves you could not be, you dirty fuckers. I was go-
ing around wanting to jump off the cliff into the ocean,
always pissed off like the devil. Lucky, yes, damn lucky I
was that I picked up and came this way I was damn fed
up of all that farting just to end up shitting piss. It's fuck-
ing cold here, but I don't have to put my butthole on the
line for some bastard to give me a job if I let him fuck me
and for you to live off what that Don Inés from hell paid
me and what he handed you to fan his conscience of what
he was doing to me. Creeps! But don't get all scared,
buddies, even if I yell at you, don't worry, you just stay
there all quiet, right there, you're all fucked now. The
devil take you! I'm going to have a good time with this
dough, I'm going to party with the gringos after I take a
few more of these pills. Tonight the joker's wild, you'll
see, so catch you later, motherfuckers.

Without really understanding why he walked out the back door with the man at two in the morning, the other guy found himself in the parking lot behind the Grand Finale. The rest of the patrons filed out by them, everyone who had waited till the last drink was served and the last song was played. They were all aware that police headquarters was across the street, where an officer would be more than willing to check who seemed too disabled to get behind a steering wheel.

The other guy's intention was to say farewell to the man and go on to his car. Something was pending.

"I never found out what you whispered in my ear."

"It doesn't matter now. We are here," the man said

"I really didn't hear you. What was it you said?"

The man swept his face with the shirt sleeve. He shook his head as if had before him a scene he refused to look at, but could not shut his eyes to keep himself from seeing it.

"I asked you whether you wanted to suck my cock in my *troca*."

The other guy laughed. He wasn't thinking. Seduced by beer and persuaded by not having anything better to do he replied:

"Not in your truck, but in your house, perhaps."

"Let's go, then, bud," the man said.

"Okay. I'll follow you in my car."

The man shook his arms as if snakes were crawling up his sleeves.

"No, bud! Why bother? Let's go in my *troca*. I'll bring you back here. You stay over and in the morning I'll drive you back."

The other guy hesitated. His slight dizziness was leading him to agree—he didn't really want to drive. He thought that with what he had drunk he wouldn't be able to drive the 29 kilometers home on the interstate highway heading north. The thought did not cross his mind that the man was also drunk. With optimism produced by alcohol-ruined reasoning he didn't think the man could crash, but he concluded instead that if the police stopped him, it would be the man who would be arrested.

"Okay," said the other guy. "You still haven't told me your name."

"Nor you yours."

"Enrique. It's actually Luis Enrique Matos, but no one calls me Luis. Just Enrique."

"Javier Montero Negrete," said the man.

"Are you related to Jorge…"

"We don't' have any singers in our family," Javier interrupted. "That's for faggots."

The pickup truck was probably ten years old, its doors rusted out at the bottom and no air conditioning. Javier opened the passenger side door for Enrique; he climbed in and Javier slammed the door before walking around to get in on the driver's side. It was hot and the night was heavy with humidity. It called for cool air, but the one coming in the broken window on the passenger side was as hot as the one coming out under the dashboard, mixed with a smell of propane gas that came from the space behind the seats. It was a stick shift. Enrique was surprised that Javier could handle the pedals and coordinate speed changes in his state. Maybe Javier wasn't as drunk as he figured.

They went out on the interstate toward the part of town known officially as West St. Paul, but actually was, according to official maps, the south side. When the city was founded it had been on the west side, but as the city grew toward the northeast, it ended up in the south. No one bothered to change its name. Only those who had not lived in the city their entire lives were confused by it.

He went over interlaced railroad tracks. The pickup truck needed a shock-absorber job, but Javier didn't seem to mind or wasn't motivated to slow down. Enrique held on to the edge of his seat, because the door puller had fallen off and was in a corner of the floorboards, worn out and punctured under his feet.

They continued to a medium-sized two-story house with an eggshell white aluminum façade, standing by itself and far from the other four houses on the block. Javier parked in the alley. Enrique had to wait for Javier to open the door. A sharp metal shaft was all that remained of what had been the handle.

They climbed up exterior steps to the second story. The upper part of the house, then, had an independent entrance and was a separate unit.

"Do you rent here?" Enrique asked as they walked up.

Javier shook his head more violently than before. He removed the door key from his pocket when they reached the top landing.

"Yes, I rent. My folks live downstairs... Pa, ma and a sister.

"Oh, that's good, that your family is here. Mine is all back in Philadelphia and Puerto Rico," Enrique said.

Javier said nothing. When they walked into the apartment Enrique was overwhelmed by a sour smell of obvious chemical origin blended with the stench of rancid nicotine. Enrique could not identify the agents mixed in with the stink that wasn't tobacco.

"You think you have a natural gas leak?" Enrique asked while waiting for his pupils to adapt to the darkness. Javier didn't bother to turn on the lights.

"No, there's no escape. It always smells like that here.

Around the living room corners Enrique saw piles of containers, glass gallons, jars and a porcelain bowl, plastic tubing stored in see-through bags and several boxes of aluminum foil. He turned around and saw a sort of still on the stove.

Enrique began to regret not coming in his own car. This didn't smell right, physically or metaphorically.

"You want a beer?" Javier asked from the bathroom, where Enrique could hear the urine stream splashing on the bowl's water surface.

What Enrique wanted to know was where the phone was. He felt all of it required a call for a taxicab, which this late at night would take a long while to arrive. He didn't even know what address he'd have to give.

"No, thank you."

Javier went to the kitchen. He returned with a bottle of Absolut vodka. He was drinking directly from it.

Enrique sat down in a chair next to the door that opened to the stairs. The windows were open, but not even a slight breeze flowed through. Javier was still sweating, but now he didn't bother to wipe it off his face. He spread out on the side of the sofa free of containers and the rest of the supplies. He looked at Enrique.

"Want to hear some music?"

"If you want," Enrique said, shrugging.

Javier took another drink from the bottle. He drank the vodka the way most people drink water, with no reaction or muted howls. He didn't let it go before approaching the record player. He lifted the player's arm. The platter started turning. Javier tried to place the needle on the first track of the album, but his hand trembled too much. The needle fell on a spot farther in than the start of the song. At once the gigantic speakers, resembling coffins on both sides of the record player started thundering. It was a metal rock band Enrique recognized, but he couldn't tell what the song was.

He thought needles were piercing his eardrums. The beer and the hour were urging him to go to bed, but by himself.

Javier held the bottle in his left hand, spilling vodka in intermittent swishes when he shook it on what would have been the neck of an invisible guitar. His right hand stroked the strings on the imaginary soundboard. Javier followed the rhythm of the song. He shook his head with eyes closed. His lips were pursed and projected forward under a gesture of forced ire. After a few bars he turned to Enrique. He started unzipping his pants with his right hand.

"Don't you think you ought to turn down the volume? You're going to upset your parents down below," Enrique suggested.

Javier lifted the bottle to drink what was left in it. His hand stiffened on his zipper.

"I pay their rent," he said, the bottle still in the same hand with which he pointed toward Enrique.

"I'm not talking about who pays the rent. It's not considerate," Enrique said, keeping his tone as low as possible but loud enough for Javier to hear above the racket on the speakers.

"Let them get used to it, those motherfuckers! If they don't like it, they can pack up and go starve to death!"

"I think you better take me back to the city," Enrique said. He rose to his feet.

"Nobody's leaving here until you give me a blow-job, you fag!" Javier shouted much louder than the music, which sounded more and more strident to Enrique.

"No, Javier, I'm sorry. Let's meet some other time... I think we both drank too much and..."

"Are you telling me what to do?" Javier yelled. He got close enough to poke Enrique in the chest. The bottle dripped on the floor, but Javier paid no attention to it. "No queer from a *gringo* colony comes to my house to order me around, you get it?"

Enrique had decided he had to placate Javier's agitation. Explaining why what Javier was saying was inaccurate would make the situation escalate.

"No, Javier, no, no way. I'm not here to order you to do anything. This is your house and you are in charge here. I just think we should postpone this for some other night. Look, I'll give you my phone number—" was all Enrique was able to say before Javier cut him off as Enrique started digging in his pocket for a pen.

"The whore of your mother is the one who needs your phone number, you motherfucking fag! You suck my dick or you don't get out, you fucking fag!"

Enrique saw that this had become impossible. No negotiation was possible.

"I'm not sucking your cock and I'm not staying," Enrique said, trying his best not to raise his voice and betray his rising anxiety.

"You are going to eat it one way or another. What do you think?"

"Turn down the music first. Then we can talk calmly," Enrique said.

Javier was still standing where he had been, but he didn't attempt to hold Enrique back. Enrique took that to mean Javier was so sure of the power of his command that he didn't need to use force to have his way. Enrique didn't know how long that would last when Javier was confronted with the imprisoned guest's determination to leave.

"Don't you fuck with me, motherfucker! You going to get like them?" Javier pointed again at Enrique's chest, but without poking him this time.

"What are you talking about?" asked Enrique, who was now feeling a lot more threatened when he saw

Javier come so close he could smell the vodka and something metallic under his breath, something Enrique could not identify, as if Javier gargled with copper filings.

Javier stretched out his arm until he had a finger against Enrique's nose. Enrique stepped as far back as the edge of the chair's seat behind him allowed.

"Put that mouth down here or you're going to end up like them!" Javier said, his finger pressing against Enrique's nose.

"What the fuck are you talking about?" Enrique shouted. In the midst of it all Enrique recognized the song, Megadeth's *Killing Is My Business*. Enrique conjectured that it was a warning, but it couldn't be. The record was already on the platter when they walked in.

"About this!" Javier shouted and walked to a corner. He lifted a bat stained with what looked like dark red paint. Enrique had gotten closer to the door and, upon seeing the improvised weapon he hurried to grab the doorknob before Javier could reach him, before rising after he stumbled on the empty bottle of vodka. This gave Enrique time to run down the steps, two at a time, until he reached street level. He could still hear Megadeth, but now farther away.

He ran like an unbridled horse up the street when he heard Javier's fast steps in the back. He assumed Javier was carrying the bat, but he was not going to stop and look back to confirm his suspicion.

The neighborhood was unknown to Enrique. He figured the safest strategy was to follow the route he remembered Javier follow, although he was not going to be able to run down the interstate, even less on bridges without pedestrian lanes.

"Stop there, you stuck-up fag! I'm going to teach you not to disrespect me! You're going to squeal like a pig when I get you on your knees, fucking fag!"

Enrique was counting on tiring him out before Javier could reach him. Maybe Javier would get his foot caught in the railroad tracks, a skein of steel rails Enrique himself had to jump with difficulty until he crossed into the other side.

"Help, help!" Enrique started shouting when he saw a neighborhood up ahead. He kept shouting while he ran up the street. He no longer heard Javier's steps. He thought he had gotten away. He slowed down and looked behind him. It had been a mistake. He couldn't hear Javier because he was running on lawns instead of the pavement.

"Help, help, for God's sake!" Enrique started yelling again until from a corner he saw the spinning red and blue lights of a patrol car. He ran to it. He didn't care now whether Javier got closer: the police would be able to subdue him.

"Someone with a bat is chasing me!" Out of breath, Enrique managed to tell the first officer that got out from the passenger side.

"Who, sir?"

"There!" Enrique said; he pointed toward the spot where he had last seen Javier. No one was there. No sign anywhere of Javier. He could be hiding behind the bushes in one of the front yards just as he could have run down a side street in that neighborhood he must have known well and returned home to lock himself in.

Without including details about the bar meeting, which, in the long run, Enrique had to provide in a deposition, he explained to the officers what had happened as his breathing allowed. His mouth begged for moisture.

The officers got him in the patrol car. They followed Enrique's directions to the house, still dark, a profile against a background of distant downtown lights and what seemed like the early-morning sun of summer.

"Stay here," the driving officer told him. The two got out of the car, guns in hand. They called Javier from down below. Nothing, no response. One of them climbed the steps. The second one was about to climb the bottom step when a voice issued a warning:

"Watch out, officer!" Enrique screamed from the patrol car.

The officer barely had time to turn around before the bat could split his head open. With a shot to Javier's leg the officer tried to disable Javier, but had it not been because the officer shifted to the side and lost his balance, he would have fallen under the weight of a certain blow. Javier was still standing, swinging the bat in the air without succeeding in striking his objective.

"Stop where you are!" yelled the other officer, who at Enrique's shouts had rushed to come down the steps.

Instead of giving up and letting the bat drop, Javier jumped toward the officer, the bat held in the air with both hands.

The officer had no time to issue a second warning. He shot Javier almost point blank, what Mexicans called a clothing burner of a shot, *quemarropa*.

Javier did not drop right away. He tried to raise the bat again and attempted another step. The third shot, from the officer who had stumbled on the curb after the first shot, finally brought Javier down. Still bat in hand as if it were glued to his hands, he fell forward. The sound of the skull cracking against the sidewalk's curb anchored itself in Enrique's memory forever.

One of the officers took Javier's pulse, probably because of a bureaucratic requirement to note the official time of death.

With all the commotion, it seemed strange to the officers that no one had turned lights on inside the lower level or at least come out to find out what was going on with Javier.

"His folks live on the first floor," Enrique informed the officers from inside the patrol car, his voice still unsettled.

One of the men rang the bell, then knocked on the door. No one answered. He knocked again. The door was cracked against the frame, not locked. When the officer grabbed the doorknob he felt a cold viscosity. He turned on his hand-held flashlight. It was blood. He tried his best to wipe it off with a handkerchief, but the sticky residue still stuck to his hand. He called from the threshold. Was someone in? Silence. He pushed the door with his foot, then shone into the interior. He was paralyzed.

"Oh, Christ!" he yelled. He turned toward his partner. "Don't come in. Call for reinforcements. This is unbelievable. Never seen the likes of it."

••••••

Coverage by the local newspaper, front page, Sunday edition, July 14, 1985.

BLOODCURLING MURDER IN WEST ST. PAUL

by Thomas Legger Romens
Special for The Morning Courier

Early today city police officers discovered a violent, bloody crime at 348 Western Drive in West St. Paul.

"Gruesome!" was how sergeant Terry Shima described the scene he witnessed when he and his partner, sergeant Edward Voigt, answered an emergency call. "Words are not enough to explain what was inside that house of horror," he stated. "In 22 years on the force I had never seen something like it."

The suspect is Javier Montero-Negrete, who lived on the second floor of the property. Montero-Negrete was shot dead by the officers after resisting address and threatening them with deadly force using a baseball bat. It is assumed it was the same weapon he used to inflict fatal blows upon his victims.

According to preliminary reports Montero-Negrete, 32, had shot and beaten to death his parents, Joaquín Montero-Félix, 62, and Raimunda Negrete-Salinas, 56, as well as his sister, Graciela Montero-Negrete, 29, possibly the afternoon or evening of Friday the 12th.

"It's impossible to pinpoint the exact time of death until forensic results are completed, said Dr. Thomas Suski of the Ramsey County Medical Examiner's office. "I would say tentatively that it took place between 7:00 and 9:00 in the evening.

The only material witness, whose name has not yet been disclosed, was unable to provide comments about the incident. Sergeant Shima explained that the witness is not suspected to be an accomplice. The witness was only interviewed in an effort to reconstruct the sequence of events that led up to the incident.

"He was there coincidentally close to the scene of the crime. I have no additional comments to make on the subject."

The presumed murderer was a legal immigrant and had done farm work in South St. Paul. He did not have a criminal record. No other relatives seem to live in this area. According to official documents he had been in the United States since 1971.

On the second story of the building where the events took place detectives found equipment and supplies for the illegal manufacture of methamphetamines, as well as 6.5 kg of marijuana. Most recently the suspect had worked for Lake Country Farms, Inc., in Dakota County between 1972 and 1981. He is not known to have had another other form of employment since then.

Detectives found the victims' bodies in two rooms on the first floor. Joaquín's cadaver was huddled with its arms crossed over his chest on a sofa in the living room. Raimunda's was collapsed in the hall to the kitchen, apparently struck from her back as she fled, according to the position of the body, explained Dr. Suski. He added that she may have struggled against her attacker. In the bathroom, whose door had signs of kicking, they found Graciela's bludgeoned body in the bathtub.

There is no evidence to indicate that someone other than Montero-Negrete is responsible for the crime or that anyone else participated in the killings.

The police announced a press conference scheduled for Monday the 15th at 10:00 a.m., where they intend to provide further details on the investigation as they become available. At press time no information is available on the motive for the murders.

A DOUBLE-MINDED MAN

*"Such a man is double-minded
and unstable in all he does."*

Epistle of James 1:8

"Tell me you love me."

"Of course I love you."

"Why don't you say it? Why do I have to ask you to say it, uh?"

"Don't be childish."

"It's just that lately I've noticed you somewhat... I don't know. Distant. As if you were thinking about something I'm not going to like if I find out what it is."

"How long have we been seeing each other?"

"How would I know? Three years? No, wait, a little more than that."

"Five years next week. Five years meeting right here every day, Monday through Friday. In this same bed. Naked. For an hour."

"Are you complaining?"

"Stop that. You know I don't like being tickled when I'm talking about something serious. I don't like it, period. Even less right now.

"Whoa. What the hell is wrong?"

"Do you think we can go on seeing each other like this for the rest of our lives?"

"Come back tomorrow and leave for the desert."

"What is that? What are you talking about?"

"I don't think about that future. Wait till we reach that bridge. Maybe I'll jump off it and drown and all your troubles will be over."

"You are not my problem. We are my problem."

"You're looking for traumaramas. Leave things as they are. If it ain't broke, you know what they say, don't fix it. 'There's a time and a season for every activity under the heavens.'"

"Have you stored away every other cliché somewhere that now you have to quote the freaking Bible?"

"Watch it! Be very careful you don't turn in the wrong direction. Do not disparage Scripture."

"That's not what I'm doing. I'm simply asking you not to quote the Bible."

"No other book is inspired by God. It is a guide in my life. And for my life, it contains a quotation for every occasion."

"I'm happy for you it gives you enough faith to anchor yourself in that belief."

"Okay, cut it out. Come kiss me. Come on!"

"I don't feel like it."

"We don't have much time left; Look, ten more minutes, and I'll have to leave. Don't deny me."

"I'll ask you again: are you planning to have us meet like this forever? Don't evade the subject to quote the Bible. You must have thought about it, haven't you?

"Let's enjoy what we have. Why are you bringing up those things? Who knows whether we'll be alive tomorrow!"

"I'm concerned because at some point we are going to have to make a decision."

"'The lips of fools bring them strife and their mouths invite a beating.'"

"There you go again with the Bible. And don't call me a fool."

"Then stop the grinding."

"Have you ever thought that the time will come when you'll have to tell your wife about this?"

"About what?"

"About this, about us."

"And why would I tell her anything about us?"

"Because of what I just said, because I don't want to go on the rest of my life like this. I love you. We have a right to be together, to our happiness."

"Together? Have you gone mad? You can't even think about it!

"So this is all that interests you?"

"I didn't say that. Don't stuff your words in my mouth."

"Doesn't this double life bother you? Hiding what you do from your wife?"

"I don't have to tell her about everything I do! This is private, yours and mine."

"What seems private, yours and mine, as you say, is digging a hole in my conscience. It's not fair for them, your wife or mine, this deceit."

"Learn to separate things. That's what I do. We are all sinners. My advantage is that I know how to repent before preaching the word of the Lord Jesus."

"White-washed tombs. Mathew 23:27."

"You're offending me. Don't you give me Bible lessons. I know my Bible from cover to cover."

"The letter, anyway. Aren't you bothered by the prohibitions in Leviticus?"

"Shut up!"

"I couldn't give a fig, but I can't go on like this. I'm telling you because I have made my decision, and it does have to do with you."

"What decision would that be?"

"I'm going to tell my wife the whole truth."

"What the fuck are you talking about? Tell her what?"

"That I am attracted to men. Not all, just you."

"You're a nut case! You've gone completely insane! Get away from me! God damn it, you sure can come up with all kinds of stupidity."

"No. I fear what comes after that, but it can't be worse that living in this two-door cage. Both are barred. I'm going to open them at last."

"Have you stopped to think of the damage you will cause with that? That your wife can go around saying that the pastor of the Pentecostal Church of God fucks her husband? You don't think, do you, God damn it!"

"You're never going to tell your wife?"

"What the fuck do I have to tell her?"

"That you too are gay."

"I am not gay! Neither are you, you hear?"

"Are you saying this while naked, with your body stuck to mine by cum and sweat after making love? Do you really believe that?

"You may be, but I'm not."

"I can't say I might be. I am. I am gay. G-a-y. Queer, homosexual, a fag, a three-dollar bill, Sodomite, as the members of your congregation say, probably led by you. I think I have been my entire life and I became completely aware of it when I first saw your face. I desired you, I felt an urgent need to be with you, to love you, something that burned my insides from my gut to my brain."

"That's your business. Move over. I want to get up. Look, look how I'm sweating. You're going to kill me of a heart attack with your foolishness."

"You're going to give yourself one with the duplicity of your life. You look at yourself. You've lost your color. You have the hue of a sheet of paper. Look at your hands, they're shaking like leaves in a storm!"

"You got me like this. Don't accuse me of being what you are. Hell, get into telling my wife about us. Do you think she's going to remain quiet? She's going to spread it to the four winds. She'll tell our kids, she'll blabber it to her relatives, to my congregation. What the fuck, this bullshit of saying anything, as if I were a fag!"

"You haven't told me what it is that we have been doing here over the last five years."

"I don't know. When I'm done getting dressed, I'm leaving. I won't return until you're over this compulsive need to self-destruct. Why don't you take Valium? Maybe a couple. You need to be locked up in the funny farm!"

."In the funny farm! Hurry up and tell me what this is that we've been doing, for God's sake!"

"Lower your voice! The neighbors... I don't know. Satan makes me do these things.

"Satan must be unrelenting."

"Don't you mock my beliefs!"

"Don't shield yourself behind them."

"Look I don't know why I've done anything with you. You... you are Lucifer's vessel of evil. 'Be alert and of sober mind. Your adversary the devil prowls around like a roaring lion looking for whom to devour.' You need to bring God into your life. You are like an enticing apple, red and shiny on the outside, but rotten to the core and full of worms."

"So I'm to blame for your two faces, you piece of shit? Go, yes, get out. Make sure you don't leave anything behind, because you're not coming back to this house."

"Come on, stop it right there. Don't get carried away. You'll get over this when you're calmer and have a chance to think things out."

"I've thought them out already. And whatever I had not thought about before you have just put in my head."

"You can't do this to me now."

"Yes, I can. I'm going to stop leading you into temptation, enticing you into sinning. I'm going to stop the Evil One from using me as a means for the eternal damnation of your unblemished soul. 'He who conceals his sins will not prosper,' right? That's *what Proverbs* says, doesn't it? You should know, you and others like you, who learn the Bible by rote and use it as a tool to judge and crush in others what they hate in themselves. The rest of that verse says, 'But he who turns his back on them and confesses will receive mercy.'"

"The devil can quote Scripture for his purpose."

"That's Shakespeare, not *Judges*. Unfortunately for you Shakespeare holds no Biblical credibility. I have nothing to confess. I have nothing to turn my back on. That Bible you preach has no mercy, and you would have it force me to deny the marrow of my being."

"On the contrary. The Bible takes you down the path of righteousness."

"Yours is righteous until it splits into two, like a cobra's tongue."

"Let's talk tomorrow, calmly, after you have reconsidered. You're not reasoning."

"I reject your false calm. I am reasoning better than ever. You have just cleared it up. Go, leave, get out. Don't come back. No, don't say anything. Save your spit for your sermons. Live happily with your secret. When you lie in bed with your wife remember this temptation that will no longer torment you. May your heart be glad and content for having abandoned it. Till never. We'll see who's happier. Or maybe I won't see it, because I don't want to know anything else about you."

***

At the second infarction in less than six months he collapsed in the midst of a Pentecostal assembly during a reawakening campaign under a circus top. He did not die. He had a stroke that paralyzed his left side. His speech is incomprehensible. No one can tell whether he is repeating biblical verses to himself or even whether he remembers them. His wife Ruth pushes his wheelchair, bathes him and dresses him. She wipes his drool and feeds him. Some of the members of his congregation praise God for giving her strength and pray for the unlikely cure of their minister. Others ask themselves what he did that God punished him that way, because he himself often quoted *Deuteronomy* and *Romans*. *Vengeance is mine, says the Lord, and I will repay.* To those most of the others reply: "'Judge not, that you not be judged.' Praise the Lord!"

In the Valley of the
Shadow of Death

He stops in front of the video booth, tokens in hand.

Before walking in to that back section he cashed in five dollars' worth of tokens from Donna, the transgender sales clerk near the building entrance. For sale at the counter are the nipple rings, the most esoteric items for sexual appetite and little bottles of amyl nitrate, labeled "Video Head Cleaner" to throw the authorities off track.

He has walked between sex toys hanging from the wall and then by the X-rated VHS tapes, in front of the magazines sealed in cellophane bags. Behind the curtain in the back are the private booths, four rows divided by two aisles under bare bulbs of few watts and dim light. The air is invaded by a pungent smell of disinfectants under which floats the unmistakable rancid smell of human fluids, urine included. The shop does not provide bathrooms for customers, who sometimes discharge their bladder in the booths.

From some of the booths, hardly big enough to accommodate one person, Pablo can hear the soundtrack of moans and screams of presumed pleasure. The clips shown last three minutes. To see the rest, patrons have to keep depositing tokens in the slot on the wall next to the TV screen. The full movie costs about four dollars. Watching the entire film is not likely. Patrons keep switching channels and see a short clip from several movies, which require more tokens. It is the living economics of pornography, based on the analytical forecast of desire for something different, a search for something perhaps more arousing, until the viewer runs out of tokens and needs to return to Donna to change more dollar bills. Initially, no one can enter the back room without first buying at least a dollar's worth of the copper coins.

Sometimes patrons find tokens sitting on top of the screen frame. They are left behind by men who do not want to get home with them in their pockets or in the car. Their memories can fail and their wives or partners are the ones who find them, with undesirable results.

Outside the sun is close to setting, but still shining. Inside it is impossible to see clearly the face of the five or six clients roaming the aisles while clinking the coins in their hands. They pretend to read the illustrated descriptions of the films running in the booths on the channels that Donna controls.

As he stands in front of one of the booths Pablo plays the same game as everyone else, pretending not to care who else cruises around them as they concentrate on the movies' tag lines. The occupant of the booth to his right has cracked open the door to afford Pablo a view of the fondling illuminated by the screen mounted on the wall opposite the one with the narrow padded vinyl seat meant for one. In the corner he sees a small trash can teeming with discarded tissue and a few previously owned condoms.

Curiosity drives Pablo to look in the booth to catch a glimpse of what the man is offering him as he holds it in his hand. The man fails to interest Pablo. He continues reading the descriptions, which should not engage the serious reader for long. Each booth offers eight channels: four for the average straight man, one for sadomasochists, one for lesbians and two gay films, one traditional and one for those interested in less ordinary acts—fisting, pissing and cross-dressing, for instance. The text is difficult to read in the dark, reduced to salacious phrases allusive to the content of each tape, besides the title, mostly sexually-charged parodies of titles of mainstream films.

No one reads anything, actually. It's just a strategy for waiting for someone attractive to walk by, enter a booth with him, deposit the tokens in the slot and then stage themselves their own life show without an audience, except for the occasional eye watching through the peep holes drilled in the partitions of double-sided booths.

Pablo feels a presence behind him. Someone is whistling a muted tune, then humming a song known only to the man humming it. Pablo thinks he detects the bars of *Rock of Ages*. It's an absurd thought, of course. Whoever he was rubbed Pablo's back with his elbow before continuing to the door of another booth. Pablo tried to identify the man in spite of the semi-darkness that obstructed his field of vision. Pablo turned his head slightly.

The man seemed in the latter years of middle age, average height, white, balding and pot-bellied. He wore black slacks and a light blue and white polo with horizontal stripes. He must have left his jacket in the car in the parking lot behind the building, where none of the drivers who go by the building on McKnight Road, always jammed, gets to see. Autumn has already set in with temperatures lower than the average.

The man is clinking the tokens in his left hand against the ones in his right hand. He continues to whistle like someone who's minding his own business, playing the standard reading-room game.

Pablo cannot see Baldy's facial features. He keeps his face close to the title sign. It is beginning to get dark outside: Pablo can tell from the dimming lights on the other side of the curtain. He knows that late evenings are best for cruising the back room behind the frayed curtain. The choices tend to be broader. Later in the afternoon he finds mostly married men on their way home, where their wives wait for them, dinner on the table for the bread-winner after a hard day at work. It was around that time that he met Ralph, the Baptist deacon who ran a nursing home with his wife. Ralph came in Wednesdays, when he had to take care of business matters downtown. This is Wednesday. Pablo needs to relief himself before Ralph shows up, which can be any minute now. He gets annoyed when Ralph brings up religion and the Bible while wiping off Pablo's semen from his folds.

Baldy could be married also. Pablo tries to look directly at him to make sure he isn't wearing a wedding band. He can't be certain, but he doesn't see any metallic glittering from Baldy's fingers.

The booth Pablo walks toward is behind Baldy. Pablo brushes against the man's back the same way the man had done to him. On his rear end Baldy has two tight globes almost as big as his belly.

Pablo steps into the booth. He leaves the door cracked open. Baldy, humming, walks tentatively toward the booth's door. He pushes it timidly, walks in and locks it. He takes the initiative to deposit a few tokens in the slot to start the video clip—which is now irrelevant: it can be a Bugs Bunny cartoon for all they care. He knows that depositing the tokens will turn on a green light over the door. It's how the tranny knows someone is using the booths in the pint-size motel room when she comes by to check whether someone's smooching, door locked and two, perhaps three, playing inside instead of the clips.

The man drops his pants and underwear, his back toward Pablo, and attempts to bend over in the scarce space he has to attempt it. Pablo pulls him up and pushes his shoulders down to indicate what he would rather have the man do.

Pablo does not look at the man's face when he starts loosening Pablo's belt and unzipping his pants. His eyes are fixed on the screen. It's his way of preserving anonymity, a rule he has violated before and provoked consequences such as Ralph's.

When the man drops to his knees and takes him in Pablo decides to take a peek. A reflex similar to a sneeze makes him withdraw from the man, his eyes close to bursting out of their sockets.

"What's wrong?" the man with the shiny scalp asks in a whisper, looking at Pablo, allowing Pablo to confirm what he has thought.

Pablo does not reply. He pulls up his pants and zips up.

"Nothing. I'm sorry, this is not going to work," Pablo replies. His face is a blaze.

"Would you rather do something else?" the man asks, already on his feet and placing a hand on Pablo's shoulder.

"No. It's just that it's late, and I have to go. I'm not into this right now. Here," Pablo says and hands the man his five-dollars' worth of tokens. "I'm not going to need them. I apologize."

Pablo unlocks the booth's door and steps out. He's stunned. Between his teeth he mutters something unintelligible to the rest of the zombies: "God, God, no, no, how horrible, I can't believe this, Jesus fucking Christ on a cross!"

Close to the main entrance he welcomes the cool autumn draft when Ralph opens the door.

"Well, Pablo! It's been a long time since…" Ralph says, blocking Pablo's exit before Pablo cuts him off.

"Yes, Ralph. Quite a while."

"I gave you my private telephone number and you never called. What is this? You're leaving? Don't you have some time? I was hoping we'd meet," Ralph says, still in Pablo's way. At that moment Pablo grasps how big Ralph really is, standing against the light and cutting a shape that takes up one of the glass-paned doors.

"You'll have to excuse me. I'm in a rush. I'm late for... uhr... a business engagement. I promise I'll call."

"You promise?" Ralph asks, looking piercingly at Pablo. "I've really missed you. A lot. You know."

"Yes, yes. Same here. I promise. Please excuse me," Pablo says hoping Ralph would pick up on his urgent need to scram. Thankfully, Ralph does. Pablo walks out and turns the corner to the back parking lot. He rushes to unlock the car door: with a trembling hand he scratches the lock, but misses the opening. He finally hits the target.

"What did I do wrong?"

Pablo turns around and recognizes the bald man, whose hair stubs he sees around the crown of his head against the setting sun. What can he say other than a trivial lie? He owes this man nothing. However, he feels embarrassed for the semi-bald man at the thought that he knows who the man is. His shame is complicated by the whirlwind in his chest because of who this man is.

"Look, really, you didn't do anything wrong. I just have to leave, you understand?" Pablo replies.

"We could meet some other time? When you have the time?" the man suggests with poorly disguised urgency. Pablo feels a tinge of pride at the man's interest, but it is a fleeting feeling. His diaphragm is in a knot. He definitely wants to get away. He is unexpectedly overpowered by the temptation to play a cat and mouse game with the miserable man.

"How about Sunday?" Pablo asks.

"It could be. Depends on the time," the man replies with evident optimism.

Pablo's desire to pursue the game any further is immediately severed. The intention to let loose a loud cackle blends with acute revulsion.

***

Three months earlier Pablo's mother had come to visit. She did every summer when she had her vacation from her elementary-school teacher job. She'd stay with him for a month or so. Sometimes she would plan a road trip or just wanted to do something she couldn't do at home without interruptions. This was usually completing a lace project on her bobbin lace wheel, something she would sew on to a linen dress on her return home.

"Pablo, here I have some money I need to deliver," she said the day after arriving while they had a light breakfast.

"For whom?"

"Mary and George Smith sent it. You remember them?" his mother asked as if it were possible to forget them. George was a dork, dull and taciturn who wore his pants up to his nipples. He had moved to Puerto Rico to work as a factory manager and ended up marrying a local woman, María. She was the empress of gossip and as such was known in the town Pablo had left, never to return.

"You're friends with them now?" Pablo asked, his words laced with derision.

"No, no, why would I. But María is a member of the Sacred Heart Sodality, and since I'm the treasurer, you know," his mother clarified.

"I see," Pablo replied without much interest. "And the money, what is it for?"

"It's that Father Albert—you remember Father Albert?"

"Yes, naturally," Pablo replied.

Father Albert had been the pastor of the Catholic church in town, the Immaculate Conception parish. He was a priest of the Congregation of the Holy Spirit, headquartered in Philadelphia. Although Pablo had been baptized by Father Manuel, he could not remember anything about him. Father Albert, on the other hand, had stood by Pablo when bishop McManus confirmed him in the faith. Father Albert had also given Pablo his first Holy Communion. The priest had been the Boy Scouts leader for Pablo's troop from Cub Scout to Eagle Scout. Pablo's four brothers had all been married by Father Albert. By the time Pablo got to college he stopped attending Holy Mass or participating in parish activities. He had put distance between him and the church after realizing that his sexual inclinations and Catholic teachings were at odds. He could not change his nature. Dogma and desire had a showdown. The former lost.

He remembered Father Albert as a very tall man, of ruddy complexion and fit even if he tended toward the heavier side of healthy. His deep voice acquired heavier density when he scolded parishioners, usually because cooperation in church fundraisers was not as enthusiastic as he expected. Father Albert had been a family friend, a guest at special celebrations and meals; otherwise Pablo's mother would take dinner to him every so often.

He was considerably closer to another family. The father taught senior high school while the mother was an elementary-school teacher. They had a daughter who made vows with the Barefoot Carmelites in Spain. Her parents traveled to Spain once a year to listen to her on the other side of a grill in the porter's lounge at the convent back in Toledo. Once or twice a year Father Albert would invite the more active members of the parish to join him for a picnic at the Holy Spirit Fathers' mother house, where the swimming pool was available to his guests. Pablo always noticed that Father Albert spent most of the time with the nun's father, who was, besides, a bodybuilder who wore a swimming suit that left little to Pablo's imagination, because the man's bulging crotch was only separated from the boy's perception by an unlined, thin yellow fabric that wet became almost transparent.

Pablo seemed to remember a time when Father Albert and the bodybuilder had traveled together to the Holy Land. Father Albert himself paid all expenses, as everyone in the parish heard from the man's proud wife: her family was singled out as a parish favorite by the popular pastor.

Father Albert's assistant with the Boy Scouts troop was Pepe Barreras. He was young, perhaps ten years older than Pablo. It was difficult to figure out exactly what his duties were: he seemed to live in the rectory judging by the amount of time he spent there, short of saying Mass and hearing confession.

During a family conversation about the parish, over something Pablo couldn't quite remember, Pepe's name came up.

"That one? That's Father Albert's wife," Pablo's father said. Pablo's brothers burst out laughing.

"Ernesto, stop saying such things!" Pablo's mother scolded him. "It's blasphemous, slander."

The comment surprised Pablo. His father never spoke ill of anyone. Anyway, it seemed to Pablo it was just idle talk by town gossips, the jealous busybodies.

"Father Albert is in a parish nearby," his mother explained. George and María are still in touch with him. They sent him money with me. Would it be too much of a bother for you to drive me over to deliver it?"

It turned out that Father Albert was assigned to a parish in Millvale, a blue-collar community some fifteen minutes from Pablo's house. He was pastor and principal of the parochial school.

The following Sunday afternoon, when Father Albert surely would be in the rectory, Pablo and his mother drove out to Millvale.

"Aren't you coming?" his mother asked when Pablo shut the engine and remained in the car.

"I'll wait for you there," he replied. "Look, the main door is over there. Ring the bell and if he doesn't answer it, ask whomever."

His mother did exactly that. Father Albert himself answered the door, which faced the church's courtyard. He didn't ask her in. Instead, he came out and talked for a few minutes. Pablo was astonished at how short he was. As a child he had seemed so tall that Pablo found it difficult to accept what now had proved to be an optical illusion from his childhood. He was portlier than Pablo remembered, with much thinner hair and a bigger belly. From the car he could hear some of the conversation without making out most of the words. Nonetheless, Father Albert's voice was still the same, perhaps a little smokier.

After giving him the money envelope, his mother and the priest shook hands and said their farewells. Pablo thought the priest was uncourteous with someone who had once been his unacknowledged cook and taught Christian doctrine in the Immaculate Conception of Mary parish. At least he could have asked her to come in and sit down. July's sun burned high in the sky. It wasn't right to leave a senior female standing in the scorching sun, particularly when the woman considered the priest a friend for so many years.

The priest turned around and walked into the rectory without noticing Pablo. His mother walked to the car and they started on the way home.

"It didn't seem that strange to me, the way he behaved," his mother said when Pablo brought up what seemed a snub to him.

"It does to me. He's a jerk," Pablo replied. HIs mother changed the subject

Three weeks later, after his mother had left, Pablo had forgotten the meeting.

***

Now Father Albert suggests they meet Sunday. Sunday afternoon, obviously after saying morning Mass. Perplexed, but so upset that he feels no discomfort at thinking of the possibility, Pablo is about to suggest instead that they meet Saturday afternoon, curious about Father Albert's reaction. They would have to meet in a confessional: Saturday afternoon is traditionally confession time, the sacrament of penance. There Father Albert would sit, forgiving the sins of others.

It occurs to Pablo that the priest is shameless, or at least very careless. The video booth arcade is not more than ten minutes from Millvale, right on McKnight Road. Is he not worried that one of his parishioners might see him leaving the parking lot? The lot is behind the building, but it has a single exit, onto the road so busy, particularly this time of day, and at the foot of Ross Park Mall, so popular with locals.

"Better not, honestly," Pablo replies. "I can't on Sunday. I don't know what I was thinking."

"Tell me when and I'll meet you here."

"I don't think it's advisable. I'm sorry. This has been a mistake," Pablo replies.

"What's wrong? Don't you find me attractive enough?" the priest asks.

"It's not that. Yes, I do find you attractive. That's not the problem. It's just that we shouldn't," Pablo insists.

"You're going to leave me hot and bothered?" the priest asks. "I really want to do it with you."

Pablo, turned into the pastor's object of desire, has no objection he can share. Then the priest says what he must have believed to be the last recourse to seduce that young man.

"I want to drink your juice."

Pablo refuses to believe he has heard that.

"What did you say?"

"I want to drink your juice," the priest repeats. "I want to drink it from the tap."

The repugnance Pablo has felt minutes before now turns into something else. What Father Albert suggests is a kind of extrafamilial incest, a betrayal of his childhood memories, a muddying of the only untarnished part that remains of his life. If his father had told him something like that Pablo would not have heard the sense of dread he feels right now. A bishop had not consecrated his father's hands to allow him to change a wafer into the body of Christ or wine into the Redeemer's blood. Pablo was no longer a believer, but his soul always kept a thin strip of respect for what had been instilled in him since he had been taken to the baptismal font.

"I can't, Father Albert, I can't," he strains himself to say. The priest looks Pablo in the face.

"You know me? Are you a parishioner?" Father Albert asks in a casual tone Pablo finds offensive.

"No, sir. You were our pastor in the town where I grew up. Immaculate Conception of Mary parish."

"Oh, yeah. I was there for many years, before I was recalled to Pennsylvania. I didn't remember you," the priest replies.

"I didn't think you had. I hadn't seen you since I was fourteen. I've changed a bit, I guess," Pablo says, his voice still wrapped in consternation.

"Whose son are you?" Father Albert asks.

"My mother is the woman who brought you the money George and María Smith sent you over two months ago," Pablo tells him.

"Oh, yeah. Now I think I remember. I see you at the swimming pool back at the mother house. You were a hot little number. Always thought you had a nice package," the priest states.

"It's been a long time since then," Pablo says. "Please, excuse me. I have to go."

"So you know where I live. There's no one else in the rectory at night," the priest goes on to say. He pulls out a small piece of paper and a ballpoint pen from his pocket. "I'll give you my phone number, you call me and we'll set up a time."

"Don't you understand I can't, that we shouldn't?" Pablo says, his voice shaking and bordering on angry.

"Why not? You already know me and I know you. It's better yet," Father Albert says. "I don't care whose son you are or how we met. I still want to drink your juice."

The priest is holding on to Pablo's driver-side door. Pablo can take no more. The reference cracks his fragile patience.

"Get away. Go on, move. If you don't walk away I'll run you over, I swear," Pablo says, his voice shaking even more, but not from fear.

The priest seems to understand at last and lets the door go. He walks away and stands against the building's back wall. He continues to look at Pablo as if hopeful the target of his passion will change his mind. Pablo carries in his chest a ton weight. He becomes aware of his jaw, hanging and almost unhinged. By a short distance he misses a car coming in his same direction and lane. He hears a horn and the cursing.

When he arrives at home, he collapses like an amorphous bundle on the study wingback chair. Dawn finds him in the same spot. The priest's words, so distant from sermons and warnings he remembers from his early youth, keep returning as if he were just hearing them.

Weeks go by before he can sleep as he usually does, without the resound of the priest's offer, an echo only he can hear and overwhelms, because he cannot cover his ears to mute it. He does not return to the video booths; when he drives home from work he chooses an alternative route to avoid driving past the building.

His mother returned on vacation the following summer, soon after getting in the car at the airport she said,"George and María sent money again for Father Albert."

He avoided making comments or letting his voice manifest what he thought about George, María and Father Albert. He preferred to remain silent for the time being. It was his mother who broke the silence.

"He's very ill. No longer at the parish."

Pablo felt no curiosity as such, but if he would be taking the gift from the dork that was George and the gossipmonger that was his wife to Father Albert, he needed to know where. That meant not going inside wherever he was.

"Where is he?"

"In a home for convalescent priests and nuns. The Vincentian Home," his mother explained. "Do you have any idea where it is?"

Pablo lived less than three kilometers from the place. It was a building set back from the road, enclosed within a tall cement wall on an estate of manicured lawns and surrounded by tall firs and oak trees. The building looked big. Its entrance was a paved road behind impressive wrought-iron gates.

"Yes, it's not far from here," Pablo said.

"When can we go? You know me with other people's money. I want to deliver it as soon as possible," his mother pointed out.

"We could go now," Pablo told her. It was still early in the afternoon. If rolling down that cliff of ill remembrance could not be avoided, better do it quick and leave the event in a new past.

They arrived at the home. His mother identified herself at the reception desk and asked the nun at the desk how she could get to see Father Albert. The nun searched through a loose-leaf binder.

"There's no one here by that name," the nun said while still reading through the pages and following names with her index finger. She shook her head. Her short veil, held on to her head by a white diadem, also shook like a tailless kite.

"I'm sorry," his mother said, the envelope already in the hand she had placed on the counter. "I don't want to contradict you, but I have a gift that friends sent him with me. They correspond with him and this is where their letters come. Could you check again?"

The nun stared at her as if surprised at the challenge. She went through the sheets again.

"No. As I said, we have no one here by that name."

His mother remained silent, wondering what to do now with the money following the nun's denial.

"Let's go," Pablo said. "If she says he's not here, he's not here. A nun would not lie about it. She has no reason to."

He then turned to the nun and asked: "Do you, now?"

The nun looked at him less than happy over the top rim of her wire-framed eyeglasses. She closed her black vinyl binder and started shuffling documents on her desk while they were still standing in front of her.

"The question is offensive," the nun said to no one in particular.

Pablo said nothing. He took his mother's arm gently and led her to the exit.

"I don't get it. George and María write him here. And the Serranos. You remember them? The ones with the daughter who's a Carmelite nun in Toledo?" his mother said. Her confusion was authentic.

"Yes, the muscle bound one. He was very close to Father Albert, wasn't he? And Father Albert to him."

"Listen, Pablo, could it be that they won't let visitors see him for some reason? I wonder what he could have," his mother wondered.

"Something that's inconvenient for them to admit," Pablo said in code for which his mother lacked the key.

"But what?" his mother asked, looking straight ahead.

They had reached the car. Pablo opened the door for her.

"Who knows. Diabetes it wouldn't be," he replied, shut her door and walked to his side. They drove off.

In March Pablo read an obituary in the city newspaper. It was for Father Albert. He had died, the obituary said, he had gone to the Lord's peace at the Vincentian Home in Allison Park. He was 58 and had been buried in Philadelphia, his hometown, at the Holy Spirit Father's cemetery. The note asked that donations be sent in cash in the name of the deceased to Holy Spirit Parish in Millvale.

Pablo spoke with his mother on the phone. She already knew: George and María had told her.

"I'm heartsick," she said. "Poor Father Albert! Don't you feel sorry for him?"

He felt like letting go and telling her everything. He wondered how heartsick she'd feel then, for different reasons. Or maybe, as she often did when reality did not match her convictions, she wouldn't believe him.

Discretion won that battle. What would he gain from saying anything? His mother would not want to hear him. She accepted Pablo in spite of what she called his defect while in the throes of fury over Pablo's revelation, but she would not be able to tolerate the sordid tale. He would let her go on thinking of Father Albert as blessed. The priest would no longer have to live on the folded edge of the duplicity of his existence. Disclosure would not be worth the effort.

Pablo hung up. He cut the newspaper to the size of the bottom of the canary cage, discarded the soiled sheet and replaced it with the clean one. There at the bottom of the cage he could see Father Albert's obituary. He threw the net over the bird cage and went to sleep. It's what he meant to do, but couldn't.

VELVET SHACKLES

Carrots were always the most difficult to slice. Daniel had replaced the knife some months back when he started adding carrots to the evening salad. He thought the knife was dull, but he was wrong. He shouldn't have thrown it out. The extra work was worth it, though. He didn't want to buy the frozen kind. Somehow they didn't taste the same. Besides, Tatito liked them better raw than boiled. "I like them crunchy," Tatito said when he asked the child how he preferred them.

Now all was ready after putting everything in the salad bowl and drizzling it with a raspberry vinaigrette dressing. When the chicken breasts were done in the broiler the only ingredient missing were the black beans, also the only thing that came out of a can. The rice, too, was ready, loose and grainy as rice had to be. He'd wait until Lorenzo came home to cook the broccoli and the zucchini for the two minutes he timed on the microwave oven's alarm, starting when the water boiled.

The table was ready. He looked at the wall clock: 6:15. Lorenzo would be home within the next fifteen minutes. Daniel went to the bathroom to take a leak. As he washed his hands he looked in the mirror and noticed a faint line on the lower eyelids. He tried to ignore it, but thought of it as another reminder of his recent 32nd

birthday. The almost invisible lines went with the gray-ing hair he had noticed on his temples. Lorenzo had joked that maybe he should dye them, like so many oth-ers. He wouldn't do that: hair dyes enslaved people who used them. Besides, vanity had never been a quality of his, aging was a natural process and most hair coloring formulas were carcinogenic. At the hospital he had al-ready seen enough cases of cancer assumed to be caused by peroxide and ammonia and the rest of the chemicals in those products. His former mother-in-law had sug-gested he apply hair straighteners to Tatito's curls.

"Those curls are part of who he is," Daniel replied to her. He was aware that what bothered his ex-wife's mother was not the curly hair, but that it was a visible sign of mixed races, that of her blonde, blue-eyed daugh-ter and his fourth-generation African ancestry. Besides the hair products his mother-in-law also suggested skin lighteners and other cosmetic procedures.

When Tatito was still two his grandmother said in a family gathering, "Such distinction! Tatito is the only one of my grandchildren with hair that black. And curly." The subtext was barely under the surface.

"Why does that woman want shared custody? I mean, besides the fact that it is unusual and probably il-legal," he asked his attorney when they were proposing the terms and conditions of his divorce from Catalina. "She has always been bothered by her black granddaugh-ter."

"That is going nowhere," Rafaela Dávila Duchesne told him.

Catalina claimed her mother was in a better position to care for Tatito than Daniel, with all the demands his nursing job put on him. Daniel's shifts were often unpredictable, and his irregular schedule could impact Tatito's welfare. Dissuaded by his attorney he abandoned the notion of pointing out that the boy had lived for four years with an alcoholic mother who had since been in and out of rehabilitation centers. Her judgment on a child's welfare would be compromised, wouldn't it?

"Don't bring that up, Daniel," Rafaela Dávila Duchesne said. "It could be interpreted as vindictiveness." Rafaela had submitted memoranda and affidavits proving that Daniel had quit his second job, the one at Hospital Damas. Now he only had the Sunday through Wednesday job, with twelve-hour shifts daily at Hospital Doctor Pila. He made arrangements for Tatito to remain in the child-care center until he picked up the child at 7:30 the evenings he worked until 7:00. Now he could spend more time with Tatito. Catalina's attempt to take the child away from Daniel had failed; she had taken a different approach.

"Ta?" he called from the kitchen. He got no answer. "Ta, can't you hear me?" he asked, raising his voice.

"Yes, Dad," Tatito shouted. He was in his bedroom watching the Cartoon Network.

"Turn that off and go wash your hands. Lorenzo will be here any minute," Daniel said in a volume that Tatito was sure to hear.

"Oh, Dad, wait a minute. He's not here yet anyway," Tatito yelled back.

"Don't talk back and shut that off now, you hear?"

"Oh, God, Dad. Okay, okay," Tatito replied.

Supper was ready. He left the chicken in the broiler after turning it off. He didn't want it to get cold. He remembered that the breasts could dry out, went to the counter oven and covered them with aluminum foil.

His entrées varied. Sometimes it was pasta with ground turkey, others vegetarian burgers in whole wheat buns, low-fat cheese and oven-cooked French fries. Once in a while he prepared something more elaborate: broiled salmon in a bourbon sauce, asparagus or artichokes. Dessert didn't change much: fresh fruit, usually berries of different types with green grapes, kiwi, mango and cantaloupe.

His routine seldom changed when he was off from work. He got up early to cook oatmeal—Sundays and special occasions he'd make French toast or pancakes mixed with egg whites, low-sugar maple syrup—hard-boiled eggs without the yolk, orange juice for Tatito and decaffeinated coffee for him and Lorenzo. After seeing Tatito off to school and doing dishes it was time to clean house, start or finish domestic chores such as mending socks and dusting, reorganizing the closets or the cupboards. He always had something to do: the process was the same, but not so the items, and he would always find something to keep him busy in the yard. He took out at least an hour daily to sit and read in the terrace. That was also when he had his ginger root or chamomile tea. He'd reheat the previous evening's leftovers to have for lunch. If nothing had remained he'd fix himself a tuna and walnut sandwich. Early in the afternoon he would call Lorenzo and get an update on work or to let him know what to shop for at the supermarket, something Daniel had forgotten from the last grocery day or that they had run out of unexpectedly and he needed for supper.

And almost at the same time each day he'd hear a car engine approach the carport. A minute later the side door opened and Lorenzo walked in. Tonight he brought his briefcase with him. That meant he had brought some work home with him from the office.

"Ta, time to eat!" Daniel called out.

"Coming, Dad! Don't call me again!" Tatito shouted from his bedroom.

"Smells good. What is it?" Lorenzo asked, his briefcase still in his hand. He kissed Daniel as usual, with a light pop and a "mmm."

"Broiled chicken. And if you hurry you will be able to eat it warm. I'm going to take it out of the oven before it turns into rubber," Daniel said.

"Almost forgot. Here's the mail," Lorenzo said. He handed Daniel several envelopes. Daniel was more concerned with the chicken than with bills and postal handbills. He placed them on the refrigerator and got busy with food.

Lorenzo took off his shoes and left them by the sofa, as every evening. He would pick them up later before going to bed. He came back from the bathroom wearing his slippers after washing his hands and hanging his tie on the back of a large chair in the living room. When he sat down Daniel put in his hands the salad bowl.

"Let me have your plate," Daniel told Tatito before serving himself.

"Did you put cooties in it?" Tatito asked his dad.

"No, here, you drop them in yourself," said Daniel and gave Tatito de small bowl and teaspoon. "And don't call them cooties. They're called croutons."

"I know, but that's an ugly word," Tatito said. "My classmates call them cooties, too."

"I don't care how anyone else calls them. Use the correct word," Daniel said.

"Yes, Big Cootie," Tatito replied.

"Stop that, Tatito. Be respectful," Lorenzo said. He made sure Tatito was not looking at him to roll his eyes toward Daniel. They both repressed a chuckle.

Lorenzo spoke of a large and significant contract they had received at the firm. The president himself, Pedro Sitiriche, had assigned it to him. Lorenzo was grateful for the vote of confidence. After all, he had been a CPA with that same organization for twelve years and thought he deserved the recognition.

"I brought the contract with me. I want to look at it carefully here without the distractions I get at the office," Lorenzo said.

"I have to work tomorrow, but only from 7:00 to noon," Daniel said. They'll pay it at time and a half, so it isn't so bad."

Tatito was done with his salad. He had left the croutons for last and was digging into the bowl with his fingers.

"Tatito! Don't be a pig!" Daniel said and took the bowl away. "Wipe your fingers with the napkin before you stain your T-shirt."

"But Dad, the cooties taste better that way!" Tatito protested.

"Don't talk back, Tatito. That's very rude. I've told you before," Daniel reprimanded him.

"I'm sorry," Tatito said. He sat on his hands and started swinging his feet, which did not reach the floor, while Daniel took his salad plate to the sink. Lorenzo stood up and took his plate to the same place. Daniel served each his entrée.

"Come get yours, Tatito," Daniel said. When the boy took his plate Daniel told him, "And be very careful not to drop anything on the floor, because if you do, you're going to have to clean it up yourself."

"The chicken is delicious, Daniel!" said Lorenzo. "New recipe, this sauce?"

"Yes. I found it in a *Good Housekeeping* at the urologist's office," said Daniel. He stopped himself in time when he was about to say he had ripped out the page, before Tatito heard it. With his hands he gestured to Lorenzo what he had done.

"Medical terrorism," Lorenzo said.

"Dad, when is my birthday, Friday?" Tatito asked.

"No, baby. It's next Sunday," Daniel said.

"Mommy said she wanted to celebrate it Friday," Tatito said.

"She hasn't said anything to me," Daniel pointed out.

Lorenzo went on eating. He tore a piece of whole wheat bread from the loaf on the dish in the center of the table.

"Then call her and ask her," Tatito said.

"Yes, baby. Go on, eat and stop talking before your food gets cold," Daniel said.

"*Avez-vous commandé le gâteau?*" Lorenzo asked.

"*Oui, bien sûr*," Daniel replied.

Daniel and Lorenzo had met in a French class when Daniel was a nursing sophomore and Lorenzo a junior in accounting. Both had had to take advanced English classes in summer school also, because their textbooks were in English, even if their major courses were taught in Spanish, causing a certain linguistic schizophrenia in students whose academic background in English was mediocre at best. Lorenzo took his studies seriously. He had no girlfriend to distract him. If he managed to speak English proficiently he could apply for a job in the continental United States. Accounting had that advantage: no matter where he went, formulas were the same; assets and liabilities went on the same columns regardless of the language. He'd still need to communicate with clients and co-workers.

Daniel was satisfying his intellectual curiosity by learning French. He had to abandon it in favor of English grammar and composition, although he didn't have much interest in going beyond that. It was a matter of understanding nursing manuals and fulfilling requirements, not of reading Shakespeare in the original. Still, he tried to keep up his French by reading short stories and novels that he checked out of the university library. As with English, it concerned education and adding a bit of sophistication, not of reading the complete works of Flaubert.

Daniel and Lorenzo became friends. Some weekends Lorenzo drove to Orocovis to visit Daniel and his family; Daniel did the same when school work allowed, but in Juana Díaz, where Lorenzo lived. They practically ate off the same plate, their friendship was so close. They were always together. For junior year Daniel suggested they share a small apartment off campus; that would cut their expenses. It would be Lorenzo's senior year. He was no longer sure he wanted to go to the States. When he graduated with high honors the most reputable tax law firm in Ponce offered him a position. Daniel then spent his last year in nursing school in the same apartment with Lorenzo.

When he was done with school Daniel was offered a job as a registered nurse in Arecibo, on the opposite side of the island to the north. Commuting between the two cities would have been impractical. Lorenzo fell apart: they had become so close that he could not bear the thought of being away from Daniel, like Siamese twins in separate bodies but joined in their minds. If his fingernails had been torn off his flesh the pain could not have been worse.

They remained in touch. Lorenzo wrote about his loneliness, of not being able to get used to his dear friend's absence, of the emptiness Daniel's laughter had once filled. He spoke of searching for a job in Arecibo. There they would be able to share an apartment again. Some three months after arriving in Arecibo Daniel began mentioning someone he had met, some woman named Catalina who was from Guayanilla, close to Ponce. He had met Catalina at a party a fellow nurse had thrown at her house. Lorenzo felt increasingly uncomfortable with the frequency of the references to Catalina, who eventually turned into the sole subject of Daniel's letters between the greeting and the farewell. The letters they had exchanged weekly began to arrive at Lorenzo's monthly, one for every three or four Lorenzo wrote Daniel.

A year later a frail thread was all that remained of their correspondence. Then Daniel gave Lorenzo the news that he was sure would make Lorenzo very happy: he was engaged to Catalina. They would soon decide on a date for their wedding—why wait? They were adults, were employed and loved each other so much. Daniel wanted Lorenzo to be best man at the wedding.

Lorenzo waited until Daniel told him the date for what Lorenzo viewed as a funeral. He wrote Lorenzo that he had a work-related commitment he would not be able to cancel on that very date, a representation he had to make in Miami for the firm. It had been scheduled months ago; impossible to skip it.

Work is work, and I understand. When you return and Catalina and I are already married we will invite you as soon as possible to visit with us, Daniel wrote back. It was the last letter from Daniel that Lorenzo read.

Lorenzo buried himself in work and studying for his CPA exams. He considered opening his own accountancy firm in Ponce, but the Pedro Sitiriche firm gave him such a raise and perquisites he decided to remain with it.

Daniel and Catalina went back to Ponce. Catalina took a job just like the one she had in Arecibo, managing a department store in a local mall. Daniel had moved to Ponce first to start a second-shift job at Hospital Damas when Catalina arrived a month later.

One evening when Daniel was having dinner a fellow nurse who had also been a classmate of his in college and was working in neonatology asked Daniel "What ever became of Lorenzo?"

"Now that you mention him," Daniel said as if it were the name of something vanished in time that required a human key from that same past to bring it back to his memory," I haven't heard from him in a very long time. I don't know whether he's still in Ponce."

"You were so close. Always together. Where we saw you, we knew that he had to be somewhere near," said the other nurse. "We took it for granted there was something between you."

"You couldn't have been more mistaken," Daniel said.

That spiked his curiosity about his old friend. He searched for Lorenzo in the telephone directory. He didn't find him.

Around that time Daniel and Catalina started becoming distant from each other. Daniel couldn't figure out what the cause was, whether boredom, a cooling of the soul, a lethargy of feelings or disappointments of uncertain origin. Catalina had started drinking at home when Daniel was at work. He would often come home and find her passed out on the sofa. They argued about money and schedules, over Tatito's day care, the electric bill, which shelf Catalina left the orange juice on in the refrigerator, where Daniel left his socks when he took them off. Often the arguments were between a sober man and a drunken woman. Daniel was worried that he'd come home one night and find Tatito injured or roaming the house while his mother slept it off.

One day he got a phone call that surprised and gladdened him. It was Lorenzo. He had found Daniel after calling Hospital Pavía in Arecibo and then was able to trace him back to Hospital Damas, where no one would give him Daniel's phone number. Lorenzo still found him in the Ponce telephone directory after calling three other numbers, because there were four Daniel Sandovals listed without a second family name.

"*Combien cela-a-t-il coûté?*" Lorenzo asked, referring to the cake's price.

"*Cinquante*," Daniel replied, $50.00

"Oh, Dad please, stop speaking that language I don't know. Is it French?" Tatito asked.

"Yes, it is," Daniel replied.

"It sounds like you're saying something bad about me."

"Don't be silly, Tatito. How am I going to say anything less than wonderful about my little angel?" Daniel said and squeezed Tatito's chin. "They're just adult matters, that's all."

"What's my share?" Lorenzo asked.

"Half, if that's okay."

That's how everything was between them, half and half, whether it was something for the house or for Tatito. Whatever the estranged wife did not pay for, they would go in together: clothing, medication, day care, private school.

After Lorenzo found Daniel again he started visiting with his old friend. Daniel's marriage was already torn into irreparable shambles. Lorenzo became an anchor that stopped Daniel's life from drifting aimlessly in his marriage. Daniel needed a friend's support. Lorenzo always agreed with him even when both were aware that up close it was obvious Daniel was wrong; Daniel reciprocated.

Catalina left and went to live with her mother in Guayanilla. Lorenzo stayed with Daniel. He did not feel secure in the house alone with Tatito. He feared Catalina would show up drunk and make an outrageous scene in an attempt to take Tatito with her after Daniel refused to let her see him, especially when she had been drinking and came to his door. She would have had the right to take him with her—the judge had not made a final custody disposition—except that Daniel called the police the last time. When the officers came to investigate they smelled the liquor on her and dragged her off to the city jail to dry out. It was one of the episodes that counted against her case for custody when the divorce had its final disposition. She was a drunk: being reasonable was not to be expected from her, even if she had been ordered to stay away from Daniel.

"Fags," Catalina told her mother after yelling it out her car window one afternoon when Daniel was walking in to work. "I'm going to spread it throughout the neighborhood! I'll tell our friends!"

"You shouldn't do that," her mother advised her. "People are going to start wondering whether you turned him that way with your bad temper and your drunkenness. Think about it, if he'd take dick up his ass rather than spend another minute with you, things are pretty bad." Catalina herself repeated that conversation to Daniel one afternoon when she waited for him at the hospital's doors to berate him in front of patients and medical personnel.

"You're drunk, Catalina. Go sleep it off," Daniel said. He looked at the few people gathered around them. He shook his head and twisted his mouth, then walked away.

"I'm going to name Lorenzo as co-respondent in my petition for divorce, you know," Catalina yelled.

Daniel stopped and walked back toward Catalina. "You are so drunk you don't realize I sued you for divorce, not the other way around. You abandoned the household, Catalina. You're in no position to claim shit." Then he walked back in and left her standing in the late afternoon sun.

Catalina still fought for sole custody of the child. She could not bring up her suspicion that Daniel and Lorenzo were involved in an affair that could have a negative impact on Tatito. She had no proof. Their irreconcilable differences had manifested themselves before Lorenzo and Daniel found each other again. At her attempts to bring up her accusations in court her lawyer would become irritated and order her to shut up. On one occasion the judge threatened her with throwing her out of court. During the turmoil of one of the final hearings her lawyer told her, "You can't bring yourself to admit to your own self that what you feel is jealousy. You are driven by vindictiveness. By drunkenness. Shut up once and for all or I'll quit your case and leave you hanging in the wind. Who the hell do you think will take this case again?"

According to Rafaela Dávila Duchesne, assuming, which she was not confirming or denying and would rather not know, if Catalina's suspicions were accurate, she could not compete with another man, even if she and Daniel worked out their difficult differences and she went away again to dry out. Catalina claimed that Lorenzo had preceded her in Daniel's life and had installed himself in her husband's heart. They were sleeping together: Catalina was sure of it. She said so to her attorney, who called Rafaela Dávila Duchesne to test the waters and see what her reaction would be to the possibility of bringing it up.

"She doesn't mean they're sleeping together, she means they are going to bed together," Rafaela replied to Catalina's lawyer. "You both need to know that they sleep in separate rooms. But I'd love for her to bring that up without evidence," Rafaela added. "Then we'd sue her for slander, too. This bitch has no interest in ever seeing her child again, does she?"

That's where it all seemed to end.

"*Et le vélo?*" asked Lorenzo. Their gift for Tatito would be a bicycle with training wheels.

"I have to pick it up at Sears," Daniel answered.

"Dad, what do you have to pick up at Sears?" Tatito asked. He was eating his grapes with his fingers and continued to swing his feet.

"Something I need," Daniel replied, looking Tatito in the face.

When there was no danger of Tatito deciphering the nature of the conversation the two men switched back to their native language.

"Tell me how much I'm going to owe you," Lorenzo asked.

"When I pick it up I'll tell you. I don't know yet," Daniel replied.

The birthday party was all planned out. Some of the guests would be Tatito's third-grade classmates. Daniel hoped that the children's friendship would be valued higher than some of the parents' bias against the possibility that the two men were more than roommates. Sonia had confirmed she would be there; she was Daniel's sister and Tatito's godmother, and would come with her husband and their four children. Carlos Alberto, they were implicitly certain, would neither come nor allow his wife, Daniel's other sister, or their children to be at the party. Daniel had ordered the balloons, the favors, the decorations for the cake table and the food. He had also contracted with the *payasita*, the clown girl who performed at children's parties; they had also made arrangements with an entertainment company to set up a bouncing cabin in the backyard. Daniel was praying that Tatito's eighth birthday would be memorable and fun for everyone. More than anything, however, he prayed that Catalina would not come to ruin their son's party with her unwanted and offensive presence.

Daniel and Lorenzo did the dishes together. They divided among each other the pots and the countertop oven grill. Lorenzo went to their bedroom to undress and slip on a bathrobe while Daniel went to Tatito's room to put him to sleep by reading him a fairy tale.

Lorenzo came back to the living room and turned on the TV set. He liked to have the background noise of cable news stations, what Shakespeare had called the sound and the fury signifying nothing. He never paid much attention to whatever was on, but when he was working on something the din alleviated the tedium. When Tatito fell asleep Daniel turned off the end table lamp and tiptoed out of the room to avoid waking him up again. He never shut the door completely, fearing that the child would wake up scared during the night and Daniel wouldn't hear him.

He came out to the living room to sit next to Lorenzo in the sofa. They had no need for conversation. Daniel followed the TV screen images while Lorenzo remained concentrated on a document in a file folder, his legs folded under his body. Every so often Lorenzo would run a highlighter over text on the sheets.

"Aren't you going to open your mail?" Lorenzo asked.

"Forgot completely," Daniel said. He stood up and went to the kitchen. He grabbed a letter opener from a tray next to the refrigerator. He returned to the sofa. He read every sender's address before opening the envelopes. One was from Rafaela Dávila Duchesne. It couldn't be a bill: he had paid off the entire balance as soon as the last statement arrived. Daniel looked at it without opening it. Lorenzo noticed the hesitation.

"Who's it from?" he asked, the highlighter in the air and his eyes fixed on the envelope.

"My attorney."

"What might she want?" Lorenzo asked.

"Let's see," Daniel said. He slipped the letter opener along the top crease. He pulled out the sheets inside and shook them to unfold the contents. Daniel read the first few paragraphs and glanced over the rest.

"Here she goes again, that pitiful nuisance," Daniel said.

Lorenzo sighed deeply. He was pretty sure he knew what this was about. He asked what the issue was anyway.

"Another petition for sole custody. Her attorney filed and sent my attorney a copy," Daniel said. Lorenzo noticed Daniel's pallor. It was an obnoxious incident that repeated itself every three or four months during the past two years. It required Rafaela Dávila Duchesne to prepare for court to oppose the petition and present arguments to deny Catalina her request. It also meant another bill for time spent on a useless attempt.

"She must have a lot of money," Lorenzo said. "All that petitioning costs a lot."

"Her mother must be giving it to her. At first her mother was perturbed and offended over Tatito's hair's texture, but now it seems she's more motivated to pursue this unfair foolishness."

The arrival of one of those letters cracked the peace of their shared domesticity. If Lorenzo didn't bring work home, they sat to watch TV when something worthwhile was on or sat silently in the semidarkness of the living room listening to music that wasn't loud enough to disturb Tatito's sleep. They liked listening to popular romantic ballads from the '60s, Lucecita Benítez's emotional interpretation of traditional songs or Braulio's bold ballads, lyrics that challenged traditional morality and social expectations. Sometimes each would read a book while the music played, their bodies touching and Lorenzo running his fingers on Daniel's thigh. Watching

TV Lorenzo would doze off. Daniel wouldn't wake him up, thinking of the exhaustion and stress he often brought home from work. Sometimes something good would come on. Daniel felt tempted to wake up Lorenzo, but didn't. He'd watch the show and let Lorenzo sleep until it was time for both to go to bed.

The passion that bound them at first had waned. Now they made love without planning for it, when they had a chance and felt shared desire, not because it was nighttime and darkness lent itself to faceless embraces, as if they had something to be ashamed of. The turbulence of the first time never repeated itself, although it was not completely dissipated. It had started with an innocent massage to alleviate Daniel's aching muscles. It had not been the first one. Daniel found them helpful; he was grateful to his friend for taking the time to administer them. Catalina had been gone for two months. Tatito was already asleep. Daniel asked his friend to rub his neck and back. Rubbing Daniel's back Lorenzo found himself caressing more than massaging. Before he could stop himself he neared his lips to Daniel's nape. He pulled away his arms and torso fearing Daniel's rejection and trying to formulate mentally an excuse to justify the abuse of his friend's trust. Daniel raised his head and looked into Lorenzo's eyes. He twisted his body toward Lorenzo, lifted his arm and with it pulled in Lorenzo's mouth to his. There would be no going back now.

"I never stopped loving you," Lorenzo said.

""And I never thought about this, even less that something like this could happen," Daniel said. He paused and looked into Lorenzo's eyes. "I'm not complaining."

A few weeks later Lorenzo began bringing more of his belongings over. Daniel explained to his child that his friend Lorenzo, who loved Tatito so much, would be coming to live with them.

"Great," Tatito said. "Now it won't be just the two of us!"

Tatito didn't seem to miss his mother much. Daniel figured it was because of the explanations he had taken the time to give the child about his parents' separation. Daniel stated that in spite of everything going on Catalina would always be his mother and Tatito would always have both of them, who loved him so and only wanted his happiness without arguments and constant yelling.

Lorenzo, of course, correctly assumed that Catalina would not be as stupid as not to conclude the inevitable. He feared Catalina would retaliate by claiming complete ownership of the marital house.

"The mortgage is in my name," Daniel said, "even if the house is titled under both. If it bothers her too much, we'll sell the house, I'll give her half of the proceeds, and we'll go wherever we please. We could go where her ghost stops hanging over us. She'll be like a cobweb. We'll scrape it off.

Catalina didn't ask for her half, however. She left her interest in the property for her son to have a secure place to live, at least for the time being. When she

regained his custody, she'd ask for a different arrange-
ment. She'd pressure Daniel to sell her his half of the
house. That was her position as her attorney communi-
cated it to Rafaela Dávila Duchesne.

"Don't get ahead of yourselves," Rafaela advised
Catalina's attorney before hanging up on him.

Aside from such periodic incursions that Catalina
made into the tranquility of their intimacy, their lives
were routine and almost boring, others would have
judged when mistaking monotony with contentment.
Those would be others looking from the outside and
without any understanding of the bond of affection between them, stripped of adolescent curiosity. To Daniel
and Lorenzo it felt as if they had found a private corner
of fulfillment in paradise. They would reassure each
other in their heart-to-heart talks, especially when Tatito
was spending the afternoon in supervised visits with his
mother and they had time for undisturbed privacy.

In the morning Daniel would call Rafaela Dávila
Duchesne. It would be a matter of dusting off, of changing the date on the same memoranda and answers to Catalina's petitions. Nothing had changed since the last
time. Catalina insisted on taking the same route each
time with the very same results; Daniel again reacted the
same way with the same recourse. If Catalina came forward to claim that her objection was to her child raised
by two men involved in a romantic relationship he would
know what he was up against. Appearances could not be
used to prove claims in court, as Rafaela Dávila Duchesne had explained. He was ready for that possibility, but

doubted it would materialize. Still Catalina would not state her true motivation. Tatito's welfare would not be it.

Lorenzo's head was bobbing. His documents were still on his lap, but teetering on the edge of his thighs and threatening to fall to the floor. Amidst Lorenzo's involuntary nodding and Daniel's thoughts on Catalina's latest legal maneuvers Daniel thought he heard glass breaking outside.

"What was that?" Lorenzo was startled. "I didn't dream that, did I?"

"No, I heard it too."

They both got up from the sofa. Daniel turned on the porch light. They peeked through the windows. There was nothing out of the ordinary out there. Most of the neighbors' lights were out; the lamppost a couple of houses down from them was still lit. They went to the kitchen door and opened it. There was glass on the carport floor. Something was broken. It couldn't be a window: both looked intact. Neither could it be the windows in Daniel's car, because they, too, looked fine. Lorenzo walked deliberately around his car, parked behind Daniel's, and stopped by the trunk. The back window's glass had shattered to pieces on the floor and over the back seat's top panel. On the trunk, in oversized letters he read "Death to queers." The graffiti artist, if indeed it was only one, must have spent several minutes there brushing black paint on the car's white trunk back in their darkened street stretch. He or perhaps she put away the painting tools before cracking the glass and taking flight. The piece of cinder block was lying on the lawn a few feet from the car. Had this person or perhaps persons fled on foot? Had he or they driven off? Was it a neighbor who just had to run a few feet back to his house after the attack? Catalina? Her mother?

"Call the police," Lorenzo asked of Daniel.

"No, wait... Better not... Do you think?"

"What do you mean if I think? This was an act of vandalism. I'm not going to let someone intimidate us this way," Lorenzo explained. "If you won't call them, I will."

"It will be a scandal, Lorenzo. The neighbors..."

"If we don't report this and have it investigated, they'll be back," Lorenzo said.

"And if you report it they will still come back," Daniel argued.

Lorenzo crossed his arms. He looked toward the car, the window cracked to pieces over the trunk and around the back of the car, the writing, so precise and clear. If they had been written on his own chest his heart wouldn't have sunken any lower. He decided it was time to confront reality without putting a lid on anything for fear of public opinion. This was the 21st century, after all. Attitudes had changed radically, even if some reactionaries were still stuck in medieval times. If they were not willing to accept or at least tolerate, that was their problem.

"I don't care what they think," Lorenzo said. "I am going to call the police. When they read what the trunk says, if they try to treat me with any less respect than I deserve, I will know what to do. I am not going to live in fear the rest of my life."

Daniel looked at him. It was obvious Lorenzo did not have a clear view of the wider panorama where they were nothing but moving targets.

"If Catalina finds out she will have more fire power that she will use against me," Daniel said. "She will claim that her son is in physical danger and will suffer rejection because his father is a fag." Daniel paused, waiting for Lorenzo's reaction. "Do you still think it is worth it?"

Lorenzo remained silent. He looked at Daniel and then turned his sight to the writing on the car trunk. "Death to queers." He turned his loving eyes toward Daniel. Their lives together ran through his mind from the moment they met to the time their friendship had not yet identified itself as unrequited love to their reencounter, to the removal of the more pressing obstacles and then to a common existence that included shared parenthood. He remembered the years of separation, days when his chest felt oppressed. He recalled the lamentations of loneliness that secretly attempted to reach for something that eluded his craving. Lorenzo thought of the paralyzing joy of finding Daniel again and how his heart really leapt to his throat as he conquered the urgency of weeping that could reveal his true feelings. He lived it all again right there, crossing through the barrier of time kept by a metronome of anguish followed by sheer euphoria, the moment when his lips received the sweet warmth of the mouth Daniel offered him freely, unrestrained.

Lorenzo said nothing. He walked closer to Daniel, who searched his eyes with the curiosity of someone who cannot see clearly whether he will be stabbed with a dagger of contempt or embraced with tenderness and love. He did not need death. He was already in a crystal coffin.

Lorenzo walked toward the kitchen door without speaking.

"What are you going to do, Lorenzo?" Daniel asked. It was more of a plea than a question.

Lorenzo stood at the threshold. He turned to Daniel and said, "Back in the shed we have some turpentine and old rags."

SELF-STOLEN IDENTITY

Alex shook his hair with his hands once he slipped out of the skis on the shore.

"You're fantastic!" Ivette said. She placed the towel in his hand. "You're incredible, Alex. Let's see whether I can do something even close to your maneuvers!

"You're going to be much better," Alex said. He wrapped himself in the towel. The breeze blowing from the west caressed his moist skin and gave him goosebumps on his chest. He slipped on the rubber sandals and walked toward the canopy where the ski club members were gathered, some sitting in on the sand and others in folding beach chairs. In the middle sat the coolers. Everyone was holding a beer or a *piña colada* that Teresita and Manolo had mixed on the improvised table. From one of the coolers Alex took out a Carlsberg. He sat in a chair between Marianita and Lourdes. An Olga Tañón *meregue* was on the cassette player.

"Alex, you are phenomenal!" Wisón said. He had pulled away the red plastic tumbler, though not much, to speak. "This year you are going to wipe out the competition. It's going to be another trophy for the club."

Lydia, in front of Alex, stirred a bloody Mary. She said nothing, but opened her eyes wide behind the thick glasses, smiled and nodded. Several, to a greater or lesser degree, gestured and emitted sounds of agreement. Only Luchy was not drinking.

"Until I'm rid of that urinary tract infection I don't want any liquor," she had said shortly after arriving in Ramoncito's convertible.

"Make it soon, because I'm smothered in this abstinence!" Ramoncito said after taking the *piña colada* straw out of his mouth. He turned to the improvised bar counter. "Hey, Teresita, are you charging for the rum? This is nothing but pineapple juice and coconut milk."

Teresita made a face. "As soon as you pay your dues you can ask for it."

"I don't know, but I don't think I'm going to ski any more today," Edgardito said. "Then I can devote my time to getting nicely drunk."

"As if you needed an excuse," Nora replied without swallowing completely her Hatuey beer. The rest laughed.

Alex sipped from his bottle. He looked toward the beach. Ivette was already on the launching pad with her feet in her skis, holding on to the towing rope. The pilot of the Mastercraft X 30 awaited her signal to take off.

"Look, there's Ivette taking off," Nora said. "Let's see if this time she doesn't crash." Most of the group guffawed.

"If sober she doesn't last a couple of minutes, drunk she's going to end up splitting her legs out like a sea ballerina," said Eileen.

"Time her, you'll see," René said with a hand over his eyes to cut the sun's glare.

"If she lasts longer than a minute, rum is on me for the next time," Eileen said. "If not, you have to buy me a bottle of Dom Perignon."

"The wager isn't worth that much," Lourdes retorted.

Alex rose to his feet and took out another Carlsberg from the cooler. Before returning to his place he turned toward the beach when he heard Eileen.

"Look at her, look at her!" Eileen yelled with Roman-circus enthusiasm. "She already crashed!"

"What a surprise," Manolito said as he was mixing his own screwdriver.

"Lydia, isn't this your turn?" Alex asked.

"Yes! I'm there," Lydia said. She rose, placed her bloody Mary on the table where Manolito was sipping his screwdriver and walked toward the dock. She crossed paths with Ivette, who was staggering toward the canopy.

"Girl, that was ugly!" Ramoncito said through laughter that made him spit the Hatuey he had in his mouth.

"What a pig, Ramoncito!" Luchy said, brushing off moisture from her chest. "You sprayed me with beer."

"I've sprayed you with worse and I never heard you complain," Ramoncito replied. The rest of them gave each other a dose of mocking laughter.

"Manolito, mix me another *piña colada*. I got to get through this with a good hit of rum," Ivette said. She removed the swimming cap and toweled off her crotch. "Today I won't be back on those deadly boards."

Alex looked toward the dock. Lydia walked to it in her flower-print bikini one or two sizes smaller than her rolls required. Her top was barely enough to contain breasts that made Alex ask himself how she could walk without falling on her face.

"She should have left her eyeglasses back here," said Eileen.

"Without them she can't see anything," said Ivette, now with her *piña colada* in hand. "She's got them strapped around the back of her head."

"If she has a blowout like you, the tide is going to rise up to here," Teresita remarked.

Laughter invaded the canopy's space and drowned Olga Tañón misandric lyrics.

Lydia, however, did not lose her balance. She performed several pirouettes, one lifting one ski while she balanced herself on the other, mastering the sudden drops with only one hand on the tow rope, waving with the other.

"At her age and after three bloody Marys, she's not bad," Eileen said.

"Old maids have nothing else to do with their time," René said.

"You really don't know a lot, you beast," Ramoncito said. "She's divorced. She says her husband was a weakling who never made decisions and she got tired of being the one who always had to make them. When she's had a few she lets all that out."

"Maybe he was queer," Cuco said.

"Or a dork, like you," Billy retorted, and everyone laughed.

"Maybe she's a dyke," Josueíto said.

"Lesbian? That one?" Luchy interjected. "I don't think those eyeglasses are good for nothing more than to look at your bulges. Haven't you noticed she always sits across from Alex and you other guys who wear Speedos?"

More laughed than remained silent or went on drinking from bottles or tumblers.

"Alfredo could tell you stories," Ramoncito said. At everyone's silence he added: "Alfredo Miranda. Alfredito."

Several shrugged and shook their heads.

"That one got on him like a one-woman plague and didn't let him breathe. Poor guy was married. His wife was this close to leaving him," Ramoncito continued.

Alex did not know Lydia's background Actually, he had never paid her much attention. He perceived a little forwardness she failed to completely conceal with feigned modesty. She seemed as if wanting to say something but instead let her glances and gestures say it for her, enigmatic without charm. She had been a club member before Alex joined.

The ski club had been organized in the capital city several years before. The members decided to change its beachside headquarters, a movable and informal setup, to the western part of the island when the *Macheteros* started beheading presumed enemies in tourist beaches with their outboard propellers. Every two weeks Alex drove west for club meetings and practice, which lasted all day Saturday, unless it was raining. In that case they would stay in the hotel lobby playing poker and taking short trips to the hotel bar between hands. They followed a routine imposed by no one in particular, just out of habit. Most arrived Friday night, had supper at the hotel restaurant or car-pooled to a restaurant in town, returned to the hotel bar and ended up at the hotel disco, after which they went to their rooms. Some went by themselves, others with someone with whom they were sharing a suite, and others with a permanent or improvised partner of the opposite sex.

Saturday by 10:00 A.M. they were under the canopy they rented. Each one went off for at least one practice; once the first round was complete, headed by the club's president, the second round would start in the same sequence as before. The number of members practicing began thinking out after the second round, until by afternoon only four or five were back on their skis. While waiting their turn, if they continued to practice, they would drink whatever Teresita and Manolito were mixing or beer from the coolers. The liquor was paid for with member dues. Alex brought his own beer with him. In Paris he had become accustomed to Carlsberg. Every other beer tasted to him mediocre and insipid or needlessly bitter, like Heineken.

Toward sunset no one practiced any longer: they were too drunk to risk breaking their neck because of lack of control over the waves. Edgardito had quite a scare two months earlier. He had learned his lesson.

"If you're drunk don't ski and if you ski don't get trunk," he would say now, imitating a TV public-service ad. "Some dreams on skis can turn into E.R. nightmares."

Alex thought it was easy to conclude that Lydia was an old maid. She had to be in her forties; the rest of the club members were in their late twenties or mid-thirties, except Ramoncito, who also seemed to be around Lydia's age, if not older.

Lydia returned and immediately grabbed a towel to wipe her eyeglasses, splashed by sea water. When she took them off she didn't look so bad, Alex thought, although she wasn't attractive either way. While she dried up she made noises that sounded vaguely like the same ones Alex made in the more intense moments of lovemaking. She let out a prolonged "Ah!" when she pressed the towel and patted her chest right where it turned into the preamble to her breasts. Before sitting down she picked up her bloody Mary, now watered down by the ice and with a withered celery stalk.

"You had perfect moves," Ramoncito said. "I suspect you have been practicing on your own."

"Nothing like that. I have no time to come out here except with you guys," Lydia replied. She drained the rest of the liquid and held down the small ice cubes in the plastic tumbler with the swizzle stick. "You must know that I'm an IT manager with no time for anything other than work during the week."

"Oh, I know nothing about such things. Only if you are a workaholic. I'd rather be an alcoholic," Eileen said.

"My job requires long working hours, darling," Lydia said. She turned toward Manolito, "Baby, hit me again. And this time use vodka instead of water."

Alex removed another Carlsberg from the cooler. The sun was already setting and soon would be time to go shower and get ready for supper.

Once the seafood meal was over they retreated to the disco. Edgardito excused himself.

"I know you are going to miss me oh so much, but I must deprive you of the honor of my presence. You all have another you by your side, and I suspect my eyes are playing tricks, aren't they? I better go lie down," he said, pulled back and made an unstable curtsy, then walked toward the elevators as if his emergency brake were stuck.

Alex felt tipsy also, but he didn't want to be the spoiler and joined the rest at the disco. Music seemed to come from every corner in the place. The dance floor was lighted with intermittent lights of many colors. Several couples were already contorting themselves to the tune of some popular rhythm, something vestigial from the '70s, music that affirmed its permanence in spite of efforts to eradicate it forever.

Alex approached the bar and asked for a Carlsberg, which, fortunately, the bar stocked. He saw Lydia standing against the counter, watching couples dancing and licking the shaker of another bloody Mary. He walked toward her, took her hand, and she placed her drink on the counter to follow him. They walked together onto the dance floor. Alex started swaying to the rhythm of the music; Lydia followed suit. The lights turned into a blurry chromatic tracking. The more he turned in one direction, the more the room turned in the opposite direction. He feared losing his balance and collapse on Lydia's breasts while she danced more restrained than he, as if her feet were too heavy. Alex clapped his hands above his head and sang along with the music. His hips were swinging to the music. He turned around Lydia. Without losing the music's beat he pressed against Lydia's back, placed his hands on her hips and tried to make them shake in synchrony with his. Lydia laughed, her head thrown back against his neck. The other club members who were watching pointed at him and laughed in an uproar. Impossible to hear what they were yelling: Bon Jovi drowned them.

The end of the song blended with the beginning of the next, something older, syncopated and familiar, *Get Down on It*, by Kool and the Gang, which Alex remembered from college in Syracuse. He pulled away from Lydia and stood with his side rubbing rhythmically against her front. He kept clapping above his head and gyrating to the music as if performing sexually in a vertical position.

"Hey, Baryshnikov!" Alex heard René yell at him from the side of the dance floor. "We're leaving! *Ciao!*"

Alex paid no attention. He went on dancing. Lydia was now clapping her hands and loosening her hips. They started approaching each other. Alex took her by her hips and pressed his lips against Lydia's. He kissed her tight, almost aggressively, with an exploring tongue, and she responded.

"Not here," Lydia whispered in his ear. "Let's go to my room."

Alex followed her until they reached her door. She slid the card key through the lock slot. The door opened. Alex remained motionless.

"I shouldn't Lydia. Please forgive me. I've had too much to drink. I'd better go to bed," he said with shame while Lydia stared confused. "I'm sorry. Some other time."

"You can bet on it," Lydia replied. It was she who approached him, threw her arms around his neck and kissed him with more passion than Alex expected, nibbling on his lips. "There won't be time tomorrow, but I'll call you Monday."

On his way back to his room he refused to believe what had just happened. It had not been a drunk's hallucination. He wasn't asleep, but he feared this might turn into a nightmare. This could be a mistake that would bear enormous consequences. He had been divorced from Elena for three years. Since then he had not slept with any woman. Theirs had been a dissolution packed with acrimony and recriminations. He had accepted the blame was all his. Alex was lucky that Elena refused to take advantage of all the rights the law afforded her in cases such as theirs. She was an architect: she had no need for the property or spousal maintenance. "A red penny from that man will be a constant reminder of his existence," she had told the presiding judge at the final hearing.

Their lives went down different paths. One of his brothers had told him that Elena had moved to Louisiana, and he had heard it from a cousin. Out there in Baton Rouge she was in a relationship with someone. Alex could not let go the feeling that his deceit and the pain he had caused her were a gloomy streak that blemished his soul with the shame of someone who is not worthy of forgiveness. He had loved her: he had no doubt about that. At first they lived in complete bliss, without doubts or shadows. Then Alex had to face reality when he found himself at an unforeseen and breathtaking crossroads.

In the ski club he was trying to find a distraction, something he could do without emotional involvement. It was more like his time of solitary and willing loneliness. He refrained from giving anyone details about his life other than superficial tidbits: his career, the sports teams he liked, the music he preferred, where he had attended college and nothing deeper than that. When someone tried to dig for more he would change the subject or say, "What an interesting question." Why do you ask?" He had learned to disarm snoops that way by putting them on the defensive and finally leave the question unanswered. For him it was a strategy for survival and depriving strangers of access to his intimacy. He would go as far as sharing the liquor-infused social activities, dinner and skiing competition, a sport he had practiced since high school. Secrets of the heart demand frontiers. Alex had traced them: he had no need to grant any of those people a passport into his personal plot.

"I've done that already. I have no interest in jumping off that cliff again," he would reply when someone reminded him that he was still young and could begin his life anew with a different woman, have children, a family. "I'm a one-woman man, and I already had mine." He had repeated the phrases when someone at the club tried to figure out the mystery of his life. None of them was married. Lucy and Ramoncito had lived together for years, but didn't seem interested in making it legal. The rest of them, as far as Alex had heard them say, were single or divorced. René had been married twice and had a girlfriend no one knew.

"I'm not bringing her along. One of these horny bastards would want to steal her from me," he said one time after the fourth cocktail.

"If she finds you desirable, she must have awful taste. I doubt she'd want someone as handsome and gifted as I," Edgardito replied. They all laughed, including René.

When the females went shopping as time allowed during the practice weekends, late in the afternoon and before supper the males went to the bar or, preferably, stayed under the canopy. They'd comment on the women who walked by in their bikinis and thongs. If the women were not in the company of men, their favorite greeting started with a whistle or a noisy air kiss.

Hey, baby, don't be like that... Look over here, beautiful... What a precious set of buttocks you got there... You wanna be my children's mom, don't you, sweetheart...? Don't leave me here wanting... You get me started and then you just walk away...? What, not even a smile, baby? A smile costs you nothing, come on... Come on, I don't bite. I just kiss... I got a beer can here for you, darling...

Sometimes one or two, if accompanied by girlfriends, would look back to the canopy and then laugh, but not to show she was taking any of it seriously; it was usually a laugh of mockery or disbelief. The ones who walked past the canopy close to the shore by themselves never bothered to look back, but neither would they stop shaking their hips, as if to say *Look at what you're not getting*, or at least that was how they interpreted the motion. This fired up the skiers and increased the aggressiveness of their speeches. Edgardito, if he was as drunk as usual at the end of the practice day, would grab his crotch or rub his genitals suggestively trying to soften the indifferent and get their attention.

Look what I got for you here, baby. You ain't getting nothing better than this, he would often say. The other men would cackle. Alex remained in the back observing without saying a word.

The morning following the disco episode Alex got up earlier than he used to when he was hung over. His mouth was pasty; his head throbbed and, when he bent over to tie his shoes he felt a dizzy spell coming on in the midst of a dry heave attack that forced him to sit on the edge of the bed and wait for it all to pass. Perhaps he had to eat some breakfast to regain his strength, but the thought alone of something more than orange juice and coffee turned his stomach and made him heave again. He went down to the cafeteria, which was virtually empty. He asked for a couple of toasts and juice. He was in a rush to eat whatever he could, pay for the room and leave before any of the others became aware of his departure.

Monday his secretary rung him up to let him know he had a phone call on line two from a woman by the name of Lydia.

"She didn't give me her last name," Marta said. "She said you knew who she was. Should I put it through?"

He hesitated, then told her to put the call through.

Lydia invited him to supper that night. Alex told her he had a previous commitment for that night. Lydia suggested the following night. Unfortunately, he told Lydia, that entire week would be difficult for him to get away.

"Well, Saturday, then. I have two tickets to *The Farce of Love's Bargain*, by Luis Rafael Sánchez, and I'm reserving one for you," Lydia said.

Alex could not refuse. He thought it best to go with her to the performance, tell her the truth when they stopped at a bar to have a glass of wine after the show and everything would end there. He thought of telling her he was still married, but that lie could be discovered without much effort. It would not be good to complicate the matter any further. He was willing to leave the club, which would be necessary once Lydia let her tongue loose and he became the target of mockery or, worse yet, a collective cold shoulder of isolation and would lead him anyway to quit.

It didn't happen the way he had planned. He stopped by her apartment to pick her up. While he waited for her to finish her coiffure Lydia had served him a glass of white wine. Alex had thanked her for the offer of red wine, but refused it because of an allergy to it.

"I assume you are not allergic also to the white kind," Lydia said, "so here you are." She placed the glass on a cocktail table in front of the sofa where Alex sat.

When the show was over they were unable to stop at the bar. She had ridden with him, a fact that had escaped Alex when he offered to pick her up instead of meeting at the theater. To avoid looking uncourteous he agreed to a drink before leaving for home.

Lydia poured him a Scotch and served herself vodka on the rocks.

"This is a very tasteful cocktail table," Alex said.

"You like it?" Lydia asked. "It was made for me by a friend of mine who's a woodworker. You are right, it's very elegant. A furniture store would have charged me around a thousand for something like this. It's ebony, you know."

Alex sipped his whiskey. It was obvious that they had nothing in common to talk about. Lydia had lain back very relaxed against a corner of the sofa, supported by the armrest. Between awkward moments of silence Alex strained himself trying to find a subject they could talk about as a prelude to what he had to say.

"What did you think of the play?" he asked her. On the way home they had talked about it, but he could not come up with anything else to ask.

"I don't think I could say any more than what I already said. It was interesting, nothing else. That type of comedy that tries to revive antiquated models doesn't interest me much. They're pretentious," Lydia said while rubbing the top of her cleavage in a circular motion with a finger. "I mean, there's a lot of newer drama under the sun, don't you think? It's cute, not much more. Kind of lame, as a matter of fact."

"Why did you buy the tickets then?" Alex asked.

"There was nothing left to see. I get the tickets for free at work. Sometimes they have theater tickets, some other times for baseball or basketball games," Lydia clarified. "They are supposed to be for important clients. If they have any left over, human resources lets management have them. You know what they say about gift horses. The price was right."

Alex nodded in agreement and sipped from the lowball glass of Scotch.

"That ceiling lamp," he paused. "It really goes well with the rest of your decor."

"You think so? I don't know... I don't much care for it," Lydia said and shrugged. "But you know, as I said about gift horses. Same sort of thing. It was chosen by a friend of mine, an electrician. He rewired my house and installed it."

"Yes, I'd say it goes well with the rest," was Alex's reply. He tried to look toward the ceiling to avoid acknowledging that if Lydia relaxed any more she would slip right off the sofa.

"I won't ask you about that sculpture on the stand, because I'm afraid you will tell me it was sculpted by a sculptor friend," Alex said and laughed.

"No, that's something I bought at Fowler Gallery. Do you like it?" Lydia asked. "

"I do. It's unusual," Alex observed. It was an amorphous bronze object with asymmetrical peaks that looked on the verge of splintering off the base. "Mimetic it isn't."

"I believe it's supposed to represent a soul both twisted and vulnerable," Lydia explained. "Another Scotch?"

Alex wanted to say no, that he had something he needed to talk to her about. He was defeated by his argument that he needed something stronger to give him courage. He said yes. Lydia went to the bar and filled up his glass again. Alex noticed she had unbuttoned her blouse almost completely. Her cleavage was visible: the light pink strapless bra she was wearing covered almost none of it. They had a few more awkward moments when neither said anything. Then Alex would start up a trivial topic about which Lydia had little or nothing to say. Between the liquor, Lydia's posture and cleavage and a sudden need to prove something to himself, he put the glass on the cocktail table and slipped over toward Lydia, almost horizontal on the sofa. He placed his hands on her breasts and kissed her deep. She fumbled through his arms and removed her eyeglasses, dropping them on the floor. *Otherwise, this is never going to end,* he said to himself. *I'll tell her some other day what I came here to say.*

They walked into her bedroom. They undressed in the semidarkness as well as they could in the midst of squeezes and caresses. Lydia lay in bed and Alex climbed on her. Close to his paroxysm he asked her, "Is it safe?"

"Yes, don't worry about it," Lydia replied panting and without freeing his neck from her arms.

After their quiver they rested silently for a few minutes. Without much encouragement from her, Alex began climbing back on her, but she turned him over to straddle him. Alex looked at the alarm clock next to the bed: it was almost midnight.

"I'm so sorry, Lydia, but I have to get going," he said in a rush and more nervous than Lydia thought necessary.

"Aren't you spending the night?" she asked, surprised.

"No, I can't," Alex replied, already hurrying to finish dressing, almost in despair over not finding one of his socks. "I have an important engagement early in the morning. Thank you, though. Some other time.

Alex got home. He undressed quickly and sped into the bathtub. He stood there under the stream cascading down his head for a long while. He couldn't explain to himself how it had all happened. It was unforgivable, a betrayal to his own self. He had no room in his life for any more culpability. He had sentenced himself already to the remorse over the matter with Elena and needed to evade becoming distraught all over again. He was glad Lydia had not asked him for his home telephone number. She had found out about his work number through Eileen, the ski club's secretary. He did not know what he would say if Lydia asked him for his home one. Perhaps she would believe him if he told her he didn't have one.

That was exactly what he told her when she called him at work Monday morning. He didn't care whether or not she believed him. She asked him to lunch on Wednesday, when she would be in a meeting near the firm where Alex was an engineer. He figured there would be no danger in that. It could be his chance to speak to her clearly.

They met at The Swiss Chalet. Lydia was already seated in a booth. When the maître d' greeted him, Alex simply said the lady was waiting for him.

They caught up with events during the previous three days. All of them had to do with work. The server approached to ask them what they wanted to drink. Lydia asked for a glass of rosé.

"Iced tea, no ice, please," Alex said. He looked at Lydia. "I have a work meeting to go over construction plans with a German bank that would soon be established in the island. I don't want to smell of booze."

"German? They'll come to the meeting after drinking a gallon of beer," Lydia said. "Their stink will overwhelm yours," she added while searching through her purse. She took out several items that looked to Alex like tickets of some kind. "Here you are. I'm giving you priority in choosing one or all before I offer them to someone else. Of course, I'd rather you'd take them all."

Lydia began pointing out what each of the five tickets was for. First she had one for a concert by the local symphony, then a second one for an exhibition baseball game between a local team and a minor league from one of the states. The third was for a charity fashion show, the fourth for a lecture on alternative medicine and acupuncture. Finally, the fifth ticket was for a wine tasting event at a restaurant that was reopening after a significant restoration.

"None is for the coming weekend, because that's a ski club practice date. I wanted to suggest that we ride together, your car or mine. We can save gas and simplify hotel arrangements. You tell me," Lydia said, her arms crossed over her chest, which Alex avoided looking at.

Alex looked through the tickets one by one. He started with the first one. Each time he refused one, he pushed it back toward Lydia. He had previous engagements each of those nights, several involving unavoidable work matters. The fashion show was the only one he rejected due to a real reason: he did not care for fashion shows, for charity or for profit.

"Well, then don't go complaining if I offer them to someone else. Or several others," Lydia said as she picked up the tickets to return them to her purse.

"Not to worry, Lydia. I won't be angry," Alex replied.

They spoke some more about subjects of no importance to either except about the weather, which would have crowned a misguided lunch date. When they were done with the main dish the server came back.

"Should I bring you the dessert menu?"

"No, just the check, please," Alex said before the server had a chance to utter the last syllable.

"We should have split it," Lydia said once the server had walked away. "After all, I invited you."

"Some other time," Alex replied.

"I'll call you later in the week," Lydia said when they were in the parking lot. "At work."

She didn't call Thursday. Alex did not find out whether she called Friday. He took the day off to take care of some matters that required a personal appearance, such as renewing his driver's license and picking up laundry.

The home phone rang. It was Saturday morning and the digital display on the alarm clock read 7:30.

"Hello?"

"Alex? This is Lydia."

He didn't quite know how to react at that specific moment.

"Are you there?" Lydia asked.

"Yes, pardon me, Lydia. How did you get my home phone number?" A thought flashed through his head that perhaps she had a friend at the telephone company.

"Your secretary gave it to me," Lydia replied unfazed.

"Then let me explain. I do not give anyone my home phone number. Don't take it personal," Alex said.

"It doesn't matter, Alex. I know how those things work," she replied. "Now we can talk when you're not at work. You have no reason for any concern. I'm not going to give it to anyone at the club. I'm calling to invite you somewhere."

Mixed up and simultaneously irritated with Marta's lack of discretion he stopped paying attention to what Lydia was saying.

"Let me check my calendar," he replied when Lydia asked him whether he was available. "I'm still in bed, so I'll have to check later.

"Well, then. And when will you be able to confirm?" Lydia asked unshaken.

"Give me a couple of hours and I will call you back," Alex said. He realized he had never asked her for her telephone number. "Where should I call you?"

He grabbed the ballpoint pen and the note pad on the nightstand to write down the number.

"I'll call you back in two hours... Good, then. Bye," he said and hung up. Then he tried in vain to remember Lydia's words referring to the invitation. He thought it was a baseball game the following Thursday night. Or perhaps it was a cocktail party Wednesday night. He opted for the baseball game on Thursday.

The telephone rang. The alarm clock's display was for 7:45. He lifted the receiver.

"Hello?"

"Did you look at your calendar yet?" Lydia asked.

"Lydia... I said I'd call you back in two... Okay, now it would be in an hour and 45 minutes," Alex said, now annoyed by the second interruption of his sleep, which, what the heck, he had not been able to go back to. Monday Marta would find out what he thought of secretaries who gave out his personal telephone number to anyone who asked for it. It was the first time in four years Marta had been indiscreet. He softened his stance toward Marta. Who knew that false information or claims Lydia had made to persuade Marta to tell her. Some people are like water drops that leak slowly from a faucet at night and rob us of sleep as they fall against a sink's bowl. Lydia was one of those, his drip. a relentless itch from a branch of poison oak he had not been able to identify before it was too late.

"I'm calling you because I have to know whether you are available in case I need to make other plans with another friend," Lydia said. Alex asked himself whether it would be the woodworker or the electrician or someone else in one of the trades she had not yet explored. Perhaps the plumber.

"I apologize, Lydia. Give me a moment," he said. He placed the receiver on the nightstand. He waited two minutes still lying down before picking it up again.

"I regret to tell you, Lydia. Thursday I'm not going to be free."

"Thursday? What about Thursday," the itchy drip asked.

"Didn't you say... something about Thursday?" Alex asked tentatively and doubtful. It was evident he had no clue what she had invited him to or when.

"Thursday may be a great day for something, but I'm not inviting you to something on Thursday. It's this afternoon."

"This afternoon?" Alex asked again. "And what is it?"

"What I told you when I called you a while back," Lydia replied. The tone was of impatient discomfort. "It's for a bugle and drum tournament at two."

"Lydia, I really am very sorry. I don't like bugle and drum bands. I doubt I would want to spend an afternoon listening to that racket," Alex told her, satisfied with the relief of being able to tell her at last something he had not made up.

"But what else could you have to spend your time on? You probably have never even attended a bugle and drum concert in your sorry life," was Lydia's reply.

After a brief pause Alex said, "I've never eaten manure, but I'm pretty sure I wouldn't want to swallow a ball of it. Besides, Saturday afternoons when we don't have ski practice I volunteer to play the piano at an old folks' home," Alex said, and was even happier that this was not a product of his imagination. "So you see, even if..."

"There's no accounting for taste, really, it's true," Lydia said. Her irritated disdain moistened her words with bile. "It's your choice. If you prefer to spend time with drooling demented old farts, it's your loss."

Alex paused as if to digest her words.

"Lydia, don't call me again. I'm not interested in drums or horns and much less in you."

He hung up. He had anticipated a difficult situation trying to end it with Lydia, and he'd end up feeling bad. On the contrary, he felt relieved. She wouldn't bother him again, or at least that was his prediction, nor would he have to make anything clear to her. She herself took care of solving his predicament. Of course, he would not return to club activities, to prevent any uncomfortable encounters. He could practice the sport somewhere closer free of clubs or derailing drunken stupors, without trips to the other end of the island. He'd only need to pay a boat pilot for the use of the vessel for half an hour whenever he wanted to put on the water skis again. If he were unable to practice the sport again, at any rate, it would be a low price he would pay for getting rid of that mosquito on two legs.

Alex felt movement next to him under the blanket.

"Who was that at this uncivil hour?" Esteban asked. It was surprising to Alex that he had not heard either conversation between Lydia and Alex. "I dreamed a bell was ringing far away, but it wasn't a dream, was it? Who was it?"

"I was ringing myself up," Alex said.

"What? What are you talking about?" Esteban asked, a single eye open and his brow knitted with confusion.

"Nothing. A very wrong number," Alex replied with complete serenity. He turned toward Esteban, lifted the blanket and slipping under it he pressed against Esteban's back, threw his arm over Esteban's chest and kissed him on the cheek. "Let's go on sleeping, maybe even dreaming."

MAN OF HIS DREAMS

The UPS man must have brought the box earlier in the day when Perry was at work. It was useless to throw the doormat over it. More than half of the package stuck out. Anyone walking by would have seen it and run away with it. No one did, and Perry could see why. Not only was it big, it was pretty heavy.

He hadn't ordered anything, not even from Amazon. He placed it on the kitchen table. No return address on the label? Then it couldn't have been the UPS man. Perry picked up the box and shook it. Maybe Sheila had started using better packaging. She and her husband Marvin had joined the Church of Latter Day Saints after they moved to Placerville, where he took a job with Pacific Sierra and she became a homemaker, taking care of their seven brats.

"I am a stay-at-home mom," she told Perry once over the phone. He laughed.

"You're just a woman who doesn't have to work, because her husband makes enough to live the middle-class life you always aspired to, Sheila."

They seldom talked, but every three months or so she would send a care package. She packed all the Campbell's soup, Vienna sausage and Spam cans with expired labels and sent them to him. Mormons were required to keep a pantry full of canned goods that they would need at Armageddon. They would be the only ones to survive and would need those ready-to-eat foods until things settled down. Expired labels had to be pulled and replaced with new items. Perry called Sheila the first time he got one of the packages.

"You people won't last until the Second Coming if you eat that crap. You'll all die of high blood pressure and cholesterol!" he mocked her. She ignored him. The packages kept arriving. This time, however, it had come earlier than he expected so he could carry them out to the trash can. Unknowingly Sheila and Marvin had joined forces with Pamalou Godfrey, his neighbor to the left. Every so often when Pamalou was outside pretending to trim down the shrubs and he was securing the pink flamingos someone took the time to knock down she would walk over and ask him "Have you accepted Jesus Christ as your savior yet?"

"You'll be the first to know as soon as that happens," Perry would reply. Pamalou would dismiss him with her limp hand and walk away.

Then there was his neighbor down the street, June Riece. Every month she would slip the latest *Watchtower* under his storm door. He sometimes felt as if under siege by people who wanted to pack superstitions down his narrow windpipe. Pamalou was a harmless nut job, Sheila was passive aggressive, sending him expired goods so they wouldn't go to waste, and June kept shoving the periodical under his door, but she stopped knocking after he posted a framed notice next to his front door, "Jehova's Witnesses: You are trespassing. I own firearms and use them to stand my ground if I feel threatened." He had added a skull and bones graphic.

Perry had never had a gun in his hands. Neither had he ever been a religious person: he considered all organized religion to be a scam based on fairy tales.

If those were Sheila's botulism-in-a-can gifts, he'd deal with them later. He picked up the box and left it on the living room floor.

Later that evening Perry was caught in that place where he was neither completely awake nor totally asleep when he opened his eyes, sure he had heard a noise. Nothing. Probably squirrels scurrying across the rooftop. He shut his eyes. That was no squirrel: the noise came from the living room. He rose and grabbed the baseball bat he kept by his dresser, the only protection he had, one that didn't require bullets or good aim in the dark. He turned on the light. He had reasoned that anyone who broke in would realize someone was in the house and flee. He heard the noise again. Should he lock his bedroom door and call 911? No, they'd laugh at him if it were just some critter banging on the door. He had heard opossums out there before.

He walked out to the hall, bat on high, and turned on the lights. He walked down the steps into the living room: it was dark except for the sliver of light that filtered through the drapes from the street lamp, but, even so, nothing seemed out of the ordinary. He turned on one of the living-room lamps. Everything was in its place. That box was in the same spot.

Perry went back to bed. Not two minutes later the sound he heard was louder than before. This time he went out without the baseball bat. As he stood in the threshold between the foyer and the living room the noise came to him loudly: it was coming from the box. Even Sheila wouldn't be stupid enough to put a live animal in a box. Now he wasn't sure that was even Sheila's box.

He walked up to the box and gave it a light kick. Nothing. It was time to open the box. He walked back to his bedroom and returned to the living room with the baseball bat in hand. He knelt by the box. The tape on the box was easy to peel off. He opened the flaps. He could not believe what he found: it was an egg bigger than his head—thrice as big, as a matter of fact—lavender and polka-dotted in purple spots. It didn't seem to do anything, so what had made the noise? It was too creepy to believe. What to do with it? Better leave it there for now. It was too dark outside and a downpour was tapping on the roof. In the morning he would trash it. How would he be able to find out who had left that for him?

Perry returned to bed. He locked his door, just in case. When he heard the noise again he looked at the alarm clock: he had slept for 28 minutes. This time it was a cracking noise, a louder version of the noise he made when he tapped an eggshell on the edge of the frying pan. He waited. He heard something like a sigh. A deep sigh. Now he really was scared.

"Who the hell is there?" he yelled from behind the bedroom door after making sure the security lock was in place. No answer, no sound. "I have a gun!" No reply. "You better leave while you can. I'm calling 911!" No sound. He thought he heard footsteps, but most likely it was his imagination. He started to sweat. His heart was threatening to pop out of his chest. He waited. Slowly, cautiously he turned the doorknob. He cracked the door, but placed a hand on it to make sure he would counterbalance any force coming from the other side. He swung the door a few centimeters toward him and placed his face against the opening so he could see a slice of the hall outside. No one. He walked out of the bedroom again with the baseball bat in his hand. He looked behind him. There was nothing back there. He turned on the hall light, looked back again. All he could see was his reflection in the bathroom cabinet mirror. He went down the steps and stood in the foyer in the dark.

Something was standing in the living room. He had no time to think. Before hitting that with the baseball bat he stretched out to the light switch. It shone into the living room. There stood a man, completely naked.

"Who are you?" Perry asked, frantic.

"Who do you want me to be?" the man replied. It was a peaceful voice. There was no rush in his voice, no breathlessness, no ill will.

"Don't play games with me!" Perry yelled. He raised the bat as if he were over home plate waiting for a pitch. "You are in my house in the middle of the night. I ask the questions, you answer before I call the police!"

"Who do you want me to be?" the man asked again.

"What are you doing here?" Perry asked, keeping the same stance.

"I will do whatever you want me to do," the man answered in an acquiescent tone, not a hint of sarcasm in his voice. Perry found it disarming and at the same time frightening.

"Where did you come from?" Perry asked impatiently.

"That I don't know, I only know my purpose and what I must do for you," the man said. He didn't sound anguished or in any way worried that he did not know what his origin was. "And I know I came out of my shell." Perry didn't think he meant to joke.

"How old are you?" Perry asked. He finally put the bat down, but did not let it go out of his hand.

"How old do you want me to be?" the man asked.

'Oh, stop the doubletalk. You are testing my patience. I need to know before I call the police," Perry said.

"Why would you call the police?" the man asked.

"Because you don't belong here, I don't know who you are, you sound crazy, you have no answers, geez, standing there naked, what else can I tell you? This is ridiculous!" Perry replied.

"I don't know who sent me here, I don't know how old I am, I don't know my name," the man replied. He stepped forward.

"Don't you move from where you are! Not another step!" Perry shouted and raised the baseball bat.

"As you wish. I am here to do anything at your pleasure," the man said. "There are things I know and things I don't know. Ask me whatever you want. If I don't know the answer I will tell you or ask you to help me answer it. My age, for instance. How old do you want me to be? Somehow I think 23 or 24, 25 tops. Am I wrong?"

"Why would I want you to be any age?" Perry asked. The bat went down again.

"Because I don't know how I know, but you have wanted me for a long time. Me or someone like me," the man said. His voice was mildly flat, never excited or totally dull—just so, but on the better side of sweet.

"How do you know that?" Perry asked. He lowered his voice. The man was endearing in his accuracy.

"I told you, I don't know how," the man replied. Then Perry focused on him. He was neither tall nor short, but rather just the right height. His skin was the color of light caramel, somewhat obscured in his chest by a shadow of hair. His green eyes were liquid pools that reflected the light from the lamp. The lustrous abundant hair that crowned his head was groomed to the back. His penis was neither compact nor monstrous: like his height, just the right size and propped on a full scrotum. The biceps and abdominal muscles were neither hardened by excessive exercise nor flaccid. Even his belly button seemed perfectly placed. And yes, he looked about 24, 25 tops.

"I'm confused," said Perry. "I really don't know what to do about this."

"Why don't you simply accept that I have been brought here to please you?" the man asked.

"Because this doesn't happen."

"Obviously it does. It has. To you, tonight," the man observed.

"Then what am I to do with you?" Perry asked.

"Whatever you wish," said the man with a smile that was neither too narrow nor too wide. His teeth were perfectly lined and white without looking bleached.

Perry's last relationship had ended almost five years before. He had gone into it without the illusion with which he had entered into such emotional entanglements in his optimistic youth. His partner then, Wendell, was not handsome, but he was about Perry's same age, worked in his own business and sounded sincere, all of which promised stability. "I couldn't cheat on you," Wendell said several times, "because I would not be able to live with myself." In less than three years he proved to be selfish and unreliable. At the end of five years Perry had also learned that Wendell had found a way to accommodate himself into a space of deceit: he had managed to live with himself.

Before Wendell there was Kevin, for three years. Kevin was not handsome: in fact, he was disproportionate in most of his physical features, measured six feet and three inches, three more than Perry; his rear end could have doubled as a cocktail table and his 300 pounds left his imprint wherever he sat. Kevin had been fooled by a married U.S. Army officer who led Kevin to believe he was single and had to travel to Tennessee every other weekend to supervise his business. The man didn't come home one day and, when Kevin called the base to inquire about his whereabouts, he learned the man had retired and had gone back to his family in Chattanooga. It made Kevin paranoid and suspicious. Perry got tired of imputations of infidelity and Kevin's sudden changes in mood. It was time to end that.

Before Kevin there was Tyndall Peacock Harris, a married man from Carrboro, North Carolina, who presided a polyamory club in Durham. He wanted Perry to come live with him, his wife and two children in a rural two-bedroom house built as a summer cabin. "Cyndi and I talk about you during sex. It enhances our orgasms," he told Perry. When it became evident to Perry that Cyndi wanted to join them in the hotel room that Perry had to pay for every other weekend to meet with Tyndall, a year and a half after their initial contact, it was time to sever ties with the couple.

His only long-term relationship that could be characterized as loving and monogamous had been with Ed Voigt. Seven years into their passionate and dedicated partnership Ed dropped dead at Perry's feet. He had a congenital heart defect that had taken his mother at an early age as well.

Before Ed were Tom, who cheated on his partner with Perry and made him believe he was married to a female; George was a mean drunk who would black out a couple of times a week and one day beat Perry up in a drunken rage; Jacob, a Baptist deacon who became enraged when Perry suggested he might be gay; Jerry, a bus driver who cheated on him with a fellow bus operator and made up conflicts just to break up with him and go live with Mr. Sylvester.

Perry had become accustomed to the idea that he would never find love again and, in a sense, he was right: at least not what he had experienced with Ed. He also got used to men who didn't measure up, but he had to admit that he didn't love them. He just respected them in the measure that they deserved respect, stuck to his promise of monogamy, felt affection for them and was attracted enough to allow for sexual excitement. Love, however, of the kind that makes one believe no one else would do nor with whom a person would be as happy, so fulfilling and passionate that the world could collapse and one would not notice? That had not made a comeback. He resigned himself to the notion that it never would. His memory of Ed and the joy they had known consoled him.

Nonetheless, Perry was not blind to his own short-comings. He tried to put himself in the shoes of the men with whom he had been involved and sometimes even justified their conduct. At least for some of those men his inability to view the world as a place where a gay man could live comfortably became a major obstacle.

And here was this man, who looked like the model of perfection. Physically, for one, but that willingness to please was unusual and seductive despite his complete ignorance of his origin. Thoughts of the danger this stranger represented surfaced in his labyrinthine mind. He dismissed them. This was the weirdest that had ever happened to him. Even though he had just turned 46, an acquaintance had recently referred to him as "soon-to-be ex-young." Perhaps the time was ripe for adventure and letting go.

"I assume whoever sent you here knows I like men," Perry said.

"It's imprinted in my brain. I surmise I wouldn't be here if you didn't," the man said.

"Can you tell me whether you have been tested for any... Any sexually-transmitted disease?" Perry asked, but as soon as he had asked the question he realized it was probably unlikely. This man had just hatched and sprung to life like the real-life version of a perfect inflatable doll.

"I'm spanking new," the man said. Somehow Perry knew the man was not attempting a funny line.

"Do you need sleep?" Perry asked. "I mean, I really don't know whether you're human, artificial, a hologram... What?"

"I'm as human as you want me to be," the man replied.

"I'm not into mannequins. I'd rather you're human," Perry replied.

"You got it," said the man.

As strange as the idea seemed initially, Perry asked the man to share his bed for the night. His bed was so big he called it a tennis court. Nothing was going to happen, not even touching by mistake, he asserted to the man. While it was true that the man could try to kill him in his sleep, he could protect himself against that. If, on the other hand, the man were left elsewhere in the house, he could sack it and then even set it on fire with Perry in it.

"Do you want me to cook?" the man asked. Perry was caught off guard. At his silence the man asked, "What do you want for breakfast?"

"You cook?"

"I told you. I will do everything you need me to do," the man replied. This had become awkward beyond Perry's grasp. He told the man what to prepare. When he got up in the morning the man was not by his side. He came downstairs. Breakfast was served. Coffee was in the pot. The man was standing by the refrigerator. Perry looked at the food on the table, looked back at the man, then sat down and started to eat.

"Have you eaten?" Perry asked him after noticing that no place had been set on the opposite side of the kitchen table.

"Do you want me to?" the man asked.

"Oh, look, you need to stop this business of doing what I want you to. If you need to eat, you eat," Perry said somewhat upset.

"Please don't be mad at me, I can only do what you want me to do. My will is controlled by your desire," he stated without raising his voice.

"Okay, I'll do that. In the meantime, two things we need to do. You need to wear clothes. I can't have you walking around the house buck naked like this," Perry said. "Second, you need a name I can call you by. What name do you prefer?"

"You have to give me the name you want to call me," the man answered.

"Okay," Perry said. He started buttering his toast, which was just the way he liked it, not too dark, not too light. He paused before putting the fork with the perfectly fried piece of egg in his mouth. "Dean. I'll call you Dean. What about a last name?" he asked, and the man looked at him again, saying nothing. "Oh, okay, that's up to me too. Okay, okay. Clyde. Dean Clyde. What do you think?

"If that's what you wish, Dean Clyde it is," Dean Clyde answered.

"You don't have a say in this?" Perry asked. "I mean, it's what you are going to be called, not me."

"I like it fine." Dean said. "What do I call you?"

"Honey," Perry said, then thought about it. "That was a joke."

"If you want me to call you Honey, I will call you that," Dean replied.

"No, it was a joke! Don't call me honey. I'm Perry. Perry Simpson. You only need to call me Perry. Please, sit down to eat."

And Dean ate.

For the time being Dean wore some of Perry's clothes. Perry ordered a bedroom suite for Dean: however this was going to work, he couldn't have guests know that the two were sleeping together. Gay friends wouldn't care and would actually assume they were. Perry, however, had none of those friends. The second bedroom, the one without any furniture in it until now, would be Dean's room.

Perry measured Dean for clothes: he and Dean were the same size. He went to several department stores and picked up what he thought Dean would need for now. Shoes would come later: Dean would wear flip-flops to the store and try on shoes. Later they both had time to shop for additional clothes, which, as expected, Perry paid for.

"Do you wear pajamas?" Perry asked Dean when they were getting ready for bed the night of the day following Dean's hatching.

"Do you want me to wear them?" Dean asked.

"Oh, Jesus," said Perry. "I don't think I'm ever going to get used to this lack of will." He thought about it. "Don't wear any."

After a few minutes Perry realized it was the first time he had shared a bed with someone for purposes other than sleeping, as he had now planned, in five years. His body started aching, what he called his arousal. Was he supposed to initiate something? Did he have to wait for Dean to make the first move? Dean was just lying there with his arms folded over his chest. If he had to give him a name and tell him what to wear, everything else most likely would have to operate in the same fashion.

"What do you enjoy doing," Perry asked, still lying on his back.

"I will enjoy everything you enjoy," Dean replied. Perry turned on his side.

"And how will you know?" Perry asked.

"I will learn from you and follow your lead," Dean said after turning on his side to face Perry.

They had talked enough. Perry reached for Dean and kissed him lightly first, then pulled away some and returned to Dean's mouth. Dean had not lied—not that lying could have been programmed in his brain. Perry felt as if he had known this man for years and that Dean knew exactly what to do to excite him, to satisfy his every whim and desire. All it took was a silent order for Dean to turn whichever way Perry wanted and to reciprocate when necessary. They were at it for a long time, took a rest and soon afterwards Perry started it up again.

"I want you to tell me that you like what we are doing," Perry whispered.

"I like what we are doing," Dean said.

"No, when we're doing it," Perry replied. "I want you to show me how much, too."

"Haven't I shown you, Perry?" Dean asked. "I'm sorry."

"No, no, nothing to apologize for. You have shown me fine. I want to make sure you don't forget that in the future," Perry said.

It was a work day. The sun had already risen some in the horizon when they finally went to sleep. Dean lay quietly, wrapped in Perry's arms. Snoring did not seem to bother Dean, whose breathing was soothing to Perry.

Before leaving for work Perry would tell Dean what needed to be done around the house. They shopped for groceries together. Dean had Perry explain to him how he liked his food cooked; he seemed to have a native understanding of how appliances big and small worked. Everything was perfect. It may not have been so for others, but everything was exactly as Perry wanted it. The yard had never looked better. Perry had shown Dean how to trim and fertilize the bushes, and it seemed Dean was blessed with the greenest thumb Perry had ever known. The tools were all where they were supposed to be. The terrace was spotless. Even the tool shed had a new coat of paint, as did the privacy fence around the sides and back of the house.

One night at the movies Perry ran into a colleague at the accounting firm. He introduced Dean as a cousin.

"A cousin? On what side?" the colleague asked. Perry had forgotten that this man knew him from the old neighborhood and was familiar with Perry's extended family.

"Oh, not really a cousin. More like a second cousin. I don't think you ever knew them," Perry said.

After they walked away Dean asked Perry "Why did you lie?"

"Sometimes you have to do that," Perry said. "People wouldn't understand."

"Because I arrived from nowhere?"

"Well, yes, that," Perry replied. "That and what we do together."

"What's wrong with that? Don't you enjoy it? Are you ashamed of me?" Dean asked.

"Oh, no I enjoy it a lot, Dean. A whole lot!" Perry replied. "I could never be ashamed of you, never. It's just that sometimes people misinterpret."

"Misinterpret? You mean they interpret correctly, but you'd be more comfortable if they interpreted incorrectly," Dean said.

"I guess. I think I know what you mean," Perry said. "Look, let's not worry about it now."

The house looked splendid. Perry had Dean paint the bedrooms a lovely peach hue that he had read was relaxing and conducive to lovemaking. He then realized that he didn't have to seduce Dean, didn't have to persuade him or wait for him to get in the mood. Dean's mood depended on his.

On a Sunday afternoon a woman stopped by unannounced. Dean opened the door. Peggy was confused.

"Who are you? she asked Dean.

"I'm Perry's cousin. Not really a cousin, more like a second cousin. I don't think you knew them," Dean said.

"On what side?"

"I'm not sure," Dean said. He had not thought about it that far. He was simply following Perry's line of thought.

"I don't know you," Peggy said at the threshold of the front door. "I'm Perry's sister Peggy. I would know if you were a cousin, trust me." She stretched her neck to look behind Dean. He still stood there with an apron on. "Where is Perry?"

"I'll call him for you," Dean said, and tried to shut the door to leave Peggy standing outside.

"Oh, no," she said. "I'm coming in." She pushed the door and crossed the foyer to make her way into the living room.

Perry was in the basement setting a mouse trap when Dean called him. "Your sister is here."

Peggy was still standing, arms crossed, in the living room when Perry walked in to greet her.

"Who is this man?" Peggy asked.

"He started working at the firm a few weeks ago. He's staying with me until he finds an apartment. I may rent him a room. I'm not sure yet" Perry replied.

"He says he's our second cousin. Whose son is he?" Peggy asked.

"He said that? What a joker!" Perry said laughing. "No, that's just the way he is. Don't worry about him."

Dean was in the kitchen making popovers when Peggy left.

"Next time somebody asks you who you are, just ask them if it's me they're looking for," Perry said. "Don't just repeat what I said before. It may not be... right."

"You mean we have to tell a different lie?" Dean asked.

"I don't think you understand," Perry said. "Look, don't worry about it. Just go along with it. I know why I'm doing it."

Every night they would reprise the sex. Every night Dean did exactly what Perry wanted. Every night they came back for seconds, for thirds on weekends.

Mr. Kasprick across the street walked over one Saturday afternoon when both Perry and Dean were working on the lawn.

"Well, Mr. Simpson, how have you been?" Mr. Kasprick asked. "I haven't seen you working outside for a while. I do see this young man out here a lot, though."

"You have? Well, of course you have, haven't you? Perry asked. He turned toward Dean. "Come here, Dean. I want you to meet someone. This is Mr. Kasprick, our neighbor across the street."

Dean shook Mr. Kasprick's hand without saying anything.

"Pleased to meet you, young man," Mr. Kasprick said. "And who might you be?"

Dean said nothing. He turned toward Perry.

"Oh, I'm sorry. His name is Dean. Dean Clyde, yes. Dean is staying with me for a while. We've known each other for years. From college," Perry said.

"Oh, my!" Mr. Kasprick said. "He sure has taken good care of himself. He looks about twenty years younger than you!"

"Yes, doesn't he? He's got better genes, I guess," Perry said. He laughed. Dean smiled, not too broad, not too tight, both of his hands holding his garden shears.

As Mr. Kasprick walked away Perry told Dean "Why didn't you talk to him?"

"You told me not to before," Dean said. "I want to wait to hear what you are going to say about me before I say anything. I don't want to get you in trouble."

"Okay, okay, don't worry about it," Perry said. They went back to spreading fertilizer on the lawn.

Every night, occasionally during the day, they made love at least once, most often twice, more often Friday and Saturday night. It started to feel to Perry as if they were starring in porn flicks whose script never changed. Even the restful sleep afterwards, sometimes when dawn was already breaking, was like being stuck in time, rehearsed. Still it was arousing and helped him make up for lost time, all those years of carnal fasting.

They were at Whole Foods a Sunday afternoon when a senior partner at the accounting firm surprised them around an aisle corner.

"Perry, fancy meeting you here!" said Mr. Graham with his characteristic jolly demeanor that sounded forced, a vocal mask for his tedious self.

"Mr. Graham! What a surprise! What are you doing here? Where's Mrs. Graham?" Perry asked. He placed himself right behind the cart handle, hoping to leave Dean behind him where Mr. Graham wouldn't see him. It was too late.

"Janet is over at the seafood counter," said Mr. Graham. "And who might this be here?" He took a few steps toward Dean, who neither smiled nor frowned.

"This is... uhr... my butler," Perry said.

"Your butler? Wow, Perry, we're paying you too much!" Mr. Graham said, laughing.

"Well, not really my butler, Mr. Graham. You see... He came here from Austria..."

"Osterreich! I had no idea they had such complexions in Austria!" joked Mr. Graham. "I've been to Austria, but I have never seen anyone who looks like this."

Again Mr. Graham choked in his own laughter and had to stop to cough and clear his throat.

"Well, not really from Austria. He lived there temporarily. He's actually from the West Indies, you see," Perry explained. "He's only been here a few months. Still doesn't speak English. He works for me doing yard work and cleaning the house until he can get himself established."

"Where in the West Indies?" Mr. Graham addressed Dean. "*Habla español? Parlez-vous français? Spreek je Nederlands?*" Mr. Graham inquired.

"He's deaf, Mr. Graham," Perry explained. "That's why he's had trouble settling down and why I'm helping him."

"Wow! You know, my brother was deaf. We had to learn sign language. I know from deafness. You sign?" Mr. Graham asked. "I mean, do you sign in an international sign system?"

"No, Mr. Graham. We manage. It's difficult, but somehow we get through to each other."

"Well done! You have a very kind heart, Perry," Mr. Graham said. "I didn't know that about you!"

On the way to the parking lot Dean asked Perry "Why do you make up a different story each time we run into someone?"

"Because, Dean, because you are difficult to explain anyway. What am I supposed to do, tell people you arrived in an egg?" Perry asked, visibly disturbed.

"Why don't you just tell them I'm your partner?" Dean asked.

"Because that's no one's business," Perry said. He started dropping grocery bags in the trunk. A jar of olives hit the rim of the spare tire. "Oh, shit, now I have broken glass and olive juice in the trunk."

"I can clean it when we get home if that is something you want me to do," Dean said.

"I want you to shut up, that's what I want," Perry yelled. "Let it stink of olive juice! Don't worry about it."

That night Perry wasn't sure he wanted to have sex. Dean was lying next to him. *He's just waiting for me to make the first move. The hell with it. I'm not that needy of affection*, he thought.

He couldn't sleep. Watching Dean sleep quietly with that breathing that evinced his innocence just irritated him. It also aroused him. He turned toward Dean. "Are you awake?"

As if activated by a mechanism Dean immediately replied, "I am always awake for you."

"Good," Perry said. He slid over and kissed Dean just like the first time, just like every time after that, without variation. He could swear that Dean's lips moved in the same direction each time, involuntarily shifting his tongue so that Perry's mouth always ended up doing the same thing. It was everything Perry had always wanted in a sex partner with none of the complications of emotional distress, the infidelity, the accommodating to someone else's needs and schedule, the demands of holidays and expectations that eventually took their toll on a relationship, in particular when the passion had dwindled and what remained was the hollow commitment, when eyes started roving and the mind wandered toward thoughts of what else could be out there that was better than what he had beside him. This was devoid of all that, of all the weaknesses of the flesh and the frailties of humanity. He had the perfect lover, the perfect housekeeper, the perfect cook, the perfect gardener, all trained according to his wishes, his preferences, his desire. Nothing out of place, nothing outside the frame of his mental painting of the flawless life.

Every night they had sex the same way, in the same sequence, a recording of the night before and the night before that, everything exactly the way he had wanted it, the way his fantasy demanded with the frequency his body required or allowed, someone he did not have to share, someone who didn't have to go home after an orgasm, someone who wasn't after him for his house or his money, someone who wasn't just bending over in a video booth for him to climax in his rectum, someone who wasn't just collecting objects of desire of which he was but a sample. What was wrong with perfection?

It was worse than being married to a woman, he realized. Perfection engendered monotony. No surprises, no divergence. Perfection, he concluded, is the petri dish of tedium, growing like a bacterium in the medium of sameness and flawlessness.

Perry grew tired of Dean. His very presence turned into a source of resentment, of inexplicable rancor. Even the smell of Dean's armpits was just perfect: not repulsive or perfumed, simply a blend of masculine aromas that aroused Perry without having to overlook rankness. Even that started irritating him. He would wake up to a kiss from Dean, a gesture that tasted of humanity without eliciting revulsion. That, too, began to perturb him, especially when Dean did not make a face at his breath.

Still every night they went to bed at the same time to do the same things, variation banished from their territory. Perry didn't want to suggest changes: it would be a betrayal of his own sexual ideal, in spite of the abominable predictability.

On a Monday night after a session of cookie-cutter sex Perry lay awake while Dean slept peacefully, his breathing now a light, annoying aspiration he could not bear to hear.

"Wake up! You're making a noise. It's keeping me up!" he yelled and pushed Dean to the edge of the bed.

"Would you like me to go to my bedroom?" Dean asked without any signs of consternation over Perry's rejection.

"No, I want you to stop that noise," Perry said.

"What noise?" Dean asked just as calm as before. That irritated Perry. No matter what the situation, Dean always had the same tone of tranquility that evinced his unnatural origin, regardless of his human appearance.

"That breathing noise," said Perry. Dean was perplexed. The only times he had been confused about Perry's actions were the occasions when he made up stories. This was different; this was a request that mystified him.

"I'd have to stop breathing," Dean said.

"Can't you do that? Stop breathing, I mean? If you came here curled up in an egg, surely you can control your breathing," Perry said even more nettled.

"I can't suspend my breathing. You wanted me to be human. You wanted me to be a human who would do everything you wanted the way you wanted. Have I disappointed you? Have I done anything wrong? Do you want me to do something differently?" Dean asked, turned toward Perry.

"Stop playing the victim! Even that you do perfectly! I can't stand this!"

"What would you want me to do, Perry?" Dean asked.

"I want you to go away, that's what I want!" Perry said, now on his knees and towering over Dean on the mattress.

"Where would I go?"

"I don't know! I don't care! Anywhere," Perry yelled. "Go be perfect elsewhere. You've made me yearn for all the men I loathed until I met you!"

"The only thing I can't do is leave, Perry. Staying by you is wired into my brain. I was sent to you. For you. You craved for someone made in your image to please you in every way. That's what I do."

"This is my house! You are an intruder. You are nothing more than a trick who overstayed his visit. Now you need to get the hell out of my life!" Perry screamed as if he had to make his point to someone a mile away.

"I won't leave," Dean said the same as if he were saying the sky was blue: it is what everyone expects it to be, no one is astonished by it.

"You will leave one way or the other. I can't take this anymore, I can't!" Perry shouted again. He jumped on Dean. Dean remained in his place without any attempt to throw Perry off him as Perry wrapped his hands around Dean's neck and squeezed as hard as he possibly could. "If you don't leave, you'll end up buried in the backyard, you miserable bastard!"

Dean stared into Perry's eyes without a blink. As if he weren't able to feel the pressure from Perry's hands, he said in a tone of voice not loud, not whispered, "I'm not leaving. You need me. That's why I'm here. Ask me for anything, but don't ask me to leave. I can't do that. It's not in my nature."

"What damned nature? You're a freak!" Perry yelled, still squeezing a neck that felt like rubber devoid of bones. "You won't leave, then you'll die!"

"I'm not leaving. I'll be here with you until the day you die, Perry," Dean said, his eyes still fixed on Perry's. "You can die when fate dictates or you can kill yourself, but I'll be here until that happens." There was no rush in his voice, no breathlessness, no ill will. It was the weather report.

Perry's hands squeezed Dean's neck until it shrank into a bundle of skin in his fist. Dean's emerald eyes continued to stare into Perry's. Dean smiled. It wasn't a broad smile, it wasn't a light one. It was just perfect.

THE HUMAN BEASTS

When they saw him approaching, they knew it was not going to be pleasant. Gloom fell on several in the neighborhood, but most of all on whomever expected and feared his visit, always untimely. To hear, "There comes Edgar!" needed no explanation. He was the boogeyman, the squeezing hand, the headless horseman, a fallen angel, evil made flesh and dwelling amongst them.

"Is your old man home?"

At those words alone, accompanied by his vertical tick of the head toward the inside of the house was like seeing the grim reaper coming for the soul of the unfortunate man, sometimes a woman. Rarely, perhaps never, was it an omen of kindness.

His mere presence was menacing. He was 1,94 meters tall and had to weigh some 96 kg. He wore round-tip black shoes like a prison guard's. He had a bouncer's shoulders and wore untucked black shirts. A tailor had to alter his pants to fit a .357 Magnum he carried in the right front pocket. Some claimed they had seen a prodigious bulge in his crotch, but it was likely to be the gun's butt. In any case, his own brother, an electrician with the state power company, encouraged the urban legend's propagation. When someone dared ask Edgar what that was he would say, "Come and grab it before I stick it up there where you'd like it."

Between half-truths, exaggerations and reality Edgar had become larger than life, a myth that Edgar never attempted to dispel.

"Don Lolo, how are you?"

"I? I am well. How about you?"

That was how the misfortunes of many usually started.

Don Lolo sat in a chair upholstered with dark brown Pantasote of the kind typical of cheap reception halls and roadside pubs. The seat was less wide than his thighs and buttocks, that hung over the edges like misshapen decorative fringes. He kept his cane on the floor, both hands on the handle.

"I was thinking that maybe you could do me a small favor, if it's not too much of a bother."

"Tell me what it's about," was the common reply. When he said that he raised a hand to turn down the front brim of his Panama hat. This cast a shadow over his eyes and made it difficult for the other person to read his thoughts. His eyes were already hidden behind prescription dark glasses. The person talking to him could not tell whether Don Lolo was looking at him. Whether he was completely bald was impossible to determine: a band of curly gray hair went around his head under the hat.

Instead of looking at the petitioner he kept his head turned toward the pool tables, always in use by someone striking balls.

"See here. I am in a bind."

"Really now? And is it binding you tight?" Don Lolo would ask mockingly. Whoever heard him often mistook his comments for empathy.

Don Lolo always sat in the same corner. No one else ever dared sit back there. No sign was necessary to point out the space was reserved for Don Lolo. The green-shaded pool lights hardly reached his corner. For years, maybe since Chucho Hernández first opened the pool hall, no one had cleaned out the webs that spiders wove from one ceiling beam to another and hung above patrons like clusters of delicate lace. The navy-blue wall behind Don Lolo looked as if the color were about to fade. It was not the intention of whomever had coated the wall in days immemorial: it was the effect of a patina of dust that also covered the other three walls, painted in a pale yellow. A greenish mold filled the crevice between the wall behind Don Lolo and the molding that divided it horizontally into two sections. On a shelf on the upper half of the intersection of two walls, a few meters from where Don Lolo sat, a fan without a grill turned slowly without alleviating the mugginess, similar to that of a grotto with a narrow entry.

"You see, I have to pay for my daughter's tuition at Puerto Rico Junior College. It's turned to be more than I anticipated, you know, and I'm like a wet chicken in a downpour."

"Oh, yes? And how much do you need for the umbrella?"

The jukebox played a ballad by a country music singer. The machine was only turned off when there was visitation at the funeral home across the street. Otherwise, it was a medley concert. It had been rigged to play without anyone depositing coins into it.

At the bar counter a minor truant sold beer and rum shots in paper cones. Don Lolo never drank: it clouded understanding. He needed his mind clear to record the details of each transaction. When the needy left he wrote them down in a small notebook he kept in one of the lower pockets of his Cuban *guayabera* shirt. When he was done memorializing the terms of the agreement he put back the pencil between his ear and the side of his head.

"My girl's grades were not good enough to be admitted at the state university. Still, she's smart, a hard worker."

"Look there, that's wonderful! Yes, the state university would have been a lot cheaper, right?"

"Yes, that's true, but if it can't be, well, you know, it is what it is."

The jukebox was playing "Orgasm," a Cuban woman by the name of Blanca Rosa Gil's signature song.

"You still live over there by Bernabé Carrión?"

"Yes, yes, right behind Yeyito Cay's butcher shop."

"Sure, there, around the corner from Don Pancho Franqui's tobacco factory, ah?"

"You're right, Don Lolo. You know where that is."

"That house, is it yours?"

"Mom and Dad left it to me. It's paid for."

"And that cute little car I saw you get out of, is it yours?"

"And yours if you need it, Don Lolo. It's old, but it chugs along."

"Your wife... What's her name?"

"Margarita."

"Ah, yes. Related to the Hernández from El Mamey, out in the country."

"She's Don Colás' daughter."

"And you have more children?"

"A boy."

"Younger than the one who's going to that expensive college?"

"Yes, Don Lolo. Younger."

"And when it's his turn to go to college, are you going to have enough for his tuition?"

"Well... We'll see. You have to get to that edge before jumping off the cliff, don't you?"

"Are you still working at the thermometer factory?"

"Yes, I've been there... Let me see... Fifteen years now. Almost sixteen.

"Oh, yeah? Look at that... And Margo, is she working?"

"She used to. She's got a bad leg. Phlebitis, doctor Collazo says. She can't be on her feet too long right now, but when she gets better she'll go back. She was working at the tannery, but, well, until she improves...

"Uh... So tell me, how much do you think the damage is going to be?"

"Well, as I see it, to get everything together... She's going to commute, you know? So for room and board I won't need any, but for transportation and lunch she'll need money. And for books. I'd say a thousand."

"Are you sure?"

"Well, that's what I calculated. What do you think, Don Lolo?"

"My girls, one went to college in Madrid and the other in Illinois. I don't know how much the Puerto Rico Junior College would cost."

"Then... Throw in $500 more."

"To repay when?"

"I leave that up to you, Don Lolo. You tell me."

"If your girl does well her first year she's going to need $1500 more the following year. You better take just a year to pay back."

"Let's see. That would be... how much?"

"For a year, 1500 bucks... At 25%... That would be $1875 at $156.25 a month."

"Dang, Don Lolo. That's a little steep."

"Did you try a bank?"

"Yes..."

"So why don't you get them to lend you the money? Or did they turn you down already?"

"They said... Well... They said I wouldn't have enough to pay with. That other lending place,

00

CommoLoco, they said the same thing. They talked about *colotral* and unsecured and a whole bunch of other stuff, and they said I'd have to renew it in a year."

"You see? More or less what I told you, that in a year you'd be back to renew it. You think about it and let me know."

In the jukebox José Feliciano was reminding some ingrate she couldn't come back home after leaving him and their child for another man, "It's a Little Too Late." One of the pool players was humming it.

"Ah, Don Lolo! I don't have to think about it. I'll do whatever I need to, but my little girl won't go without college. It's a deal."

Two neighbors gossiping in front of a house saw Edgar's car climb up the hill behind Yeyito Cay's butcher shop.

"May he strike elsewhere and stay away from us," one said, making the sign of the cross.

"Who's he going to mortify?" the other one asked when Edgar's armored tank of a black Lincoln Continental approached them. "You think your husband may have agreed to something with Don Lolo?"

"*Ay, mija*, don't you even joke about it!"

Edgar got out of the car, a much bigger car than the powder-blue Toyota he had been driving and in which he barely fit.

He knocked on the door of the one-story wood-frame building. The front door would open into a cement step on the sidewalk. No one came to the door. He punched the shut slat window next to the door, but no one answered. He thought it was strange for everything to be shut: it was already the end of May and a premature infernal heat had even his eyelids bathed in sweat. He walked to the alley between the house and Yeyito Cay's butcher shop. In the bare clay backyard he found a skinny barefoot boy who had climbed to the lowest branch of a breadfruit tree; he held a rooster in his hands. Behind the tree he saw a shed that he assumed was the outhouse. Edgar had grown up just downhill in the same neighborhood, but the city had installed sewer and tap water services down there. Up the unpaved road all houses had such sheds.

Edgar made a visor with his hand to shield his eyes from the sun and looked up at the treetop. It was 4:00 in the afternoon. Not a cloud covered the sky.

"Is your old man in?" he asked, followed by his characteristic movement of the head, which could be either a greeting or an inquiry.

The boy fixed his eyes on Edgar, but didn't answer.

"Did you hear me? Is your old man home?"

"Who wants to know?" a female voice asked from inside the house, on the other side of Persian window slats where the kitchen should be. Under the window grew huge elephant ear plants, probably fertilized by the phosphates from dishwashing water pouring out of a pipe hanging over the ground with no connection to anything.

"I am," Edgar said without telling her his name, sure that the woman would know who he was.

"He's at work."

"What time does he get home?" Edgar asked, his hand withdrawn from his forehead.

"Around six."

"Then tell him I was here and that I have a small matter I need to discuss with him."

"Alright," the woman said. She turned the window handle and shut the slats.

Edgar had worked as a laboratory assistant at the Eastern Sugar mill in town. The first thing that angered him was all the orders he had to take. He was as allergic to being pushed around as an asthma patient to pollen. Then there was the unbearable smell of rotten bagasse surrounding the plant. It was a pestilence like fermented cheese mixed in with toe jam. When the wind blew from the northwest, usually in the evening, that side of town became saturated with the stench. He could not understand how the families of the mill's administrators, the sugar-cane field foremen and the rest of the settlers annexed to the mill's land could stand the odor. They claimed they no longer noticed it. Perhaps smelling that all day long fatigued their sense of smell. His, however, was still very active.

The third issue that repelled Edgar about the job was the little it paid for all he had to do. He didn't have to run any tests: that was what the licensed chemists did; he was more of an errand boy between the lab's sections. He was given the hundredths he needed to reach a passing grade-point average for high-school graduation. That was not the result of getting in the good graces of his high-school counselor. The school principal could not bear the idea of having him around for another year, getting into fist fights with classmates and challenging teachers. He did not stand out in any academic subject except arithmetic: for high school he needed algebra and geometry, neither of which he liked. He failed to see their usefulness for earning good money after graduation. At the mill he decided there had to be an easier way to make lots of money, although his former teachers were surprised he could have been hired anywhere other than as a sugar-cane cutter. The more time he spent in the lab the fewer opportunities he would have to make a lucrative future for himself.

He quit. He spent his days in a rocker in the front porch, a leg over an armrest, looking across the street, where Wilfredo lived. Freddy was a tall, slender blond man with bedroom green eyes, married to Tatin, a drunken bitch who treated him like dirt. When Edgar was rocking back and forth Freddy would often come out to hose down the sidewalk, one hand stuck in a back pocket where his fingers rubbed his butt when he had his back to Edgar. Once in a while he would smile toward Edgar, who waved back and wouldn't miss a step Freddy took.

Edgar lived with the unfaltering hope that some day Freddy would tire of Tatin's abuse and ask Edgar to take him in. He would gladly do so. They'd have to share a bed, though.

No one at home disparaged him for his lack of employment. Sometimes he would walk with his mother to the Adventist church on the other side of town. His sister Tere taught math in the local high school; her salary was enough to support, Edgar, their mother and her stepfather, a drunk pervert who wore eyeglasses thin as Coca-Cola bottoms. Whatever else they still needed for their expenses was covered by their electrician brother Pinto, famous for keeping his wife on the straight and narrow with punches to her face, and Falle, another brother who had moved to Manhattan. They also received occasional contributions from two stepsisters, Luz and Gloria, who took some of what they made in a shoe factory in Brooklyn to help the family back home.

"Don't you have a job?" Don Lolo asked him one afternoon when Edgar was playing pool where Don Lolo kept his unofficial office.

"Naw," Edgar replied after striking the seven ball and dropping it in a corner pocket. It was exactly where he had predicted it would go. He addressed his pool partner, "This is all a matter of patience and chalk, bud."

"And how do you support yourself?" Don Lolo inquired.

The other player failed in his attempt to drop the six ball on a repeated angle in the center left pocket. Not even by a fluke was he able to get the carom shot as he should have. It was Edgar's turn again.

"I manage," Edgar replied to Don Lolo and struck the eight ball to roll it into the pocket he had called.

"Come here when you're done. I'd like to talk with you," Don Lolo said.

Edgar collected his five dollars from the losing player. He went to the bar to pick up the Rheingold bottle he had left on the counter, and went back to sit in Don Lolo's penumbra.

The loan shark started by praising Edgar's body: tall, robust, barrel-chested, with big hands and an intimidating presence. His arms? Not even Popeye. It was a shame to waste all that testosterone. Wouldn't Edgar be interested in putting all those attributes to work for him?

"Doing what?" Edgar asked. He sipped from the Rheingold bottle.

It was a matter of collecting from his debtors, who occasionally swallowed more than they had room for and then wouldn't pay as agreed. Sometimes they had to be scared into paying, a sort of reminder like the ones banks send out when the debtor missed a payment date, but not in written form, because letters just ended up in the trash bin. When debtors evaded their obligation a week after the due date, then it was necessary to sweep their faces a bit if they were men and, in the case of women, shake them two or three times and shout at them in public to shame them in front of their neighbors and friends. The interior of churches was an exception, but not their front yards or porticos.

The law did not see Don Lolo's kind of business with much consideration. They called that usury, a very ugly word to label what he did. He provided a service, of course. He helped those to whom banks denied credit, and that was worth a great deal. Instead of vilifying him and calling him bad names they should have paid him tribute and given him an honorary post in city hall. It was necessary to keep his eyes open and look after himself, because no one else would look after you: me first, me second and, finally, me last. The world is teeming with ingrates.

But no, the world would not see it the way he did. Bureaucratic shysters objected because the interest rate he charged was higher than what the law allowed. They said he was exploiting the vulnerable. And between them here, what really bothered them was that he didn't pay income taxes—now, that was the real issue.

"The risk is mine, understand? This is how I earn a living. If they can't pay or just don't want to, because some are nothing but deadbeats even when they have money to pay with and go spend their money on crap they don't need, well, then I have to protect my interest, don't you think?"

"Sure, yeah, I get it. You want me to go do what you don't have the *cojones* to do."

Don Lolo's expression changed.

"Shit, man, don't get fresh," he said. "More respect. That's not the fucking point."

It was not a matter of not daring to collect. The problem was that while he was out collecting he wouldn't be available for clients to look him up to pay on time or request another little loan, *otro prestamito*. He had had an assistant who collected from the feckless, but he had gone to New York.

"He eloped with the wife of one of the guys who owed me, the son of a bitch. He collected the debt all right. The fucker bought the plane tickets with that same money and took the guy's wife with him, a whore of a bitch. Her husband borrowed from me to buy her expensive jewelry and clothes. That's life for you, a boxful of surprises. And all of them smeared in shit."

"When do you want me to give you my decision?" Edgar asked.

"Well... Think about it. You know where to find me."

"No, what the hell, I don't have to think it over. Tell me when you want me to start."

"Hold it, now. We have to talk about money first," Don Lolo said. "Keeping straight accounts is the best way to keep your friends, as my departed wife used to say, may God have her in his holy bosom."

Don Lolo would pay him minimum wage, payable every Friday regardless of whether work was heavy or light. For every payment Edgar collected Don Lolo would give him 10%. Sometimes collections of cash could not be made. In such cases they would make arrangements to get back Don Lolo's investment: the title to a house, land or a car and even a boat, for which Don Lolo would give Edgar 15% of the value of the seized property. Otherwise, when possible, depending, of course, Edgar could have one of the units he took. Some people didn't have a pot to piss in. Then he would have to clean out their house or business, including the enema bag. If it were a furniture business Edgar would take pieces whose value amounted to what was owed; the same if it were an appliance shop or a beauty parlor. When it was land, between the two of them they would arrange to subdivide or pass title, but, unless payment were made with horses, Edgar was not to accept animals like chickens or pigs, cattle even less. There would be no place to store the beasts to eat and shit until they could get rid of them. Horses could be traded or sold later and in the meantime put away in stables that Don Lolo had confiscated from one of the Solás, back there in Celada, in the town of Gurabo.

On occasion some bastard would want to pay with one of his daughters. Regardless of how hot they were, no, Don Lolo was not going to slip on that banana peel. Money is money and tits are something else. If he took one of the girls as payment he'd eventually have to support her and even her family. No, no fucking way. If the father wanted to let him have her after paying what he owed, well, that was a different story, and he would only keep her a short while.

"I'm telling you for the obvious reason," Don Lolo said. "I don't want anyone to try to do the same with you, you understand? You with that face and that body, you'd be at risk of them approaching you with sexual intentions. Besides, what you collect in flesh you'll have to make up in cash, you get it?"

Don Lolo could not understand Edgar's long face on hearing his warnings. Was it disappointment, maybe?

"Once in a while they'll get tough and think they are going to intimidate me into leaving them alone. Of course, they know much too well I don't have any recourse under the law and can't take them to court to force them to pay. That's where you come in handy. They won't dare fuck around with you. I think a good shiner will put an end to the shamelessness. Just as backup you can get yourself a gun. That would be even better, but only to scare them with it, you understand?

"As I asked you before, when do I start?"

A little before 6:00 Edgar returned to the delinquent debtor's house. Instead of driving the Lincoln he came in a semi with an open bed. He smacked the front door three times. knocked on the window again, this time with three smacks. Nobody answered.

"What do you want?" the debtor asked. He had cracked the door just enough to show the middle of his face. His nose was wide enough to fill the crevice.

"You know what I'm here for," Edgar shouted for the neighbors to hear. It was cooking or dining time: someone would hear and the fear of embarrassment would make the debtor open the door.

The debtor, however, did not open the door any wider.

"No need to shout. Look," he said in a low tone, his mouth between the frame and the edge of the door, "tell Don Lolo that I am too tight right now, but that his business is coming."

"He's waited as long as he was going to. Now you have to deal with me," Edgar yelled. From the corner of his eye he could see one of the neighbors, a woman who had come out to pretend she was sweeping the sidewalk.

"But I don't have a red cent on me. Come back on Friday and I'll pay what I can."

"What do you take me for, an asshole, you cocksucker? Don't give me that bullshit. You know what the deal was. If you're a month behind, your interest rate climbs to 30%. If you're a month and a half late, you have to pay the full amount you owe. I warned you when a week was up, then two. You're fucking with me.

"No, look, I swear on my children's health," the debtor said. "Friday I'll have the payment for you. Today I have nothing, not even enough for a cigarette pack."

Edgar climbed the step. He leaned back, jerked forward and with his shoulder pushed the door open. The debtor had been holding on to the doorknob, ready to shut the door if Edgar tried to come in. He fell on his back against a chair upholstered in green oilcloth in the living room. There were no signs of anyone else in the house.

"If you don't pay, let's see what I'm going to take with me," Edgar said, looking around.

The debtor rose to his feet. Edgar didn't think he'd be able to carry off much. It would be he alone taking all that junk to the truck, including a china cabinet that Columbus himself must have brought with him. The debtor's wife had a lady's Bulova watch he had bought her for Mother's Day; jewelry he wouldn't find any, except for a neck chain with a medal of Our Lady of Perpetual Help. The TV set weighed more than he. The ramshackle record player was coming apart and was no less than twenty years old—it had 16 and 78 rpm settings. The debtor had bought it from his friend Don Ramón for $50; he doubted it had appreciated in value.

What would this bully take, a plateful of rice and beans? The chifforobe? The Parcheesi board with the missing dice? The debtor almost burst out laughing at the thought of the scene.

Edgar's situation had improved considerably less than two years after working for Don Lolo. He had not even suspected the number of people who borrowed from the usurer and passed for moneyed citizens of the upper classes. The debtors came from all social spheres: the daughter of a Spanish entrepreneur who had wasted all of the capital she had inherited from her frugal father; the police chief, who was under the gun to buy a used car for his son so that he could go visit his girlfriend in the town of Humacao, after Banco Roig had already found that, irrespectively of his title and position, he was so overextended he would not be able to fulfill his payment obligation for another debt; a teacher who needed money with the same urgency as the police chief, to buy a dress for her daughter's debutante ball at the Lions Club; the owner of a cock-fighting hall who had received a unique offer for the purchase of Jerez gamecocks with a pink comb, animals he had considered exotic and aggressive, sure to win every match; a young taxi driver who was his bed-ridden mother's only means of support and had run out of any financial resource to pay for her medical care.

Edgar invaded the heiress' home, pushed her around a few times and took her living-room furniture. He forced the police chief to sign over the car's title from his son to Don Lolo. The teacher had gathered all she had to pay Don Lolo, but without the late fee, which required her to give Edgar an emerald 14-karat gold ring to cover the balance. The cock fighter tried to give him the five remaining gamecocks. Edgar thought these were more than ordinary chickens, and he took them: he sold them to another cock fighter for the same amount he had tried to collect. The taxi driver sold his cab at a loss to pay Don Lolo and went to work as a bus driver for don Benigno Rosario's line when his mother died.

Edgar owned a parcel of land in a place called Guardarraya. It was a fourth of the twenty acres Don Lolo had forced a small farmer to title over to him. Don Lolo had given Edgar the five acres, an award for the efficiency and zeal he displayed in increasing the loan shark's assets. Everything Edgar owned had to be under the name of his sister Tere and his mother: he had no official source of income with which to justify ownership. He kept his cash in *Sultana* soda-cracker tins at his mother's house. He had parked the Toyota indefinitely in front of his house, where he no longer lived. Don Lolo had sold him, at a discount, a six-year old Lincoln Continental, part of the booty Edgar had recovered from a mechanic who, according to street talk, needed extra money to finance marijuana shipments from Colombia.

The reward Edgar treasured the most was a country house in a rural area known as Montones 2 in the town of Las Piedras, a building whose thick hedges afforded him great privacy, surrounded by lemon, mango and acerola trees. It was a wooden house with a metal roof and a wrap-around porch. When he had nothing pending he would retire to the house. He got there in an old Jeep he had bought for the purpose of climbing the steep hills of Montones 2 on an unpaved road that ended at the house's iron gate and a barbed-wire fence. He slept in one of the two bedrooms at the end of a hall that ran back from the living room. He had furnished it with confiscated pieces Don Lolo had given him and some new ones.

The decor included lace curtains, bows, rugs, framed pictures and vases holding cloth flowers. It was Freddy's work. Edgar had no interest or ability for that kind of thing. If he were going to the house in the evening during the week he picked up Freddy at the city park. Freddy couldn't spend the night there, but they could be together for a couple of hours away from his wife and the neighbors' prying eyes. Freddy told Tatin he was going out drinking with the boys.

Edgar had seduced Freddy without Freddy noticing it. When his wife was out Edgar used to bring Freddy bags of Spanish limes and mangos from the country house, and even sausage that he had expropriated from Yeyito Cay, the butcher up the street. He didn't want to get Freddy in trouble by giving him anything he would have to explain to his wife. The afternoon he brought Freddy Payco ice cream from Vitín Torres' corner store, just a couple of blocks away, Edgar entered the house after learning from his sister that Tatin had gone to her mother's for a few days. Freddy asked Edgar to share the ice cream. It came in a round plastic dish and was sold with small wooden spoons. Freddy took a bite and then asked Edgar to lick the spoon. Edgar didn't bother with the utensil. He cast the dish to the side and kissed Freddy hard on the lips, his arms under Freddy's to bring him as close as possible to him. First Freddy opened his green eyes the way only a surprise can, but before long Edgar noticed how he yielded to Edgar's advances and closed them again, letting himself go. Freddy threw his arms around Edgar's neck without even taking the time to play coy or resisting: Edgar felt at home.

Without a word they walked to the same bed that Freddy shared with Tatin. They left no traces of anything that could reveal what happened during the three hours they spent making love, initially a tentative and awkward enterprise that did not take long to evolve into intuitive maneuvers leading to shared pleasure.

"One of these days I'm going to kidnap you so you will never leave me again," Edgar would tell Freddy when they lay naked in bed at the country house, trying to recover the energy they expended fiercely during the little time they had to enjoy each other's company.

"You'd have to kill Tatin first," Freddy always said when Edgar expressed the threat with no possibility of executing it.

"That's why I bought the gun," Edgar told him one day.

Freddy looked at him with eyes so wide they seemed about to pop out of their sockets. Edgar laughed and kissed him on the lips, caressed his face and, his hand on Freddy's cheek said, "An occupational hazard. It's for protection from muggers and scaring Don Lolo's clients. I don't have to kill your wife. I can wait."

"If you have nothing to pay with, I'm going to take everything you have here," Edgar told the debtor.

"But what are you going to take? There's nothing here worth anything."

"Leave that to me. I know how to get something out of it. And if this junk isn't enough to liquidate the balance, I'll come back and take your house away, too," Edgar replied.

"Lord in heaven, have some compassion," the debtor asked with the same voice someone asks God in the most abject despair. He made the mistake of starting at the end of the process of absolution; he could not increase now the intensity appropriate for him who cannot debase himself any more. Edgar did not miss the error, not that any of it made a difference.

"Look, miserable slob, you're not going to get to my weak side. I don't have one. If you're so sure you have no money to pay with, start helping me to load up this garbage on the truck."

"Fuck, Edgar, have some pity," the debtor pleaded with the same quivering voice. He knelt in front of Edgar and tried to hold his hands, but Edgar shook him to the side. He struck the debtor on the side of the head. The debtor lost his balance and fell against a corner of the green chair. He was able to get on his feet again. The top of his head only reached up to Edgar's chest. He took two steps backwards.

"I have nothing other than this house, Edgar. What's in here is worth nothing, Maybe if you let me talk to Don Lolo..."

"Don't be an idiot on top of being a deadbeat. Why do you think I'm here? Don Lolo pays me so he won't have to deal with bums like you," Edgar replied.

Without Edgar knowing where the debtor got the courage, he squared off intending to assault Edgar, fists up. Edgar reached into his pocket for the gun. He aimed at the debtor's chest.

"Let's see if your balls are big enough to come fight this."

No sooner had Edgar said it than from one of the rooms that opened into the living room, behind two flower-print curtain panels, came out the debtor's wife, screaming at full lungs.

"Oh, please, my God, God mine, no, no no, don't Edgar! Put that away, oh, Lord, sweet Lady of Perpetual Help!" wept and pleaded the debtor's wife without daring to come near Edgar. "No, no he's not going to do anything against you, Edgar, put that away! Can't you see how desperate he is? Are you going to make orphans out of my children and end up in prison over a couple of bucks? Edgar, search in your heart for a little mercy!"

Edgar saw something moving behind the half-open curtains. It was the same skinny boy he had seen on the tree branch. The boy was sobbing and hiccupping, trying to keep his noise down.

"This is business. If you wanted compassion over not paying what you owe, you should have borrowed from a priest," Edgar said, gun still in hand, but with the barrel pointing down while he looked at the debtor from the corner of his eye, in case he tried to grab the gun. "I bet your daughter is out in Río Piedras attending college, isn't she? And you know who's paying for that, right? Then make yourself believe you owe Satan and he's coming to drag you to hell's fire, because that's exactly what this is.

Don Lolo was in his corner, under the flowing stalactites that spiders left on the ceiling. He had asked a boy who was pacing in the pool hall to walk to the corner to Goyito's drug store to buy him some bicarbonate. He handed the boy a one-dollar bill, 75 cents for the bicarbonate and 25 for the errand. He asked the bartender for a glass of water and a spoon. He mixed the powder with the water and drank with repugnance the salty and slimy liquid. Don Lolo belched something deep and bitter, but felt no respite from the acute pain in the middle of his chest, close to the pit of his stomach.

It was close to his supper time, but he was waiting for Edgar to arrive with the results of the collection. He had no doubt Edgar would come back with something. Money he was almost certain that Edgar would not bring him, because that guy would have none. His was a difficult line of work, not because he felt remorse for his collection methods, but because of the debtors' lack of respect and seriousness. For every ten people to whom he lent money, five would pay according to their agreement, two would be late, but paid, and the rest needed a hard squeeze to get them to let go something to compensate for the cash they would not pay. He, because he was so kind-hearted, let people whom you could tell from a distance were not going to pay, and they abused his charitable nature. He had developed already, in his mind and through experience, his actuarial tables to determine the likelihood of payment one way or another. He never lost. If he let it go the news would spread and others would come to take advantage of his weakness.

Anyway, he didn't think he'd be able to eat. Doña Melo would have sent already the lunch pail to his house with her youngest child. He paid her for a double ration, usually four fried pork chops with their fat skirt on, rice, stewed kidney beans with pig feet and French fries or *tostones*, fried plantains. On special occasions she would prepare mashed plantain with *mojito* sauce and *chicharrones*, fried pork cutlets. Dr. Porras had told him already that he needed to cut out the lard and stop eating so late at night. Those were the reasons for waking up in the middle of the night in pain and bathed in sweat. What could he do? If he skipped anything he'd go to bed hungry; the waste bothered him. He never ate anything left over and refrigerated from the previous night. Whatever he could not eat he would throw in the oil can outside, where he kept the pig slop that Dolores Alverio picked up from the alley every morning.

Lately he felt the pain during the day as well. He broke out in a cold sweat and his lower back ached as if a mule had kicked him. The discomfort made him feel full, as if his lunch had rolled up into a ball in his stomach. That was what he had had at Marquito's, the bus with passengers on the fenders he had for lunch—the name the cooks gave a mound of rice and red beans, steak in an oil sauce and two fried eggs. He was sweating more than usual in that corner of the pool hall. The heat could not be from bulbs, because there was none where he was seated. He wiped his forehead and his nape with a rolled-up yellowing handkerchief he kept in a pocket of his Cuban *guayabera* shirt.

What was taking Edgar so long? He had taken much longer than was customary. By that time he should have been able to empty out a house or slap his way into getting the car keys, registration and title. Surely he had arrived early and the deadbeat wasn't home yet. Maybe he was with that guy people said he was fucking out there in Montones 2, but it wasn't like Edgar to postpone his duties just to go get laid. Besides, that all sounded like idle gossip. A man with Edgar's body and looks couldn't be queer. If he were, he'd have to be the guy on top, that was certain, a *bugarrón*. It was well known that the queer was the guy who took it up his ass, not the one who stuck it up there.

Now what the hell was this? I'm passing out and...

The bartender looked toward the dark corner where Don Lolo had been sitting after two pool players called his attention to the loan shark.

"Hey, Mingo, something's wrong with the old man!"

The man had tried to get up. His cane hit the floor tiles in a dry strike. He had grabbed his chest with his right hand, as if something where piercing him and impeded his breathing. Something like a labored whine escaped from his mouth before falling on the floor, his hat rolling briefly before coming to a stop with the brim against the floor a few feet from Don Lolo's head. Everyone noticed that he was, indeed, bald except for the thin ribbon of greasy gray curls. The pencil remained where it had been, behind the ear that did not hit the floor.

The bartender approached him slowly, as if fearing that Don Lolo would abruptly rise and jump on him to bury his fangs on the bartender's neck. When he was sure the body was not moving he came closer.

"Don Lolo, hey, Don Lolo. Is anything wrong?"

"Fuck, man, can't you see something is? What a stupid question," one of the pool players leaning against a table said, the cue stick propped on the floor between his legs.

The bartender crouched down. He placed a hand on Don Lolo's shoulder and shook him. Nothing. He wasn't breathing.

"Oh, Jesus. I don't know whether to call a doctor or Cariño," said the bartender, referring to the man who owned the funeral home across the street.

"Call the police," said one of the players who was looking from a table, a toothpick hanging from his lips. "If he died here they can't take him to the funeral parlor. They have to investigate. Take him to forensics."

"Investigate what?" the bartender asked. "You all saw it. He was sitting there like a blob, he drank the bicarbonate and fell all fucked up."

"Maybe it was rat poison that they sold him," the one with the toothpick said, and laughed.

"Stop being disrespectful. This is not the time," the bartender said.

"No one's going to be at this one's wake," said another pool player in a sleeveless undershirt who had sat on the edge of a table. "His own mother didn't like this son of a bitch."

"Don't speak ill of the dead," the bartender reprimanded him.

"That's not speaking ill. It's telling the truth. Many are going to be very happy, especially the people who owed him," the player replied while he tried to make himself comfortable on the edge of the table and adjusted his crotch.

"That's going to be a short-lived happiness. Edgar's going to take care of it," the bartender observed.

"Look there," said the player who first called the bartender, a filterless cigarette stuck to the corner of his mouth and the pack within a rolled-up sleeve, "he's got the notebook in the shirt pocket. That's where he kept the names of his debtors. Pull it out and throw it away."

The bartender stood up and stared at the player who made the suggestion.

"I won't touch a corpse."

He walked back to the bar and started dialing police headquarters from a list of emergency numbers taped to the side of the register. From the jukebox they could hear the Ortiz-Lara duo singing "Fog in the Brook."

Edgar was coming around the corner when he saw a group of people looking into the pool hall. He was bringing with him the title to the house that the debtor had given him on the promise he would show up the next day at the law office of Oscar Brizzie, Don Lolo's lawyer, to finalize the title transfer. Don Lolo would then rent the house back to the debtor.

He had to make his way through the throng of snoopers. He came in the side opposite the back. The people who had gathered around parted into two sides and opened a path for him after those in the front saw him and nudged the ones toward the back to indicate Edgar was coming.

"What happened to him?" Edgar asked no one in particular. The small crowd remained silent. The bartender explained. It was difficult to determine whether what they saw on Edgar's face was sadness or worry. Without explaining himself he came near Don Lolo's body and noticed the limp tongue hanging out of Don Lolo's mouth. He knew right away Don Lolo had died of a heart attack. He stuck his hand in Don Lolo's shirt pocket, took out the small notebook and put it in his gun pocket.

He stepped back. The bartender told him the police were on their way. He heard the noise of a cue stick that broke the ball triangle with a flawless strike on the side of the front ball. Edgar was not in the least surprised at the indifference toward the body lying on the gritty floor. Don Lolo wouldn't have died from excessive love. The players would have to remain in the hall to give their testimony when the police arrived. They had to entertain themselves with something in the meantime.

He had nothing to declare: he hadn't been there to see any of it.

Edgar promised Freddy he was going to take him to the country to live together. Now the business was his alone. Don Lolo was a widower; his daughters had given up any claims to anything that could link them to their father, of whom they were ashamed now that one was a professor of Spanish literature at the University of Puerto Rico and the other an attorney in Chicago. Don Lolo's only male child had died of meningitis at the age of four. A quick search of Don Lolo's house before a judge shut it down was all Edgar needed after forcing a side door open with a butter knife. The slit on the headboard side of a mattress on a spare-room bed gave Edgar access to its interior. It had been Don Lolo's bank.

Edgar did not need to run off with Freddy. Without suspecting anything previously Tatin found out what was going on from street rumors. She wouldn't have stood for being abandoned for another woman, but, in the long run, she couldn't give Freddy what Edgar could. With a great deal of beating around the bush Tatin led Freddy to assume that she didn't care what he did with Edgar. Then Freddy started giving Tatin expensive presents: diamond rings, gold necklaces, a latest model TV set for the living room and another for the bedroom, a frostless freezer refrigerator, an electric stove. All of it, except for the expensive Velasco gowns and shoes, came from seizures effected on deadbeats. Tatin drove the Toyota exclusively.

Now, when people see Edgar approaching they feel their bowels loosen and the air becomes redolent of Sulphur. They know he isn't coming as Don Lolo's messenger. He comes to collect whichever way he has to. He now has much more to lose.

Becoming One with the Mask

She became a luminary of the big silver screen. Later she did likewise on the small screen. Meantime she was also outstanding on stage: no national award eluded her talent and longevity in her profession. Towards the end of her life her face was a cushion of sculpted silicone, her skin whitened with bleaching treatments and her hair, whenever she did without a wig, had yielded the tight curliness of her childhood to chemical processes. Her eyes, no longer blinking, seem to express a fear she never felt, the effect of Clostridium botulinum injections.

"She was embalmed prematurely," observed a fellow actor at her funeral-home wake. "Her decomposition will be delayed for a long time, like mummies."

She blended her physical façade with the identity she ignored until a few weeks before her death. Perhaps her passing was accelerated by the encounter that forced her to face her true past with whom she had never surmised would do so.

A few months before she had published a notable autobiography. However, that one had been preceded by an illustrated biography overflowing with her own statements about her origin and the way she arrived in New York City. She had repeated those expressions consistently in magazine and newspaper articles.

"I wish to invite you to come to Puerto Rico." The invitation must have seemed strange to the actress. She did not know the man who was offering to cover travel expenses for her and her husband. The host established his credentials: he was a distant relative, the great grandson of one of her biological father's aunts. He presided his own company, an agency that promoted tourism in the island. She could verify the firm's prestige and the standing of the man who was extending the invitation.

"Your acceptance would be a great honor to me. It's only for two or three days. Give me a call once you have made your decision," the promoter said before saying good-bey and ending the call.

Two days later he had the actress' answer. She was accepting the invitation, but required details on the itinerary and the stay. Her husband would be unable to travel with her—previous engagements. She, on the other hand, had had nothing to film for some months, except for an introductory presentation she had made for one her movies on a classic-film cable channel and a motivational speech she had given for an industrial association in Topeka, Kansas.

"If Friday sounds good for you to travel, I will make all flight arrangements. I will let you know flight number and time, and you can check in at the San Francisco International Airport," the host advised the actress. "Once you arrive in the island, you will be staying at the Caribe Hilton Hotel in San Juan. I will take care of any other arrangements and will consult with you about them when you get here."

At dusk the following Friday her host greeted her at the baggage-claim exit of the Luis Muñoz Marín International Airport after she was escorted on a wheelchair by an airline representative from the arrival gate. She was wearing an oyster head scarf and large sunglasses that reminded the host of a role she had played in the early 1960s. Her host called a luggage porter to carry the actress' four suitcases. The host was somewhat confused at the number of pieces, considering this was a weekend trip and the actress had brought enough luggage for a one-month visit.

They headed for the limousine that took them to the hotel. It was evening. The host suggested that the actress rest from her long trip and order whatever she wished for dinner from room service.

"I can come for you in the morning around eleven, what do you think? That way you won't be as jet-lagged. After all, it is a four-hour difference between California time and Puerto Rico's," the host said.

The actress agreed.

"Say," the actress said, calling him by his first name, "I can call you by your first name, can't I?"

"Of course, ma'am," the host answered.

"Perfect. Are you a real Puerto Rican?" she asked.

"Yes, ma'am," answered the host, a little perplexed.

"Oh, my, God bless you! You look American with your blond hair and blue eyes!" she said with enthusiasm.

The host could not think of anything to say at first. He did not think it was a compliment worth gratitude.

"I've been told before," he lied.

Once the actress was installed in her suite the host left. Just as he had promised, at exactly eleven o'clock the next morning the host knocked at her room door. When she opened it he noticed she was not ready. She was wearing a bathrobe and had yet to apply any makeup.

"Oh, child, I'm not ready yet! I thought you had given me Latino time. You know, half an hour after what they say?" the actress said with a broad smile.

"I'm sorry, ma'am. I guide myself with the hands of the clock, which knows of no cultural expectations. If you wish I can wait for you out here," the host told her.

"Oh, no, no way! I will be done in a New York minute. Come on in, come on!" the actress said in an encouraging tone.

The host came in and when the actress disappeared behind the bathroom door, since he had no invitation to sit down, he remained on his feet. He looked at the other side of the glass sliding doors. He saw a sectin of the urban landscape, the Miramar district to the left. To the right he saw Hotel Normandie and part of Parque Muñoz Rivera. Extreme right was the Atlantic glimmering under a bright sun and a cloudless sky unusual for an early November day.

Fifteen minutes to noon she reappeared in a sky-blue blouse down to her thighs and peach slacks. Her heels made her look somewhat taller, but she still came only as high as his chest.

"*Ay, chico*," she said. I'm so sorry! Why didn't you sit down?"

"Don't worry, ma'am. I'm alright like this," the host said.

They came down to the hotel's ground floor. There the host called the limousine.

"Do you wish to have something special for lunch?" the host asked.

"You choose," the actress said. "The other time I was here I was a judge at the Miss Universe pageant in Dorado. They took me from one place to another, so I don't know where anything is. *Sabes*? You know, I was fur when Mom and I left for New York on the Borinquen."

"Good. Then let's go to a restaurant that specializes in local food, in Caguas," the host suggested.

"*Bueno*, the actress said, before giggling in apparent surprise at her knowledge of a word in Spanish. "If you don't mind, could you tell me what's on the schedule for today? I am fascinated, you're doing so much ,and I still don't know exactly why."

"Well, you see, ma'am," the host said. "You have mentioned the city where you were born and where you lived before leaving for the mainland. Before your mom took you to New York City. I don't know how much you know of that city or your biological father's hometown."

"*Es verdad*!" the actress exclaimed. "All I know is what I was told by Mom, may she rest in peace."

"That's what I thought. I intend to take her to those places. Then you'll be personally acquainted with them," the host replied.

"Oh, darling! You are so generous! Thank you so much! Tell me, how are we related?" the actress asked. The limousine was on the freeway, reaching the Hato Rey distriet, then on the outskirts of the city of Río Piedras, all part of the San Juan metropolitan area. The actress intermittently looked out the tinted winsow at the places they drove by. She did not seem as interested in any of them as she did in the conversation with the host.

"My maternal grandmother was your dad's cousin. My great grandmother was your dad's aunt."

"*Ah, sí*? How interesting!" the actress said in what sounded like a sincere tone. The host remembered, however, that she was an actress. "So is this the way to Humacao?"

They had just gone by the old state prison near the borough of Monacillos, the crossroads for the old highway to Río Piedras and the cities of Bayamón and Guaynabo. It was difficult to tell where each ended or started: no road signs indicated where any of them were, only what direction to take to reach them.

"Yes, ma'am. Caguas is the next city before we go on to Humacao," the host replied.

"Who'd think!" Puerto Rico looks so tiny on maps, you could never imagine that it had so many roads and that nothing is as close as it seems, isn't that true?"

"I wouldn't know what to say, ma'am," the host said. "Except to the time I spent in the Marine Corps in North Carolina, I have lived here. Everything there is larger and cities are bigger, but Puerto Rico has never seemed small to me."

"Oh, for sure! Everything is relative, right? Yes, he said it. Einstein said it," she said, putting her hand on the host's shoulder. He jerked a little at the surprise of physical contact from the actress.

They reached the outskirts of Caguas, close to the Villa Blanca development. The chauffeur, previously informed and instructed, entered the restaurant's parking lot. He opened the actress' door. The host opened his own, walked around and joined his guest.

"Wait a minute," the actress said. She reached for a pair of sunglasses from her purse and put them on. "Sometimes I want to be recognized, but other times, not so much. Today is one of those days."

The glasses had their intended effect: no one recognized her or at least did not acknowledge her presence. The host suspected it was probably due to her fans' expectation of her as a tall woman, the way she seemed on the screen, instead of someone some five foot two. He chose a table away from foot traffic, where he sat the actress with her side toward the rest of the clients. She ordered a daiquiri and *mofongo*, mashed plantains, in a mortar with shrimp. The host asked for a glass of bottled water with wedge of lemon and mofongo with pork. When the server brought the entrées, she lifted her empty glass and clinked her index fingernail on it . The server understood.

"Certainly, *señora*. Right away!"

"As long as I'm here, I might as well drink the local cocktail, don't you think? When in Rome and all." the actress said. Again she smiled and flashed her bleached teeth. The host blushed and nodded. He could not find a tactful way to tell her the daiquiri was Cuban. "How charming!" the actress said.

"What?"

"This restaurant. Even the oilcloth table covering adds local color," the actress explained, running her hand over the red and white checkerboard tablecloth. In her other hand she held the daiquiri the server had brought her.

"Yes, that's right," the host said, chewing his words together with a morsel of fried pork. He swallowed. "They know me here. I often come with clients."

"Oh, yes? Interesting. Listen, *chico*, this *mofongo* is exquisite," the actress said. "And where do you live, in Old San Juan?"

"No, ma'am. I keep an apartment in Santurce, a borough of metro San Juan. I only stay there when I have late-night engagements. I live in Juncos, where you lived as a child," the host clarified.

"Oh, no, no, that's not right!" the actress said with an obvious urgent need to correct the host. " I lived in Humacao, where I was born, before we left for *Nueva York*."

"Oh, yes? Interesting," the host said without adding anything else.

The actress slurped the daiquiri at the bottom of the glass.

"What, you think I'm from Juncos?" she asked.

The host looked at this wristwatch. "I think we should take a ride around and let's see what we find."

"*Ay*, I'm intrigued!" the actress said in a tone devoid of conviction.

"Not for long. You'll see, ma'am."

The host noticed she once again raised her glass, trying to catch the server's attention. He asked, before the server noticed the empty glass in air, "How would you like guava shells in syrup with *queso fresco*?"

"Oh, how sweet of you. And how sweet that dessert, but no, thank you. That's too many calories," she said.

That seemed strange to the host. She was counting calories, but not those in Don Q rum and the sugar added to the daiquiri.

"Then, ma'am, if you don't mind, we should be heading out. That will give us more time to reach the places I have planned for you to visit. Is that alright?" the host asked.

"You're in charge!"

"No, ma'am, you're in charge. I'm only suggesting. The power is all in your hands," the host lied. He would have to come up with some subterfuge if she took him at his word.

"*Ay*, how chivalrous! Well, then, yes, let's go."

When she rose from the chair that the host pulled away from the table, he thought he had noticed the actress was wobbly. That compact constitution could not absorb so much liquor that fast. On top of it, she was burdened by her eighty years plus of age. Just in case, he put out his arm for her to hold.

"*Ay, gracias*! You are so courteous! This is what I like of Latino men, you know?" the actress said. "American men aren't like that. Well, not all." She was dragging out her words some.

Back in the limousine they rode out toward Gurabo, the town just before Juncos.

"Aren't we going to Juncos?" the actress asked when they passed the road sign that pointed to the freeway exit to the town.

"No, not yet. We will when we return from Humacao," the host said.

"Ah, alright."

Some twenty minutes later they entered Humacao, on the southeastern coast of the island. Humacao had grown and changed much since the actress had been absent—not that she would have recognized any of the changes, of course. They would be met by downtown traffic, a nightmare of excessive vehicles in streets too narrow to accommodate them. They came in from the noreastern side of the city, Fonot Martelo Street. The host asked the chauffeur to park in front of a building on a hill on the other side of the street.

"This sector was known as *Las Moscas,* The Flies, at the time when you were born. It was a slum known for its prostitutes," the host said. He pointed to the right, to a street and rows of houses that hardly resembled what the *barrio* had been. "At the end of this street is Humacao River, that flooded the whole neighborhood during periods of heavy rain. In 1960 many drowned on the other side of town, people who lived on the banks for the river. They had no idea of what was going to happen.

"Oh, yes? How awful! What month was that?"

"I believe around September," the host answered.

"Let me see… Around that time I was shooting… Oh, *Life in Paradise*! It was a TV series, very popular, you know? I only did guest appearances. I remember I played a Polynesian girl. That was when they were still making me play indigenous people, before I got a break with roles better suited to my talent. In that series they had an actor, *ay, mi madre*. That was a *papi*, you know? Charles McKee. My girlfriends envied me. One of the perks of playing those roles."

The host stared at her, baffled.

"*Ay, chico*, but why tell you about such things, if you are a man and don't understand?" the actress said and guffawed.

"Actually, I do understand your feelings. I am not heterosexual," he said.

"Oh, how interesting!" the actress said with a certain degree of awkwardness. "One of my boyfriends back when, you kno2? Gay, too. I would have never guessed. In fact, I didn't!" The actress guffawed again.

"More than two-hundred people drowned in that flood. They lived in shacks in slums by the river and Mariana Creek. Thousands lost their homes," said the host, attempting to take the conversation back to the original topic.

"Oh, yes? That's why I won't live close to rivers or beaches, you know?"

"But don't you live in San Francisco?" the host asked without succeeding at getting the actress to grasp his intention.

"Yes, sure, but no at the beach," she replied.

The host paused. He was about to remind her of the fault that ran through the area. He remained silent.

"The building we have to our left is Ryder Memorial Hospital, founded in 1914. It's where you were born," the host said.

"Don't you say! I had never seen it," the actress said, with evident emotion. "So this is where my roots are." The host thought he saw her eyes dampen when she removed the sunglasses to get a better look at the building. "Driver, please, roll down the window. I want to have a better view."

Once the window was down the host said, "Of course, like everything else in the city, the hospital has changed a great deal. When you were born it was a modest building painted green, with a small maternity ward for several women and some double rooms. It had a wrap-around balcony, southern style. Now you can see even apartments for assisted living and a convalescent home."

"Look at that, I had no idea. Thank you so much for bringing me here," the actress said. She put her hand on his thigh and left it there long enough to convey her emotion and gratitude with her hand's pressure.

"Chauffeur, let's go to Barrio Junquito," the host instructed.

The chauffeur rolled up the window and took off in a U-turn. He took the section of freeway that bypassed the city's traffic congestion and ended in the road to Humacao Beach.

Going past Palma Real Shopping Mall, with its Walmart and JC Penney, the host pointed out that all that was new. There was not a single Puerto Rican-owned business in the strip mall.

"This area was all sugar-cane fields. All of this construction is relatively new," he said. He pointed to the crowded hillside, full of more businesses, gas stations where housing developments had been some years before. Although it was the other side of downtown, traffic moved slowly, and cars were parked on the side of the road as well as in the overflowing parking lot. It all reminded the host that back in the 1960s Lady Bird Johnson, flying over San Juan, had called the metropolitan area a cement jungle. That could be said now of most urban areas in the island.

"So much progress!" the actress said, who looked attentively at buildings, an opportunity afforded her by the traffic jam across the street from Sam's Club and Chili's. "I had no idea Puerto Rico was so modernized!"

The host remained silent. On the rearview mirror he could see the chauffeur's eyes, squinting at the actress' statements.

"Back here there was little traffic except in times of sugar-cane *zafra* and summer, when people went down the road to the beach.

"*Zafra?*" the actress asked.

"Harvest and milling. There used to be a long line of trucks on this road heading to Pasto Viejo Sugar Mill, farther down the road."

"So much local color!" the actress asked. "That is what Hawaii must have been like. That was where *Pacific Native* was set, you know, but it was filmed in Hollywood. I also used to play Indians in movies shot in Los Angeles. Very realistic, wouldn't you say?" the actress said amid laughter.

They reached the road to Barrio Junquito, perhaps the midpoint between the urban zone and the public beach in Playa Humacao. The chauffeur turned left into the road and followed a narrow paved road on whose left side stood a row of medium-sides homes. Five minutes later they got to a curve on the road.

"Here is where Barrio Pasto Viejo begins, where the old sugar mill was," the host mentioned. "Please, let's go outside. I want you to see something," said the host.

The chauffeur opened the acvtress' door. The host led her to the front of the limousine and pointed to the horizon stretching before them.

"Do you see any mountains?" the host asked her.

"No, none. Everything is flat here," the actress replied. "Was there sugar cane planted here also?"

"That's right. No sugar cane is planted anywhere around here any longer. No sugar mills, either," the host said. "Now they build summer houses all over and eat up open spaces. But that's not what I wanted you to see. Take a good look. Do you see any mountains anywhere near here?"

"As I said, none. Well, except for those hills there in the distance," the actress replied.

"Ah, that is true. This is the point in Humacao where the northeastern part of the island can be seen best," the host said in a docent tone. "You have stated in your biography and in interviews that you were raised in Humacao, at the foot of the El Yunque Rain Forest, that your mom hung laundry in the backyard of the house, that you both used to sing together while you helped her hang clothes."

"Well, yes. I don't remember," the actress clarified, "but that is what Mom used to tell me when I was a child back in Long Island."

"Did she ever tell you where in Humacao you could see El Yunque?

"No, she never told me. I assumed you could," the actress said.

"I mention it because you cannot see the rain forest from Humacao. If she had told you Naguabo, on the other side of the beaches, maybe. And even from Las Piedras, between Humacao and Juncos. Some barrios in Las Piedras do extend up to the southeastern limits of El Yunque, ma'am. Barrio Río Alto, for example. Its Río Blanco flows from the rain forest."

"Then?" the actress asked, evincing a slight daze perhaps aggravated by rum, "What are you trying to say?"

"That it was not in Humacao where you lived as a child. That there were no musical afternoons while hanging laundry at the foot of El Yunque. That maybe you were born in Humacao, but your house was not here."

The host seemed the actress' face sketched what was going through her mind. It would be a vital dissonance she could not have expected from this excursion with a total stranger claiming to be a relative of some kind. What if he were a madman who had brugh her to this countryside to assault or stab her to death? That was what the host read in her face.

"I don't mean to offend you, ma'am. Or confuse you. The truth? I think you were sold a past as true as those Disney TV shows you did".

"But why would Mom make up those stories? Why would she?"

"Perhaps because the truth was painful and uglier. She would have looked as if under a dim light."

The actress was pensive. She took her hand to her forehead and let it slide to her lips in slow motion. The host could not tell whether it was histrionics or true confusion.

"Do you by any chance have water in the limousine?" she asked.

"But of course," the host replied. He gestured toward the chauffeur, who immediately walked to the vehicle, opened a small refrigerator and removed a bottle of water. He pried open a compartment where the tumblers and cups were, uncapped the bottle, poured some in the tumbler and handed it to the actress.

The host noticed the lipstick stain on the tumbler's edge. She held it in her hand after taking a swig. One of the actress' fans would have preserved the tumbler without washing it in a glass case to brag about having a vessel from which the famous star had drunk.

"Would you like to see where you really lived?" the host asked.

"How do you know that?"

"I heard it from my grandmother and my great grandmother. They used to tell the story much differently from yours. We would have to start with the assertion…"

"Assertion?" the actress asked, cutting in.

"Affirmation, statement, declaration," the host said. "You have asserted that your mom left Juncos because she was tired of both her husband and the town."

"Ah, she always told me that," she said, offering the tumbler back to the chauffeur. He placed it in a receptacle for used glassware, to wash later.

"Then it's the only time you have said something that doesn't match the narrative of your past. If it was her husband and Juncos she was tired of, what was she doing in Humacao?"

The actress did not reply immediately. After a while she said, "Now I really don't understand."

"I want to help you understand, ma'am. It doesn't seem fair to me that anyone should go through life convinced of having lived a fictitious past," the host said.

"But that's only a small detail! Okay," the actress replied, "we didn't live at the foot of the rain forest or in Humacao. So what?"

"Aren't you interested in the rest of the puzzle?"

"The what? What puzzle?" the actress on the verge of agitation.

"Your jigsaw puzzle of a life, ma'am," the host said in a flat-lined tone.

That she did understand.

"You are being disrespectful. You are taking advantage of my vulnerability. You are offending me because I am at your mercy."

"Not at all, ma'am. I have no intention of offending you, only to make some things clearer for you. And do you know why? Because if I don't make things more transparent for you, some day someone could do it, someone with the cruel intention of sabotaging your career and making you seem like a phony," the host said.

"But how could they? I have never lied. Someone told me those stories and I repeated them," the actress protested.

He felt compassion toward her, and a trace of shame clouded his thoughts. A life of intentional manufacture is already a form of vital counterfeit, but one manufactured to justify oneself and seem heroic is cowardice. This woman had no clue about who she was, but she had lived happily in her mythical bubble. The host hesitated and questioned his motives. He dismissed his doubts: he had come too far and letting the actress leave without facing the truth would leave him feeling like a fool and her confused at the suspicion that something was not clear yet she never did discover what it was.

"Let's go to Juncos, please," the host said with a hand shake to indicate to her that they would go back on the limousine.

The afternoon was beginning to turn into dusk. It was the middle of tropical autumn, almost just as hot and muggy as summer, but featuring an earlier arrival of night.

No one said anything until they reached Juncos. The chauffeur took a detour from the freeway and entered on the south side of town past a development initially meant for low-income families and now full of two-story mansions in minute lots. On every side stood a strip mall featuring loudspeakers blaring *salsa* music that blended stridence and nonsensical refrains at decibels dangerously close to the threshold of human tolerance. A locally-owned supermarket stood next to a Banco Popular branch. Farther down they drove by a conglomerate of *comeivetes*, Burger King and Church's Chicken next door to a Walgreens drugstore.

They entered the town on a two-lane bridge on the Valenciano River, of which only a shallow thread flowed from boulders surrounded by bamboo trees. To the right stood the remains of a cement wall. It had been built in the 1930s to keep floods from destroying the low-lying areas of the town; it had collapsed some thirty years later, revealing that the structure had never been reinforced. Now the absurdly named river was no threat to anyone.

The host provided historical details for the actress.

Around the time when the actress was born during the day there would be at least a dozen women at the river doing laundry. Most of the washing women took in laundry from families who were better off: back then a washing machine would have been a luxury few would have been able to afford, if any had been available. Some of the women, however, were residents of La Marina and the other slum across the way from the bridge, to the left of the limousine. In time the people who lived there had improved their houses and the municipality had installed water service and electric power. That other slum, *Manchuria*, had been a poverty-stricken inhabited by indigents and the unskilled working class. While La Marina had an unpaved hilly Street that separated two rows of houses, Manchuria had something the width of an alley to keep apart the hovels, some of which had an outhouse. Tap water came from a communal faucet at the slum's gateway, at the bottom end of Muñoz Rivera Street, where it joined Agüeybana Street. Slum dwellers would fill up large cans, mostly discarded large oil and lard metal containers, and carry them home on their heads.

Manchuria's people were not delinquents: they lived barefoot and in misery. From bathing in the river many of them contracted bilharzia, a fresh-water parasite that broke through the bottom of feet and lodged itself incurably in the human liver; its victims eventually died of hepatic cirrhosis. Waste of every kind ran from streets down the wide alley; the stench was unbearable. Even after the island's fiscal situation improved toward the end of the 1940s and in the early 1950s. Manchuria remained the same.

The chauffeur parked the limousine next to what had been *Colmado Flores*, a small grocery store facing the bridge. The entrance to Manchuria cold be seen from a diagonal angle. Only the houses closest to Muñoz Rivera Street were visible from the limousine.

"That is where you lived as a child until you were four," the host said.

"There? You must be mistaken!" the actress objected.

"No, ma'am, I am not mistaken. You lived there. When your parents divorced and your mother went to New York to live with her sister, the little house was taken over by a cousin of your father's with her husband and two young daughters."

The actress again pressed her fingers against her lips.

"Let's stop playing games," the actress said after a few seconds. "This is either truly a tasteless joke or you persist in making me feel bad. Tell me once and for all what you want to tell me without taking me through Humacao or Juncos or any other town," the actress demanded.

"A joke, hardly, and I do not wish to make you feel bad, okay?" the host said, staring at her eyes, now bare after she had removed her sunglasses before they entered Juncos. "Look here, ma'am, when my grandmother lived in New York, your biological father and she went to see you perform at Teatro Puerto Rico. They tried to see you in your dressing room. They walked to the stage door and identified themselves. Someone went to let you know your father wanted to speak with you. You sent word back, 'I do not know anyone named like that. I don't know who he is.'"

"*No me arrecuerdo*," I don't remember none of that, the actress said.

"*No me acuerdo,*" the host said. I don't remember any of that.

"But why should you not remember none of that?" the actress asked.

"No, I meant that in Spanish we say, '*No me acuerdo,*" replied the host. "The verb you used is incorrect."

"Now you're going to correct my Spanish, too?"

"Please accept my apologies," the host said. "The fact is that Grandma became very sad whenever she told me that story. She never forgot your contempt and the embarrassment your dad suffered for trying to see you. She always thought your mom had poisoned your mind against your dad. Now I am certain that it was precisely that way. Then you had adopted your third or fourth stepfather's last name.

"He was not a good man to her. He mistreated her," the actress asserted.

"I cannot speak to what happened in their home, ma'am, just as neither can you assure it. Life is like a coin, with its two sides. Perspectives differ and tend to alter reality when it comes to human relatioinships, specially marriage. Everyone talks about the party according to the time they had at it," continued the host. "Or as they want others to think they did."

"I'm not sure I can even understand what you're trying to say."

"To be blunt, ma'am, your mother knitted a gigantic yarn of a tale. Let's start with the travesty of the ship your mom and you took to New York," the host said.

"Hey, watch it!" she protested. "*Yo me arrecuerdo* about that trip perfectly. *Me arrecuerdo...* Sorry, *me acuerdo*, I remember, when we went past the Statue of Liberty, and I said to myself, 'Wow, a lady gives the orders in this country.' You're not going to tell me I made up that memory, *o sí*?"

"Your memories may be true, but what led to that impression, no, ma'am. If you let me, I want to take you somewhere else," the host replied.

"What for? So I can see something uglier than this?" the actress asked. Her distress was obvious to the host. "Look, before night falls, you can just take me back to the Caribe Hilton and forget the rest of your itinerary. You have upset me greatly, just so you know."

"It's nothing uglier," the host clarified. He did not want to sound less than calm. The actress could suffer some sort of dramatic breakdown, with unknown consequences. "It's the place from where you left for New York with your mom."

That seemed to cool her down. The chauffeur turned the engine and climbed Agüeybana Street; he was unable to go up Almodóvar Street, now one way in the direction opposite to the town's central park.

The chauffeur drove on streets just as narrow as Humacao's, but with medium-sized one-story houses whose façades lacked a porch and were perpendicular to the narrow sidewalks. They looked like boxes covered with gabled zinc-sheet roofs. When the limousine was on Baldorioty de Castro Street, the host pointed to several rectangular buildings, white-washed structures that occupied whole blocks. They had identical large, boarded up brown windows on all three stories.

"Many years ago tobacco was stripped in those buildings. The tobacco was sold to the Consolidated Tobacco Company, in Caguas, at the other end of the city from where we ate lunch. Nothing goes on in there now. The tobacco industry in Puerto Rico came to an end with industrialization in the 1950s. These buildings are worth remembering, though. I'll explain in a minute," the host said.

The limousine went down Escuté Street. A large building painted blue and white with a well-manicured patio called the actress' attention.

"Hey, what is that? It looks important," the actress said.

"City hall," the host replied. It used to be an elementary school, Tomás Hernández. I was there from first grade to third.

"*Ah, sí?* Hmm. Interesting."

Toward the end of Escuté Street the limousine turned onto Teodomiro Delfaus Street. It followed down some four blocks before coming to where the street crossed Betances Street. The chauffeur was able to park across the street from a modest dwelling on the corner. The walls were covered in metal sheets painted light blue with a white trim. Like so many other houses in town, the roof also consisted of corrugated zinc sheets. A double door faced Delfaus Street and the other opened to Betances Street at the top of two cement steps. The original lattice double windows had been replaced with metal Persian ones framed in unfinished wood.

"That is where my great grandmother lived. Your dad's aunt," said the host.

"Then she was my grandaunt, right?"

"That is correct. Her name was Justina. I knew her as Mamá Justina, as my grandmother also called her," replied the host. "She and her husband Papá Soto had three children. They owned a trucking company."

The host pointed to a house on the opposite diagonal corner. It was a relatively large cement building with a porch that went from one side to the other in front of the house.

"An aunt of yours lived there. María, although we called her Mary. She was father's sister. She died a year ago," the host said, then paused. "Your dad died five years ago. I don't know whether anyone told you."

'Okay, that's good to know, but what does any of this have to do with Mom or me?" the actress asked.

"You left with your mom from Mamá Justina's house to go to New York."

"From my grandaunt's house? "Might you be wrong?" the actress asked. "As far as I know, Mom and I left together, so it must have been from our own house, I would think."

"Your mom did not live in Puerto Rico, ma'am. She was living with her sister, who could have also been her cousin, because I don't know whether they were sisters from the same set of parents," the host said.

"A cousin? What? I don't understand."

"Your maternal grandfather was married to one woman, but that woman's sister was also your grandfather's mistress. He had children with both. That made the children siblings and cousins."

"What are you talking about? Mom never told me that!" the actress said, visibly upset.

"No, it's obvious she neglected to tell you a lot of tings," the host told her.

The actress seemed stunned. With one blow the host had revealed a life she ignored she had. It was like being born again or reincarnating from another life without dying first. She had been forced to stand before a mirror that reflected someone she never knew. She shook her head as if chasing away an indiscreet bug.

"What else are you going to tell me?" the actress asked in a tone that betrayed her curiosity masquerading as fear.

The host took no time in replying. The actress' mother and father had divorced, yes, but not because she was sick of her husband and Juncos, as her mother alleged and the actress claimed in her biographical accounts and contrived memoirs.

Her grandmother, Dolores, was a woman of a remarkable ill humor, relentless and heavy handed. Her
close relatives used to tell that she did not think twice
before slapping her husband or whipping her children to
discipline them. The entire family came from rural areas:
they wore shoes only when they came down to town.
Aunt Dolores' house was always spotless. It was a large
palm-hatch structure on a plainin Barrio Mamey, in Juncos. Photos of the house, the land and their livestock
were still at the host's mother's house. The family was
known for their unflinching tradition of honesty and hard
work from sun up to sun down. When time allowed,
Dolores would take a break to teach her daughters nee-
dlework, said Dolores, tasks required of decent women
and dedicated homemakers: their handiwork was cele-
brated as legendary in intricacy and originality, from knit
tablecloths and bedspreads to doilies shaped like swans.
The daughters also learned to cook, slaughter hogs for
the open pit roast on the Feast of the Epiphany. They had
a small fortune amassed from farming and cattle raising
and sustained with extreme thriftiness. To them their
whiteness was a matter of pride: they rejected anyone of
African origin.

The actress' mother's hair was suspiciously, tightly
curled despite her facial features and her light skin. It
was obvious that there were blacks in her lineage. That
by itself was enough to be denied access to the family as
a member of equal worth. The matter of her father's
promiscuity weighed heavily on her lack of suitability.
She was, additionally, in her mid-teens when she married
the actress' father, six years her senior. She was known
to be lively in an impudent manner. When her mother-
in-law refused to let the newlyweds live in the main
house, they ended up setting up house in one of the
shacks in Manchuria.

"To be honest," the host added, interrupting his narration to issue an opinion, "for the longest time I doubted you were actually born at Ryder Memorial Hospital or anywhere other than Juncos. Back then the hospital required an advance payment. It was not cheap by local standards. Your dad must have had to work long hours and save most of his pay in the middle of the Great Depression to have his wife deliver a baby there instead of summoning a midwife to come to the Manchuria dwelling."

The actress listened to the host's assessment without uttering a word. The host was not sure whether she understood what he was saying. He thought about asking her whether she knew what a *comadrona,* a midwife was, but his gut feeling was that in that context the meaning could not have escaped her.

When the actress was about three, her mother became pregnant. Puerto Rico was under the dire effects of a world depression complicated by immense losses in the wake of a catastrophic hurricane, San Ciprián, which had decimated the island in 1932. Supporting his family was the reason the actress' father had to migrate to Dutch Guyana, where Puerto Rican construction workers were recruited. He remained in that country during his wife's pregnancy.

"She was pregnant? Did the baby die?" the actress asked.

"No, ma'am. She had the baby before your dad could return from Guyana."

"I do not understand. I never knew of any brother."

"If you allow me, I can explain," the host said. He had noticed the actress' choppy breathing and the frequency of her sighs. She jerked her arms with subtlety; sometimes she crossed them, some other times she clutched a hand within the other, as if making a fist.

While her father was away her mother started going out to party. She left the newborn and the toddler with a sister. People in town, then a lot smaller than it now now, ahd where the scarce opportunities for entertainment mvited gossip, started rumors about an affair the actress' mother was having with the owner of one of the tobacco stripping plants.

"I asked you to take a close look at those buildings we saw. Their owner of one of them was your mom's lover. Your mother was not yet twenty and already had two children," the host explained.

"That cannot be!" the actress protested. Her chest quivered and an artery in her neck seemed to throb.

"Pardon me, ma'am Your mom lived with three men in New York, married two of them and finally married the man whose surname you use. I don't want to be a gossip, but it seems there was evidence of the affair."

Color had escaped from the actress' countenance.

"Would you like something to drink, ma'am?" the host asked.

"Do you have anything stronger than water?" the actress asked.

"There is whiskey in that compartment," the host said. He pointed to a small door behind the seat in front of them. "Unfortunately, we have no ice."

"I don't care," she replied, anxiety unleashed in her voice.

"Allow me," the host said. He took out a bottle of Chivas Regal and a cocktail glass from the compartment. He poured her the drink. She downed it like water at the end of the day in the desert.

As soon as she had emptied the glass, she raised it again to let the host know she wanted a refill. Once again the host filled it halfway. This time the actress waited before speaking again. They were still sitting in the limousine. Early evening darkness had fallen. The incandescence of bulbs and the spectral luminosity of television screens shone from inside neighborhood houses. Traffic was light. With the extension of the town into what had been rural areas business had dwindled and, with it, so had automobile traffic.

"Rumors about your mom's infidelity reached her mother-in-law," the host explained. Right away the actress gulped down her whiskey.

When the baby was about two months old the actress' father returned from Guyana. He had meant to go back to some construction project in what had been the jungle and was turning into urbanized deforestation. A few days after his return he received an anonymous letter. Its author had revealed his wife's affair. "Look in her dresser drawers. Under her bras she keeps jewelry her lover has given her," the message read.

"Who wrote that?" the actress wanted to know.

"Many suspected it was your grandmother, but the details about the exact location of the jewelry pointed to someone else. Maybe her own sister."

The husband searched where the letter indicated and found the jewelry. Your mom's betrayal was in the open. They divorced. Because the actress' mother was judged unfit, the court gave the children's custody to their father.

"Where did Mom go?"

"To New York, to live with the sister whose apartment she would later bring you to," the host replied.

"Yes," the actress said. Again she drank from the glass the host had refilled for her while he narrated the sordid events. "In a room divided into a bathroom and a kitchen. No privacy whatsoever. Mom and I slept in a rollaway."

Her voice had changed from the comfort of the adventure she had undertaken with this trip to something unlike the bitterness of memory, but shaded in soiled hues. The host wanted to avoid her becoming lost in memories without first listening to the rest of her story.

"My great grandmother sat with you while your dad was at work, often twelve hours under the sun. Your brother, Frank, was looked after by the woman who was then your dad's girlfriend," the host said.

"My brother Frank," the actress said as if absent from her body.

"Yes. He died some twenty years ago in a motorcycle accident in New York."

"No one told me anything about a brother!" the actress yelled. "How horrible! You are hurting me deeply. If you had stabbed me with a knife you couldn't have wounded me any worse," said the actress. It sounded like an authentic appreciation of her pain.

"Please forgive me, ma'am. I did not want to hurt you. We have started this…" the host said, and the actress cut him off.

"You started this."

"Yes, I started this. Now I'm going to end it,"the host countered. "Or would you rather not hear anything else?"

After a brief silence, the actress raised her glass. The host filled it halfway once more. She downed it. She tightened her eyes before answering.

"Go on. Now I can't remain without knowing the rest," the actress said.

When the actress was four, in 1935, once day she was at Mama Justina's house when her mother poked her head in the door from the Delfaus Street side. The house's doors were kept open during the day for the sake of ventilation. Mama Justina was in the rocking chair, next to the radio; she sat there during her breaks from house chores to listen to radio dramas. The actress, always shorter than the average child her same age, was playing with a rag doll on the floor. She saw her mom first; Mamá Justina was immersed in the afternoon soap-opera plot.

Her mom greeted the child. This startled Mama Justina: that woman was the last person she expected to see again at her door. The child recognized her mother and ran to hug her as much as the child guard at the door allowed her.

"*Doña* Justina, may I come in?" asked the woman who had been married to Mamá Justina's nephew, the woman who had cheated on him.

Mamá Justina at first considered denying her access to the house, but the child's happiness at seeing her mom softened her repugnance.

The child's grandaunt went to the kitchen under the pretext of taking care of something she had left unfinished. In the kitchen she sat on a stool from which she could see what was going on in the living room.

"Would you allow me to take my daughter to Laudelino Alonso's store? I want to buy her a pair of shoes. The ones she's wearing are pretty scuffed."

Mamá Justina remained silent for a short while. She looked at the child and read in her eyes a request from an innocent anxious expectation She decided in favor of the outing.

"That was the last time Mamá Justina or anyone else saw you. Your mom kidnapped you and took you on the sailing ship Borinquen to New York," the host said. "Your dad lacked the means to stop her and follow her to New York. He sought assistance from the local police, but they could do nothing. By the time one of her relatives said where she was headed you and your mom were on your way to New York."

The actress asked for a refill.

"The only contact your dad had with you was from images on movie screens and photos in magazines," the host continued. He noticed a certain languor in the actress' eyes. The host could not truly tell if that was due to the liquor or his revelations. Or perhaps it was both. "That was why your rejection after your stage performance at Teatro Puerto Rico wounded him so deeply.

"Today my picture would be on milk cartons instead of show business publications," the actress said, her words staggered. "She took only me. Why didn't she try to get her son, too?" The question seemed directed at her mother more than at the host.

"Frank was little more than a year old. He didn't know her," the host replied. "Besides, Sylvia took care of him. That was your dad's girlfriend. Your mom would not have been able to trick her into taking the baby. Her escape would have been much more difficult with two children in tow, one of them in diapers and needing formula."

"She left a child behind," the actress said in a tone of bewilderment. She asked the host, "Do you have children?"

"Yes, ma'am. My partner and I adopted a girl who's now nine and a boy, three. They were my sister's. She died in a car accident and their father could not raise them by himself."

The actress had no reaction. She twisted her mouth and took a deep breath.

"Have you been together long?" she asked the host.

"Twelve happy years," the host said.

"You are both parents to those kids?" the actress asked.

"Both. We share their care."

"And if you and your partner were to separate, would you leave any of your children behind for someone else to raise while you ran off?" the actress asked.

Her body was there next to the host, but her thoughts were distant in time and tone.

"I have never thought about it, ma'am, but I am sure I would not," the host replied.

"Of course not! Who the hell does that?" the actress shouted, waving around the arm with which she was not holding the glass. With her body movement she was unable to control the glass. Some of the whiskey splashed out onto her blouse. She did not seem to notice or care. "If she could not take both children, why the fuck did she bother with one? God damn it, who leaves her own flesh and blood with another woman?" the actress shouted, again shaking one arm in the air.

"Even in Puerto Rico she would have been able to take them. Neither you nor your brother. The courts would not have allowed her," the host replied. "She could not have done any better than supervised visitation.'"

The actress ignored him. She drank the rest of the whiskey before going on.

"She dragged me everywhere on auditions. To recitals, selling me to buy her lunch ticket. It was not my talent she was so concerned about. She wanted to live through me!! I was the facsimile of what she could have been, so provincial, so mediocre. So unfaithful. She was all woman. A mother only when it was convenient."

"Don't judge her so severely," the host advised. "She suffered the scorn of the family she had planned to belong to and share in its wealth. She married too young. And she lived in a four-street town. Her world must have seemed too small for her. Perhaps she wanted something better for you."

"Yeah, yeah, sure, you could be right. That does not excuse her not even telling me I had a brother," the actress protested. I can't forgive her either for filling my heart with so much undeserved garbage about my dad, when she was the actual trash."

The host could not think of anything to say. It was decidedly night outside. Following a silence only intermittently broken by the actress' sobs he asked the chauffeur to take them back to the hotel. No words were exchanged during the trip back to San Juan. The host had his doubts about his actions, but he convinced himself that knowing the truth was better for the actress in the long run. She would no longer wonder where she came from or who her forebearers were nor would she have to weave lies abut her past. Her mother was dead; she would have to forgive her posthumously or live with bitter resentment. Fortunately for her, her husband was a psychiatrist: she could have at-home on-the-spot therapy. With his help she would be able to resolve the issues that now upset her.

At the hotel the host was about to step out of the limousine when the actress told him, "You don't have to. I can go up by myself."

"But ma'am, you have had a little too much to drink, and I'm afraid that…"

"Then let the chauffeur escort me," the actress said. "You can stay here."

"I'm sorry if I made you feel bad, ma'am," the host said.

The chauffeur had stepped out of the limousine and opened the actress' door.

"No need to apologize, *chico*," the actress replied. "Somehow I feel I should be grateful for what you have done. Going through all this trouble. It's water under the bridge. We can't go back into the past to fix what went wrong," she added, philosophy soaked in whiskey.

"What time should we come by tomorrow to pick you up?" the host asked. "We need to be at the airport at noon."

"Look,, *chico*, I'd prefer that you not come to pick me up. Just have the limousine come by for me and I'll take care of the rest," the actress stated, sounding tired, but imitating a gesture that the host recognized from several of her films and two television series.

"But…"

"No, no buts. Just forget about it. Thanks for bringing me here and for filling out the blanks in my autobiography. I don't think the publisher will allow for corrections, so as far as history and the public go, what's written is the truth," the actress said.

She walked away. The chauffeur cam back. He did not get to accompany her to her suite, although he waited until he thought it was useless to stick around. As soon as they entered the lobby several people recognized and surrounded her. A small mob of curious guests formed a small mob, all asking for her autograph on napkins from the hotel bar.

"I loved you in *I'm Latina*! You were a divine dancer!" one said.

"Oh, I wish my mom could see you! She remembers you on Broadway, in the show they gave you the Tony for!" someone else cheered.

"You were so lucky to be in a movie with Jack Nicholson! Well, the luck was his," yet another one yelled before guffawing.

A middle-aged woman with a heavy Brooklyn accent yelled, "My kids grew up watching you on that children's show, what was it called? Anyway, you were fabulous!"

All sorts of comments blended to the point where the words became gibberish of which only "… thought you were taller," "… visiting relatives," "… he didn't deserve you," "… he's dead,, but you're not," "… next to you Jennifer Lopez is nothing!" The actress replied at everything with "Thank you," "*Ay, qué linda,*" "Really?" "*Ay*, how sweet!" She only diverged from her shorter statements to ask a young woman whether she was *Boricua*, because, God bless her, she looked like an American girl.

The next morning the host read one of San Juan's newspapers. The front page ran a photo of the actress in the same outfit she had worn the previous day. Among the people in the lobby was a reporter who had been assigned to interview Puerto Rico's resident commissioner in Washington, D.C., who was in the island on official business. The reporter mentioned that detail in an account that exposed his awe at the actress and the remarkable serendipity of coinciding with her that night in the lobby. He changed his assignment; instead, he convinced the actress to give him an interview. It would have to be in private, because the fans in the small crowd kept interrupting them. The newspaper's photographer joined them at the suite. The reporter asked her what she was doing in the islad, whether she was going to shoot there or had an engagement for a musical revue like the ones she performed in New York.

"No, oh, no, nothing like that," the actress replied, according to the news item:

In this unscheduled and felicitous interview, completely improvised, we were lucky enough to speak with the actress, so praised, so recognized for her work in film, television a,d the theater with so many national awards *Boricua* pride, this great figure of international fame! She honored us by granting us this interview during a few minutes she took out of her busy schedule, out of the immense love she feels for her birthplace, a place she never forgets, just as she loves her *Boricua* public.

Reporter: Tell us, please, what brought you to our little island this time, then?

The Actress: Well, can I call you by your first name?

Reporter: Of course, madame.

The Actress: Oh, good! Well, ha, ha, ha, I was invited here by a well-known Puerto Rican promoter to spend a few days recovering from a short-term illness. I only came for a few days, and I'm leaving tomorrow.

Reporter: You did not let the press know. We would have greeted you at Luis Muñoz Marín Airport to give you the welcome you deserve. The governor certainly would have organized a reception for you.

The Actress: Oh, how kind! Very sweet of you to say that. That's something I have always loved about my people. Such chivalry!

Reporter: Tell us, then, what have you been doing during your time here?

The Actress: Well, look... I was invited, as I said, to take a break and reconnect with places I had visited as a child and had not seen since then.

Reporter: So you went to Humacao?

The Actress: Yes, of course. You know it's where I was born, at Ryder Memorial Hospital. Then I was taken where I lived before moving to New York with my mom. As I have said before, we lived in the countryside, at the foot of the rain forest. It was something dreamlike I remember very little about, so many years have gone by, but I never forget the happy time we had there. Later, well, with my parents' divorce my mom and I were by ourselves, and she decided we were better off migrating to New York. We went by sea, you know? When we went past the Statue of Liberty I remember thinking, "Wow, this country is ruled by a lady!" Ha, ha, ha. The rest is, as they say, history. Or herstory, ha, ha, ha.

"How interesting," the host said to his partner as they had their morning coffee that Sunday, before the children woke up. He folded the newspaper in half to look at local baseball standings.

Two weeks later the actress' husband found her dead in the attic of her house outside of San Francisco, but not close to the Pacific. She was hunched over a cardboard box; as she fell she knocked over the bottle of Jack Daniels. Her silk pajamas were soaked in liquor. She had taken the lids off several boxes stored in the attic. She had torn off the tape on the box where her head and her upper torso had fallen. The box contained a dozen photo albums. Her hands were curled in, holding one of the volumes. It had photographs of her childhood in New York, except for one in which she was in Mamá Justina's rocking chair at the age of two. Someone's arm held her back by the waist from behind the chair. Her hair was gathered in small tight-curled buns, her skin was dark and her almond-shaped eyes popped out, as if she were scared of something behind the camera.

SURVIVED BY THOSE WHO LOVED HIM

Climb up the steps and go find out once and for all what's going on up there—that's what I should do. But why should it matter to me anymore? Other than my sleep, what else can they disturb? Certainly not the dead, although they seem to have tried that also. I can hear them clawing through Fred's files, organized chronologically and alphabetically. First, the nearly distant clicks of metal-drawer locks; then the rolls of bearings, roo-eep, roo-eep. If only their imprecise whispers five feet above my head could come through as identifiably as the rest of the rumbling. I can even hear their fleshy pincers flipping through the folders. Maybe all along he had planned to make it easier for them to cash in on his death without too much inconvenience.

At least tonight I cannot hear the cringing wheelchair. They must have left her at Sanac. So she is not with them—to spare themselves the trouble of carrying her up the steps. She's not heavy, but she must be an awkward bundle. She will not be ringing our doorbell as she did last time, interrupting our fragile conjugality still haunted by images of death and painfully unexpected self-doubt, to ask me, the intrusive Mrs. Gustafson, where her grandfather's silver trumpet went. And what of the little silver purse with a blue velvet lining, from the Weyerhauser estate sale? And what of the thirty silver coins, whose symbolic possibilities her defective mind had not considered? No, she had never seen any of it, but Fred had told her everything was in the condo.

And the silver coins, the silver coins, whatever happened to them? I had never seen them either, I insist. But I—you—had kept his key. But unlike you three I didn't go through Fred's files or closets or cupboards, nor looked under his bed, under his mattress—your pristine hands isolated from the phantom of his presence by gloves from some medical supply company—under the rugs, in his laundry bag, in his tin cans, in his desk drawers, in his bank account, his bank statements, union papers, travel guides to places he never went because he didn't want to leave you in the incompetent hands of the county nurse, Mrs. Gustafson. Yes, but you—I—could have seen it. But I didn't. Not the silver trumpet. Excuse me, Mrs. Gustafson. I'm tired. "Poor Freddie. I'm sure he wanted all that for me." Yes, I am sure, too, I said mechanically, barely detached from her words, adhesive like cobwebs. And I hope you find the trumpet and the silver purse, and the coin collection, and the stamp collection, and some legal statement that makes it all, all yours, Mrs. Gustafson.

It would make sense, after all. Warped sense, like everything else in his life. She was the last relative with whom he lived before he joined the U.S. Navy. She reportedly took care of him. That must have been before she started to keep him home from school to run errands for her. That must have been when he and his two sisters were too young to do anything other than play with empty cans and discarded boxes in the middle of the triangle whose vertices were the wheelchairs. Then Martha was still Martha Schulz, not Martha Gustafson—Mrs. Gustafson. Back when, to look at the Hormel stockyards across the snow-covered street, Fred climbed the armrest of Agatha's wheelchair and hopped onto a ledge. As he'd come back down, Agatha wheeled herself out of his skinny let's way. Fred was always sure that this time she would not try that. The fall always left a bruise on his skinny elbows. But if on its way to the floor the sack of bones struck one of the shelves of five-and-dime figurines, Martha shrieked, Agatha cackled and Karola howled. The vertices closed in and formed a circle around the vertical axis of under nourishment and clipped wings. Back then Martha could still move her hands and grasp the rim of the wheels. She could also wrap the leather belt around her hand and snap the buckle on Fred's back after he, like an icicle, stood motionless in a post she would designate. His lungs filled with a suffocating scream whose physical reverberations only found his vocal cavity minutes later.

She would teach him respect in harsher terms when he asked questions that only a little *Affenarsch* like him could ask.

"Why are all of you in wheelchairs? Is God angry with you, too?"

Even Agatha and Karola joined then in a circular gauntlet, jerking themselves into turning the wheels as their alternating hands chopped the air crookedly and slammed their clumsy might over Fred's disproportionate head and the narrowness of his back.

"Because they were born from animals, the *Schweine*, that's why," Fred's father used to say when Fred took advantage of the man's intoxicated indiscretion to develop an image of the past on which his own present had been shaped. When Fred was nine, his father filled in the gaps in his awareness of heritage.

"Your grandfather was your grandmother's brother. And they made a bunch of loonies. Your mama wasn't sick like Martha, but she died on me. Bad ticker," words chewed out from the side of his drooling mouth.

Fred didn't know that other children sat at the table to eat with their parents until his father married a third time and took him to live with the new bride on an abandoned farm in Stillwater. ("*Scheisse* don't sit with people, Martha said, and Agatha and Karola agreed.) That stepmother seemed to care more than the previous one: when Fred's father brought him to visit, the other stepmother had made him head cheese and blood sausage sandwiches, then would sit across the table to laugh and watch Fred get queasy just looking at the filling between the two slices of stale pumpernickel. The third wife— what was her name? he would wonder aloud when he talked about her. But the third wife tired also of bill collectors that came around for their share, in dollar bills, of what Fred's father had already liquefied in alcohol. She left him and took her two children. Fred was working for the railroad before he saw just one of those half-brothers again—by chance, at the Union Depot in St. Paul.

During moments of unfathomable darkness on the interminable nights when he shared the only bed in the South Side hotel room with his father, back from a vigil at a corner tavern, Fred missed Martha. He would often dream that he was pedaling a boat on Como Lake, toward the shore where Martha waited for him in her wicker-back wheelchair. Suddenly the boat filled with dark-green water. He pedaled lethargically, as if he had all the time in the world. The boat wasn't sinking: the water level of the lake rose, and Martha would wheel herself farther from the shore, as if her chair were motorized, up the hill, farther from him, higher that he could hope to reach before the warm water soaked him through. Fred would wake up frightened, searching for Martha, amazed that he could still breathe in the darkness of the bottom of the lake. His underside was damp and cold as far as his unconscious father's urine could reach. And Fred would spend the balance of his restless night crawling toward the drier corners.

He soon went back to the cellar apartment with Martha. He only saw his father again one more time, on an autumn night at Ramsey County Hospital, after Fred's discharge from the Navy. His father had sent for him to tell him that he wanted to have his life insurance policies changed to make Fred his beneficiary. Fred refused.

"Leave them to your wife and your other sons, so that they can take care of medical expenses."

Fred's father left the certificates as they were, and that night, in spasms and gags from his own collapsing insides' search for expulsion from his disintegrating body, carbonized old-man Doppler for the last time shared of himself in bloody spittle sprayed on his son. The dismay of his anxiety kept Fred from thinking to shake his father's entrails off his bespattered clothing. The widow and her sons decided that they had suffered enough, kept the insurance money, and sent the bills for the hospital and funeral to Fred. Three years he spent, paying them off to the Northland Finance Company.

At least Martha was not as bad as Fritz. Fred's sisters had gone to his house, to their aunt Agnes and her own children. Her husband Fritz did not allow children to occupy chairs around a dinner table either, and Fred did not mind standing at the table while he ate. But Fred certainly was startled when one of Fritz's children did something that Fritz did not like—talking before breakfast, sitting in a chair he wanted for himself, forgetting to close the storm door, clutching their noses to avoid smelling his beer *Fürze*. Then Fritz stood the derelict on the top step of their front door and kicked him on the back with his work boots to make the child hit the sidewalk face first. Regardless of the time of the year, the child could only come back in when Fritz decided. He would give Agnes a shiner if she opened the garage door for one of the little *Arschficker*.

And Uncle Emil out in St. Louis Park did not seem to want them around. He was the only one of the Schulzes who did not live in South St. Paul, and the only one of the Schulzes who was not then visibly crippled. He had a nice house—Fred and his sisters had visited once on Easter, when Fritz and Agnes had come by and managed to load the Doppler children and the three Schulz sisters in their wicker-back wheelchairs on the bed of a pickup truck, for the ride across town to St. Louis Park—but his wife Janice did not much care for the Schulzes. Right in front of him Janice had said she did not want Fred in their house.

"I just don't have the facilities to raise a child like... this one. I have enough with mine, trying to keep them from bad influences."

And when Agatha died a month after Karola, some weeks before Fred's eighth-grade graduation, Martha told Fred that he could not leave her without help after all she had done for him. He had to see it her way. At any rate, the streets in winter would be much worse.

They have separated and gone in different directions, like cockroaches when the lights go on. Divide and conquer. Two of them must be in the living room. One of them is nailing high heels onto the bare hardwood floor. Janice, most likely: Beverly wears those shoes designed in hyper-sensible space, perhaps perfect for stepping on scorpions in the Big Sandy desert. She's opening one of the drawers of the chest in the hall. The cherry-wood chest of drawers that Fred bought at the auction last spring. The same one where we bought the Queen Anne secretary. I can hear the screeching drawer close, and the hardware handles bounce off, click-clink. Another one opens. Clink, clink. Even more Maggie's breathing—rhythmic sighs she takes when she sleeps deeply—I know that Janice is going through the manila envelopes, the ones with the photographs. Sailor Fred, white strips ending in a knotted neckerchief, his blue eyes almost black behind Navy supply eyeglasses and above air-brush-peach cheeks. Ensign Fred again with the U.S. Naval School group in Great Lakes. Best man Fred standing at a wedding. Usher Fred laughing in the line-up at someone else's wedding, Chuck and Rusty, NAS Chapel-Corpus Christi, 7/4/58, Always the clown, thanks, Fred. Instructor Fred with his U.S. Naval Medical Center group 1963. 1964. 1965.

One of them shut the bathroom door. Maybe disconsolate Chester or gifted Carl or helpful, loving Uncle Emil. Something they must have eaten earlier. I doubt they would want to touch any of the food Fred left behind, even if he was obsessed with cleanliness. I bet I know what's going through their misinformed minds. There, a flush. Water running. He is washing his hands. But he won't find a towel. I threw them in the laundry basket last Thursday. Let him dry them on his double-knit pants.

Had he been conscious, he would have known what the steady signal meant. Now somewhere someone has written that the comatose don't really lose their hearing. It's the last sense to abandon us. One of those things we won't get to verify until--. So maybe he did know what was going on and what I whispered in his ear. For all the good the knowledge could do him.

"We've done our best," Dr. Bowers said, and I noticed, etched on his face, the characteristically, despicably studied expression of feigned compunction so representative of the worst of his profession. And what was I supposed to reply, "Sure"? Five hours earlier the grave-yard-shift desk nurse sat in front of Fred's clear spinal-fluid sample, wondering out loud (he loves me, he loves me not, he loves...) whether she should even touch the tube in case he did have meningitis. For an unknown length of time I had been biting my lip unconsciously but angrily as I read her lips from the other side of the see-through panel in the visitors' waiting room. She glanced at me, I glared, but undeterred she let the sample sit in the eight-tube rack.

But then again, Fred had not seemed to want much to be done either.

"Just don't go shooting things into his heart, please. Let him go with dignity."

He had convulsed throughout the night, at least the times I disguised myself in aseptic gowns and masks and went into his isolation chamber.

"Maybe he's responding to you. H wasn't to me," said a nurse in an unflattering, enormous blue gown, her head poking Archimboldesquely through the top opening. His eyes and mouth widened and shut close again when I touched his hand, "I'm here, buddy." Like an automaton activated with an electric charge that lasts two seconds, ceases, and repeats the cycle a moment later. His eyes would expand again, the way they did when my mischievous sons (giggling, scaring him out of his nodding sleep, then he would lead them on, pretending to doze off so they could startle him again and laugh) interrupted his irregular sleep during a nap, stretched out peacefully on our sofa, after a holiday meal that most other people spend with relatives. Perhaps he was trying to get a glimpse of the two rubber hoses disappearing into his nostrils.

"I understand." Dr. Bowers' mouth emitted the words—teeth on repetitious gears—as he completed a chart in several ink tones and handwritten scribbling.

Like hell. Like hell you—he—understood. Like sheer hell, this sudden mess caused by unknown enemies no one could see or control or vanquish or even understand.

"We've notified his sister."

His sister?

"How did you find her?"

"His aunt Martha called the hospital this morning and gave Mrs. Beverly Roberts' name as the next of kin."

I felt relieved. Nothing remained that I could do for Fred, as frustrating as that was to admit. Once Mrs. Roberts flew in from Texas I would be able to delegate the responsibility I had assumed, and pass it on to the people who had the legal duty to take over in spite of their preferences. But Mrs. Roberts would only come, Dr. Bowers explained with a skeptical smirk, if her congregation in Big Sandy received a supernatural command during a prayer meeting conducted by her husband, the spiritual leader and minister of some unknown, to me anyway, Christian group in the Texan desert, where her husband also ministered to inmates at the nearby state prison.

Joyce, the other sister, had died the same way Fred's mother had died, of congenital heart failure, at twenty-eight, leaving three children. Dr. Bowers could not see why the hospital had to call the three nieces. I agreed. Fred had never met them.

The history of failing—broken, could almost be said—hearts explained why Fred kept track of his cardiac health. His last biannual physical exam had been the

previous November. "The pump of a teenager," Dr. In-
gram had told him. Everything checked out. Perfect."

The pallor had set in later, at the hospital. Even the
night I found him lying on the sofa he looked healthy. As
healthy and young-looking as the forty-four year-old
("I've already outlives my father by a year") Maggie and
I had met four years before at a condo owners meeting:
the single owner, our neighbor upstairs. We can always
tell when you're coming home. The whistling. Always
the same one, too. "Lili Marlene." Stop by and visit us
sometime. You've done great things with this place—I
like the bare brick fireplace. Super artwork, too. Wow.
So this is the piano. You play beautifully, Maggie. Oh,
no, never a bother. I sit in the balcony to hear you better.
And these are the two tikes I hear all the time. Oh, God,
no, they don't bother me. It's monotonous around here,
with all of these couples without children. They hide the
BMWs and Volvos in the garage, put the lid on them,
then put a lid on themselves. I don't know the people
here. Great stuffing, Maggie. How did you bake this
scrumptious ham? Hmm. Delish. Who made your birthday cake, Jerry? Dad? Dad should open a bakery. Did
you like your present, Little Al? Oh, it's nothing. Glad
to. These are my children too. Like my children, anyway.
I know, corny, but true. That's how I feel. Stand here and
pose with Uncle Fred—smile and say cheese. Great
Asti—cheers. Are they in bed yet? Here are my presents
for them. Oh, nonsense, sure I had to. I was worried it
might not clear the door. Sure he's old enough to ride a
bike. You're too protective. Enough already, so let me
spoil them.

"Not completely."

A sweat spot marks the pillow where his head has
been resting until he lifts it to look at the intruder. Suddenly his shaking returns, uncontrolled.

"Are you sick?" My face alone must betray my fear.

"Just a chill. Nothing to worry about."

The television set is on, but he doesn't seem to be following the images on the screen, "...or behind door number two? Number two? Let's see what..."

"How long have you been sick?"

"Couple of days." His teeth, click-click.

His temperature has been consistently four or five degrees above normal. Oh, no, no, he has just taken analgesics, thanks just the same. The cough? A chest cold. (Three empty bottles of cough syrup of different brands lie empty on the floor.) Does he want a blanket? That would be nice.

I pull two quilts out of his linen closet and throw them on him, tucking the top one under his feet and shoulders. He has crossed his arms over his chest beneath the quilts.

"You look like a mummy."

He smiles. "I feel like one. A wound-up mummy." He pauses. A gagging cough overtakes him. He signals at a plastic pail in a corner. I run for it and bring it to the sofa. He raises his head to clear the edge of the cushion and a mixture of drool and bile ejects from his mouth onto the pail. He hasn't eaten for two days, nothing stays down.

"This sounds like something you need to be seen for."

"Oh, I suppose. I'm trying to give it a few days. I'm on vacation, you know." As if his vacation had been mandated by a heavenly edict to cause the railroad company—"Twenty-eight years with them next May"—as little disruption as possible when he became ill.

I push his feet back and sit by them. He looks flushed. His legs begin to shake, then his whole body. I slide up the edge of the sofa and feel his forehead. Under it a ball of fire threatens to melt his skin and bolt through.

"What is wrong?" I'm more desperate than curious. "Why haven't you called us? Why haven't you called your relatives?"

Fred manages to laugh lethargically, avoiding another coughing fit. "What for? I'm too old to whip. I haven't seen any of them in so long. Except Martha. And I don't want her to worry."

"Do you want me to drive you to the hospital?"

"Oh, no, no. It isn't that serious."

He'd know if it were, wouldn't he?

Tension has been building up in my chest. Helplessness is only apprehended through experience, like catching your naked fingers in a slamming steel door.

The shaking increases. He hums an involuntary wail through the intermittence of gnashing teeth. I throw myself over him gingerly, hoping that my body warmth will chase away the chill, and hug him, hold him tight against me, my ear pressed against his, a fleshy lump of burning coal, his breath halitus from an iron furnace on my shoulder, the smoothness of his skin roughened by the viscous remnants of unceasing sweat. "Oh, Lord, Fred, you need someone to see you for this." I loosen my embrace with unsuspected reluctance and run home for an ice bag. More analgesics. Nothing helps.

I stay by him that night. Impossible that either he or I could rest. I wipe his face when the chills impolitely yield again to a fever. We make small talk. I don't want to encourage him to say anything: perhaps the effort of articulating sounds depletes his energy.

"Stop looking at my crotch, you pervert."

"Trust me, Frederick Doppler," I laugh, my nerves all concentrated in my throat. I laugh, yes, but self-conscious and uncomfortably confused. "That's one part of you I don't want."

The knot loosens some. He must be better if he's joking.

368

But my heart leadens again: he is delirious. I touch his moist head, a warm mass of fine strands plastered to his skull like a realistic recreation of a hominid in a diorama, and he jumps, startled.

"I thought you were speaking to me."

He is shaking again. I slip a towel under the layers of sweaters to dry his sweat.

"Uh dream'n uf Martha's husband. He work'n circus."

"Are you awake?"

His eyelids uncover bloody patches diffused through convex slime. His dim pupils are set deeply behind. "Uhmm."

"I didn't know Martha had been married. I knew, but it was knowledge at odds with imagination. I don't want to explain it to Fred. Martha Gustafson, whom I had met one night when I drove Fred to her apartment at Sanac, the Special Adult Needs Apartment Complex on the North End of St. Paul. She could barely move her hands and needed help to move her head up, controlled by the corrosion of progressive sclerosis.

"Oh, uh-humm. Man work in circus, then for Salvash'n Arm. He stare my crotch all uh time, licked's lip. They marr. Mart got pregn't. Babe kill Marth. Spinuh bifith. Mess. Always shak'n bed'n Marth pick up. Live three yirs."

"And the husband?"

"He died. Left her penshn. Hes good fe'er."

They sound like rodents in the old tenement on Cedar Avenue ten years ago. At night when I sat to read, whenever a Chippewa woman wasn't running down the street yelling for help, I could hear the light, scratchy crompcroomp of teeth and claws in a genetically determined conspiracy to strip me of my sanity. I'd get off my over-stuffed chair—panels of corrugated cardboard between my back and its rusty springs—and hit the book against the ceiling, and for a few minutes I'd have uninterrupted peace even as the book's pages lay on the floor like over-sized confetti from a carnival long since over and forgotten.

Steps come from all directions and converge in the hall. She must have found something she was looking for. Or that she wants after seeing. Certainly not the photographs. Maybe the trumpet. Maybe sterling pounds. Scrapes and clicks alternate on the floor. They're heading for the front bedroom. What had they left unturned in there from the last time?

When the faint natural light made the lamp unnecessary, I helped him to his bed, went home to take a shower, call my secretary and bring Maggie up to date—Maggie, who worries and stops by to order him to get well, preferably by the close of the business day or else—and came back with a tray of orange juice, toast, and tea. Fred sat in bed awkwardly and drank the juice while I held the glass to his lips. The same yellow fluid came back and into the pail a few minutes later.

"You can't go on like this. I'm taking you to the emergency room."

"I'm dirty," he said, now that the fever was back but the tremors were gone, if only for a while. "I need a shower. But I'm too weak."

"Who cares if you're dirty? I'm sure they've seen worse."

"I care. I can't."

"Fine, Mr. Anal Retentive. On with it, then."

His body was lighter than it seemed. The toilet seat complained with a cracking squeak when I plopped him on it. I helped him out of the sour-smelling sweaters and the warmth-soaked T-shirt he had worn for three days and the jeans he said he felt glued to after two.

I lifted him again and sat him on the tub's warm water.

"That feels so good," he said quietly.

"Are you going to need more help?"

"I really can't do anything. I feel like my arms fell off. And I'm dizzy." He shook his head lightly, as if to cast off a creeping insect.

I shampooed his hair while massaging his scalp, then rinsed it off. I lathered him from his neck to his toes, squeezing the soap bar under his arms to catch the parts he was most worried about. He rested with my arm thrown across his back, my hand propping him up while I washed his legs and avoided his groin.

"I guess your things are yours to scrub?"

"He seemed to smile. "If I had the energy I'd laugh. No. But you've done enough already, so you can skip my smelly *Piller*.

Gently I slipped my hand into the water to reach for his groin and lathered him the same way I had washed his ears, his back, his hands. "Isn't this stupid?" I asked.

"I told you you didn't have to."

"That's not it, Fred. I feel stupid for having asked." I was perhaps revealing more than I was clarifying. This, however, was not the time for my concerns.

"Then wash them well and reach all the way behind them, too. And don't look like you're enjoying it, or I'll start rumors." Humor without the usual euphonic laugh—he tried and the cavernous hacking took over again.

He lay in bed as I dressed him. I ran down and changed clothes, then came back up for him.

I put him on my back, the way Jerry and I played cowboy. I held him by his thighs and leaned forward as far as I could without losing my balance to keep him from sliding off. My arm held him up until he could ease himself onto the back seat of my car. He lay down and thunder cracked in the cave of his chest.

"Mr. Doppler has to be admitted," the nurse told me in the emergency room two hours after an orderly had wheeled him in, making Fred vanish between the flowing sails of the ward's compartments, all in low tide. "Can you sign the admission form as a witness? I mean, you know, for health insurance. Mr. Doppler's hand can't hold the pen."

One of them just walked out. Must be a man. His steps are chasing themselves down the stairway, thump-thump-thmp-tmp on the other side of the hall that runs along our bedroom wall. Maggie's turning. Her eyes are shut across the fault between the two pillows, and a tress crosses her cheek. In her sleep she rubs her forehead where I've blown, unsuccessfully hoping she would wake up without a startle, that together we might trace the steps above and hypothesize aloud about the goal of this search.

The one who slammed shut the building door some minutes ago is back. The stride is shorter, the steps are slower. He kicks the door upstairs, and another set of steps advances to the door. His hands must be full. What's he bringing in? They plunder in reverse.

We really are not sure exactly what happened," Janice would say. None of the other relatives standing with her by the coffin could add any details either. They were packed tightly together by the pine coffin, individual to-tem poles whose gestures and mouths were equally in-scrutable, rubbing their hands nervously as if to remove filth from them. "But he knows: he was with him when, well, when==" Janice, alternating between cicerone and band leader, would point at me in the back of the funeral parlor, surrounded by veteran clerks from the railroad company. The gang, the old guard. Janice's finger, more than guidance for the interested, was an accusation. Hundreds of people seemed to be coming through. I didn't know any of them. "Fred used to lend me money." "Remember, Shirley, how he stayed with me when I had the operation?" "When he played the drum with the company clown band, we used to go to foster homes together." "We didn't see much of him outside of work the last couple of years." "He never forgot my birthday. Boofdays, he called them. I always found a card from him on my desk." "I didn't know he had family here. And twenty-five years I knew him." "A good man. A good man"—a nod followed by the nods of others around, eyes fixed on parquet, embarrassment being the inescapable consequence of recognizing human goodness. "But how did this happen? He looked so good last week!"

I had wanted to avoid becoming an echo chamber for platitudes at the viewing. At first I'd state the background in carefully chosen words. As the night progressed and the scores of strangers flowed through, and Janice's Zolaesque finger increased its activity, I shrugged into a condensed version: the necessary details, no more, no less, like a school assignment on conciseness. He got sick suddenly. Right on his second day of vacation. He thought it was the flu. I took him in. Lasted two days. And here we are.

"At least you were there and can fill people in," Mrs. Roberts, Beverly, observed uncomfortably, perhaps in appreciation or in resentment of herself, for herself, of me, for me—of Fred or for Fred. I gave her my best imitation of a grin, looking past her at the backdrop of truncated gardens and the open lid behind Fred's head raised on a white satin pillow. Not a single rose. This was not the way to pay homage to a man who cultivated the plot in our backyard, the rose garden for which he paid the condominium association to maintain: forty rose bushes that he uprooted carefully in late October, buried in rows under dirt and mulch, and again cleared and raised to replant early in the spring. In summer his bouquets of American beauties always sat in our tall green vase, the obliquely refracted sunlight cutting a tunnel through stems and water, making useless attempts to blind Maggie when, albeit the moisture of temple beads in languorous Sunday afternoons, she refreshed our love with Mendelssohn.

"No roses in the arrangements."

"Did he like them?" Beverly asked. And revealed.

She had flown in Sunday afternoon and joined the swarm of Schulzes and Dopplers at Martha's. She had had to decide: open or closed casket. Then Sunday night Emil and Janice had driven her to the funeral home to give her approval for the clothes he was wearing, the suit, shirt and tie I had picked from his wardrobe. Beverly would also have to approve the cosmetic reconstruction of his boyish face, beauty still chiseled onto his features even in his illness and despite the pallor.

"But what would they need to reconstruct?" My naive question got lost, just like indifference had smothered my other comments.

Why is he here? seemed to be the question none of them had the guts to ask openly. Now that our Beverly is here, what's he still doing around?

I had reasons. For one thing, I had not surrendered Fred's condo key. I also had his attorney's name and address, and had called him to inform him and to inquire what my role would be in all of this. Yes, Fred had appointed me executor of his estate with the Brotherhood, but he had left no will. Would I want to do it? How would that benefit Fred now? Yes, Fred trusted me—but I really didn't know how he wanted his funeral or to whom his property should go. We never talked about death. Yes, but from what I've heard I don't think I want to become easy prey.

"Then don't do it: no law compels you to, more trouble than it's worth, lots of paperwork, lots of time. They'd pay you for it, but it gives you few rewards and many headaches, no one is ever satisfied and most relatives go to their own graves suspecting that the executor cheated them out of a larger share."

Then why bother, especially for the Saturday morning pack at Martha's.

Emaciated snow pellets had blurred the neon-lit Friday night, and by the early hours of Saturday morning, during the time I wasn't checking for signs of Fred's unlikely recovery, I'd look out the window in the visitor's lounge to the uneven sheets of drifting snow, three-dimensional graphs opening upward against clay brick walls. I slipped while walking out of the hospital late that morning, and Fred's clothes flew like crazed birds out of the paper shopping bag the nurse had handed me two or three minutes after the monitor's continuous signal warned us unceremoniously, with the distinct sonotechnics demanded by medicine for such an artifice, that only a stillness encased in cold flesh, absurdly and needlessly invaded by hoses and needles and fluid-filled tubing remained on his austere and aseptic bed.

My car skidded often on the streets where snow had staked an obtrusive claim, but made it to Martha's. Some of the relatives had already gathered there, complaining about messy streets, all those nuts on the road, where the hell they done going on a Saturday morning, they themselves wouldn't have come out if it wasn' for—. Jackie, Martha's most recent county-assigned nurse, her head thrown back and her eyes constantly blinded by the smoke of a cigarette spit-glued to her lower lip, introduced me to two of Fred's cousins and an uncle. Above the uneven horizon of the assembly of survivors she made repeated circular motions with her finger to her temples and dismissed them with a fallen hand-fan gesture of contemptible worthlessness.

"Oh, poor Freddie, my poor Freddie," Martha whined with her had propped toward heaven and her praying mantis hands against the dinette table. Her image was incomplete without Fred's profile under the overhead factory lamp, a painting on which a vandal had blackened out the balancing figure from the focal scene.

Who would shop for her now, who would take three bus transfers to bring her more food after she had had her dinner, because she had called him to say she had a craving for chow mein, who would listen patiently to her stories about cousin Peggy, going at it, the sow, with her own retarded brother Carl before God and everybody right there in their mother's living room when she wasn't out doing it in alleys with truckers and bikers down in West St. Paul?

"I took care of him since he was just a baby. I promised his mother I'd always look after him," she sobbed nasally, the same expression of pain she always had furrowed behind her wrinkles, the same tearless ache carved into her eyes, her mouth, her waxy jowls. "I promised when they brought him to me. He was so little he fit in a shoe box. And his little head, tiny, tiny like a crab apple. I didn't think he'd make it." She stopped to clear the secretions accumulating in her throat from so many complications, some of them worsened by the carelessness of nursing assistants provided to her by Ramsey County.

After the Navy Fred wanted his own place, but no one else could take Martha in. He signed her up for county assistance and rented a room for himself at Maury Neumann's on Summit Parkway, a huge house that had previously been a Catholic convent and whose bedrooms were all labeled with one of the Virgin Mary's names. Maury, who owned several flower shops and evergreen farms in Wisconsin, had left the labels on the door frames; Fred's was Shelter of Sinners, across the hall from Mother Most Chaste.

Fred tried to keep an eye on Martha's helpers—the halfway-house resident who hid shoplifted merchandise in Martha's chair's bag, the parolee hustler who brought his sex clients to Martha's, the obese woman who'd throw Martha's food on the table if she refused to eat when the caretaker wanted her to, and all the rest of the grotesquerie, sometimes ten in one year, but he'd only find out the truth after they had vanished or arrested, when Martha was free of their silencing threats. He felt guilty, but he, too, needed distance from Martha's constant demands. He could almost see her pushing the buttons on the nursing misfits. He, too, wanted to choke her once or twice.

"Oh, Freddie, my poor Freddie."

"Hey!" cousin Chester addressed me from a corner in the living room. "Did he shoot dope?"

The question was so distant from anything Maggie or I admired and loved in Fred.

"Who?"

"Fred, my cousin, dammit." Chester gestured and scanned the room for consensus on his suspicion that I was 'tarded.

My head shook. A repressed pressure kept waiting for someone with whom I could feel free to release it. Rather than this overwhelming scene in whose midst I suddenly found myself, I had feared I'd come into a roomful of anguished relatives waiting for details, Achilleus narrating an account of defeat in a lost battle, not trusting himself to restrain his enraged sorrow at losing Patroklos, and simultaneously hoping he could finally let it flow freely.

Janice and Emil walked in noisily. Pain was rubbed like black greasepaint on every line of her face, sketched in an unintentional caricature. Above the mask sat a hairpiece, a flattened beehive riveted with bobby pints to her natural hair, or maybe into her skull itself like staples on compressed wood chips. Emil limped his way around two cousins and shook my hand after Jackie told them who I was. I had identified them as soon as they walked in from Fred's descriptions, apt and surprisingly accurate: they could not be mistaken for anyone else.

Janice stood by him with one hand holding up her clay-caked cheeks, her brow wrinkled—"I just can't believe it"—and her jaw fallen to form a darkening tunnel behind her varnished dentures.

Someone wanted to know who was going to be in charge of the reception. Janice suggested that Beverly take care of that when she came in.

"What's she coming up for?" Emil asked, still bitter that Saturday at Beverly's apostasy over that cult her husband led in Big Sandy. Like Jews, fasting Fridays, sitting in the dark.

"Emil, honey. Her little brother's dead. Go get me a glass of water."

"Besides, she's going to have to take care of the legal matters," I interjected without any attempt at boldness.

Janice's eyes lost the vague hint of modest mourning. "Legal matters."

"Did he leave a big one?" Chester yelled as the beer can stuck to his mouth allowed.

"I don't know. But big or small... You need to think about something more pressing now," I clarified, trying to get these people to focus on what I had stupidly assumed was their main concern.

"You have no idea? I imagine, though. A single man like him. A confirmed bachelor, no wife or children to claim anything." She paused to return to the moment. "Oh, poor Frederick," Janice said as if to alert others that she knew what she was doing there and smacked her lips, staring blankly at the room's opposite wall, tenant-proof gold.

"Yeah, I bet he left a hefty stash," Chester snorted.

"Do you know where he left the little silver purse he told me about?" Martha asked with syllables funneled through her nose.

"I don't know." With the expanding group of people in a place meant for five or six at a time, the proximity of Emil and Janice and the overheated apartment, I broke out in an unhealthy sweat and my head began to slide into a slow spin. I closed my eyes as if I could look into my mind and find something crucial I had wanted to take care of before running out for something to breathe.

"Fred's body is in the hospital's morgue. They need relatives to make arrangements today to have him removed. Do you know any funeral directors you could call before Mrs. Roberts arrives?" asked Janice. She should have known at least one: she was thrice widowed before she married Emil. According to Jackie, the third husband was not altogether dead when Janice was running around with Emil. And at this moment, what could that matter to me, except for the possibility that she might make the arrangements?

"Oh. Right. I can call some. Right here on Snelling. You know, closer to the Schulzes." Janice lowered her voice and spread a black wing over my shoulders to pull me down closer within her ravenous span. "Who has his keys and his files? Did he have a will? Do you know where his will is?"

I pulled away from her surreal face to recover my verticality.

"Whatever," I said as if I had not heard any of her words. "A funeral director here or in Minneapolis. I thought you might want someone in South St. Paul, where he grew up. As long as someone is taking care of it. I can't. I'm not a blood relative. Are you also going to call the pastor?"

Agnes had escaped my field of vision when she entered the room. She had walked in with incestuous nephew Carl. His tongue seemed to prevent his lips from meeting. "He never went to church when he was alive. Why bother to take him to it now?" Agnes asked as she removed her coat.

I wanted to say that once I had made a disparaging remark on the artistic merits of some ecclesiastical music, especially "Faith of Our Fathers," a hymn Fred had sung since Martha used to force him to walk to Sunday school two blocks away from their cellar. It was the only time Fred had been offended enough to snap at me. No, he didn't go to church on Sundays, but his tender presence had often reminded me of the life-size statues that crowded the churches in Ansbach and Ulm.

I remained silent, overcome by the stunning power of the commanding dwarf Agnes had turned out to be. Eventually, for $75 charged against the Estate of

Frederick K. Doppler by a (Mrs.) Emil H. Schulz, they contracted a preacher who read Sermon No. 4 for Funeral Services, followed by the five-minutes' worth of eulogy I had begged Beverly to allow me on behalf of my family, a hymn sung by the restrained coloratura of the preacher's wife ($35 in additional charges), and the privilege Beverly gladly granted me to lower the lid over Fred while I whispered a farewell burnished in love from my shredded heart. A good-bye over my Fred. Our Fred, now no one's.

"Who is his lawyer?" "Where did he keep his bank accounts?" "What kind of insurance did he have at work?" "Lucky Beverly has us to help her with all that"—Janice so wanted to assist, even as the casket rolled into the velvet penumbra of the hearse. She was available. Always on call, even when a call had not been issued.

Monday at the reception in Sanac's party room I handed Beverly the key Maggie kept for Fred in the first drawer of the secretary. Janice had hovered with obviously staged discretion from a prudent distance, following me around the room, stopping to perch her arms on a folding chair's back behind some relative if I stopped to refill my disposable coffee cup or to look at the compact droves of Dopplers and Schulzes. I had tried to talk privately to Beverly to offer my help to contact Fred's attorney, to locate the most important documents, and just to tell her, amidst tears that I had hoped to share with her, refused as I had to permit them to slide out of my eyes at the funeral service and at the graveside ceremony, briefly eternal in the blustery subzero wind, and tell her that we'd miss Fred, that our lives were so enriched by his presence in them, that no one knew what Fred had meant to us, that nothing would be the same without Fred—all of those clichés that leave us searching for fewer commonplaces and more original statements to make as we realize that we are saying exactly what we mean, but that the words we have uttered cannot possibly match what we honestly feel, stripped as they are of everything other than the vacuity of syllabic strings as cuttingly senseless as the good man's death. I would fail to transcend his formulaic obituary: Mr. Doppler is survived by sister Beverly Roberts, aunts Martha Gustafson and Agnes Wendt, Uncle Emil Schulz, beloved Aunt Janice (Mrs. Emil E. Schulz), nephews, nieces, cousins and other relatives.

During a brief moment I found Beverly alone, picking her teeth with her fingernails across the table from three orphaned shreds of cooked ham on a melting, fingered gelatin mold, and from Martha's crippled hands, like a pale ant's forelegs juggling a flat crumb, employed in shaking the condolence cards that Jackie handed her, hoping for a minted delicacy of dollar bills and bank checks to float down onto her lap. "If you need any help getting..."

"We're here for support, Beverly dear," Janice crowed from above the gripping umbrage she cast over Beverly's shoulders, all the while staring at me. "All she needs right now is to be allowed to grieve, and we are here to see she has all she needs."

"Oh, I'm certain of that," I said, vanquished and looking at Beverly added, "In the name of the friendship that bound me to your brother, I wish you the best, which is what he would have desired for you." That shallowness needed no expansion. I did not know what Fred would have wished for any of them, but I knew he never wanted anything other than goodness to come their way. It was, after all, Fred, whose body lay in a wooden box, but whose spirit was alive and clinging to my grateful heart.

On my way home I stopped at a flower shop that years ago had been Maury Neumann's and bought forty-eight red roses. One for each of his years in the physical world, a prodigious dozen for each of our family members. Behind the door Maggie waited on her feet against brick and mortar; Jerry and Little Al played in their bedroom—they know, but should we help them talk about it?—I never had—maybe we should have taken them after all—so difficult—how was it? I held her tight, she threw her arms around me and caressed my nape, and I in turn anointed her hair with the tears I had saved, slipping out from my burning eyelids. I gave her the roses. "From Fred. For Fred."

They're leaving now. Their feet hammered their descent into the lobby, and now are crunching snow on the icy steps outside. I rise to peek out, pressing against the edge of the window frame. My shadow looms three or four times larger than the original it copies against the eggshell wall behind, outlined unevenly and distorted against the harsh, unbounded clarity of the lamppost. Each of the three carries a cardboard box that couldn't have been in Fred's apartment before. Emil unlocks the trunk and, suppliants from a pagan rite, Beverly and Janice follow after him to deposit an encased offering in the sunken altar. Emil slams the sanctuary shut. I hear it a fraction of a minute later. (Into my mind crawl obversions and extensions of one of those fruitless arguments that questions or confirms assumptions of our centric importance in the universe. Had I not heart it, would it have not mattered? Had Fred's sobs not been soldered eternally onto my eardrums, the panic of abandonment infinitely more agonizing than the certainty of death, "Don't leave me alone. Not until I can't tell whether you are here anymore," would I have cared? What would I have felt?) They shuffle their inflexible legs mechanically to the sides of the car, careful, dear, this is sheer ice, don't slip and fall now. My shadow withdraws from the threshold of the glare and dissolves as it fuses with the rest of me under the blanket.

They're gone, slowly, tire tread biting hesitantly on the fresh coating of snow. On my night stand, on a small dish, the slightly tarnished brilliance of a dozen silver coins vanishes into a phosphorescent outline against the deepening darkness of the wall.

Maggie has slept through it. The withered velvet of a rose petal perhaps detached itself from its crisp sepal and rolled perhaps onto a piano key. Perhaps now we can all get some rest. For a while, anyway. Perhaps.

AND NOW, WHAT?

The Day before Yesterday

They've left you behind in the dark. The British-Italian tour guide had been explaining to you and the rest of the excursionists that you were facing the cell where Giacomo Casanova had been imprisoned in Pombi, in the *Palazzo del Doge*. Who knows for sure, you asked yourself. She might as well have said Washington slept there, too. Venice, like the rest of Italy from Bolzano to Puglia, is filled with anecdotes impossible to verify and implausible fictions that pass for indisputable facts.

When the cowbell-deprived herd moved on, they left you behind. It was the main feature of European excursions. The guide was Little Bo Peep herding tourists like *pamperos* with cattle. You know from this: you have seen those also. She went ahead of everyone holding up a parasol, that she could be found in the tourist maelstrom. For all the good her gesture did, she might as well have rolled off on a wheeled pedestal all over *Piazza San Marco*. You need to look where you're stepping, not where the infertile pigeons fly. In St. Mark's Cathedral, worse yet: the uneven tiles made you stumble and even fall on a prie-dieu kneeler.

"*Aiuto, aiuto! Sono qui senza vedere niente!*" you have shouted, hoping someone will come to your rescue.

A guard has appeared at your screams, because the rest of the excursionists can no longer hear you, fearful that they will lose sight of the shepherd, clustered like a malleable masses in a lava lamp, avoiding the risk of losing their way in a place where of the language they know nothing but *arrivederci* and even that they mispronounce. You have explained to the *polizotto* that you can't see in that darkness, that your pupils don't dilate and that you have been left behind by your group. He takes your arm, the one not holding the cane, and takes your breath away when you feel the impossibly solid bicep under a heavy drill sleeve.

The yearling herder offers no apology nor has she noticed your absence. You walk away from the group without explanation, not that anyone would ask for it. Free of the mule driver you sit at an outdoor table of Caffee Florian to drink an espresso.

With what I have paid for this I could have bought six pounds of coffee and brewed it at home, you have thought to yourself, then feel shame at your pedestrian provincialism. The price of the cup of coffee includes the history, the location, the view, the distance you have put between your routine and this adventure. The price could have been higher, you decide, and leave the *camariere* an excessive bourgeois tip to make up for your unvoiced slight.

This afternoon you have gone by *vaporetto* to Alberoni Beach, on the Lido. You have rented a folding chair, a *lettino*, and have laid in it on the sand, under the giant umbrella in the colors of the Italian flag. You think of Gustav von Aschenbach when the young man approaches. He greets you with a *Ciao* and a splendid smile that shows, that even you can see, a set of teeth forged in the anvil of cosmetic odontology.

"*Sei qui da solo?*" the young man asks the redundant question, as no one else is with you, obviously. He holds the ends of a rolled towel against his nape.

"*Si. Lo preferisco cosí*," you answer.

"*É romano?*" he asks, unshaken. *il mantenuto*, flashing the same smile.

"*Si, romano,*" you lie. "*Per favore, non sono interessato a comprare,*" you say, hoping he will understand you are not shopping for his services.

The treacherous smile has not left his face.

"*Non ha bisogno de una guida a la spiaggia? Conosco posti…*"

"*Non sei uno stronzo,*" you yell at him, because that is what he is, an asshole.

He walks away crestfallen and when you see his back from shoulders to buttocks you are almost sorry you sent him off, in spite of your commitment to voluntary and salubrious celibacy, even if only for your body, because in your mind, deprived of pleasure, you have lain dozens of Italian males. It's sunny, but not hot. It's the first week in May. The waters of the Adriatic are still too cold for quick dips in it, but it doesn't stop the hustlers in low-cut Speedos from coming to make their living. That one must be experienced in reading his targets' faces and persuasions: he has failed to decipher your will, not your desire.

He keeps walking along the shore of the beach, almost deserted, but every so often he looks back, you have noticed from the corner of your eye, perhaps hoping you will change your mind or vulturing around for easier carrion.

Because it is remote and lacking in any particular appeal, Alberoni is not a popular beach even in season, much less right now. That is precisely why you have chosen it. You only want to look at the sea, watch the waves, so interestingly different from the ones that bathe the beaches of your island. The waves do not withdraw and then rise in heavy folded foam to collapse on the shore as if uselessly gathering strength in an attempt to reach farther in. These are like displacements made by a mythical and invisible giant while stirring asymmetrically a huge cauldron of cold greenish soup. These waves are closer to what you have seen often in San Juan Bay against the dock when you have ridden the Cataño ferry or strolled along the old San Juan Gate, behind the governor's mansion. If you want to see something more like Playa Azul in Luquillo, albeit without the palm trees, you will have to return to Amalfi, where you have not taken time to go this time around.

And tomorrow you will check out of the hotel to return to Florence. You have seen enough of Venice on this visit. You hadn't seen it since you could see. You know you have come to confirm how much more vision you have lost in the past fifteen years. Now you can leave without denying to yourself that you can ever travel by yourself to places you knew when your vision was normal. That's why you canceled the trip to Murano. You have come too far to verify what you could have confirmed by staring into the horizon from your house on the mountain. You have, actually, and you have refused to convince yourself. Of course, back there you wouldn't have gotten compliments from Italians who hear you or bragged mentally of your skilled mastery of the Italian language as you listen to yourself speak it with the musicality of whom has spoken it since childhood as his native language unless you talked to yourself. That wouldn't be anything new. That's also how you have kept your fluency in French and German.

"*Wie geht es Ihmen heute?*" That's how each morning you greet your spoiled dog Melampo.

"*Mon amour, as-tu dormi cette nuit, enfin?*" That's how you greet the ghost in your fantasy, where Alejandro remains. Alejandro's face the way you saw it last and not the way it looked when you met. Viral decrepitude has imposed itself over the memory of his beauty.

***

Years Ago

I prepared myself for death. It's been, heck, how long? *Quindici anni?* No, more. Almost twenty. This is how it all started.

I went to the clinic to get tested. Alejandro refused to go

"Why would I want to know? If there's no cure, what do I gain, more anguish? My affairrs are all in order and whatever isn't, well, the devil take the rest.

His reasoning was tinged with validity, but I gathered all the courage I could muster and, why deny it, the hope that the result would be non-reactive, but suspecting that it would be. As far as I knew my previous partner remained uninfected, although it was impossible to know for sure. Before Alejandro and I met he had been a test tube for every bacterium and bacillus known to humanity to be sexually transmitted, including two cases of syphilis and a bout of hepatitis B. Who'd know whether in one of his incursions into what was not known then as unprotected sex he had caught something less curable. I knew it early on and didn't care, even though by then the whole world had heard the plague's blast. I fell in love, erased old accounts and opened a new ledger, monogamy hence. The rest was in the past. We made no room for the intrusion of the condom's asepsis.

No one knew for certain about these things, as we discovered when Pablo Cofresí, so full of life, from one day to the next turned into a walking cadaver who in no way resembled his old self. Just the same, I have never liked surprises, not even for my birthday.

And precisely on mine I went for my results. I was called to a small room where a small magazine bookcase stood against the wall next to a table and two chairs. A box of Puffs tissue sat on the table. The health educator walked in wearing a face serious as a bad diagnosis. She pulled out a chair and sat down across from me, her hands off the table.

"I'm sorry," she said. As if in a stage scene that required a dramatic pause she added, redundantly: "The result was reactive. You tested positive."

I can't recall the expression etched on my face. Disappointment, maybe? Horror? I don't know. My head was in flames, my neck was stiff. That no one forgets. On the window behind the woman an air conditioner missing a front panel blew cold air in all directions without placating the sweltering.

The health educator slowly pushed the box of Puffs closer to me. A blue ply, dizzy and collapsed, stuck out its opening.

"This is not a death sentence, you know?" she told me. It was the tone of someone reading a hackneyed libretto.

"No, really? What is it, exactly?"

"You can't lose hope. A lot of research and development is going on, there's been progress, each day we know more about the virus, we are told of forthcoming treatments and—"

"But right now there are none. The mortality rate for the infected is of 100%," I cut her off. "Don't patronize me. I didn't climb down a crib to come here."

She said nothing right away, but after a while she gave me a line I have since learned was standard:

"Not everyone who's been exposed goes on to develop symptoms. The worst thing you can do is losing hope. Be positive!"

"I thought I was," I said, not wanting to miss the opportunity to point out the inappropriate cliché under the circumstances.

"You know what I meant."

Of course I knew. How not to know of the uselessness of the dialogue. She was going to suggest the same recommendations she had given others: support groups, counseling services and other banal and impotent suggestions for dealing with the plague. I held back the temptation to poison her with my imputed negativity.

I left. I climbed in my car. I think some tears slipped out of my eyes. Oh, who the hell am I kidding? Yes, as a matter of fact, I shed lots of tears. Lots. I covered my face with an old rag Alejandro had left on the back seat. I don't know how long I sat there, my face contorted against the piece of cloth and crying deep and relentlessly, coupled with screams that the rag drowned.

Remain positive, keep your chin up, Pollyanna; optimistic, Maria von Trapp. No one of any fame had been more optimistic than Anne Frank. We all know how life took care of crushing her positive outlook before typhoid fever finished her off at Bergen-Belsen.

In this situation, once I began processing the stupidity of that useless resource, I concluded that remaining positive (in that other sense) would be equivalent to living in denial or going around repeating superstitions: that the Lord will help you, that he won't let you die, seek his comfort, that you cannot lose your faith in God, that God closes a door but opens a window, that you need to pray a novena to St. Jude, patron saint of desperate cases, that you need to pray to the Holy Child, that you have to go to the church of Our Lady of the Well, that you need to drink *jagua* tea, that you need to drink infusions of rue herbs, that you need to bathe in rosemary branches, that you need to go to the *santero* to have him do a cleansing and a bad-spirit removal rite.

Those were not the types of positive perspectives I needed, even less the ones he would get from Mother, commanding me to do penance, pray the rosary twice a day and stating as a matter of fact that it was the consequence of running around looking to catch that disease to afflict me when I did the nasty things I obviously did. She had not raised me to go do those things. I needed to look at the example she gave me, a decent woman of unblemished morals, a good wife and an even better mother. She had no idea where I had learned those bad habits. Now not even God was going to save me. I needed to repent before it was too late to expect God to have mercy on me.

Yes, if I had told the health educator of my skepticism she would have looked at me with her own brand of incredulity, measuring my cynicism the same way others check engine oil levels, surprised they are running so low. Since adolescence I had been missing three quarts.

What would have been necessary here was to cover myself in proaction. Avoid exposing myself from the start was what I should have done. Now the issue was how to go on living until one of those fatal illnesses attacked me and I would die from a death that went beyond the limits of a terrible nightmare while I was cared for by a nurse in an astronaut costume who administered everything tentative and from a distance. I already knew what dying from this was like. I had heard the stories about those who tried to strangle themselves with their own hands in a hospice bed when they were not even strong enough to raise a plastic spoon, of those who suffered from unexplainable fevers and an uncontrollable amebiasis diarrhea, about those who drowned from the inside out with pneumocystis and were eaten up alive by sarcoma. I knew of those who were evicted from their apartments, of the mothers and siblings who went to hospital rooms to read from "Leviticus," "Judges" and "Proverbs" out loud, of those who lost their job or collapsed from toxoplasmosis in a hall at work, of those who turned into ambulatory skeletons, of those who were re-moved from airplanes when other passengers com-plained of the looks of someone on an oxygen tank, of hospitals that threw bodies in plastic bags into alleys be-cause no one claimed them nor funeral parlors wanted to process them, of those who could not disguise their ill-ness because they had lost so much weight or had such spots on their face that restaurants would deny them ac-cess or teach or continue to work as Catholic priests.

That was what awaited me, I thought as I went on screaming with the rag stuck in my mouth to absorb my screams in the parking lot.

What gave a health educator the right to speak to me as if I were uninformed or ignorant of the future? I had attended workshops, lectures, informative sessions about the virus and its means of transmission. I knew as much as medical professionals knew. I had also witnessed the rebellion among those who refused to accept that they could become infected through sexual contact: they claimed that it was a myth to frighten them and force them back into another closet, that it was all a heterosex-ual plot, that the evidence was not there.

I had chosen to turn my back on what I knew. I based what I did solely on my right to happiness, refusing to believe anything could happen to me if I did it out of love. Contagion was the result of the logic of desire, which knew nothing about syllogisms, sophisms or crit-ical thinking. And even when the moment of passion had ended and I fell in the abyss of doubt, it was too late and my flesh was recidivist in spite of my intellect.

I had to remain optimistic, she said. That could only come out of the mouth of someone who was not in my precarious place.

Finally I turned the engine. Although I had not gone into a church in a long time I parked close to the cathedral. Against my own reasoning and disbelief of the possibility that anyone could help me, I climbed the steps to the building's doors. I felt close to asphyxiated. I remembered that as a child I went to the darkened church and looking at the statue of Our Lady of Providence provided me a sense of peace. I stared at her in the face and its surroundings vanished. Her eyes seemed to leave their sockets and approach me until I shut my own, because they filled me with overwhelming fear. Back then I asked for her help, because I was struggling against my instinct and needed divine reinforcements to stop thinking of the ugly things I wanted to do with the boy across the street from us. It worked then, although it was not a permanent remedy: eventually I stopped thinking of Mary, the pope and the rest of the sanctimonious quackery.

I grabbed the handle on the main door. At the same time a priest on the other side held the door. Without looking me in the face he said:

"It's closing time."

He pulled the door shut. From the outside I could hear the locking mechanism turning and the muted thud of the bar that secured the door.

It was affirmation from a heaven in which I did not believe of my reasoning while I cried like Mary Magdalene of Christian fairy tales.

I got home. Alejandro was waiting for me with a cup of coffee on the kitchen table. I sat down and told him. He said nothing right away. He took my hands in his. We talked about how I felt, the patience we would need. I asked him whether the mail carrier had stopped by already and he started weeping. A miniature brook of tears formed on both sides of his face.

"I don't want you to die!" he said. He stood up and came to me. He held my head tight against his chest, whose sobs I could hear. "Oh, please, don't die on me, don't!"

Yesterday

You have decided never again to travel on excursions. You have been to Madrid so many times. Your vision is enough to orient yourself without being spurred on by the guide, like that Australian in Granada, when you went on a skiing trip to the Nevada Range four years earlier. He didn't rush anyone because he had to stick to the schedule, but rather because he had a date with the first of a stream of Foster's he would drink at the Hotel Carmen bar, in lieu of the *paella* reserved for the excursionists. He stayed at the bar making a fool of himself, cackling and yelling incoherently until the bar turned into a disco and you went down there. Then he came to squeeze you and twist your nipples. He confused you. You had no idea whether those were the antics of an insomniac adolescent soaked in alcohol or a sign you could not ignore, because at your age you had learned that a man who travels by himself is most likely not heterosexual. You found out two years later that he had married an Italian woman when you ran into him in Capri while he worked as a tour manager for the same Trafalgar Tours in Naples.

This time you stayed again at the Tribeca Hotel: it was close to Castellana Parkway and the Santiago Bernabéu metro station, there, almost in front of the Ministry of Defense.

It's a glorious April afternoon, the sun's heat abated by a breeze that cools your face, perfect for going to the Prado Park and taking long walks down Serrano Street or Plaza Mayor in a light jacket. You, however, have spent sixteen years without sexual contact with anyone other than yourself. You crave a dark space perfumed by the rancid aromas of sex. You have become aware of the complications and the embarrassment of having to explain to someone your seropositive status. You hit your nose against the reality of fictitious tolerance and discovered the fear, the ignorance and suspiciousness, and experienced rejection. You only need to rent a porn video and sit down to pleasure yourself with selfish involution. Your hand does not need a warning, disclosure or protection. Fingers require no asepsis to deprive lust of the sensitivity of your skin. In the end, you don't need to ask yourself when the hell he'll leave without hinting that you have to be up early; you have no need to pretend you enjoyed it so much you are going to give him your telephone number and at the same time hope he never calls and then, in fact, he never does anyway. And if he does, you have to look for excuses to postpone or cancel the possibility of another meeting until he finally forgets you.

Those you know who are also positive—the ones you met in the support group you decided to join only to cross them out of your life, regret and repent of having allowed your solitary weakness to compel you into that facsimile of a shelter—want to bareback, which you refused to do. The encounter turns into mutual dissatisfaction. You fear the so-called reinfection, wondering whether the other party had a mutation they could transmit and strengthen your own virus, or vice versa.

The virus thrusts you into stark Darwinism: it involves the survival of the best informed, of the one who always carries with him a condom that has not yet expired, of the one who will not allow anyone to ejaculate in his rectum and with the best access to capsules. To anyone equipped with a moral conscience the virus is the bridle that holds back the horse of instinctive passion before someone else is kicked over the hurdle of life.

You have had times when your conscience has gone on holiday or has looked the other way. You have to live with that, because remorse does not count when actions are free, but the consequences never are.

Today you are fed up with the lack of fingers running down your skin and the absence of contact with a body other than yours. Today you are where no one knows you. No explanations are required. Passion shared in anonymity begs for no justification. The risk will be mutual, shared in halves or thirds or fourths or whatever fraction is necessary, where everyone will be responsible for his on will.

The gay travel guide you have brought with you includes an entry for a promising place. You have exited the metro at the Gran Vía stop and reached Puerta del Sol. The crowd overwhelms you: you fear that a pickpocket with the looks of a businessman will extract your euros from your pants' pocket. As soon as you can you stop and stick them inside your shoe when no one is looking. In your left pocket you have left only the metro return ticket and in the shirt pocket, a minimum of folded bills.

You can't see the place, but you know it's around here. You will not stop looking for it. You tried to go to Sauna Paraíso, back there on Norte Street in Chueca. "The baths are for young men," the sign over the entrance reads in a sort of Dantesque mockery, meant to make those of your generation lose all hope that their self-image of vigor and youth match the perception of others You've experienced enough discrimination: you have no need to take it also from those in your own ghetto. Walking toward Sauna Paraíso you stopped in front of a disco to listen to the music. An oversized man with a head too small for the rest of his body yelled at you from the door "This is for young men only!" as if your ears were of any age or required any reminder that you were over fifty, an age you had not thought you would ever reach.

At the A Different Life bookstore you commented to Carlos, the bear cashier, about the emphasis on youth.

"They do it to keep hustlers out," he replied. "If they allow mature daddies, the hustlers follow them to strip them of their dough. Have you been to Black and White?"

"No. What is it?" you asked.

"Man, a bar that mature foreign men favor. Hustlers come in to pluck their feathers and to have the patrons take them to their hotels to get them laid," Carlos explained. "And look here, some of those should have the chance to get in bed with you, 'cuz you're not at all bad, not at all, and if I wasn't coupled with someone, you were going to see!"

You go on looking for the movie house the guide mentions. Could it be that it's no longer there? You go toward the McDonald's next to kilometer zero, the starting point of all state highways in Spain. No sign of the movie theater. What you do see next door to Sephora is a souvenir shop, trinkets for tourists exhibited in the window, where prices are stated in euros on top and in pesetas at the bottom. You don't get it. Spaniards don't buy tambourines illustrated with the figure of a bullfighter about to give the bull the final *estoque* with his sword or castanets or paper-leaved fans and foreigners only pay with euros, not pesetas.

Out of curiosity you have stopped in front of the window, just steps away from the famed kilometer zero and from where you can see the Tío Pepe billboard and the Osborne bull, posing his toughness with petulance. In the showcase are key chains of the Royal Basilica of the Virgin of Atocha, molded plastic figurines of Don Quixote, imitation nacre high combs for veils no one wears any longer, a color photograph of King Juan Carlos without Sophia, post cards and guide books in languages you recognize and others you don't. Czech? Bulgarian?

The handsome black-haired man at the shop's door has smiled at you. He's wearing a pullover and black slacks too tight for the thickness of his *serrano* ham thighs. You smile back. You notice he has his hand on his bulge and runs it up and down while staring at you, still holding the smile. You turn youu head and keep on walking. You've never liked explicit gestures in public, regardless of how magnificent they may be.

You finally see the place, clearly trying to efface itself for everyone except those who are looking for it. Nothing on its façade identifies it, but its architecture speaks of a former theater of the type you remember, dubbed into Castilian, in which Elizabeth Taylor used purely peninsular words and called Richard Burton son of a female dog instead of son of a whore, as Spaniards did. They were visual and audio reminders of Franco's omniscience.

A red neon sign, barely visible from the outside, in what would have been the lobby of the old theater, identifies the place simply as XXX. You are sure it doesn't stand for kisses.

The woman in the ticket booth looks to you like your grandmother as you remember her from your teenage years. A cardboard sign indicates that they have continuous shows 24 hours a day and that a ticket costs 10 €, less than the seventeen posted on the bath house sign for fewer hours.

You hand her the ten-Euro bill, 1660 pesetas, the equivalent according to the sign of the store with the bulge for tourists next door.

"You don't need one, *caballero*," the retiree tells you. She points to an opening in the wall behind the booth.

You move the frayed velvet purple curtain to the side: it begs for a wash. You walk down a hallway that is almost lit by the sunlight outside. The farther in you walk, the less you can see what surrounds you. On the left you hear what sounds like a German soundtrack. You get close to a cracked door. You pull it open and, sure enough, you hear clearly. It is German. On a screen that does not cover entirely what used to be the proscenium of the old theater you see the images of a movie with faded colors that is most likely a video projected from a booth: you can see the diffuse ray that starts out concentrated from a hole in the upper side of the back wall and becomes progressively diffused, an expanding horizontal smoke stack that is eventually captured in a more or less precise reflection on the small screen.

"Fick mich, fick mich, härter, härter, ja, ja, fick mein Arsch!" says the thick-haired blond, trying to encourage a man in his fifties with swollen cheeks, half bald and pot-bellied to penetrate her anally while she holds on to the banister of an interior staircase and his hand holds her hair high in a bundle.

The light bouncing off the screen is not enough for you to see. You stand by the door to wait for your eyes to get used to the darkness. This will take a while, because your pupils no longer react to the opacity of darkness in normal time, as you well discovered in Pombi, back in Venice, a few years back.

Someone stands next to you. Somewhere in there you have heard rhythmic and continuous snoring. The man beside you has started rubbing your buttocks. You dislike the idea of a total stranger touching you. With the little you have begun to see of the seats you walk forward and find an empty one at the end of a row toward the back.

You don't know what happened with the man pawing you.

The snoring is louder. You look to the side, to the row behind yours, and are able to see a man almost completely sliding down from his seat, his head thrown back against the wall.

There are some twenty rows of seats, divided in herringbone by a hall between two sets of about sixteen seats on each side. The padded seats make a loud noise when someone sits down or moves in them. You see nine heads spread out around the main floor, all looking toward the screen. You are not sure, but their shoulders all seem to be shaking.

You hear the teeth of a zipper mesh. A man rises one or two rows from you to the left and heads for the exit door, which you can now see completely. Two men walk in and sit on opposite ends of the same row, where one is already sitting in the middle, shoulders shaking. Somewhere behind you to your right a belt buckle clinks against the bare floor. One of the two who came in is now sitting two seats away from the one shaking his shoulders. Not two minutes later he is sitting next to the shaker and suddenly his head and back disappear toward the shaker's lap.

Half an hour later you can see there are more bodies pacing in the back, to your right. There are more seat rows back there, some occupied by men looking in your direction. The faces are blurred, but they must be men: a sign in the lobby over the ticket booth clearly states, "No women allowed."

You get up, then walk in their direction, toward a door in the back, leading who knows where. You stand against a column from which you can see someone with an erect penis above his pants, stretched out between his knees. He looks at you and points with his head toward his crotch. You become afraid: your heart is jumping rope. The column seems like a mast to which you are tied by a cord of ambiguous purpose: you cannot tell whether to save you from the mermaids beckoning with muted voices or for you to decide to untie yourself and run to them.

You turn your head to the left. Against the wall you see a man who looks young, wearing eyeglasses, his penis also hanging out of his pants while he fondles his erection and looks your way.

You walk to the back to explore what may be behind the door you have seen before. You push it. No one's there, just empty seats a level above the seats on the other side of the wall. Against a wall you see a metal staircase that climbs up to a black door. It must be the projection booth.

You return to the column. It's more of a pillar, but not virginal like the one you kissed in the church in Zaragoza as a child. The man sitting in the middle of the row to your right rises and comes to you. He takes your hand to place it on his penis. You have not pulled it away. You don't mind touching him. After all, wasn't this what you came for?

The one standing against the wall also approaches you. You have no objection to his massaging. He grabs your left buttock. He may be the same one who stood by the door when you first arrived. He digs into your crack and attempts to explore as much as your pants' fabric will allow him.

The German video has ended. Now it's a British movie on the screen. "Oh, yeah, baby, suck that cock, yeah, eat that shit, all the way, baby, right there, swallow it, yeah, yeah, you like that cock..,?" a black man in an Afro, his face crossed by acne scars and flat assed addresses a woman made up to look twenty, but with the actual looks of a fifteen-year old girl. The movie's coloration, his hair and the shirt the man is holding up to his nipples look like something from the '80s. The girl is naked except for the red brassiere the black man rubs.

Another man approaches, one with a few extra kilos on him. He stands in front of you. He unzips and fondles himself. The one on your right has grabbed your shoulder and without uttering a word instructs you to kneel.

You have spent three and a half hours at the XXX. The German video ran again followed by an American one of a threeway, one woman and two men who penetrated her simultaneously, and the man behind her has his hand on the waist of the one who penetrates her vagina, as if he needed support. By the time you push the exit door you hear French spoken on the speakers, but you can no longer tell what they are saying, although it's porn-speak, universal and filled with exclamations and phony moans that could just as easily be Russian, Mandarin or Swahili—and you don't much care.

You have made up in one afternoon for all of the appetite you have repressed for years. The one who caressed your buttocks brought with him a condom, lubricant and even moistened towelettes. It has been your first time with more than two at the same time. You have not allowed anyone to make Onan's mistake: that would have been a waste. Once you satisfied the first three, five more came along. No, six, actually, with the man in a uniform whose affiliation you could not recognize but wanted to know whether it was a civil guard or an exterminator on break.

You have learned a new orgasm phrase, "I'm running, I'm running!" which you had not heard before, because you had never done it with a Spaniard. You heard it several times in spastic whispers, once in a duo.

You have returned to the XXX three times. After traveling by train to Valencia, where you knelt for a stranger in an alley close to the Fallero Museum, and back in García Lorca's Granada and Hotel Carmen you went to the XXX, which turned out to be a porn theater chain. The cashiers were two really ugly transgendered women who carried on their lively chat without even looking at you when they took your money. You may have been the most wanted ripper for all they knew.

One you were unfortunate enough to have seated next to you had his genitals smeared in Vaseline. Not even after washing your hands with hand soap while two had anal sex by the urinals and two others looked on were you able to remove that grease you had not used since you were thirteen, following a suggestion made by Jesús Arturo Collazo, a fellow student who fancied himself a connoisseur of all things sexual.

Back in Madrid it has been sheer coincidence that the stud was there in the bathroom at El Corte Inglés department store in Puerta del Sol inviting you with a look to use the WC as a miniature motel room for awkward sordidness during which you have discovered another practice you had not had the opportunity to try before.

You pay a farewell visit to the same XXX, where one of the three has asked you in a whisper why you had not come in the shop to buy a souvenir, and you realize it is the bulger at the trinket store. With a common act he shows you that the ordinary can turn into the extraordinary when you have access to the appropriate instrument. Were it not because you must return to the island, you would be there still, dragged down by decadence unchained from considerations of emotional preoccupation.

You fear you have contracted one of those diseases that, though curable, their origin is difficult to explain to your physician.

Valiantly you have gone to Dr. Abigaíl Robles, not the doctor who treats you for viral matters, that you had sex with an unknown female and are taking preventive measures. The doctor has replied, "Preventive measures would have been not having sex with a stranger. This is a diagnostic issue. Take off your pants and let's do a gonorrhea smear."

Years Ago

He did not die. He was close to coming to his end, but no, it didn't come to that.

For seven years he ignored the possibility that his immunological system was shutting down or at least of becoming so depressed that he would decide to slash his metaphorical veins. He felt fine and, hell, he had no symptoms of anything! Why fix what wasn't broken?

Alejandro was not as lucky. Four months after he got his own results from the health educator, Alejandro told him he was feeling tired. He began waking up at night soaked in sweat that went right through to the bed sheets. The very day Alejandro started his vacation he had to stay in bed with a high fever, malaise and a relentless dry cough. His doctor did not bother with therapies. He had to wait two days for a lung biopsy. Three days later he had choked in his own lung fluid, at dawn, his body invaded by tubes and needles in an intensive care unit.

He feared his depression would finish off his CD4 cells, then called T cells, the ones that fought off the virus. He went to the Medical Center to have blood drawn to determine where his levels were. They were at 550, above what was known as "full-blown AIDS."

He felt certain he would not end up like everyone else he knew, all in wheelchairs or buried.

"I suggest you go see my physician. He's a family friend. I know him really well," a co-worker told him one afternoon. "He specializes in respiratory problems. He treats my asthma. You're going to like him."

She could not avoid hearing him cough. Her office was next to his. He sucked on cough drops, that alleviated the problem only momentarily and could not be taken constantly, because they caused diarrhea.

He went to see Dr. León. The doctor found thrush in his throat and on his tongue. The doctor performed an endoscopy.

"Your trachea is blooming with candida. This must be due to an immunological problem," said Dr. León some four feet away and his hands in his gown's pockets.

He said nothing. He thought the doctor would ask him whether he had had the ELISA test.

"Are you a homosexual?" the doctor asked instead.

He nodded.

"And have you been tested for HIV?" the doctor then asked, and he nodded again.

"It was reactive."

"Your immunology must be compromised if you have a case as severe of candidiasis as this," the doctor stated and took another step back. "I assume you are not being seen by an infectologist."

"No," he answered, still somewhat groggy from the procedure, still lying there in the recovery room.

"Then I'm going to refer you to a specialist. You need to see one soon. In the meantime I'm going to prescribe Flucanazole. It will take care of that infection. You're going to have to keep taking it or the candida will make a comeback."

He returned to the doctor's office three days later for a follow-up. After asking him to open his mouth wide while holding a flashlight from a prudent distance at his desk, the doctor said that it was already starting to look better. He turned to the side and dialed a number on the phone. He said he was calling Dr. Marcano, the specialist in infectious diseases.

"I have a patient for you... Yes, isn't it? The opposite of what always happens, I have one for you instead of you one for me... Positive... He has admitted he is homosexual... Yes, get me your receptionist and I'll give her his information... Good... Thanks, Raúl.

He waited until the receptionist gave Dr. Marcano the appointment date and time.

"Thank you, Dr. León," he said and stood up. He didn't stretch his hand to shake the doctor's for fear the doctor might refuse to touch it. "I want to clear something up. You asked me whether I am homosexual. Just the same you could have asked me whether I am an intravenous drug user or had received a transfusion."

Dr. León had no discernible expression on his face, but continued to stab the patient's eyes with his.

"I didn't admit anything. You are not a detective and I am not a criminal. I only informed you of my sexual orientation."

His blood boiled when someone categorized him with words that aspired to cover up biases, but more so yet when the person was supposed to be intelligent and sensitive but were clueless when it came to perceiving how their words betrayed their prejudice. He had put one of his cousins in her place when he found out that she had told aunt Puruca that he had confessed his homosexuality.

"I haven't confessed anything," he told her in a tone that left no doubt he was pissed. "No one has ordained you a priest. I only wanted you to know to stop you from trying to set me up with your homely friends."

He went to see Dr. Marcano. After examining him thoroughly and drawing blood himself the doctor told him he needed to get in an immediate AZT regimen. It was the only medication on the market to treat AIDS. Now this was the case, not just an infection, but what was called "full-blown AIDS."

"Don't you love the flowery metaphor? I guess it's appropriate, that blowjob theme, isn't it?" asked Dr. Marcano in jest. Looking at him, the doctor raised his eyebrows and pretended to flicker the ash of an imaginary cigar in his mouth. It was shorthand with which to communicate his own sexual orientation.

"And have you admitted it to Dr. León yet?" he asked the doctor. Dr. Marcano laughed. "He carries his homomisia on his sleeve. I don't think he wants to know, nor is it convenient. I tolerate him for professional reasons, period. Be glad he referred you to me and you don't have to see him again. Flucanazole is very effective. If you need refills, I'll call them in."

A week later he was back to see Dr. Marcano.

"Your T cells are down to 138. Stay on the AZT and the Flucanazole. You also have to go on a daily dose of Bactrim DS. It prevents pneumocystis, and you are at risk for it. I prefer to be aggressive with this. I'm going to refer you to the retinologist, to have him look in the back of your eyes. You are on the verge of being hit by cytomegalovirus retinitis.

He left Dr. Marcano's office, headed to Walgreens to buy his medication and returned home. He sat in the darkened family room, staring outside. He didn't cry. When he took the bar exam he had been studying for months. He arrived at the exam room and began writing his answers with such stress that the edges of the hexagonal pencil buried into his skin and formed a callous that deformed his left middle finger. When he returned to his apartment he sat in a corner of his bed. He couldn't go to sleep, He felt his soul had slipped out of him and he had to wait until it returned to his body. Therefore, this numbness of the spirit was not unknown to him. He had to be patient again. With any luck it would not take the wrong turn and leave him forever.

He consulted a colleague at the law firm and, without saying why, put him in charge of writing his will and a power of attorney to appoint his physician as the person in charge to make medical decision for him in case he was unable to do so. He specified that he did not want heroic measures used on him: DNR, he made clear his desire not to be resuscitated was respected in the event a loss of consciousness was suspected to be permanent.

He saw Dr. Marchán, the retinologist. Dr, Marchán examined him once a month over a period of several months to make sure no cytomegalovirus was affecting his retina. He thought it was funny that Dr. Marchán wore double latex gloves on each hand to instill dilation drops. Dr. Marchán extended his arms to stretch his eyelids when examining him with the ophthalmoscope. Once the exam with the slit lamp Dr. Marchán grabbed two alcohol-soaked cotton balls to wipe anything that had been in contact with the patient's face. He was surprised that Dr. Marchán had not ripped out the entire instrument when done with the exam. Maybe he should have felt grateful that the eye guy condescended to tolerate the presence of a body polluted with a virus common among junkies and fags. In a way he didn't blame Dr. Marchán: he expected it and the retinologist did not disappoint.

"You have active cytomegalovirus," Dr. Marchán said during a visit. "Treatment has to begin now. Dr. Marcano takes care of that."

At Auxilio Mutuo Hospital he had a catheter port implanted, a device that connected an external needle to a subcutaneous disc that pumped the liquid medication directly into his subclavian artery. He had to take a taxicab home: nobody would pick him up without expecting details about the procedure. He could lie and make up a story, but he didn't. He had done that when he was circumcised at 27 and someone eventually figured out why he was limping and sitting gingerly. Besides, he really did not care to see anyone.

Twice a day he had to connect a bag of Ganciclovir to the needle he had on his chest for an infusion with a manual pressurized counter that took an hour to empty out the bag. He felt the cold flow travel from his access port to his bloodstream, a fluid armed with microscopic machine guns to stage an assault on the cytomegalovirus enemy, rahtahtahtah, poom! poom! and its ally the human immunodeficiency virus.

At the end of the process he had to inject heparin into the needle's tube to prevent clots on the line. Once a week he had to go to an ambulatory facility to have the needle removed, his chest shaved and disinfected and the bandage changed after reinjecting a fresh needle.

"How do you bathe?" Miguel asked him. Miguel was the infusion nurse.

"Very carefully," he said with halfhearted mirth.

"You should get a hand-held shower head. That way you can shower without fear you will get the bandage wet," Miguel suggested. "Wall shower heads are difficult to control."

"Yes, I'm very careful to keep it dry. Still, I'm going to get me one of those hinkymagiggies," he said and rose from the gurney. Whenever the needle was changed he felt an itch that was almost erotic as the nurse shaved the stubs on the bandaged side. The sensation was as he remembered the tingling of his penis on his first masturbation, a feeling that never returns, as happens to the heroin addict who chases the dragon of the first high without ever experiencing it again. Miguel's disposable razor gave him back the feeling, but now distant from his genitals. He was tempted to scratch even if it exposed him to contamination. The incipient erection neutralized the pain of the needle stick.

He had to keep the bandage dry. Water could not leak into the needle opening to prevent an infection. The subclavian artery was connected directly to his heart: any infectious agent would achieve what the virus had not.

He rose early in the morning to complete the infusion before leaving for work. He did the second one twelve hours later. During the hour-long procedure he went over paperwork he'd bring home from the office. Even if the Ganciclovir was effective, he noticed the floaters in his left eye, where the infection was active, and the reduction in the visual field of the same eye.

By then he also developed a relentless obsession with leaving everything up to date and organized in his office and at home. *What would I leave undone if I died in half an hour?* was his guide at the end of each day. He adopted an attitude he talked about with a colleague, on Zen, yoga and meditation, although he refused invitations to join a group that met for yoga exercise a few minutes away from the firm. "Enjoy what you have today, because tomorrow it may be gone, dead or broken down." He took comfort in another thought he invoked when someone became anxious and agitated over a conflict or got on a lamentation binge: "Considering the boundless dimensions of the universe and all its complications, how big can this be that merits such oppressive concern?"

He wanted to reserve his peace of mind for matters truly worth the expenditure of energy. Resolving a legal problem for a client, fighting for a fair judgment on a case, convincing a jury that his reasoning was solid and

convincing, helping someone who needed financial aid
to give someone hope and encourage similar actions in
others, not injuring or hurting anyone, not abusing someone's trust: those were all worth it. They helped reestab-
lish the moral order in the world without biblical quotes
and bromides. Death can be neither avoided nor resisted.
Everything else had some kind of a solution, even if only
resignation and acceptance.

Mariological recitative of mystical pharmacology

> O Mary, mother mine,
> o consolation of us mortals!
> Virgin of virgins,
> pray for us.
> "You are going to die,"
> Dr. Bowers said
> when Raúl Marcano
> died in a car crash,
>   (Solo: *arrogantte*0
> a car driven by a drunk
> on old highway 1.
>   (*Solo arrogantte*0
> "You'll die, like my brother
> you will. Brain cancer,
> he has. You and he. Dead.
> Six months from now.
> Less, maybe."
> (Chorus, *largo disperato*.)
> T cells at 138.
> AZT,
> Flucanazole,
> Bactrim DS,
> Videx,

ddI.

Mother of divine grace,
pray for us.
    (Solo: *timoroso*)
"You're here on a lark,
don't fool yourself,"
said the new doctor
when the one before him
collapsed with a stroke.
(Chorus, *largo e troppo funebre*.)
T cells at 50, with a viral load > 25000.
Flucanazole,
Bactrim DS,
3TC,
Combivir.

Incorruptible Mother,
pray for us.
"I'm giving you no hope,"
the doctor ordered his chest
opened and stabbed with
an intravenous catheter.
"But you'll go blind,"
said the retinologist.
(Chorus, *larghissimo*.)
At 36 your T cells,
viral load at 32000.
Flucanazole,
Bactrim DS,
Sulfadiazine,
Ganciclovir IV,
Neurontin.

Mother of Good Counsel,

pray for us.
    (Solo: *allegro, ma con avarizia*)
"We'll buy your life
policy, $250 thousand
for $90 thousand and that
helps with your treatment,
because you're not leaving
any of it to anyone,
are you?"
It does you no good if
you're dead.
And it's only one. You
have two more you can leave to...
A niece? The free clinic? ASPCA?"
So said the viatical company
and he sold it.
(Chorus, *largo, ma con speranza.*)
CD4 cells at 180, viral load >6500:
    Sustiva,
    Isentress,
    Epivir,
    Gancíclovir IV,
    Sulfadiazine,
    Neurontin,
    Lyrica.

Mirror of Justice,
pray for us.
    (Solo: *allegro vero*)
"Astonishing! You
give me hope.
This is what we want
to achieve and it's possible
when the patients do their share
and take their medication,"
so said Dr. Claudio,

reinstated after his retirement
when his only son died of
the infection's simple complications.
(Chorus, *allegro, ma scettico.*)
CD4 at 215, viral load at <300.
    Norvir,
    Crixivan,
    Tivicay,
    Sustiva,
    Lyrica.

Mother Most Admirable,
pray for us.
"I'd kiss you, but
I'm not into men, ha ha ha,
no offense. I'm so proud
what we have achieved together,"
said Dr. Claudio
and kissed him anyway on his forehead.
(Chorus, *allegro, ma non troppo.*)
CD4 at 425, undetectable viral load.
    Triumeq.

Comfort of the Afflicted,
pray for us.
    (Solo: *grandioso*)
"You are going to live. We all
die sooner or later,
but you, you're like Sisyphus,
you won't let the boulder
crush you.
You are going to live,"
said Dr. Claudio.
(Chorus, *brevissimo*
con brio ma con attenzione

e misurato:)
CD4 at 550, undetectable viral load.
    Triumeq.

Ark of the Covenant,
pray for us.
Queen of Christians who judge,
pray for us.
Mother of those who no longer believe,
pray for us.
Throne of unending anguish,
pray for us.
Mother of the truncated paroxysm,
pray for us.
Patron of saving inhibitors,
pray for us.
Queen of the gold it takes
to remain alive,
pray for us.
Refuge of those who sin
because they are human,
pray for us.
Comfort of the damned and accursed,
pray for us.
Mother of the Precious Blood
that shall not be donated,
that shall not be shared,
that shall be wiped off with bleach,
that shall be drawn,
that shall be analyzed,
that shall have atrophied cells,
pray for us.
Give us this day our daily
caramelized bile,
turn it into ointment
turn it into light,

turn it into bread of life,
turn it into calm,
turn it into pleasure,
turn it into humanity.
And lead us not into temptation
as long as we can sublimate,
as long as we can repress,
as long as we can deny ourselves,
as long as we are not undetectable,
as long as we don't develop resistance,
as long as pharmacogenic anemia strikes,
as long as our viscera are not turning,
as long as we have a rash with pruritus,
as long as we can become eunuchs
and when we do fall into temptation
be mother most gracious mother,
be mother most prudent
be worthy of praise
and leave us alone,
for though I walk in the valley
of the shadow of death
and *de profundis clamem,*
Gilead is my shepherd:
I shall not want.

Today

No, he's not dead. He lives and now asks himself
why.

When the virus stabilized and remained undetectable the doctor had the access port removed from his
chest. The scar remained as a reminder, his Hester
Prynne scarlet A. Dr. Claudio feared that the fragility of
his skin after two years of perforations, penetrations and
removal of needles it would become infected. He had

only been giving it maintenance care: he had not used the device for six months, because a new intravenous medication was available to be administered once a week. Dr. Claudio had left the port in in case things changed, but it was a risk. Instead of choosing the precaution against a possible relapse Dr. Claudio had a surgeon take it out. Later an oral medication became available.

His other seropositive friends are all dead, with one exception, Mario, who has gone blind, not from cytomegalovirus, but from another opportunistic brain infection that killed his optic nerves. Mario's doctor has asked him to get rid of the macaw: the birds are carriers of the bacterium that causes toxoplasmosis, but Mario says he'd rather die than lose Paco, his only company. His partner, Arturo, tired of the fear of contagion, remodeled the house to make it suitable for a blind person and went off to live with a younger funeral director.

Santiago, a dentist disabled because of his status at 42 was one of his few friends with whom he compared the side effects of medications and progress in keeping the disease in check. One day Santiago told him, "I don't know why going on living is worth it just to take all these pills."

He tried to explain that what they called the pillage was what allowed them to enjoy the rest of the time. Among his complaints Santiago referred to Marinol, which he took to open up his appetite and prevent physical wasting. He had always had the thickness of a femur, but the virus had him so thin he looked as if he were about to vanish. He claimed Marinol had made him grow pubescent breasts, which was one of its unfortunate side effects of the hormone.

"I don't believe in quantity. That's what this is, not quality," Santiago told him while following an ice cube that melted in a liquid smoke spiral, contorting voluptuously as it blended with the whiskey.

Santiago took a vacation from his forced idleness and flew to San Francisco. for a weekend.

"I anesthetized myself with gin, went to the baths and let myself go into dissipation of the worst irresponsible and decadent kind," Santiago told him through his laughter. The following day he shot a bullet into his temple. The cleaning women found him three days later in a viscous puddle of blood at the foot of his grand piano.

After so many years of living unconcerned with the possibility of developing symptoms, he had become used to the new prospects of going on in relative health with the new medications. He took up again his activities outside of work, where no one knew of his status. He returned to the gym. There his brain could drool over so many youthful and vigorous bodies, but he held back when one of them signaled interest. He signed up for a charitable marathon, a race to raise funds for breast cancer research, and was able to finish it.

He has cut back on the volume of legal work a bit at a time without calling anyone's attention to it. He has been a full partner for a while and has no need to prove himself. He rarely litigates in court: he prefers mediation and resolution without reaching that point and consults in civil cases. Family law he never practiced. He feared working cases where couples used their children as pawns in a cruel and traumatizing game. He didn't have the stomach to face people who had loved each other, shared a bed, and later turned into adversaries, merciless, bitter and vindictive.

He was tempted by the idea of getting a dog to keep him company. He did not yield to it. If the dog survived him, what would become of him? Would someone caring adopt it or would they let him get lost in the hills before reaching the valley and be run over by a truck? If he survived his pet he would have to endure again the pain

Melampo's death and absence caused him, a sorrow almost equal to losing Alejandro. Melampo had been with him longer than he had been with Alejandro.

He climbs the mountain home, where he can only hear crickets and *coquíes* at night, every so often also an airplane flying low toward the regional airport. He watches the sun set in the distance, afternoon after afternoon, a semicircle reverberating with heat until it turns into a waning secant aligned against the horizon line before disappearing and leaving behind a faded orange luminosity, soon to become a vague cerulean tinge. It's the sun itself that reminds him that the magnetic field continues to make the planet turn on its axis, whether he lives or dies or the desperate and impatient who cannot accept anything less than a total cure take their own lives. The vegetation surrounding him will go on growing unless someone comes to destroy it. The fauna will be the same unless human or beastly predators achieve their destructive goals. He is then assailed by the doubt that living with death sitting on his shoulder is worth it. Today he cannot even consider himself immunocompromised. His antiviral cocktail keeps his immune system the same as that of someone who is not infected. That, however, could change at any time and without warning. The virus could become resistant to drugs. The medications could have deleterious side effects that would give him chronic diarrhea, impotence, nausea, anemia, loss of appetite, neuropathy, a teratological hunchback.

Sometimes he feels victimized by luck. He wants to seek his revenge against life. On one of those isolated beaches he knows about but has never had the courage to visit, he would expose a married and ignorant man, one of those who believes that because he is married, lays women and has made his wife pregnant seven times, he isn't a faggot and therefore he cannot be infected by a disease that can only be suffered by junkies, whores and those who are exclusively fucked in the ass, not the ones who do the fucking—which is why he's not afraid of taking dick up his butt occasionally. What would he feel afterwards? Remorse? Sadness? Unrest? Insomnia? Anxiety over having to return to a confessional? Only the release of a tight sexual spring? The pleasure of sociopath vengeance? Would he celebrate his felony and be glad that the anonymous fool will expose his wife, who had no clue about what he was doing when he left home to visit his mom, he, so macho, so Pentecostal, so homophobic? He will never know.

When he goes to Walgreens to pay $1750 for his three-in-one bottle of antiretroviral tablets he asks himself whether someone out there will have to be happy with outdated and ineffective medications from the '80s because he can't afford the newer ones or someone newly diagnosed who will have to wait powerlessly for death to come because he doesn't have health insurance or the money to buy them? Someone, yes, someone there must be. Perhaps thousands, especially those who are not eligible for public assistance but don't have enough money with which to buy the pills. Those have to choose between eating and paying their mortgage or buying tablets, one of life's sarcastic smiles, prolonging their lives but keeping them from affording food.

Then he feels something like impotent resentment against pharma, but it doesn't last. He sits back in his loneliness and the distant threat of a death that rides bareback on a squalid and tired horse, but which can unexpectedly change over to an Arabian stallion that will bring it when he least expects it. For that reason he will not lower his guard: he knows not how or when. Perhaps Santiago was right on the irony of it all, going on medicating oneself to keep death behind the finish line and at the same time wonder at what particular moment it will surprise him.

He does not suffer the guilt of those who claim they have survived the plague while their friends, their partners, their spouses have died.

"Why? Why me?" they ask.

"*Pathetique! Perdenti, che miseria contropro-ducente!*" he says aloud to himself when he considers it as an attitude laden with uselessness and hypocrisy, expressed to seek pity and provoke commiseration. No one can be blamed if genetics and better physiological resources retard the collapse. If nature made some less resistant, why does anybody have to feel compunction over something they can't control? It's not the same to wax nostalgic over those who are gone as to run around like Margherite Gautier. Given the choice, would they trade places with a ghost who returns to claim his place among the living?

"It's another form of victimage," he adds as he reflects and talks to himself on the terrace in between sips of ginger root tea. "*Il est une form autodestructice de rester une victime.* Jeremiahs."

And yet he, isn't he a victim also for living with the worry of the possibility of the arrival of death, which for thirty years has kept him from enjoying the time pharmacology has provided him?

He gets on his feet. He locks the back door and turns down the windows, which he never shuts completely unless the rain comes down in windy droves. He enters his study, with a view of the brush growing unchecked and insolent a few meters from his house, bordering uncontrolled the entrance to the garage. Although his field of vision is somewhat reduced and he is losing visual and manual coordination, he sees on his desk a stack of correspondence he has yet to address and several folders he has not filed away. Only an undefined vestige of sunlight remains and in the distance the city lights have acquired the brightness of fixed fireflies. He turns on the banker's light with the luminescent bulb on the desk. The rest of his study is in the dark. He sits within the boundaries of a hemisphere of light, isolated from the blurry shadows. Before going to bed he has to clear his desk. No one knows what might happen.

WANDERING SOUL

I think I heard the digital alarm. It informed the nurse on call that my heart had stopped. They call it something like plainlining. Flat? I have no idea how I got there, whether I got sick or a train rolled over me. I know even less whether I was unconscious or for how long.

It all happened the way lightning strikes. My body's vital chemical processes ended instantaneously and those of putrefaction set in for me to inject myself in a new stage of the nitrogen cycle. Whoever said it was possible to end a life has no knowledge of that process. When the electrical impulses that made blood run through my veins ceased, on the eve of decomposition, my bladder loosened and my sphincters retook their will—that is, I urinated and defecated. Something like a vaporous substance detached itself from that same sulfuric and septic fecal matter and dispersed; anemic smoke the color of lead from a cigarette in repose that the wind will not oppose. Like all vapor in a high state of heat, it rose until it was no longer visible to the living.

That turned out to be the soul.

That is what I am now, an incorporeal conscience, perhaps pestilent (I lack any sense of smell), light and almost transparent smog that obeys the law of conservation of matter in the universe, deprived of free will.

No angels or demons appeared to transport me to the famous great beyond. Actually, there is one, but not of the kind I had been told: sometimes it is far beyond, then sometimes it is close by.

No heavenly pearly gates where anyone greeted me. No eternal fire, no Nirvanas or seventh heavens or virgins waving palm fronds when they perceived my arrival. No god, in capital letters or lowercase, like Micaelangelo Bounarotti's on the famous ceiling or as depicted in murals. No gods or goddesses. No feeling of the presence of Odin or Buddha or Allah, Vishna or Isis.

I am part of a universal network of evanescence interweaving, in a true vaporous and asexual miscenegation, both men and women, children and adults, maybe even dogs and turtledoves, giraffes and walruses. No one recognizes a self or others: we are in perpetual anonymity without knowing whether whoever went through us was Edith Piaf or Einstein or Pope John XXIII, Ethel Rosenberg or Roy Cohn, Dante or Rafael Leonidas Trujillo, Socrates or Kruschev, Eva Duarte de Perón or Patrick Lumumba or Crazy Pablo, the town's nutcase who screamed at the moon from the park. It is possible that at some time I may have touched what were the buttocks of Errol Flynn or Carol Dada's breasts or Jon Dillinger's notorious penis o Cleopatra's mouth. Perhaps at some instant I crossed through Augusto Piinochet, in which case, if I were to still have emotions, I would be happy not to know it. Here no one knows who penetrates us or when, nor do they know.

In this state nobody has any more or less influence than anyone else; there are no hierarchies of any type. We have no peace or eternal rest, no quarrels or tensions. We have nothing here. I suppose the rest of these vapors are those who at one time wandered on Earth, because that is how I go and it is impossible that I am the only one. I harbor some doubt, however, because just as neither that nor the certainty matter, I continue to slide here and there without anyone's notice or complaint.

When cosmic forces I can no longer aspire to control fan me toward Earth, I notice people I never knew and others I did, and others who make me feel what I used to call lucky, because they no longer cross my path.

If someone is reading a Bible or the Koran or any other books such as those, that is when I would like to have a voice to whisper in their ear that it is a waste of time to live judging others or feeling guilty for suffering from weaknesses that lead them, as they say on Earth, to commit sins of the flesh. It is when I wish, if I still had the neural connections that made me feel that, I could spread the warning. The time spent on Earth worshipping an inexistent divinity I could have spent helping others to improve their lives regardless of their place of origin or the color of their skin: maybe I did that, but I cannot remember; if I did not do it, I should have. If I did not, I could have enjoyed what evolution gave me and appreciate what while alive I called beauty. And if I did not, it would have been better to praise the efforts of scientists to document our past and formulate a vision of our future, instead of reading the falsified history of humanity in apocryphal religious tracts. Now I will never know. Maybe I could have. No, I will never know; here there is no room for remorse or regret, and thus it matters not a bit if I did not.

When I sneak among the members of a religious congregation and notice they do good that they may reach the kingdom of heaven there is tension among the molecules of my vapor, I suppose vestigial remains of my carbon-based days. They know not that doing what is right and just out of hope or fear is masquerading pettiness, that in the long run they will be what I am, the detachment of rectal gas floating without living or dying no matter how they lived on Earth. Being fair and honest is its own reward; after expelling the final fart, neither punishment or pats on the back. Hell is lived while the heart beats in the shadow of a conscience. Fortunate are the sociopaths, for they inherit premortem peace.

It is the great mystery of the universe: it will not be revealed until de soul detaches from the intestines. Not even *The Book of the Dead* could have had a glimpse of it.

I have no idea what they did with my corpse, whether it was cremated or they left it outdoors where the vultures could feast on it. Did I live in opulence or on what I found in trash cans near the bridge under which I lived? Was I dedicated to honesty in the midst of a corrupt government or was I the manipulator of accounts to hide my embezzlement? Was I insane? I know not whether I had a wife or children, whether I lived alone with in someone's company, someone of the opposite sex or my own, whether I was well educated or was a dunce. I must have known something to be able to tell to whom the ethereal remnants I cross are. Who knows, and what does it matter now?

That is indeed the paradox of this, the purest existence, because I am somewhere without being anyone. Now I know everything, but it is all useless. I cannot issue alerts, I cannot return to enlighten those who have no clue, because they cannot even suspect everything they ignore. This could also be called a true sentence, but, fortunately, it neither bothers nor upset me nor do I pull the blanket or push it nor is it mine. Some day they will find out, but not while they breathe.